#1 *NEW YORK TIMES* BE

JODI PICOULT

SING YOU HOME

COMPANION SOUNDTRACK

1. Sing You Home
2. The House on Hope Street
3. Refugee
4. The Last
5. Marry Me
6. Faith
7. The Mermaid
8. Ordinary Life
9. Where You Are
10. Sammy's Song

Original music by Ellen Wilber
Lyrics by Jodi Picoult
All songs performed by Ellen Wilber

Not for individual sale

ATRIA BOOKS

Sing You Home

Sing You Home

A NOVEL

Jodi Picoult

ORIGINAL MUSIC COMPOSED AND
PERFORMED BY ELLEN WILBER
LYRICS BY JODI PICOULT

DOUBLEDAY LARGE PRINT HOME LIBRARY EDITION
ATRIA BOOKS
New York   London   Toronto   Sydney

ATRIA BOOKS
A Division of Simon & Schuster, Inc.
1230 Avenue of the Americas
New York, NY 10020

First Atria Books hardcover edition March 2011

ATRIA BOOKS and colophon are trademarks of Simon & Schuster, Inc.

Manufactured in the United States of America

ISBN 978-1-61129-289-3

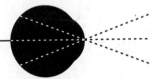

This Large Print Book carries the Seal of Approval of N.A.V.H.

ACKNOWLEDGMENTS

The mark of intelligence is being able to surround yourself with people who know more than you do. For this reason, I have many people to thank who all had a hand in helping me create this novel. I am grateful to my brilliant medical and legal minds: Judy Stern, Ph.D., Dr. Karen George, Dr. Paul Manganiello, Dr. Michelle Lauria; Corporal Claire Demarais, Judge Jennifer Sargent, and the attorneys Susan Apel, Lise Iwon, Janet Gilligan, and Maureen McBrien. Thanks to the music therapists who allowed me to pick their brains and to tag along and share some remarkable moments: Suzanne Hanser, Annette Whitehead Pleau, Karen Wacks, Kathleen Howland, Julie Buras Zigo, Emily Pellegrino, Samantha Hale, Bronwyn Bird, Brenda Ross, and Emily Hoffman. I'm also indebted to Sarah Croitoru, Rebecca Linder, Lisa Bodager, Jon Picoult, Sindy Buzzell, Focus on the Family's Melissa Fryrear, and the *Box Turtle Bulletin*'s Jim Burroway.

I always thank my mom, Jane Picoult, for being an early reader, but this time I'd also like to thank my grandmother Bess Friend. We should all be so open-minded in our nineties.

Thanks to Atria Books: Carolyn Reidy, Judith Curr, Mellony Torres, Jessica Purcell, Sarah Branham, Kate Cetrulo, Chris Lloreda, Jeanne Lee, Gary Urda, Lisa Keim, Rachel Zugschwert, Michael Selleck, and the dozens of others without whom my career would never have reached the heights it has. And David Brown—it is really nice to have you back on Team Jodi. I am so grateful that (when I announced we'd be publishing this book with original music) your first reaction was a wild buzz of excitement—not utter panic.

To Laura Gross—remember how you told me about the dead guy on the train? And remember how I said one day I was going to use that? Here it is. I knew you'd be a wonderful agent, but I think I underestimated what a good friend you would become.

To Emily Bestler—I just don't think there are very many editors who can move seamlessly in a discussion with their authors from why the SATs are a tool of torture to how to fix the ending of a novel. Or in other words, I really hit the jackpot. We've been together so long now I think we'll have to be surgically removed from each other's hips.

My publicists, Camille McDuffie and Kathleen Carter, are the best cheerleaders an author could ask for. Over the past thirteen years, you've taken me from "Jodi who?" to having fans spot me in the grocery store and ask for autographs on their shopping lists.

There is something pretty remarkable about this book—it's musical. When I knew I was writing in part about gay rights, I wanted my readers to literally hear the voice of my main character; to take this from a political arena to a personal one—and so you get to hear Zoe pouring out her heart and soul to you through her songs. To that end I have to thank Bob Merrill of Sweet Spot Digital, who produced the CD; Ed Dauphinais and Tim Gilmore, who played mandolin and drums respectively; and Toby Mountain of Northeastern Digital, who mastered the CD. But most of all I have to thank Ellen Wilber, who agreed to be the voice of Zoe—and the creator of her music. Ellen is one of my dearest friends, and we've written over a hundred songs together for original children's musicals that are performed to raise funds for charity. She has more musical talent in her pinkie finger than I could hope to have in a lifetime, and she has the biggest heart. She wrote the songs you'll hear; I wrote the lyrics—and it's her crystalline voice you're listening to on the CD. There aren't enough words for me to use to thank her—for thinking that this project would be something fun to do . . . and, more important, for our friendship.

Finally, as always, thanks to Tim, Kyle, Jake, and Sammy. You guys are the soundtrack of *my* life.

For Ellen Wilber—Your music has completely enriched my life; your friendship has meant so much to me and my entire family. I'm not sure I can remember which one of us is supposed to be Louise and which one is supposed to be Thelma, but I don't think it matters as long as we're on the road together.

And for Kyle van Leer—From the moment you were born in a hurricane I knew you were going to be one of a kind. I don't think I could possibly be any more proud of you if I tried—not just for who you've become but for the individual you have always been.

Somehow, I know you two won't mind sharing a dedication page.

AUTHOR'S NOTE

The CD that accompanies this book was created to bring the character of Zoe to life for the reader by giving her a real voice. There is no "right" or "wrong" way to mix the music with the novel, but while Ellen Wilber and I were writing the songs and lyrics, we envisioned each track paired with a chapter. You'll see section breaks between the chapters that identify where we placed each song, just in case you'd like to play them in the places where they correspond to what Zoe is feeling and thinking at that moment. Enjoy!

No man has a natural right to commit aggression on the equal rights of another, and this is all from which the laws ought to restrain him.

—THOMAS JEFFERSON

✓	**TRACK 1**	**SING YOU HOME**
	TRACK 2	THE HOUSE ON HOPE STREET
	TRACK 3	REFUGEE
	TRACK 4	THE LAST
	TRACK 5	MARRY ME
	TRACK 6	FAITH
	TRACK 7	THE MERMAID
	TRACK 8	ORDINARY LIFE
	TRACK 9	WHERE YOU ARE
	TRACK 10	SAMMY'S SONG

ZOE

One sunny, crisp Saturday in September when I was seven years old, I watched my father drop dead. I was playing with my favorite doll on the stone wall that bordered our driveway while he mowed the lawn. One minute he was mowing, and the next, he was facefirst in the grass as the mower propelled itself in slow motion down the hill of our backyard.

I thought at first he was sleeping, or playing a game. But when I crouched beside him on the lawn, his eyes were still open. Damp cut grass stuck to his forehead.

I don't remember calling for my mother, but I must have.

When I think about that day, it is in slow motion. The mower, walking alone. The carton of milk my mother was carrying when she ran outside, which dropped to the tarred driveway. The sound of round vowels as my mother screamed into the phone to give our address to the ambulance.

My mother left me at the neighbor's house while she went to the hospital. The neighbor was an old woman whose couch smelled like pee. She offered me chocolate-covered peppermints that were so old the chocolate had turned white at the edges. When her telephone rang I wandered into the backyard and crawled behind a row of hedges. In the soft mulch, I buried my doll and walked away.

My mother never noticed that it was gone—but then, it barely seemed that she acknowledged my father being gone, either. She never cried. She stood stiff-backed through my father's funeral. She sat across from me at the kitchen table that I still sometimes set with a third place for my father, as we gradually ate our way through chipped beef casserole and mac-and-cheese-and-franks, sympathy platters from my father's colleagues and neighbors who hoped food could make up for the fact that they didn't know what to say. When a robust, healthy forty-two-year-old dies of a massive heart attack, the grieving family is suddenly contagious. Come too close, and you might catch our bad luck.

Six months after my father died, my mother—still stoic—took his suits and shirts out of the closet they shared and brought them to Goodwill. She asked the liquor store for boxes, and she packed away the biography that he had been reading, which had been on the nightstand all this time; and his pipe, and his coin collection. She did not pack away his Abbott and Costello videos, although she always had told my father that she never really understood what made them funny.

My mother carried these boxes to the attic, a place that seemed to trap cluster flies and heat. On her third trip up, she didn't come back. Instead, what floated downstairs was a silly, fizzy refrain piped through the speakers of an old record player. I could not understand all the words, but it had something to do with a witch doctor telling someone how to win the heart of a girl.

Ooo eee ooo ah ah, ting tang, walla walla, bing bang, I heard. It made a laugh bubble up in my chest, and since I hadn't laughed all that much lately, I hurried to the source.

When I stepped into the attic, I found my mother weeping. "This record," she said, playing it over again. "It made him so happy."

I knew better than to ask why, then, she was sobbing. Instead, I curled up beside her and listened to the song that had finally given my mother permission to cry.

Every life has a soundtrack.

There is a tune that makes me think of the summer I spent rubbing baby oil on my stomach in pursuit of the perfect tan. There's another that reminds me of tagging along with my father on Sunday mornings to pick up the *New York*

Times. There's the song that reminds me of using fake ID to get into a nightclub; and the one that brings back my cousin Isobel's sweet sixteen, where I played Seven Minutes in Heaven with a boy whose breath smelled like tomato soup.

If you ask me, music is the language of memory.

Wanda, the shift nurse at Shady Acres Assisted Living, hands me a visitor pass, although I've been coming to the nursing home for the past year to work with various clients. "How is he today?" I ask.

"The usual," Wanda says. "Swinging from the chandelier and entertaining the masses with a combination of tap dancing and shadow puppets."

I grin. Mr. Docker is in the final throes of dementia. In the twelve months I've been his music therapist, he's interacted with me twice. Most of the time, he sits in his bed or a wheelchair, staring through me, completely unresponsive.

When I tell people I am a music therapist, they think it means I play guitar for people who are in the hospital—that I'm a performer. Actually, I'm more like a physical therapist, except instead of using treadmills and grab bars as tools, I use music. When I tell people *that,* they usually dismiss my job as some New Age BS.

In fact, it's very scientific. In brain scans, music lights up the medial pre-frontal cortex and triggers a memory that starts playing in your mind. All of a sudden you can see a place, a person, an incident. The strongest responses to music—the ones that elicit vivid memories—cause the greatest activity on brain scans. It's for this reason that stroke patients can access lyrics before they remember language, why Alzheimer's patients can still remember songs from their youth.

And why I haven't given up on Mr. Docker yet.

"Thanks for the warning," I tell Wanda, and I pick up my duffel, my guitar, and my djembe.

"Put those down," she insists. "You're not supposed to be carrying anything heavy."

"Then I'd better get rid of this," I say, touching my belly. In my twenty-eighth week, I'm enormous—and I'm also completely lying. I worked way too hard to have this baby to feel like any part of the pregnancy is a burden. I give Wanda a wave and head down the hall to start today's session.

Usually my nursing home clients meet in a group setting, but Mr. Docker is a special case. A former CEO of a Fortune 500 company, he now lives in this very chic elder-care facility, and his daughter Mim contracts my services for weekly sessions. He's just shy of eighty, has a lion's mane of white hair and gnarled hands that apparently used to play a mean jazz piano.

The last time Mr. Docker gave any indication that he was aware I shared the same physical space as him was two months ago. I'd been playing my guitar, and he smacked his fist against the handle of his wheelchair twice. I am not sure if he wanted to chime in for good measure or was trying to tell me to stop—but he was in rhythm.

I knock and open the door. "Mr.

Docker?" I say. "It's Zoe. Zoe Baxter. You feel like playing a little music?"

Someone on staff has moved him to an armchair, where he sits looking out the window. Or maybe just through it— he's not focusing on anything. His hands are curled in his lap like lobster claws.

"Right!" I say briskly, trying to maneuver myself around the bed and the television stand and the table with his untouched breakfast. "What should we sing today?" I wait a beat but am not really expecting an answer. "'You Are My Sunshine'?" I ask. "'Tennessee Waltz'?" I try to extract my guitar from its case in a small space beside the bed, which is not really big enough for my instrument and my pregnancy. Settling the guitar awkwardly on top of my belly, I start to strum a few chords. Then, on second thought, I put it down.

I rummage through the duffel bag for a maraca—I have all sorts of small instruments in there, for opportunities just like this. I gently wedge it into the curl of his hand. "Just in case you want to join in." Then I start singing softly.

"Take me out to the ball game; take me out with the . . ."

The end, I leave hanging. There's a need in all of us to finish a phrase we know, and so I'm hoping to get him to mutter that final *"crowd."* I glance at Mr. Docker, but the maraca remains clenched in his hand, silent.

"Buy me some peanuts and Cracker Jack; I don't care if I never get back."

I keep singing as I step in front of him, strumming gently. *"Let me root, root, root for the home team; if they don't win it's a shame. For it's one, two, three—"*

Suddenly Mr. Docker's hand comes flying up and the maraca clips me in the mouth. I can taste blood. I'm so surprised I stagger backward, and tears spring to my eyes. I press my sleeve to my cut lip, trying to keep him from seeing that he's hurt me. "Did I do something to upset you?"

Mr. Docker doesn't respond.

The maraca has landed on the pillow of his bed. "I'm just going to reach behind you, here, and get the instrument," I say carefully, and as I do, he takes another swing at me. This time I stumble, crashing into the table and overturning his breakfast tray.

"What is going on in here?" Wanda cries, bursting through the door. She looks at me, at the mess on the floor, and then at Mr. Docker.

"We're okay," I tell her. "Everything's okay."

Wanda takes a long, pointed look at my belly. "You sure?"

I nod, and she backs out of the room. This time, I sit gingerly on the edge of the radiator in front of the window. "Mr. Docker," I ask softly, "what's wrong?"

When he faces me, his eyes are bright with tears and lucidity. He lets his gaze roam the room—from its institutional curtains to the emergency medical equipment in the cabinet behind the bed to the plastic pitcher of water on the nightstand. "Everything," he says tightly.

I think about this man, who once was written up in *Money* and *Fortune*. Who used to command thousands of employees and whose days were spent in a richly paneled corner office with a plush carpet and a leather swivel chair. For a moment, I want to apologize for taking out my guitar, for unlocking his blocked mind with music.

Because there are some things we'd rather forget.

The doll that I buried at a neighbor's house on the day my father died was called Sweet Cindy. I had begged for her the previous Christmas, completely suckered by the television ads that ran on Saturday mornings between cartoons. Sweet Cindy could eat and drink and poop and tell you that she loved you. "Can she fix a carburetor?" my father had joked, when I showed him my Christmas list. "Can she clean the bathroom?"

I had a history of treating dolls badly. I cut off my Barbie dolls' hair with fingernail scissors. I decapitated Ken, although in my defense that had been an accident involving a fall from a bicycle basket. But Sweet Cindy I treated like my own baby. I tucked her each night into a crib that was set beside my own bed. I bathed her every day. I pushed her up and down the driveway in a stroller we'd bought at a garage sale.

On the day of my father's death, he'd wanted to go for a bike ride. It was beautiful out; I had just gotten my training wheels removed. But I'd told my father that I was playing with Cindy, and maybe we could go later. "Sounds like a plan, Zo," he had said, and he'd started to mow the back lawn, and of course there was no *later.*

If I had never gotten Sweet Cindy for Christmas.

If I'd said yes to my father when he asked.

If I'd been watching him, instead of playing with the doll.

There were a thousand permutations of behavior that, in my mind, could have saved my father's life—and so, although it was too late, I told myself I'd never wanted that stupid doll in the first place, that she was the reason my father wasn't here anymore.

The first time it snowed after my father died, I had a dream that Sweet Cindy was sitting on my bed. Crows had pecked out her blue-marble eyes. She was shivering.

The next day I took a garden spade from the garage and walked to the neighbor's house where I'd buried her. I dug up the snow and the mulch from half of the hedgerow, but the doll was gone. Carried away by a dog, maybe, or a little girl who knew better.

I know it's stupid for a forty-year-old woman to connect a foolish act of grief with four unsuccessful cycles of IVF, two miscarriages, and enough infertility issues to bring down a civilization—but I cannot tell you how many times I've wondered if this is some kind of karmic punishment.

If I hadn't so recklessly abandoned the first baby I ever loved, would I have a real one by now?

By the time my session with Mr. Docker ends, his daughter Mim has rushed from her ladies' auxiliary meeting to Shady Acres. "Are you sure you didn't get hurt?" she says, looking me over for the hundredth time.

"Yes," I tell her, although I suspect her concern has more to do with a fear of being sued than with genuine concern for my well-being.

She rummages in her purse and pulls out a fistful of cash. "Here," Mim says.

"But you've already paid me for this month—"

"This is a bonus," she says. "I'm sure, with the baby and everything, there are expenses."

It's hush money, I know that, but she's right. However, the expenses surrounding my baby have less to do with car seats and strollers than with Lupron and Follistim injections. After five IVF cycles—both fresh and frozen—we have depleted all of our savings and maxed out our credit cards. I take the money and tuck it into the pocket of my jeans. "Thank you," I say, and then I meet her gaze. "What your father did? I know you don't see it this way, but it's a huge step forward for him. He connected with me."

"Yeah, right on your jaw," Wanda mutters.

"He *interacted*," I correct. "Maybe in

a less than socially appropriate way . . . but still. For a minute, the music got to him. For a minute, he was *here*."

I can tell Mim doesn't buy this, but that's all right. I have been bitten by an autistic child; I have sobbed beside a little girl dying of brain cancer; I have played in tune with the screams of a child who was burned over eighty percent of his body. This job . . . if it hurts me, I know I am doing it well.

"I'd better go," I say, picking up my guitar case.

Wanda doesn't glance up from the chart she's writing in. "See you next week."

"Actually, you'll see me in about two hours at the baby shower."

"What baby shower?"

I grin. "The one I'm not supposed to know about."

Wanda sighs. "If your mother asks, you better make sure you tell her I wasn't the one who spilled the beans."

"Don't worry. I'll act appropriately surprised."

Mim reaches out her hand toward my protruding belly. "May I?" I nod. I know some pregnant women think it's an in-vasion of privacy to have strangers reaching to pat or touch or offer par-enting advice, but I don't mind in the least. I can barely keep myself from rubbing my hands over the baby, from being magnetically drawn to the proof that this time, it is going to work.

"It's a boy," she announces.

I am thoroughly convinced that I'm carrying a girl. I dream in pink. I wake up with fairy tales caught on my tongue. "We'll see," I say.

I've always found it ironic that some-one who has trouble getting pregnant begins in vitro fertilization by taking birth control pills. It is all about regulat-ing an irregular cycle, in order to begin an endless alphabet soup of medica-tions: three ampoules each of FSH and hMG—Follistim and Repronex—in-jected into me twice a day by Max, a man who used to faint at the sight of a needle and who now, after five years, can give me a shot with one hand and pour coffee with the other. Six days after starting the injections, a transvaginal ultrasound measured the size of my ovarian follicles, and a blood test measured my estradiol levels. That led to Antagon, a new medication meant to keep the eggs in the follicles until they were ready. Three days later: another ultrasound and blood test. The amounts of Follistim and Repronex were reduced—one ampoule of each morning and night—and then two days later, another ultrasound and blood test.

One of my follicles measured twenty-one millimeters. One measured twenty millimeters. And one was nineteen millimeters.

At precisely 8:30 P.M. Max injected ten thousand units of hCG into me. Exactly thirty-six hours later, those eggs were retrieved.

Then ICSI—intracytoplasmic sperm injection—was used to fertilize the egg with Max's sperm. And three days later, with Max holding my hand, a vaginal catheter was inserted into me and we watched the embryo transfer on a blinking computer monitor. There, the lining of my uterus looked like sea grass swaying in the current. A little white spark, a star, shot out of the syringe and fell between two blades of grass. We celebrated our potential pregnancy with a shot of progesterone in my butt.

And to think, some people who want to have a baby only need to make love.

My mother is on her computer when I walk into her house, adding information to her recently acquired Facebook profile. DARA WEEKS, her status says, WISHES HER DAUGHTER WOULD FRIEND HER. "I'm not talking to you," she says, snippy, "but your husband called."

"Max?"

"Do you have more than one?"

"What did he want?"

She shrugs. Ignoring her, I pick up the phone in the kitchen and dial Max's mobile number. "Why isn't your cell on?" Max asks, as soon as he picks up.

"Yes, honey," I reply. "I love you, too."

In the background I can hear a lawn mower. Max runs a landscaping business. He is busy mowing in the summer, raking in the fall, and snowplowing in the winter. *What do you do during mud season?* I had asked the first time we met.

Wallow, he'd said, smiling.

"I heard you got hurt."

"Embarrassing news travels fast. Who called you, anyway?"

"I just think . . . I mean, we worked so hard to get to this point." Max stumbles over the words, but I know what he means.

"You heard Dr. Gelman," I tell him. "We're in the home stretch."

It seems ironic that, after all these years of trying, I am the one who is more relaxed about the pregnancy than Max. There were years when I was so superstitious I counted backward from twenty before getting out of bed, or wore the same lucky camisole for a week in an effort to ensure that particular embryo would be the one that actually stuck. But I've never made it this far before, where my ankles are blissfully swollen and my joints ache and I cannot see my feet in the shower. I've never been so pregnant that someone could plan a baby shower.

"I know we need the money, Zoe, but if your clients are violent—"

"Max. Mr. Docker is catatonic ninety-nine percent of the time, and my burn victims are usually unconscious. Honestly, this was a fluke. I could just as easily get hurt walking across the street."

"Then don't cross the road," Max says. "When are you coming home?"

I'm sure he knows about the baby shower, but I play along. "I have to do an assessment of a new client," I joke. "Mike Tyson."

"Very funny. Look, I can't talk right now—"

"*You* called *me*—"

"Only because I thought you were doing something stupid—"

"Max," I say, cutting him off. "Let's not. Let's just not." For years, Max and I were told by couples with children how lucky we were; how our relationship had the luxury of being all about us, instead of who was cooking dinner and who was carpooling to Little

League. But the flame of romance can be just as effectively doused by dinner conversations that center on estradiol levels and appointment times at the clinic. It is not that Max doesn't do everything right—from massaging my feet to telling me I look beautiful instead of bloated. It's that, lately, even when I am pressed up close against him, I feel like I cannot get close enough to touch him, like he is somewhere else. I have told myself that I'm imagining things. That it's nerves on his part, raging hormones on mine. I just wish I didn't have to keep making excuses.

Not for the first time, I wish I had a girlfriend to confide in. Someone who would nod and say all the right things when I complained about my husband. But my friendships had dwindled as Max and I began to devote ourselves entirely to combating infertility. Some relationships I'd ended, because I didn't want to hear a friend talk about her baby's first words, or go to a couple's home for dinner and be confronted with sippy cups and Matchbox cars and stuffed bears—details of a life that eluded me. Other relationships had simply fallen by the wayside, since the only person who really could understand the cyclone of emotions involved in IVF was Max. We'd isolated ourselves, because we were the only pair among our married friends who didn't have kids yet. We'd isolated ourselves, because it hurt less.

I hear him hang up. My mother, I see, has been hanging on every word. "Is everything all right between you two?"

"I thought you were mad at me."

"I am."

"Then how come you're eavesdropping?"

"It's not eavesdropping if it's my phone and my kitchen. What's wrong with Max?"

"Nothing." I shake my head. "I don't know."

She schools her features into an expression of open concern. "Let's sit down and unpack this feeling together."

I roll my eyes. "Does that really work with your clients?"

"You'd be surprised. Most people already know the answers to their problems."

My mother, for the past four months, has reinvented herself as the owner and sole employee of Mama Knows Best Life Coaching. This profession comes on the heels of her earlier incarnations as a Reiki instructor, a stand-up comedienne, and—for one very uncomfortable summer of my adolescence—a door-to-door saleswoman for her entrepreneurial invention: the Banana Sack (a fitted pink neoprene suit that shimmied over the fruit to keep it from going brown too quickly; unfortunately, it was mistaken repeatedly for a sex toy). By comparison, becoming a life coach is fairly tame.

"When I was pregnant with you, your father and I fought so much that one day I left him."

I stare at her. How is it possible that, in the forty years I've been alive, I never knew this? "Seriously?"

She nods. "I packed and told him I was leaving him and I did."

"Where did you go?"

"To the end of the driveway," my

mother says. "I was nine months pregnant; that was the maximum distance I could waddle without feeling as if my uterus was falling out."

I wince. "Do you have to be quite so graphic?"

"What would you like me to call it, Zoe? A fetal living room?"

"What happened?"

"The sun went down, and your father came out with a jacket for me. We sat for a few minutes and we went back inside." She shrugs. "And then you were born, and whatever it was that we'd been arguing about didn't seem to matter. All I'm saying is that the past is nothing but a springboard for the future."

I fold my arms. "Have you been sniffing the Windex again?"

"No, it's my new tagline. Look." My mother's fingers fly over the keyboard. The best advice she ever gave me was to take a typing course. I'd fought her furiously. It was in the voc-tech side of my high school and full of kids who were not in my über-academic classes— kids who smoked outside before school,

who wore heavy eyeliner and listened
to heavier metal. *Are you there to judge
people or to type?* she'd asked me. In
the end I was one of three girls who got
a blue ribbon from the teacher for mas-
tering seventy-five words per minute.
Nowadays I use a keyboard, of course,
but every time I type up an assessment
for one of my clients, I silently thank my
mother for being right.

She brings up her business's Facebook page. There's a picture of her on
it, and her cheesy tagline. "You would
have *known* that was my new motto if
you'd accepted my friend request."

"Are you seriously going to hold social networking etiquette against me?"
I ask.

"All I know is that I carried you for
nine months. I fed you, I clothed you, I
paid for your college education. Friend-
ing me on Facebook seems like a small
thing to ask in return."

"You're my *mother.* You don't have to
be my friend."

She gestures at my belly. "I just hope
that she gives you the same heartache
you give me."

"Why do you even *have* Facebook, anyway?"

"Because it's good for business."

She has three clients that I know of— none of whom seem perturbed that my mother has no degree in counseling or consulting or anything else you'd want from a motivational coach. One client is a former stay-at-home mother who wants to rejoin the workforce but has no skills beyond making a mean PB&J sandwich and separating lights from darks. One is a twenty-six-year-old guy who recently found his birth mother but is afraid to make contact with her. And the last is a recovering alcoholic who just likes the stability of a meeting every week.

"A life coach should be on the cutting edge. Hip," my mother says.

"If you were hip, you wouldn't use the word *hip*. You know what I think this is about? The movie we went to last Sunday."

"I didn't like it. The book's ending was better—"

"No, not that. The girl at the ticket booth asked if you were a senior, and you didn't say another word for the rest of the night."

She stands up. "Do I *look* like a senior, for God's sake? I color my hair religiously. I have an elliptical machine. I gave up Brian Williams for Jon Stewart."

I have to give her this—she looks better than most of my friends' mothers. She has the same poker-straight brown hair and green eyes that I do and the kind of funky, eclectic style that always makes you look twice at someone, wondering if she planned the outfit meticulously or just rummaged in the depths of her closet. "Mom," I say, "you are the youngest sixty-five-year-old I know. You don't need Facebook to prove it."

It amazes me that someone—anyone—would pay my mother to be a life coach. I mean, as her daughter, isn't her advice the very thing I've tried to escape? But my mother insists that her clients like the fact that she's survived a great loss herself; it gives her credibility. She says the vast majority of life coaches are nothing more than good listeners who, every so often, can give a procrastinator a kick in the pants. And really, what are the best credentials for that, outside of being a mother?

I peer over her shoulder. "Don't you think you should mention me on the site?" I say. "On account of the fact that I'm your primary qualification for this job?"

"Imagine how ridiculous it will look if your name is on the site and there isn't a link to your profile. But"—she sighs—"that's only for people who've accepted my friend invitation . . ."

"Oh, for God's sake." I lean down and type, my hands between hers, this baby pressed to her back. I log in to my profile. The live feed that fills the screen contains the thoughts and actions of people I went to high school with or other music therapists or former professors; a former college roommate named Darci I haven't spoken with in months. *I should call her,* I think, and at the same time I know I won't. She has twins who are just going to preschool; their smiling faces are her profile photo.

I accept my mother's pending friend

request, even though it feels like a new low in social networking. "There," I say. "Happy?"

"Very. Now at least I know I'll be able to see new pictures of my grandchild when I log in."

"As opposed to driving a mile to my apartment to see her in person?"

"It's the principle, Zoe," my mother says. "I'm just glad you finally got off your high horse."

"No horses," I say. "I'm just not in the mood to fight until it's time to leave for my baby shower."

My mother opens her mouth to respond, then snaps it shut. For a half second, she contemplates going along with the ruse, and, just as quickly, she gives up. "Who told you?"

"I think the pregnancy is bringing out a sixth sense in me," I confide.

She considers this, impressed. "Really?"

I walk into her kitchen to raid the fridge—there are three tubs of hummus and a bag of carrots, plus various indistinguishable clots in Tupperware containers. "Some mornings I wake up and I just know Max is going to say he wants Cap'n Crunch for breakfast. Or I'll hear the phone ring and I know it's you before I even pick up."

"I used to be able to predict rain when I was pregnant with you," my mother says. "I was more accurate than the weatherman on the ABC news."

I dip my finger into the hummus. "When I woke up this morning, the whole bedroom smelled like eggplant parmigiana—you know, the really good kind that they make at Bolonisi's?"

"That's where the shower's being held!" she gasps, amazed. "When did all this start?"

"About the same time I found a Kinko's receipt for the invitations in Max's jacket."

It takes my mother a moment, and then she starts to laugh. "And here I was planning the cruise I was going to take after I won the lottery with your number picks."

"Sorry to disappoint you."

She rubs her hand over my belly. "Zoe," my mother says, "you couldn't if you tried."

Some cognitive scientists believe human response to music provides evidence that we are more than just flesh and blood—that we also have souls. Their thinking is as follows:

All reactions to external stimuli can be traced back to an evolutionary rationale. You pull your hand away from fire to avoid physical harm. You get butterflies before an important speech because the adrenaline running through your veins has caused a physiological fight-or-flight response. But there is no evolutionary context within which people's response to music makes sense—the tapping of a foot, the urge to sing along or get up and dance, there's just no survival benefit to these activities. For this reason, some believe that our response to music is proof that there's more to us than just biological and physiological mechanics—that the only way to be moved by the spirit, so to speak, is to have one in the first place.

There are games. Estimate Zoe's Belly Size, a purse scavenger hunt (who would have guessed that my mother had an overdue utility bill in her bag?), a baby-sock-matching relay, and, now, a particularly disgusting foray in which baby diapers filled with melted chocolate are passed around for identification by candy bar brand.

Even though this isn't really my cup of tea, I play along. My part-time book-keeper, Alexa, has organized the whole event—and has even gone to the trouble of rounding up guests: my mother, my cousin Isobel, Wanda from Shady Acres and another nurse from the burn unit of the hospital where I work, and a school counselor named Vanessa who contracted me to do music therapy earlier this year with a profoundly autistic ninth grader.

It's sort of depressing that these women, acquaintances at best, are being substituted for close friends. Then again, if I'm not working, I'm with Max. And Max would rather be run over by his own lawn-mowing machines than identify chocolate feces in a diaper. For this reason alone, he is really the only friend I need.

I watch Wanda peer into the Pampers. "Snickers?" she guesses incorrectly.

Vanessa gets the diaper next. She's tall, with short platinum blond hair and piercingly blue eyes. The first time I met her she invited me into her office and gave me a blistering lecture on how the SATs were a conspiracy by the College Board to take over the world eighty dollars at a time. *Well?* she said when she finally stopped for a breath. *What do you have to say for yourself?*

I'm the new music therapist, I told her.

She blinked at me, and then looked down at her calendar and flipped the page backward. *Ah,* she said. *Guess the rep from Kaplan is coming tomorrow.*

Vanessa doesn't even glance down at the diaper. "They look like Mounds to me," she says drily. "Two, to be exact."

I burst out laughing, but I'm the only one who seems to get Vanessa's joke.

Alexa looks devastated because her party games aren't being taken seriously. My mother intervenes, collecting the diaper from Vanessa's place mat. "How about Name That Baby?" she suggests.

I feel a twinge in my side and absently rub my hand over the spot.

My mother reads from a paper Alexa has printed off the Internet. "A baby lion is a . . ."

My cousin's hand shoots up. "Cub!" she yells out.

"Right! A baby fish is a . . . ?"

"Caviar?" Vanessa suggests.

"Fry," Wanda says.

"That's a verb," Isobel argues.

"I'm telling you, I saw it on *Who Wants to Be a Millionaire*—"

Suddenly I am seized by a cramp so intense that all the breath rushes out of my body.

"Zoe?" My mother's voice seems far away. I struggle to my feet.

Twenty-eight weeks, I think. *Too soon.*

Another current rips through me. As I fall against my mother, I feel a warm gush between my legs. "My water," I whisper. "I think it just broke."

But when I glance down, I am standing in a pool of blood.

Last night was the first night Max and I ever talked about baby names.

"Johanna," I whispered, after he turned out the light.

"Sorry to disappoint," Max said. "But it's just me."

In the dark, I could see his smile. Max is the sort of man I never imagined would be attracted to me—big, broad, a surfer with a shock of blond hair and enough wattage in his smile to make grocery clerks drop his change and soccer moms slow down near our driveway. I was always considered smart, but by no stretch of the imagination am I a looker. I am the girl next door, the wallflower, the one whose features you cannot recall. The first time he talked to me—at his brother's wedding, where I was filling in for the lead vocalist in the band, who'd developed a kidney stone—I turned around, certain that he was speaking to someone else. Years later he told me that he never knew what to say to girls but that my voice was like a drug; it had seeped into his veins and given him the courage to come up to me during the band's fifteen-minute break.

He didn't think a woman with a master's degree in musicology would want anything to do with a college dropout / surf rat who was scraping together a landscaping business.

I didn't think a man who could have taken home his pick of anyone with two X chromosomes would find me even remotely attractive.

Last night he put his gentle hand over our baby, an umbrella. "I thought talking about the baby was bad luck."

It was. Or, at least, it always had been, to me. But we were so close to making it to the finish line. This was so real. What could possibly go wrong? "Well," I said, "I changed my mind."

"Okay, then. Elspeth," Max said. "After my favorite aunt."

"*Please* tell me you're making that up . . ."

He laughed. "I have another aunt named Ermintrude—"

"Hannah," I countered. "Stella. Sage."

"That's a spice," Max said.

"Yeah, but not like Ground Cloves. It's pretty."

He leaned over my belly and pressed his ear against it. "Let's ask her what she wants to be called," Max suggested. "I think . . . wait . . . no, hang on, she's coming in loud and clear." He looked up at me, his cheek still against our baby. "Bertha," he pronounced.

The baby, as if to comment, gave his jaw a swift kick; and I was sure at the time that this meant she was fine. That it hadn't been bad luck at all.

I am being turned inside out; I am falling through blades. I have never felt so much agony, as if the pain is trapped under my skin, and trying desperately to slice its way out.

"It's going to be all right," Max says, clasping my hand as if we are about to arm-wrestle. I wonder when he arrived. I wonder why he is lying to me.

His face is as white as a midnight moon, and, even though he's only inches away, I can barely see him. Instead, there is a blur of doctors and nurses crowded into the tiny delivery room. An IV is fed into my arm. A band is wrapped around my belly and hooked up to a fetal monitor.

"I'm only twenty-eight weeks," I pant.

"We know, honey," a nurse says, and she turns her attention to the medical personnel. "I'm not getting anything on the monitor . . ."

"Try it again—"

I grab the nurse's sleeve. "Is she . . . is she too little?"

"Zoe," the nurse says, "we're doing everything we can." She fiddles with a knob on the monitor and readjusts the band around my belly. "I'm still not getting a heartbeat—"

"What?" I struggle to a sitting position as Max tries to hold me back. "Why not?"

"Get the ultrasound," Dr. Gelman snaps, and a moment later one is wheeled in. Cold gel squirts onto my abdomen as I am twisted by another cramp. The doctor's eyes are trained on the ultrasound monitor. "There's the head," she says calmly. "And there's the heart."

I look frantically, but I see only shifting sands of gray and black. "What do you see?"

"Zoe, I need you to relax for a moment," Dr. Gelman says.

So I bite my lip. I listen to the blood pounding in my ears. A minute passes, and then another. There is no sound in the room except for the quiet beeps of machines.

And then Dr. Gelman says what I've known she'll say all along. "I'm not seeing a heartbeat, Zoe." She looks me in the eye. "I'm afraid your baby is dead."

Into the silence rips a sound that makes me let go of Max's hand and cover my ears. It is like the strafe of a bullet, nails on a chalkboard, promises being broken. It's a note I have never heard—this chord of pure pain—and it takes a moment to realize it is coming from me.

This is what I have packed in my hospital bag for delivery:

A nightgown with tiny blue flowers printed all over it, although I haven't worn a nightgown since I was twelve.

Three pairs of maternity underwear.

A change of clothes.

A small gift pack of cocoa butter lotion and soap leaves for a new mom, given to me by the mother of one of my recently discharged burn victims at the hospital.

An incredibly soft stuffed pig, which Max and I bought years ago, during my first pregnancy, before the miscarriage, when we were still capable of hope.

And my iPod, loaded with music. So much music. While doing my undergraduate degree at Berklee in music therapy, I had worked with the professor who first cataloged the effect of music therapy during childbirth. Although studies had been done linking music to breathing, and breathing to the autonomic nervous system, nothing had been done until that point to formally connect Lamaze breathing techniques to self-selected music. The premise was that women who listened to different music at different parts of labor could use that music to breathe properly, to remain relaxed, and to subsequently reduce labor pain.

At nineteen, I had found it amazing to work with someone whose research had become widespread practice during childbirth. I didn't realize it would be another twenty-one years before I got the chance to try it myself.

Because music is so important to me, I selected the pieces to use during labor and delivery very carefully. For early labor, I would relax to Brahms. For active labor, when I needed to stay focused on my breathing, I chose music with a strong tempo and rhythm: Beethoven's "Moonlight Sonata." For transition, when I knew it would hurt the most, I had gathered a combination of music—from the songs with the strongest positive memories from my childhood—REO Speedwagon and Madonna and Elvis Costello and Wagner's "Ride of the Valkyries," whose angry lifts and falls would mirror what was going on in my body.

I wholeheartedly believe that music can alleviate the physical pain of childbirth.

I just don't know if it can do anything for the grief.

While I am delivering the baby, I am already thinking that one day I will not remember this. That I will not remember Dr. Gelman talking about the submucosal fibroids that she had wanted to remove before this IVF cycle—a surgery I declined, because I was in too big a hurry to get pregnant—fibroids which are now so much bigger. I will not remember her telling me that the placenta had sheared away from the uterine wall. I will not feel her checking my cervix and quietly saying that I'm at six centimeters. I will not notice Max hooking up my iPod so that Beethoven fills the room; I will not see the nurses gliding in somber slow motion, so different from every giddy and raucous labor and delivery I've ever seen on *A Baby Story*.

I will not remember my water being

broken, or how so much blood soaked the sheet beneath me. I won't remember the sad eyes of the anesthesiologist who said he was sorry for my loss before he rolled me onto my side to give me an epidural.

I won't remember losing the sensation in my legs and thinking that this was a start, wondering if they could fix it so that I didn't feel anything at all.

I won't recall opening my eyes after a knotted contraction and seeing Max's face, twisted just as hard as mine with tears.

I won't remember telling Max to turn off the Beethoven. And I won't remember that, when he didn't do it fast enough, I lashed out with one arm and knocked the iPod dock station to the floor and broke it.

I won't remember that, afterward, it was silent.

I will have to be told by someone else how the baby slipped between my legs like a silver fish, how Dr. Gelman said the baby was a boy.

But that's not right, I'll think, although I won't have the recollection. *Bertha is supposed to be a girl.* And how, on the heels of that, I wondered what else the doctor had gotten wrong.

I won't remember the nurses wrapping him in a blanket, crowning him with a tiny knit cap.

I won't remember holding him: his head, the size of a plum. His blue-veined features. The perfect nose, the pouting mouth, the smooth skin where his eyebrows were still being sketched in. The chest, fragile as a bird's, and still. The way he nearly fit in the palm of one hand; the way he weighed nothing at all.

I won't remember how, until that moment, I really did not believe it was true.

In my hazy dream I spin back one month. Max and I are lying in bed after midnight. *You awake?* I ask.

Yeah. Just thinking.

About what?

He shakes his head. *Nothing.*

You were worrying, I say.

No. I was wondering, he says soberly, *about olive oil.*

Olive oil?
Right. What's it made from?
Is this a trick question? I ask. *Olives.*
And corn oil. What's that made from?
Corn?
So, Max says, *how about baby oil?*
For a moment, we are both silent. Then we start laughing. We laugh so hard that tears come to my eyes. In the dark, I reach for Max's hand, but I miss.

When I wake up, the shades in the room are drawn but the door is ajar. At first, I cannot remember where I am. There is noise in the hallway, and I see a tangle of family—grandparents, children, teen-agers—floating along on the trail of their own laughter. They are carrying a rainbow of balloons.

I start to cry.

Max sits down beside me on the bed. He awkwardly puts his arm around me. Playing Florence Nightingale is not his strong suit. One Christmas, we had the flu together. In between my own bouts of vomiting, I would walk to the bathroom and get him cold compresses. "Zo," he murmurs. "How do you feel?"

"How do you think I feel?" I am being a bitch. Anger burns the back of my throat. It fills the space inside me that was formerly home to my baby.

"I want to see him."

Max freezes. "I, um . . ."

"Call the nurse." My mother's voice comes from the corner of the room where she's sitting. Her eyes are red and swollen. "You heard what she wants."

Nodding, Max gets up and walks out of the room. My mother folds me into her arms. "It's not fair," I say, my face crumpling.

"I know, Zo." She strokes my hair, and I lean against her, the way I did when I was four years old and teased for my freckles, or fifteen and getting my heart broken for the first time. I realize I will not have the chance to comfort my own baby this way, and that makes me cry even harder.

A nurse steps into the room with Max at her heels. "Look," he says, handing me a photo of our son. It looks as if it were snapped while he was asleep in a bassinet. His hands are curled on either side of his head. His chin has a tiny dimple.

Beneath the photo are a handprint and a footprint, too tiny to look real.

"Mrs. Baxter," she says softly, "I'm so sorry for your loss."

"Why are you whispering?" I ask. "Why are you *all* whispering? *Where the hell is my baby?*"

As if I have summoned him, a second nurse enters, carrying my son. He is dressed now, in clothes that are swimming on him. I reach for him.

For a single day, I worked in an NICU unit. I was playing guitar with the preemies, and singing to them, as part of developmental care—babies who are exposed to music therapy show increased oxygen saturation and decreased heart rate, and some studies have even shown preemies doubling their daily weight gain when music therapy is part of their routine. I'd been working with one mother, singing a lullaby in Spanish to her baby, when a social worker came in and asked for my help.

"The Rodriguez baby died this morning," she told me. "The family's waiting for their favorite nurse to come in and do the last bath."

"The last bath?"

"It helps, sometimes," the social worker said. "The thing is, it's a big family, and I think they could use a hand in there."

When I walked into the private room where the family was waiting, I understood why. The mother was sitting in a rocking chair with the dead infant in her arms. Her face looked as if it had been carved from stone. The father was hovering behind her. There were aunts and uncles and grandparents milling in silence, a direct counterpoint to the nieces and nephews, who were shrieking and chasing each other around the hospital bed.

"Hello," I said. "I'm Zoe. Would it be all right if I played?" I gestured at the guitar hanging by its strap across my back.

When the mother didn't answer, I

knelt down in front of the chair. "Your daughter was beautiful," I said.

She didn't answer, nor did anyone else, so I pulled my guitar around and began to sing—the same Spanish lullaby I'd been singing minutes before:

Duérmete, mi niña
Duérmete, mi sol
Duérmete, pedazo
De mi corazón.

For a moment, the kids who were running in circles paused. The adults in the room stared at me. I became the focal point, the center of all their energy, instead of that poor infant. As soon as the nurse arrived and undressed the baby for its last bath, I slipped out of the room and went to the administrative offices of the hospital and quit.

I had played at the bedsides of children who were dying dozens of times; I had always considered it a privilege to swing them from this world into the next with a string of notes, a sweet refrain. But this had been different. I just couldn't play Orpheus for a dead baby, not when Max and I were trying so hard to get pregnant.

My own son is cold to the touch. I lay him down between my legs on the hospital mattress and unsnap the blue pajamas in which some kind nurse has dressed him. I cover his torso with my hand, but there's no heartbeat.

Duérmete, mi niño, I whisper.

"Would you like to keep him here for a while?" asks the nurse who was carrying him.

I look up at her. "I can do that?"

"You can keep him as long as you like," she says. "Well . . ." She doesn't finish the rest of the thought.

"Where does he stay?" I say.

"I beg your pardon?"

"When he's not here. Where does he stay?" I look at the nurse. "In the morgue?"

"No. He stays with us."

She's lying to me. I know she's lying. If he had been in a bassinet with the other babies, his skin wouldn't have a chill to it, like an autumn morning. "I want to see."

"I'm afraid we can't—"

"Do it." My mother's voice crackles with authority. "If that's what she needs to see, let her."

The two nurses look at each other. Then one of them steps outside and brings in a wheelchair. They help me swing my legs off the bed and sit down. The whole time I am holding the baby.

Max wheels me down the hallway. Behind one door I hear the grunt of a woman in labor. He pushes me a little faster.

"Mrs. Baxter would like to see where her son has been," the nurse says to a colleague behind the desk, as if this is the kind of request she fields daily. She leads me past the nurses' station to a row of shelving units stuffed with plastic-wrapped tubing and stacks of swaddling blankets and diapers. Beside it is a small, stainless steel refrigerator, the kind I used to have in my dorm room at college.

The nurse opens up the refrigerator. I don't understand at first, and then when I look inside and see the empty white walls and the single rack, I do.

I grab the baby closer, but he is so small that it's hard to feel as if I've got him soundly. I might as well be holding a bag of feathers, a breath, a wish. I stand up without a plan in my head—just knowing that I cannot look at that refrigerator anymore—and suddenly I cannot breathe, and the world is spinning, and my chest is being crushed in a vise. All I can think, before I fall to the ground, is that I won't drop my son. That a good mother wouldn't let go.

"What you're saying," I tell Dr. Gelman, my OB, "is that I'm a ticking time bomb."

After I fainted, was revived, and told the doctors my symptoms, I was put on heparin. A spiral CT scan showed a blood clot that had traveled to my lung—a pulmonary embolism. Now, my doctor's told me that my blood tests showed a clotting disorder. That this could happen again and again.

"Not necessarily. Now that we know you've got AT III, we can put you on Coumadin. It's treatable, Zoe."

I am a little afraid to move, certain

that I will jar the clot and send it right to my brain and have an aneurysm. Dr. Gelman assures me that the shots of heparin I've had will keep that from happening.

There's a part of me, the part that feels like I've swallowed a stone, that is disappointed.

"How come you didn't test for it before?" Max asks. "You tested for everything else."

Dr. Gelman turns to him. "Antithrombin three deficiency isn't pregnancy-related. It's something you're born with, and this thrombophilia tends to show up in younger people. We often can't diagnose a clotting disorder until someone's aggravated it. A broken leg can do that. Or, in Zoe's case, labor and delivery."

"It's not pregnancy-related," I repeat, grabbing on to that statement with all my might. "So technically I could still have a baby?"

The obstetrician hesitates. "The two conditions are not mutually exclusive," she says, "but why don't we talk about this in a few weeks?"

We both turn at the sound of the door closing behind Max, who's left the room.

When I am discharged from the hospital, I am wheeled to the bank of elevators by an orderly, with Max carrying my overnight bag. I notice something I didn't notice during the two days I've been there—a single buttercup in a little glass vase that is suctioned to my hospital room door. My room is the only one in the hallway that has a vase. I realize this is some kind of sign, a cue for the phlebotomists and the residents and the candy stripers entering the room that this is not a zone of happiness, that, unlike in every other new mother's room, here something terrible has happened.

As we are waiting for the doors to open, another woman is wheeled up beside me. She has a newborn in her arms, and attached to the arm of her wheelchair is a CONGRATULATIONS balloon. Her husband follows, his arms full of flowers. "Is that Daddy?" the woman coos, as the baby stirs. "Are you waving?"

A bell dings, and the elevator doors open. It is empty, plenty of room for two. The woman is wheeled inside first, and then my orderly begins to pivot the wheelchair, so that I can be wheeled in beside her.

Max, however, blocks his way. "We'll take the next one," he says.

We drive home in Max's truck, which smells of loam and freshly cut grass, even though there are no mowers or weed cutters in the flatbed. I wonder who is covering the business. Max turns on the radio and sets it to a music station. This is a big deal—usually we argue over the programming. He will listen to *Car Talk* on NPR, *Wait Wait . . . Don't Tell Me!* and just about any news show . . . but he doesn't like music playing while he's driving. Me, I can't imagine even a half-mile trip without singing along to a song.

"It's supposed to be nice this weekend," Max says. "Hot."

I look out the window. We're at a red light, and in the car beside us is a mother with two children, who are eating animal crackers in the backseat.

"I thought we could take a ride down to the beach, maybe."

Max surfs; these are the last days of summer. It's what he'd normally do. Except nothing is normal. "Maybe," I say.

"I thought," Max continues, "that might be a good place for, you know." He swallows. "The ashes."

We named the baby Daniel and arranged to have him cremated. The ashes would come back in an urn shaped like a tiny ceramic baby shoe with a blue ribbon. We didn't really discuss what we would do with them once they arrived, but now I realize Max has a point. I don't want the urn on the kitchen counter. I don't want to bury it in our backyard the way we buried our canary when it died. I suppose the beach is a pretty place, if not a meaningful one. But then again, what is my other option? It's not like my baby was conceived in a romantic place like Venice, where I could float the urn down the river Po; or under the stars in Tanzania, where I could open the urn to

the wind of the Serengeti. He was conceived in a lab at an IVF clinic, and I
can't really scatter the ashes through
its halls.

"Maybe," I say, which is all I can give
Max right now.

When we pull into our driveway, my
mother's car is already there. She is
going to be staying with me during the
day to make sure I'm all right when Max
goes to work. She comes outside to
the truck to help me down from my
seat. "What can I get you, Zo?" she
asks. "A cup of tea? Some chocolate?
We could watch the episodes of *True
Blood* you've got TiVoed . . ."

"I want to just lie down," I say, and
when she and Max both rush to help
me, I hold them off. I walk down the
hall slowly, using the wall for support.
But instead of entering our bedroom at
the end of the hall, I duck into a smaller
room on the right.

Up until a month ago, this had been
my makeshift office—the place where,
once a week, Alexa came to do my
books. Then, over the course of one
weekend, Max and I painted it a sunny

yolk-yellow and lugged in a crib and a changing table we'd scored from a charity shop for a grand total of forty dollars. While Max did the heavy lifting, I organized books—my favorites from when I was little: *Where the Wild Things Are, Harry the Dirty Dog,* and *Caps for Sale*—on a shelf.

But now, when I open the door, I draw in my breath. Instead of the crib and changing table, there is the old drafting board I used as a desk. My computer is hooked up and humming again. My files are neatly stacked beside it. And my instruments—djembes and banjos and guitars and chimes—are lined up against the wall.

The only indication that there might ever have been a nursery here are the walls, which are still that sunshine yellow. The color you feel inside you, when you smile.

I lie down on the braided rug in the middle of the floor and curl my knees into my chest. Max's voice drifts down the hall. "Zoe? Zo? Where are you?" I hear him open the door to the bedroom, make a quick sweep, and leave. He does the same thing in the bathroom. Then he opens the door and sees me. "Zoe," he says. "What's wrong?"

I look around this room, this not-nursery, and I think of Mr. Docker, of what it means to become aware of your surroundings. It's like waking up from the best dream to find a hundred knives at your throat. "Everything," I whisper.

Max sits down beside me. "We have to talk."

I don't face him. I don't even sit up. I keep staring straight ahead, my eyes level with the radiators. Max forgot to take the safety plugs out of the outlets. They are all still covered with those flat disks of plastic, to make sure no one gets hurt.

Too fucking late.

"Not now," I say.

You lose keys, your wallet, your glasses. You lose a job. You lose weight.

You lose money. You lose your mind.

You lose hope; you lose faith. You lose your sense of direction.

You lose track of friends.

You lose your head. You lose a tennis match. You lose a bet.

You lose a baby, or so they say.

Except I know exactly where he is.

The next day, I wake up and my breasts have become marble. I can't even breathe without them aching. I have no newborn, but my body doesn't seem to know that. The nurses at the hospital had warned me about this. There used to be an injection to dry up breast milk, but there were serious side effects, and so now they could only send me home with fair warning about what would come to pass.

The covers on Max's side of the mattress are still tucked in. He did not come to bed last night; I don't know where he slept. By now, he will have left for work.

"Mom," I call out, but no one comes. I sit up, wincing, and see a note on my nightstand. *Gone grocery shopping*, my mother has written.

I shuffle through the discharge paperwork I was given at the hospital. But no one thinks to send the woman who's delivered a stillborn home with the contact information for a lactation expert.

Feeling stupid, I dial the office number for Dr. Gelman. Her receptionist—a sweet girl I've seen monthly now for over half a year—picks up. "Hi," I say. "This is Zoe Baxter—"

"Zoe!" she says enthusiastically. "I heard you were being admitted on Friday! So? Boy or girl?"

I can tell, from the bubbles in her voice, that she has no idea what happened over the weekend. The words in my throat rustle like leaves. "Boy," I manage. I can't say the rest.

Even the fabric of my T-shirt is causing me excruciating pain. "Can I speak to a nurse-midwife?"

"Sure, I'll put you through . . . ," the receptionist says, and I hold the line praying that the nurse-midwife, at least, knows what happened.

There is a click on the line. "Zoe," the nurse says gently, "how are you doing?"

"My milk," I choke out. "Is there anything I can do to dry it up?"

"Not really—you have to sort of ride it out," she says. "But you can take some ibuprofen. Try putting refrigerated cabbage leaves inside your bra—we don't know why, but there's something in them that helps reduce inflammation. And sage—if you have any, cook with it. Or make a tea. Sage inhibits milk production."

I thank her and hang up the phone. As I am putting down the handset again, it falls against the clock and inadvertently turns on the radio. I have it tuned to a classical station because it's somehow easier for me to wake up at 6:00 A.M. to orchestral strains rather than a rock beat.

The flute. The seesaw of the string section. The pumping grunt of the tuba and the horn. Wagner's "Ride of the Valkyries" wings from wall to ceiling to floor, filling the room with chaos and drive.

This track is on a CD still in a birthing bag I have not unpacked.

This track was never played during my delivery, although I had a baby.

In one quick move I grab the clock radio and yank it out of the electrical socket where it's plugged in. I hold it high over my head and hurl it across the room so that it smashes onto the wooden floor in a crescendo that would have done Wagner proud.

When there is only silence, I can hear the tatter of my breath. I imagine explaining this to Max. Or my mother, showing up with a grocery bag and stumbling into this scene. "Okay," I say to myself. "You can do this. You just have to pick up the pieces."

In the kitchen I find a black trash bag and a dustpan and broom. I take the remnants of the radio and clean them up. I sweep all the tiny fragments and the innards into the dustpan.

Pick up the pieces.

It's that simple, really. For the first time in forty-eight hours I feel a shift, a purpose. I dial Dr. Gelman's office for the second time in ten minutes. "This is Zoe Baxter again," I say. "I'd like to schedule an appointment."

There are several reasons that I went home with Max the first night I met him:

1. He smelled like summer.
2. I was not the kind of girl who went home with guys she just met. Ever.
3. He was bleeding profusely.

Even though it was Max's brother's wedding, he spent all his time waiting for me to have my next band break. While the other guys went out for a smoke or to grab a glass of water from the bar, I'd look down and find Max waiting for me with a soft drink. At the time, I assumed that he wasn't drinking alcohol out of solidarity: I was working, and not allowed to, so neither would Max. I remember thinking that was awfully sweet. Something most guys would not have done.

I didn't know the happy couple, since I was a last-minute substitute singer, but it was hard to believe that Reid and Max were related. Not just in looks— Reid was tall and athletic in a golf-and-racquetball kind of way, whereas Max was sheer brute size and strength—but also in demeanor. Reid's friends seemed all to be bankers and lawyers who liked to hear themselves talk; their girlfriends and wives had names like Muffy and Winks. Reid's new wife, Liddy, came from Mississippi and seemed to thank Jesus a lot—for the weather, the wine, and the fact that her grammy Kate had lived long enough to see a ring on Liddy's finger. Compared to the rest of the wedding party, Max was much more refreshing: what you saw was what you got. By midnight, when we were scheduled to stop playing, I knew that Max ran his own landscaping business, that he plowed snow in the winter, that his older brother was responsible for the silver scar on his cheek (line drive with a baseball), and that he was allergic to shellfish. He knew that I could sing the alphabet backward, that I could play ten instruments, and that I wanted a family. A big family.

From my spot on the podium, I turned to the band. According to the playlist, our final song was supposed to be Donna Summer's "Last Dance." But this didn't seem like a disco crowd, so I turned to the guys behind me. "You know Etta James?" I asked, and the keyboard player launched into the beginning strains of "At Last."

Sometimes when I sing, I close my eyes. There's harmony in every breath I take; the drums become my pulse, the melody is the flow of my blood. This is what it means to lose yourself in music, to become a symphony of notes and rests and measures.

When I finished singing, there was a thunder of applause. I could hear Reid clapping loudly: *Brava!* And Liddy's twittering girlfriends: . . . *best wedding band I've ever heard . . . must get their card from you.*

"Thank you very much," I murmured, and when I finally opened my eyes, Max was staring into them.

Suddenly, a man came crashing toward the stage, smacking his hand against the drum set as he stumbled forward. He was completely trashed and, from the sound of his Southern accent, one of Liddy's relatives or family friends. "Hey, girlie," he crowed, grabbing at the hem of my black dress. "You know what you are?"

The bass player took a step forward, shielding me, but Max was already coming to my rescue. "Sir," he said politely, "I think you should leave . . ."

The drunk man shoved him and grabbed my hand. "You," he slurred, "are a fucking nightingale!"

"You don't swear in front of a lady," Max said, and he punched the guy. The drunk collapsed against a shrieking cotillion of bridesmaids, their long gowns breaking his fall to the floor.

In an instant, a tuxedoed behemoth grabbed Max and spun him around. "This here's for beatin' on my daddy," he said, and he knocked Max unconscious.

It was pandemonium—Hatfields versus McCoys, tables being overturned, old ladies tearing ribbons off each other's hats. The band grabbed up their instruments, trying to keep the fray from destroying their equipment. I leaped off the stage and crouched over Max. He was bleeding from his mouth and nose, and also from a cut on his forehead where he'd struck the stage as he fell. I pulled his head onto my lap and huddled over him, shielding him from the rest of the commotion. "That," I said, as soon as his eyes fluttered open, "was idiotic."

He grinned. "I don't know about that," Max said. "It got your arms around me."

He was bleeding so much that I insisted he go to the emergency room. He gave me the keys to his truck and let me drive while he pressed a napkin to his forehead. "Guess no one's ever going to forget Reid's wedding," he mused.

I didn't answer.

"You're mad at me," Max said.

"It was a compliment," I said finally. "You punched a guy for giving me a compliment."

He hesitated. "You're right. I should have let him tear your dress off."

"He wouldn't have torn my dress off. The guys in the band would have stopped him before—"

"I wanted to be the one to save you," Max said simply, and I stared at him in the green glow of the dashboard.

At the hospital, I waited with Max in a cubicle. "You're going to need stitches," I told him.

"I'm going to need a lot more than that," he said. "For starters, I'm pretty sure my brother will never speak to me again."

Before I could respond, a doctor pulled aside the curtain and entered, introducing himself. He snapped on a pair of rubber gloves and asked what had happened. "I ran into something," Max said.

He winced as the doctor probed the scalp wound. "Into what?"

"A fist?"

The doctor took a penlight from his pocket and instructed Max to follow the tiny beam. I watched his eyes roll up, then from side to side. He caught my glance and winked at me.

"You're going to need stitches," the doctor echoed. "You don't seem to have a concussion, but it wouldn't be a bad idea to make sure someone stays with you tonight." He pulled aside the curtains of the cubicle. "I'll be back with the suture tray."

Max looked up at me, a question in his eyes.

"Of course I'll stay," I said. "Doctor's orders."

One week later, I go back to work at the burn unit of the hospital. The first patient I see is Serena, a fourteen-year-old girl from the Dominican Republic who is one of my regulars. Burned severely in a house fire, she was treated locally and wound up disfigured and scarred. She hid in the dark in her family home for two years before coming to Rhode Island to have reconstructive skin grafts. I've met with her for an hour each time I am scheduled to be at the hospital, although at first, no one really understood what good music therapy could do for Serena. She was blind because of cataracts that developed when her scarred eyelids wouldn't shut, and has limited movement in her hands. At first I just sang to her until she began to sing along with me. Eventually, I modified a guitar for her, tuning it to an open chord and then fitting it with a slide so that she could play. I put Velcro patches on the back of the neck of the guitar so that she could literally feel her way into the chords she was learning to play.

"Hi, Serena," I say, as I knock on the door to her room.

"Hey, stranger," she answers. I can hear the smile in her voice.

I am grateful, selfishly, for her blindness. For the fact that, unlike minutes ago, when I was talking to the nurses at their desk, I will not have to be responsible for putting her at ease when she doesn't know how to offer condolences. Serena never knew I was pregnant; therefore, she has no reason to know the baby died.

"Where've you been?" she asks.

"Sick," I say, pulling up a chair beside her and settling my guitar across my lap. I begin to tune it, and she reaches for her own instrument. "What have you been doing?"

"The usual," Serena says. Her face is swathed in bandages, still healing from her most recent operation. Her words are slurred, but, after all this time, I know the patterns of her speech. "I have something for you."

"You do?"

"Yeah. Listen. It's called 'The Third Life.'" I sit up, interested. This term grew out of therapy sessions we'd had over the past two months, where we'd talked about the difference between her first life—pre-fire—and her second, after the fire. *What about your third life? I had asked Serena. Where do you think of yourself, when all the surgeries are finished?*

I listen to Serena's reedy soprano, punctuated by the beeps and whirs of monitors attached to her body:

No hiding in the darkness
No anger and no pain
The outside may be different
But inside I'm the same

On the second verse, when I have her melody tangled in my mind, I begin to pick out harmony on my own guitar. I finish when she finishes singing, and as she slides her hand up the neck of the guitar, I clap.

"That," I tell Serena, "was the best present ever."

"Worth getting sick for?"

Once, during a session, Serena was playing with a rainstick, turning it over and over and getting progressively more agitated. When I asked her what it reminded her of, she told me about the last day she had been outside in the Dominican Republic. She was walking home from school and it started to pour. She knew, because she stepped in the puddles that were forming, and her hair was wet. But she couldn't feel drops on her skin, because of the scar tissue. What she'd never understood was why she could not feel rain, but something as insubstantial as a classmate's sneer about her Bride of Frankenstein face felt like a hot sword running through her.

That was the moment she decided not to leave her house again.

Music therapy is not supposed to be about the therapist, it's supposed to be about the patient. And yet, a small splash on the belly of my guitar suggests I must be crying. Like Serena, I haven't felt the tears on my cheeks at all.

I take a deep breath. "Which verse do you like the most?"

"The second, I guess."

I fall back into the familiar: teacher to student, therapist to patient, the person I used to be. "Tell me why," I say.

I don't know where Max has found the boat, but the rental is waiting for us when we get to Narragansett Bay. The weather report was wrong; it is cold and damp. I am quite sure we are the only people booking a motorboat this morning. Mist sprays against my face, and I zip my jacket all the way up to my chin.

"You go first," Max says, and he holds the boat so that I can step into it. Then he hands me the cardboard box that has been on the seat between us for the drive down to the beach.

Max guns the engine, and we go spitting out to sea, puttering through the no-wake zone around buoys and the sleeping hulks of sailboats. Whitecaps reach their bony fingers over the hull of the little boat and soak my sneakers.

"Where are we going?" I yell over the motor.

Max doesn't hear me, or he pretends not to. He has been doing a lot of that lately. He comes home hours after the sun has set and I know he couldn't possibly be pruning or planting or mowing or even surfing. He uses this excuse to sleep on the couch. *I didn't want to wake you up,* he says, as if it is my fault.

It's not even really morning yet. It was Max's idea to come out here when the ocean was quiet—no fishing trawlers, no weekend sailors. I sit on the center of the bench of the boat with the box on my lap. When I close my eyes, the churn of the engine and the slap of the waves rearrange themselves into a rap beat. I drum my fingers against the metal seat, playing in time.

After about ten minutes Max cuts the engine. We bob along, tossed by our own wake.

He sits across from me, his hands

tucked between his knees. "What do you think we should do?"

"I don't know."

"Do you want to . . ."

"No," I say, thrusting the box at him. "You do it."

He nods and takes the small blue ceramic shoe out of the box. A few packing peanuts flutter away on the wind. It makes me panic—what if a big gust of wind comes along at just the wrong moment? What if the ashes wind up in my hair, on my jacket?

"I feel like we ought to say something," Max murmurs.

My eyes fill with tears. "I'm sorry," I whisper.

For not knowing anything better to say.

For having to do this in the first place.

For not being able to keep you safe inside me a few more weeks.

Max reaches across the space between us and squeezes my hand. "I am, too."

The reality of my baby, it turns out, is no more than a breath in the cold, a puff of smoke. The ashes are gone almost the very moment they hit the air. If I'd blinked, I could easily have pretended that it never happened.

But I imagine them settling on the frantic surface of the ocean. I imagine the Sirens on the sea floor, singing him home.

Max is late to the appointment with Dr. Gelman. He comes skidding into her paneled office, smelling of mulch. "Sorry," he apologizes. "Job ran late."

There was a time when he was ten minutes early for our appointments. When, once, his truck broke down and he jogged with a semen sample to the clinic so that it would arrive in the window of time necessary to fertilize the harvested eggs. But in the two weeks since I've been discharged from the hospital, our conversation has been limited to the weather, the grocery list, and what I'd like to watch on TV at night. He slides into the chair beside me and looks at the obstetrician expectantly. "Is she okay?"

"There's no reason to think that Zoe's

not going to be fine," Dr. Gelman says. "Now that we know about the thrombophilia, it's manageable with medication. And the fibroids that we saw beneath the placenta—we'll hope that, without the hormonal fluctuations of pregnancy, they shrink again."

"But what about next time?" I ask.

"I honestly don't anticipate another clot, as long as we keep you on Coumadin—"

"No," I interrupt. "I mean, the next time I get pregnant. You said I could try again."

"What?" Max says. "What the *hell*?"

I face him. "We have three embryos left. Three frozen embryos, Max. We didn't give up before when I miscarried. We can't just give up now—"

Max turns to Dr. Gelman. "Tell her. Tell her this is a bad idea."

The obstetrician runs her thumb along the edge of her blotter. "The chance of you having a placental abruption again is between twenty and fifty percent. In addition, there are other risks, Zoe. Preeclampsia, for example: high blood pressure and swelling that

would require you to take magnesium
to prevent seizures. You could have a
stroke—"

"Jesus Christ," Max mutters.

"But I can try," I say again, looking
her directly in the eye.

"Yes," she says. "Knowing the risks,
you can."

"No." The word is barely audible, as
Max stands up. "No," he repeats, and
he walks out of the office.

I follow him, hurrying down the hall
to grab his arm. He shakes me off.
"Max!" I yell after him, but he is headed
toward the elevator. He steps inside,
and I reach the doors just as they are
closing. I slip in and stand beside him.

There's a mother in the elevator, too,
pushing a stroller. Max stares straight
ahead.

The elevator bell dings, and the doors
open; the woman pushes her child out.
"That's all I've ever wanted," I say, as
soon as we are alone again. "To have a
baby."

"What if it's not what *I* want?"

"It's what you used to want."

"Well, *you* used to want a relationship with me," Max says, "so I guess we've both changed a little."

"What are you talking about? I still want a relationship with you."

"You want a relationship with my sperm. This . . . this baby thing . . . it's gotten so much bigger than the two of us. It's not even us, in it together anymore. It's you, and it's the baby we can't seem to have, and the harder it gets the more air it sucks out of the room, Zoe. There's no space left for me."

"You're jealous? You're jealous of a baby that doesn't even exist?"

"I'm not jealous. I'm lonely. I want my wife back. I want the girl who used to want to spend time with me, reading the obituaries out loud and driving for forty miles just to see what town we'd wind up in. I want you to call my cell to talk to me, instead of to remind me that I have to be at the clinic at four. And now—now you want to get pregnant again, even if it kills you? When do you stop, Zoe?"

"It's not going to kill me," I insist.

"Then it just might kill *me.*" He looks

up. "It's been nine years. I can't do this anymore."

There is something in his gaze, some bitter pill of truth, that sends a shiver down my spine. "Then we'll find a surrogate. Or we'll adopt—"

"Zoe," Max says, "I mean, I can't do *this.* I can't do *us.*"

The elevator doors open. We are on the ground floor, and the afternoon sun streams through the glass doors at the front of the clinic. Max walks out of the elevator, but I don't.

I tell myself the light is playing tricks on me. That this is an optical illusion. One minute I can see him, and the next, it's like he was never here at all.

	TRACK 1	SING YOU HOME
✓	**TRACK 2**	**THE HOUSE ON HOPE STREET**
	TRACK 3	REFUGEE
	TRACK 4	THE LAST
	TRACK 5	MARRY ME
	TRACK 6	FAITH
	TRACK 7	THE MERMAID
	TRACK 8	ORDINARY LIFE
	TRACK 9	WHERE YOU ARE
	TRACK 10	SAMMY'S SONG

MAX

I always figured I'd have kids. I mean, it's a story most guys can identify with: you're born, you grow up, you start a family, you die. I just wish that, if there had to be a delay somewhere in the process, it would have been the last bit.

I'm not the villain, here. I wanted a baby, too. Not because I've spent my whole life dreaming of fatherhood, but for a reason much more simple than that.

Because it's what Zoe wanted.

I did everything she asked me to. I stopped drinking caffeine, I wore boxers instead of briefs, I started jogging instead of biking. I followed a diet she'd found online that increased fertility. I no longer put the laptop on my lap. I even went to some crazy acupuncturist, who set needles dangerously close to my testicles and lit them on fire.

When none of that worked, I went to a urologist, and filled out a ten-page form that asked me questions like *Do you have erections?* and *How many sexual partners have you had?* and *Does your wife reach orgasm during intercourse?*

I grew up in a household where we didn't really talk about our feelings, and where the only reason you went to a doctor was because you'd accidentally cut off a limb with a chain saw. So I don't mean to be defensive, but you have to understand, the touchy-feely part of IVF and the poking and the prodding isn't something that comes naturally to me.

I had a hunch that it wasn't just Zoe who had infertility problems. My brother, Reid, and his wife had been married for over a decade and hadn't been able to conceive yet, either. The difference was that, instead of forking over ten thousand dollars to a clinic, he and Liddy prayed a lot.

Zoe said that Dr. Gelman had a better success rate than God.

As it turns out, I have a total sperm count of 60 million—which sounds like a lot, right? But when you start figuring in their shape and speed, all of a sudden I'm down to 400,000. Which—again—seems like a pretty big number to me. But imagine that you're running the Boston Marathon along with more than 59 million drunks—suddenly it gets a little more challenging to cross that finish line. Add Zoe's infertility issues to mine, and we were suddenly looking at IVF and ICSI.

And then there's the money. I don't know how people pay for IVF. It costs fifteen thousand dollars a pop, including the medications. We are lucky enough to live in Rhode Island, a state that forces insurance companies to cover women between twenty-five and forty who are married and can't conceive naturally—but that still means our out-of-pocket expenses have been three thousand dollars for each fresh cycle of embryos, and six hundred dollars for each frozen cycle. Not covered: the ICSI—where sperm are directly injected into the eggs (fifteen hundred dollars), embryo freezing (a thousand dollars), and embryo storage (eight hundred dollars per year). What I'm saying here is that, even with insurance, and even before the financial nightmare of this last cycle, we'd run out of money.

I can't really tell you the moment it went wrong. Maybe it was the first time, or the fifth, or the fiftieth that Zoe counted out the days of her menstrual cycle and crawled into bed and said, "Now!" Our sex life had become like Thanksgiving dinner with a dysfunctional family—something you have to show up for, even though you're not really having a good time. Maybe it was when we started IVF, when I realized there was nothing Zoe wouldn't do in her quest to get pregnant; that *want* had become *need* and then *obsession.* Or maybe it was when I began feeling like Zoe and this baby to be were on the same page—and that I had somehow become the outsider. There was no room in my marriage for me anymore, except as genetic material.

A lot of people talk about what women go through, when they can't have a baby. But no one ever asks about the guys. Well, let me tell you—we feel like losers. We can't somehow do what other men manage to do without even trying . . . what other men take precautions to *not* do, most of the time. Whether or not it's true, and whether or not it's my fault—society looks at a guy differently, if he doesn't have kids. There's a whole book of the Old Testament devoted to who begat whom. Even the sex symbol celebrities who make women swoon, like David Beckham and Brad Pitt and Hugh Jackman, are always in *People* magazine swinging one of their children onto their shoulders. (I should know; I've read nearly every issue in the waiting room of the IVF clinic.) This may be the twenty-first century, but being a real man is still tied to being able to procreate.

I know I didn't ask for this. I know I shouldn't feel inadequate. I know it is a medical condition, and that if I suffered a cardiac arrest or a broken ankle I wouldn't think of myself as a wimp if I needed surgery or a cast—so why should I be embarrassed about this?

Because it's just one more piece of evidence, in a long, long list, that I'm a failure.

In the fall, landscaping is a hard sell. I do my fair share of leaf blowing and buzz cutting lawns, so that they're prepped for the winter. I prune deciduous trees and shrubs that flower in the autumn. I've managed to talk a couple of clients into planting before the ground freezes—it's always something you'll be glad you did come spring—and I'm pretty sold on some red maple varieties that have spectacular color in autumn. But mostly this fall, for me, will be about laying off the guys I hired during the summer. Usually I can keep on one or two, but not this winter—I'm just too far in debt, and there isn't enough work.

My five-man landscaping business is going to morph into a one-man snow-plowing service.

I'm pruning a client's roses when one of my summer help comes loping down the driveway. Todd—a junior in high school—stopped working last week, when classes started up again. "Max?" he says, holding his baseball cap in his hands. "You got a minute?"

"Sure," I say. I sit back on my heels and squint up at him. The sun is already low, and it's only three-thirty in the afternoon. "How is school going?"

"It's going." Todd hesitates. "I, um, wanted to ask you about getting my job back."

My knees creak as I stand up. "It's a little early for me to start hiring for next spring."

"I meant for the fall and winter. I've got my license. I could plow for you—"

"Todd," I interrupt, "you're a good kid, but business slows down a lot. I just can't afford to take you on right now." I clap him on the shoulder. "Call me in March, okay?"

I start to walk back to my truck. "Max!" he calls out, and I turn. "I really need this." His Adam's apple bobs like a cork. "My girlfriend—she's pregnant."

I vaguely remember Todd's girlfriend driving up to the curb of a client's house this July with a car full of giddy teens. Her long brown legs in her cutoff jean shorts, as she walked up to Todd with a thermos of lemonade. How he blushed when she kissed him and ran back to her car, her flip-flops slapping against the soles of her feet. I remember being his age, and panicking every time I had sex, certain that I'd be in the two percent of cases where Trojans failed.

How come, Zoe used to say, *the odds are that, if you're sixteen years old and desperate to not get pregnant, you will . . . but if you're forty and you want to get pregnant, you can't?*

I won't look Todd in the eye. "Sorry," I mutter, "I can't help." I fiddle around with some equipment in the flatbed of my truck until I see him drive away. I still have work to do, but I make the executive decision to call it a day. I'm the boss, after all. I should know when it's time to quit.

I drive to a bar that I've passed fifty times on my way to this job. It's called Quasimodo's and sports a bad paint job and metal grilles across the one window, which doubles as a lit Budweiser sign. In other words, it's the sort of place nobody ever goes in the afternoon.

Sure enough, when I first walk inside and my eyes are adjusting to the light, I think it's only me and the bartender. Then I notice a woman with bleached blond hair doing a crossword at the bar. Her arms are bare and ropy, with crepe paper skin; she looks strange and familiar all at once, like a T-shirt washed so often that the picture on the front is now just a blotch of color. "Irv," she says, "what's a five-letter loamy deposit?"

The bartender shrugs. "Something that calls for Imodium?"

She frowns. "The *New York Times* crossword's too classy for that."

"Loess," I say, climbing onto a stool.

"Less what?" she asks, turning to me.

"No, *loess*. L-O-E-S-S. It's a kind of sediment made by layers of silt that the wind's blown into ridges or dunes." I point to her newspaper. "That's your answer."

She writes it in, in pen. "You happen to know six across? 'London street-cars'?"

"Sorry." I shake my head. "I don't know trivia. Just a little geology."

"What can I get you?" the bartender asks, setting a napkin in front of me.

I look at the row of bottles behind him. "Sprite," I say.

He pours the soft drink from a hose beneath the bar and sets it in front of me. From the corner of my eye, I see the woman's drink, a martini. My mouth actually starts to water.

There is a television above the bar. Oprah Winfrey is telling everyone about beauty secrets from around the world. Do I want to know how Japanese women keep their skin so smooth?

"You some kind of professor at Brown?" the woman asks.

I laugh. "Yeah," I say. Why the hell not? I'm never going to see her again.

The truth is, I don't even have a college degree. I flunked out of URI a hundred years ago, when I was a junior. Unlike Reid, the golden son, who'd graduated with honors and had gone on to work as a financial analyst at Bank of Boston before starting his own investment firm, I had majored in Beer Pong and grain alcohol. At first it was parties on the weekends, and then study breaks midweek, except I wasn't doing any studying. There is an entire semester I cannot remember, and one morning, I woke up naked on the steps of the library without any recollection of what had led up to that.

When my dad wouldn't let me move back home, I crashed on Reid's couch in his Kenmore Square apartment. I got a job as a night watchman at a mall, but lost it when I kept missing work because I was sleeping off that afternoon's bender. I started stealing cash from Reid so that I could buy bottles of cheap

booze and hide them around the apartment. Then one morning, I woke up,
hungover, to find a handgun pointed at
my forehead.

"Reid! What the fuck?" I yelped,
scrambling upright.

"If you're trying to kill yourself, Max,"
he said, "let's speed it up a bit."

Together we dumped all the alcohol
down the sink. Reid took the day off
work to come with me to my first AA
meeting. That was seventeen years
ago. By the time I met Zoe, when I was
twenty-nine, I was sober and had figured out what a guy without a college
degree could do with his life. Thinking
back to the only classes I'd really liked
in college—geology—I figured I'd better stick to the land. I got a small business loan and bought my first mower,
painted the side of my truck, and printed
up flyers. I may not be living the lush
life, like Reid and Liddy, but I netted
$23,000 last year *and* I could still take
days off to surf when the waves were
good.

It was enough, with Zoe's income, to
rent a place—a place that she's now

living in. When you are the spouse that wants out of the relationship, you have to be willing to actually *leave.* Sometimes, even though it has been a whole month, I find myself wondering if she's remembered to ask the landlord about getting the furnace cleaned. Or whether she's signed a lease for another year, this time without my name on it. I wonder who carries her heavy drums up the entryway stairs now, or if she just leaves them in the car overnight.

I wonder if I made a mistake.

I look over at the crossword woman's martini. "Hey," I say to Irv the bartender, "can I get one of those?"

The woman taps the pen against the bar. "So you teach geology?"

On the television, Oprah is talking about how to make your own salt scrub, like the ones Cleopatra once used.

"No. Egyptian," I lie.

"Like Indiana Jones?"

"Kind of," I reply. "Except I'm not afraid of snakes."

"Have you been there? On the Nile?"

"Oh, yeah," I say, although I do not even own a passport. "A dozen times."

She pushes her pen and newspaper toward me. "Can you show me what my name would look like in Egyptian?"

Irv sets the martini down in front of me. I start to sweat. It would be so easy.

"I'm Sally," the woman says. "S-A-L-L-Y."

It's amazing what you'll do when you want something bad. You are willing to do anything, say anything, be anything. I used to feel that way about drinking— there were things I did to get cash for booze that I am sure I've blocked out permanently. And I certainly felt that way, once, about having a baby. Tell a stranger the details of my sex life? Sure. Jab my wife in the ass with a needle? My pleasure. Jerk off in a jar? No problem. If the doctors had told us to walk backward and sing opera to increase the chance of fertility, we would not have batted an eyelash.

When you want something bad, you'll tell yourself a thousand lies.

Like: The fifth time's the charm.

Like: Things between Zoe and me will be better once the baby's born.

Like: One sip isn't going to kill me.

I once saw a TV documentary about giant squid, and they filmed one shooting its ink into the water to get away from an enemy. The ink was black and beautiful and curled like smoke, a distraction so that the squid could escape. That's what alcohol feels like, in my blood. It's the ink of the squid, and it's going to blind me so that I can get away from everything that hurts.

The only language I know is English. But on the edge of the newspaper, I draw three wavy lines, and then an approximation of a snake, and a sun. "That's just the sounds of the name, of course," I say. "There isn't really a translation for Sally."

She rips off the corner of the newspaper, folds it, and tucks it into her bra. "I am totally getting a tattoo of this."

Most likely the tattoo artist will have no idea that these are not real hieroglyphs. For all I know, I might have written: *For a good time, call Nefertiti.*

Sally hops down from her stool and moves onto the one beside me. "You gonna drink that martini or wait till it becomes an antique?"

"I haven't decided yet," I say, the first truth I've offered her.

"Well, make up your mind," Sally replies, "so that I can buy you another one."

I lift the martini and drain it in one long, fiery, mind-blowing gulp. "Irv," I say, setting down the empty glass. "You heard the lady."

The first time I had to leave a semen sample at the clinic, the nurse stepped into the waiting room and called my name. As I stood up I thought: *Everyone else here knows exactly what I'm about to do.*

The literature Zoe and I had been given said that the wife could "assist" in the sample collection, but the only thing that seemed more awkward than jerking off in a clinic was having my wife in there with me, with doctors and nurses and patients just outside the door. The nurse led me down the hallway. "Here you go," she said, handing me a brown paper bag. "Just read the instructions."

"It's not so bad," Zoe had told me over breakfast. "Think of it as a visit to *Pee-wee's Playhouse.*"

And really, who was I to complain, when she was getting shots twice a day and having constant pelvic exams and taking so many hormones that something as simple as crossing the street could make her burst into tears? By comparison, this seemed like a piece of cake.

The room was freezing cold and consisted of a couch that had been covered by a sheet, a TV-VCR, a sink, and a coffee table. There were some videos—*Pussy in Boots, Breast Side Story, On Golden Blonde*—various issues of *Playboy* and *Hustler* and, weirdly, a copy of *Good Housekeeping*. A small window that looked like it belonged in a speakeasy was to the right—this would be where I left the sample when I was done. The nurse backed out of the room, and I pushed the lock in the door handle. Then I opened it, and pushed it again. To make sure.

I opened the paper bag. The sample cup was enormous. It was practically a *bucket.* What were they expecting from me?

What if I spilled?

I started to leaf through one of the magazines. The last time I'd done this, I'd been fifteen and had shoplifted the December issue of *Playboy* from a newsstand. I became incredibly aware of how loudly I was breathing. Maybe that wasn't normal. Maybe that meant I was having a heart attack?

Maybe I just needed to get this over with.

I turned on the television. There was already a video playing. I watched for a moment, and then wondered if the person waiting on the other side of the trapdoor for the sample was listening.

It was taking forever.

In the end, I closed my eyes, and I pictured Zoe.

Zoe, before we'd started talking about a family. Like the time we'd gone camping off the grid in the White Mountains, and I woke up to find her sitting on a boulder playing a flute, wearing absolutely nothing.

Afterward, I stared at the sample in the cup. No wonder we couldn't get pregnant; there was hardly anything there, at least in terms of volume. I wrote my name and the time on the label. I slipped the sample into the drop-off zone and closed the door, wondering if I should knock or yell or somehow let the technician know that it was ready and waiting.

I decided they'd figure it out, and I washed my hands and hurried into the hallway. The receptionist smiled at me as I left. "Thanks for coming," she said.

Seriously? Shouldn't that phrase be banned from use at an IVF clinic?

As I walked to my car, I was already thinking of how I'd tell Zoe what the receptionist had said. How we'd laugh.

When I wake up, I am lying on a pillow covered in purple fur, on the floor of a bedroom I do not recognize. Gradually, ignoring the sledgehammer at my temple, I sit up and see a bare foot, flame red polish. My tongue feels like it's carpeted.

Staggering upright, I look down at the woman. It takes me a full minute to remember her name. I can't really recall how we got here, but I do have an image of another bar, after Quasimodo's, and maybe even another after that. I can taste tequila, and shame.

Sally is snoring like a longshoreman—the only saving grace. The last thing I want to do is have a conversation with her. I tiptoe out of the room, holding my pants and my shirt and my shoes in a ball at my groin. Did I drive here last night? I hope like hell I didn't. But God only knows where I left my car.

Bathroom. I'll go to the bathroom, and then I'll sneak out of here. I'll go home and pretend this never happened.

I pee and then wash up, dunking my head under the faucet and scrubbing my hair dry with a pink hand towel. My gaze falls to the counter, to a foil snake of condoms. Oh, thank God. Thank *God* I didn't make that mistake, too.

Get a grip on yourself, Max, I say silently.

You've been here before, and you don't want to go back.

Everyone messes up from time to time. Maybe I've had a few more instances than others, but that doesn't mean that I'm down for the count. This wasn't falling off the wagon. It was just . . . a speed bump.

I open the bathroom door to find a toddler sucking his thumb and staring up at me, with his older sister—a teenager—standing just behind him. "Who the fuck are *you*?" she asks.

I don't answer. I run past them, out the front door, down the driveway that does not have my car in it. I run all the way out of this suburban cul-de-sac in my boxers. At the juncture of the state highway, I throw on my clothes and dig in my pocket for my cell phone, but the battery's dead. I keep running, certain that Sally and her children are going to chase me down in the minivan that was in the driveway. I don't stop until I see a strip mall. All I need is a phone; I'll call a taxi service to get me back to Quasimodo's to pick up my car (which is, I hope, where I left it) and then I'll take refuge at Reid's house.

It's not really my fault that the first place I find open is a restaurant whose proprietor is doing inventory on a Saturday morning. That the guy shakes his head when I ask to borrow the phone, and says I look like I've had a rough night. That he offers me, on the house, a drink.

Normally, we would have been home. After all, the progesterone shot had to be given between 7:00 and 7:15 each night—and it was easy enough to plan our evenings around that, since we didn't have any spending money to go to a movie or out to dinner anyway. But Zoe had been invited to the wedding of two seniors who'd met in one of her group therapy classes at a nursing home. "If it wasn't for me," she'd said, "there wouldn't even *be* a wedding."

So I came home from work and showered and put on a tie, and we drove to the nursing home. In her purse, Zoe had the progesterone, alcohol wipes, and syringes. We watched Sadie and Clark, with their combined age of 184, get united in holy matrimony. And then we ate creamed beef and Jell-O—the food had to be denture-friendly—and watched the residents who were still mobile dance to big band records.

The happy newlyweds fed each other cake. Leaning toward Zoe, I whispered, "I give this marriage ten years, tops."

Zoe laughed. "Watch it, buster. That could be us one day." Then her watch beeped, and she looked at the time. "Oh," she said. "It's seven." I followed her down the hall to the bathrooms.

There were two, one for men and one for women, each big enough to accommodate a wheelchair—or a husband who had to give his wife a progesterone shot. The women's room was locked, so we ducked into the men's instead. Zoe hiked up her skirt.

There was a bull's-eye on the upper part of her butt, drawn in Sharpie marker. Every day for the past week, since we began these shots, I'd re-drawn the circle after her shower. I didn't want to hurt her by sticking the needle somewhere more painful than it had to be.

I had believed there was nothing worse than giving Zoe shots in her belly—mixing up the powder and the water and pinching the skin to inject the Repronex; dialing the dose on the handy-dandy syringe-pen that con-tained the Follistim. The needles were tiny and she swore they didn't hurt, even though they left bruises on her abdomen—so many that sometimes it was hard to find a fresh spot for the next shot.

But the progesterone was different.

First, the needle was bigger. Second, the medicine was in oil, and just looked thicker and creepier. Third, we'd have to do it every night for thirteen weeks.

Zoe took out the alcohol swabs and a vial. I swiped the top of the vial clean, and then rubbed the center of the bull's-eye on her bottom. "Are you going to be okay standing up?" I asked. Usually, she was lying on our bed.

"Just get it over with," Zoe said.

Quickly I screwed the big needle onto the syringe and withdrew the dosage from the vial. It was tricky, because of the oil—sort of like sucking molasses through a straw. I waited till the fluid was a bit past the number on the syringe and then pushed on the plunger, to get it just right.

Then I twisted off the needle and attached a new one we'd use for the injection. It wasn't as wide a bore, but it was equally nasty—a good two inches had to get jabbed into Zoe intramuscularly. "Okay," I said, taking a deep breath, even though it was Zoe having the shot.

"Wait!" she cried out. She twisted toward me. "You didn't say it."

We had a routine. "I wish I could do this for you," I told her, every night.

She nodded, and braced her hands against the wall.

No one ever tells you how resilient skin is. It's meant to be tough, which is why it takes a little leap of courage to jam a syringe through it. But it was worse for Zoe than for me, so I kept my hands from shaking (a real problem at first) and plunged the needle into the center of the bull's-eye. I made sure there was no blood mixing into the medication, and then came the hard part. Can you imagine the force it takes to push oil into the human body? I swear, no matter how many times I did this to my wife (and I did look at it that way—as something I *did* to her), I could feel every bit of resistance that her flesh and blood put up against the progesterone.

When, finally, it was done, I pulled out the needle and stuck it into the Sharps container that was next to the sink. Then I rubbed the injection site, trying to keep Zoe from getting a hard knot there. Usually, now, I'd get her a heating pad, too, but that obviously wasn't going to happen tonight.

Zoe put everything back into her

purse and pulled down her dress. "Hope we didn't miss the bouquet toss," she said, and she opened the bathroom door.

An elderly man in a walker was patiently waiting. He watched Zoe emerge from the men's room, followed by me, and he winked. "I remember those days," he mused.

Zoe and I burst out laughing. "Not unless he was a diabetic," I said, and we walked back into the reception holding hands.

The Kent County Family Court isn't that far from Wilmington, where Zoe and I have rented an apartment for years; but it's a good distance from Reid's house in Newport. Clutching the copy of the marriage certificate I got from the town hall, I walk the length of a covered portico from the parking lot into the building.

Every few steps, I hear a bird.

I stop walking, look up, and notice the speaker and the motion sensor. The

courthouse has some weird nature recording following me with every step.

It's kind of fitting, actually, to be
headed in to file for divorce and to learn
that something I thought was real is just
smoke and mirrors.

The clerk looks up at me when I enter the office. She has curly black hair—
and that's just her mustache. "Yes?"
she says. "Can I help you?"

These days, I don't think *anyone* can.
But I take a step toward the chest-high
counter. "I want a divorce."

She flattens her mouth in a smile.
"Honey, I don't even remember our
wedding." When I don't respond, the
clerk rolls her eyes. "Just once. Just
once I'd like someone to laugh. Who's
your attorney?"

"I can't afford one."

She hands me a packet of papers.
"You own property?"

"No."

"You got kids?"

"No," I say, looking away.

"Then you fill out the paperwork, and
bring it to the sheriff's department down
the hall."

I thank her and take the packet out to a bench in the corridor.

In re: the Marriage of

Plaintiff: that would be me.
And *Defendant:* that would be Zoe.

I carefully read the first item to be filled out: my residence. After hesitating, I put down Reid's address. I've been there for two months now. Plus, the next item is Zoe's address. I don't want the judge to get confused and think we're still living together and decide not to grant the divorce.

Not that it works like that, but still.

Number three: On _____, in _____ (city), _____ (country), _____ (state), the Plaintiff and Defendant married. An official copy of the marriage license is attached to this complaint for divorce.

Zoe and I had gotten married by a justice of the peace with a speech impediment. When he asked us to repeat our vows, neither of us could understand him. "We've written our own," Zoe said, in a flash of inspiration, and, like me, she made them up on the spot.

On the divorce form, there are four spaces for children, and their birth dates.

I feel myself break out in a sweat.

Grounds for No-Fault:

I have only two choices here, and they are listed for me. Carefully I reprint the first option: *Irreconcilable differences that have caused the irremediable breakdown of the marriage.*

I do not really know what all that means, but I can guess. And it seems to describe me and Zoe. She can't stop wanting a baby; I can't stand the thought of trying again. Irreconcilable differences are the children we never had. They're the times she would sit at dinner, smiling, when I knew she wasn't thinking about me. They're the baby name books stacked for reading by the toilet, the crib mobile she bought three years ago and never unpacked, the finance charges on our credit card bills that keep me awake at night.

Just above the spot where I sign my name is a vow: *The Plaintiff prays for an Absolute Divorce.*

Yeah, I suppose I do.

I'd worship anyone and anything who could turn my life around.

In a way, I get along better with my sister-in-law than with my own brother. For the past two months, every time Reid asks me if I have a master plan, a goal to get back on my feet, Liddy just reminds him that I'm family, that I should stay as long as I want. At breakfast, if she cooks an uneven number of slices of bacon, she gives me the extra, instead of Reid. It's like she's the one person who really gives a crap whether I live or die, who either doesn't notice that I'm a colossal fuckup or, better yet, just doesn't care.

Liddy grew up with a father who was a Pentecostal preacher, but when she's not acting all churchified, she can be pretty cool. She collects Green Lantern comic books, for example. And she's totally into B movies—the more outrageous the better. Since neither Zoe nor Reid ever understood the attraction of this kind of pulp film, Liddy and I have had a tradition of going to a midnight showing each month, at a dive of a theater that does crappy-director film festivals honoring people you've never heard of, like William Castle or Bert Gordon. Tonight, we're watching *Invasion of the Body Snatchers*—not the 1978 remake but the 1956 original by Don Siegel.

Liddy always pays for my ticket. I used to offer, but Liddy said that was ridiculous—in the first place, she had Reid's money to spend and I didn't, and in the second place, I was keeping her entertained while Reid was at some client dinner or church meeting and so this was the least she could do. We always got the biggest bucket of popcorn—with butter, because when Liddy and Reid went out, he insisted on being heart-healthy. That was about as rebellious as Liddy got, frankly.

I've been out drinking three times this

week—just a quick beer here and there, nothing I can't handle. But knowing I was meeting Liddy for this movie is what kept me dry tonight. I don't want her running back to Reid, telling him that I reeked of alcohol. I mean, I know she likes me and we get along, but she's my brother's wife first and foremost.

Liddy grabs my arm when the main character, Dr. Bennell, runs onto the highway at the climax of the film. She closes her eyes, too, at the really scary parts, but then demands that I tell her every last detail of what she missed.

They're here already! the actor says, looking right into the camera. *You're next!*

We always stay for the credits. All the way to the end, when they thank the town that allowed filming. Usually, we're the last ones out of the theater.

Tonight, we're still sitting in our seats when the teenage boy with zits comes in to sweep the aisle and pick up the trash. "Have you ever seen the 1978 remake?" Liddy asks.

"It sucks," I say. "And don't even get me started on *The Invasion.*"

"I think this might be my favorite B movie ever," Liddy replies.

"You say that about every one we see."

"But I mean it this time," she says. She leans her head back against the seat. "Do you think they knew what happened to them?"

"Who?"

"The Pod People. The aliens. Do you think they got up one morning and looked in the mirror and wondered how they got to be that way?"

The kid who's sweeping stops at our aisle. We stand up, walk into the dingy theater lobby. "It's just a movie," I tell Liddy, when what I really want to tell her is that no, the Pod People don't ask what's happened.

That actually, when you turn into someone you don't recognize, you feel nothing at all.

Seventy-seven.

That's how many days after filing the divorce petition I'd have to show up in court. That's how long Zoe would have, after being served this summons by the court, to join me there.

Since I filed the divorce papers, it's been hard for me to get back into the swing of work. By now, I should be putting up my flyers for plowing. I should be cleaning and storing my mowers for the winter. Instead, I've been sleeping in, and staying out late, taking up space in my brother's house.

So when Reid asked me to help him by picking up Pastor Clive at Logan Airport the next morning after a red-eye from an evangelical conference at the Saddleback Church, I should have said yes immediately. I mean, it wasn't like I was busy. And after everything Reid had done for me, the least I could do was repay him with time, if not money.

Instead, I just stared at him, unable to respond.

"You," Reid said quietly, "are really something else, little brother."

Liddy came up to the kitchen table, where I was sitting, and poured me a glass of orange juice. As if I needed any reminder that I was just a black hole in the middle of their home, sucking away their food, their money, their private time.

I may not have been able to say yes to my brother, but I couldn't say no to her.

So now it's dawn, and I'm fully planning on driving to Logan to meet the 7:00 A.M. plane arrival, but as I'm heading past Point Judith, I notice the waves. I check the clock on my dashboard. I've got my board and wet suit with me—they're always in my truck, just in case—and I'm thinking that there's no point in getting up this early if I'm not going to get in fifteen minutes of surfing on my way to Boston.

I pull on my wet suit, hood, and gloves, and head toward a bar that has proven itself in the past for me—a fairy godmother made of shallow sand that can take a long, low wall and turn it into a screaming curl.

Paddling out, I pass a pair of younger guys. "Jerry, Herc," I say, nodding. Fall and winter riders are a unique breed, and we mostly know each other simply because there aren't many people crazy enough to head out surfing when the water is fifty degrees and the air temperature is forty-one. I time it just right and catch a decent six-footer. On the way back out I watch Herc's wave go vertical, see him skirt the inside break.

I can feel my triceps burning, and the familiar icy headache that comes from being slapped in the face by a freezing, teasing ocean. It's harder to pull myself up on the board, easier to nod to the others to take that particular wave while I wait out the next one. "You sure, Gramps?"

I am forty. Not ancient by any means, but a relic in the world of surfing. *Gramps my ass,* I think, and I decide I'm going to catch the next wave and show these toddlers how it's really done.

Except.

No sooner have I pulled myself upright and stuck my first turn than I suddenly lose my footing, tumbling backward. The last thing I see is the flat hull of my board, coming at me with lightning force.

When I come to, my cheek is pressed into the sand and my hood's been yanked off my head. The wind has turned my wet hair into icicles. Jerry's face slowly comes into focus. "Hey, Gramps," he says, "you okay? You took a hard knock."

I sit up, wincing. "I'm fine," I mutter.

"You want a ride to the hospital? To get checked out?"

"No." I'm bruised and battered and shivering like mad. "What time is it?"

Herc lifts up the neoprene edge of his wet suit to check his wristwatch. "Seven-ten."

I've been surfing for over an hour? "Shit," I say, struggling to my feet. The world spins for a moment, and Herc steadies me.

"There someone we should call?" he asks.

I can't give them the number of one of my employees, because I've laid them all off for the winter. I can't give them Reid and Liddy's number, because they think I'm picking up the pastor. I can't give them Zoe's number, because of what I've done to her.

I shake my head, but I can't quite

bring myself to say the words: *There's nobody.*

Herc and Jerry head back out one more time, and I walk slowly to the truck. My cell phone has fifteen messages on it. I don't have to call voice mail to know they are all from Reid, and they are all angry.

I call him back. "Reid," I say. "Look, man, I'm really sorry. I was just about to hit Ninety-three North when the truck broke down. I tried to call, but I didn't have service—"

"Where are you now?"

"Waiting for a tow," I lie. "I don't know how long it's going to take to fix."

Reid sighs. "I'll get Pastor Clive a limo," he says. "Do you need a ride, too?"

I don't know what I did to deserve a brother like Reid. I mean, anyone else would have written me off long before now. "I'm good," I reply.

Zoe had wanted me to quit surfing. She didn't understand the obsession, the way I couldn't pass by a beach with a rip curl. *Grow up, Max,* she had said. *You can't have a child if you are one.*

Was she right?

About everything?

I picture the sheriff showing up at her house. *Zoe Baxter?* he'd say, and she'd nod. *You've been served.* Then he would leave her holding the little blue folder, the one she must have known was coming sooner or later, and yet still would feel like a kick in the gut.

In the truck, I am still shivering, even with the heat turned up high. I hesitate . . . and then reach into the glove compartment. The bottle of Jägermeister is really just for medicinal purposes. You see it all the time in movies—the guy who's got frostbite, the one who's fallen off a bridge into the water; the fellow who's been left out in the cold too long . . . they're all confused and frantic until they take a nip to get their blood flowing again.

One sip, and suddenly they're healed.

Two months later

If not for the garbage truck, I would have missed my court date.

I wake with a start when I hear the high-pitched beeps, jumping upright and smacking my head against the roof of the car. The garbage truck backs toward the Dumpster I'm parked beside and hooks its teeth into the metal loops so that it can lift the receptacle. All I know is that it sounds like freaking Armageddon.

The windows are steamed up and I'm shivering, so I turn on the ignition and blast the defroster. That's when I realize that it's not 6:00 A.M., like I figured, but 8:34 A.M.

In twenty-six minutes I am getting divorced.

Obviously, I don't have time to go back to Reid's and shower. As it is, I will have to break the land speed record to get to the Kent County Courthouse on time.

"Shit," I mutter, throwing the car into reverse and peeling out of the parking lot of the bank where I must have fallen asleep last night. There's an Irish pub around the corner, and last call is 3:00 A.M. I have a vague recollection of a bunch of guys having a bachelor party, of being invited to do some tequila shots.

Fortunately, there's no snow yet, or for that matter an overturned truck on the highway. I park illegally in a spot that isn't really a space (not a bright idea at a courthouse, but really, what am I supposed to do?) and run like hell into the building. "Excuse me," I mutter, my head pounding as I run up the stairs to Judge Meyers's courtroom. I bump into a woman with her two kids and a lawyer reading a brief. "Sorry . . . pardon me . . ."

I slide into the back row of the benches. I am sweating, and my shirt's come untucked from my pants. I haven't had a chance to shave, or even wash up in the bathroom. I sniff my sleeve, which smells like last night's party.

When I glance up again, I see her staring at me.

Zoe looks like she hasn't slept in seventy-seven days, either. She has dark circles under her eyes. She's too thin. But she takes one look at my face, my hair, my clothing, and she knows. She understands what I've been doing.

She turns away from me and fixes her gaze straight ahead.

I feel that dismissal like a hole punched through my chest. All I ever wanted was to be good enough for her, and I screwed up. I couldn't give her the kid she wanted. I couldn't give her the life she deserved. I couldn't be the man she thought I was.

The clerk stands up and begins reading through a list. *"Malloy versus Malloy?"* she says.

A lawyer stands up. "That's ready, Your Honor. Can we have the process on that, please?"

The judge, a woman with a round, sunny face, has decorated her bench with seasonal items—Beanie Babies dressed like Pilgrims, a stuffed turkey.

"Jones versus Jones?"

Another attorney rises. "Ready, nominal."

"Kasen versus Kasen?"

"Your Honor, I need a new date on that. Could I have December eighteenth?"

"Horowitz versus Horowitz," the clerk reads.

"That's a motion, Your Honor," another lawyer replies. "I'm ready to go."

"Baxter versus Baxter?"

It takes me a moment to realize that the clerk is calling my name. "Yes," I say, standing up. As if there's a thread connecting us, Zoe rises, too, all the way across the room.

"Um," I say. "Present."

"Do you represent yourself, sir?" Judge Meyers asks.

"Yes," I say.

"Is your wife here?"

Zoe clears her throat. "Yes."

"Are you representing yourself, ma'am?" Judge Meyers asks.

"Yes," Zoe says, "I am."

"Are you both ready to go forward with the divorce today?"

I nod. I don't look at Zoe to see if she's nodding, too.

"If you're representing yourselves," Judge Meyers says, "you are your own attorneys. That means you have to put your case on if you want to get a divorce today. I highly recommend watching these other nominal divorces to see the procedure, because I can't do it for you. Is that clear?"

"Yes, ma'am," I say, but she might as well be speaking Portuguese for all I understand.

We are not called again until over two hours later. Which means I could have showered, since, even though I've now sat through five other divorces, I have no idea what I am supposed to do. I walk past the gate at the front of the courtroom into the witness box, and one of the uniformed bailiffs comes up to me holding a Bible. "Mr. Baxter, do you swear to tell the truth, the whole truth, and nothing but the truth, so help you God?"

From the corner of my eye, I see the clerk directing Zoe to take a seat at one of the tables in front of the bench. "I do," I say.

It's funny, isn't it, that you have to speak the same words to get married as you do to get divorced.

"Please state your name for the record . . ."

"Max," I say. "Maxwell Baxter."

The judge folds her hands on her

desk. "Mr. Baxter, have you entered your appearance?"

I just blink at her.

"Sheriff, have Mr. Baxter enter his appearance. . . . You want a divorce today, Mr. Baxter?"

"Yes."

"And you're representing yourself today?"

"I can't afford a lawyer," I explain.

The judge looks at Zoe. "And you, Mrs. Baxter? You're representing yourself as well?"

"I am."

"You're not fighting the divorce today, is that correct?"

She nods.

"Sheriff, have Mrs. Baxter enter an appearance on her own behalf, please." The judge turns back to me and sniffs. "Mr. Baxter, you smell absolutely pickled. Are you under the influence of alcohol or drugs?"

I hesitate. "Not yet," I say.

"Seriously, Max?" Zoe blurts out. "You're drinking again?"

"It's not your problem anymore—"

The judge bangs her gavel. "If you

two feel like having a counseling session, don't waste my time."

"No, Your Honor," I say. "I just want this to be over."

"All right, Mr. Baxter. You may proceed."

Except I don't know how. Where I live, and whether I've lived in Wilmington for a year, and when I was married, and when we separated—well, none of that really explains how two people who thought they'd spend the rest of their lives together one day woke up and realized they did not know the person sleeping beside them.

"How old are you, Mr. Baxter?" the judge asks.

"I'm forty."

"What's the highest grade of school you completed?"

"I got through three years of college before I quit and started my own landscaping business."

"How long have you been a landscaper?"

"For ten years," I say.

"How much money do you make?"

I look into the gallery. It's bad enough

to have to say this to a judge, but there are all these other people in the courtroom. "About thirty-five thousand a year," I say, but this is not really true. I made that *one* year.

"You allege in your complaint for divorce that certain differences arose between you which caused your marriage to fall apart, is that true?" the judge asks.

"Yes, Your Honor. We've been trying to have a baby for nine years. And I . . . I don't want that anymore."

Zoe's eyes are glittering with tears, but she doesn't reach for the tissue box beside her.

We got together two months ago— after she was served with divorce papers—to hash out all the details the judge was going to need. Let me tell you, it's a strange thing to go back to the house you used to rent, to sit at the table where you used to eat dinner every day, and to feel like you're a total stranger.

Zoe, when she'd opened the door, had looked like hell. But I didn't think it was right for me to say that to her, so instead, I just shuffled at the threshold until she invited me in.

I think that—at that moment—if she'd asked me to come back home, to re-consider, I would have.

But instead Zoe had said, "Well, let's get this done," and that was that.

"Do you own any real estate?" the judge says.

"We rented," I say.

"Are there any assets that are worth some monetary value?"

"I took my lawn care equipment; Zoe took her instruments."

"So you're asking that you be awarded the items in your possession, and that your wife be awarded the items in her possession?"

Isn't that what I said, but more clearly? "I guess so."

"Do you have health insurance?" the judge asks.

"We've agreed to each be responsi-ble for our own insurance."

The judge nods. "What about the debts in your name?"

"I can't pay them yet," I admit. "But I'll take care of them when I can."

"Will your wife be responsible for any debts in her name?"

"Yes," I say.

"Mr. Baxter, are you in good health?"

"I am."

"Do you understand what alimony is?" I nod at the judge. "It states here that you're asking the court to allow you to waive alimony today?"

"You mean, so Zoe doesn't have to pay me anything? That's right."

"Do you understand that it's a permanent waiver? You can't go back to this court or any other court and be granted alimony?"

Zoe and I had never had much money, but the thought of having her support me is completely humiliating. "I understand," I say.

"Are you asking for an absolute divorce today from your wife?"

I know it's legal lingo, but it makes me stop and think. Absolute. It's so final. Like a book you've loved that you don't want to end, because you know it has to be returned to the library when you're done.

"Mr. Baxter," the judge asks, "is there anything else you want to tell the court?"

I shake my head. "Not the court, Your Honor. But I'd like to say something to Zoe." I wait until she looks at me. Her eyes are blank, like she's looking at a stranger on the subway. Like she never knew me at all.

"I'm sorry," I say.

Because we live in Rhode Island, which is a predominantly Catholic state, it takes a while to really get divorced. After the seventy-seven days we waited to go to court, it's about ninety-one days before the final judgment, as if the judge is giving a couple just one more chance to reconsider.

I admit, I've spent most of that time shitfaced.

Bad habits are like purple loosestrife. When that plant pops up in your garden, you think you can deal with it—a few pretty purple stalks. But it spreads like wildfire, and before you know it, it's choked everything else around it, until all you can see is that bright carpet of color, and you're wondering how it got so out of control.

I swore I'd never be one of the eighty percent of recovering alcoholics who wind up making the same mistakes all over again. And yet, here I am, stashing bottles up in the ceiling tiles of Reid's bathrooms, behind books on his shelves, inside a corner I've carefully slit open in the guest-room mattress. I'll spill full cartons of milk down the sink when Liddy's not home, then gallantly volunteer to run out at night to get more so we have it for breakfast—but I'll stop at a bar on the way home from the convenience store for a quick drink. If I know I have to be around people, I'll drink vodka, which leaves less of an odor on the breath. I keep Gatorade under my bed, to ward off hangovers. I am careful to go out to bars in different towns, so that I look like someone who drops in every now and then for a drink, and so that I don't get recognized in my own backyard by someone who'd narc to Reid. One night, I went to Wilmington. I drank enough to get the courage to drive by our old place. Well, Zoe's *current* place. The lights were on in the bedroom, and I wondered what she was doing up there. Reading, maybe. Doing her nails.

Then I wondered if there was anyone else there with her, and I peeled away with my tires screaming on the pavement.

Of course, I tell myself that since no one seems to notice my drinking, I don't have a problem.

I am still living at Reid's, mostly because he hasn't kicked me out. I don't think this is because he enjoys having me living in his basement, really—it's basically Christian charity. Before marrying Liddy, my brother got "born again" (*Wasn't the first time good enough?* Zoe had asked) and started attending an evangelical church that met on Sundays in the cafeteria of the local middle school; eventually, he became their finance guy. I'm not a religious person— to each his own, I figure—but it got to the point where we saw less and less of my brother and his wife, simply because we couldn't get through a simple family dinner without Zoe and Reid arguing—about *Roe v. Wade,* or politicians caught in adultery scandals, or prayer in public schools. The last time we went to their house, Zoe had actually left after the salad course when Reid had criticized her for singing a Green Day song to one of her burn victims. "Anarchists," Reid had said—Reid, who listened to Led Zeppelin in his room when we were kids. I figured it was something about the lyrics his church objected to, but as it turned out, it was the character of the songs that was evil. "Really?" Zoe had asked, incredulous. "Which notes, exactly? Which chord? And where is that written in the Bible?" I don't remember how the argument had escalated, but it had ended with Zoe standing up so quickly she overturned a pitcher of water. "This may be news to you, Reid," she had said, "but God doesn't vote Republican."

I know Reid wants me to join their church. Liddy's left pamphlets about being saved on my bed when she changes the sheets. Reid had his men's Bible group over ("We put the 'stud' back in Bible study") and invited me to join them in the living room.

I made up some excuse and went out drinking.

Tonight, though, I realize that Liddy and Reid have pulled out the big guns. When I hear Liddy ring the little antique bell she keeps on the mantel to announce dinnertime, I walk up from my guest-room cave in the basement to find Clive Lincoln sitting on the couch with Reid.

"Max," he says. "You know Pastor Clive?"

Who doesn't?

He's in the paper all the time, thanks to protests he's staged near the capital building against gay marriage. When a local high school told a gay teen he could take his boyfriend to the prom, Clive showed up with a hundred congregants to stand on the steps of the high school loudly praying for Jesus to help him find his way back to a Christian lifestyle. He made the Fox News Channel in Boston this fall when he publicly requested donations of porn movies for day care centers, saying that was no different from the president's plan to teach sex ed in kindergarten.

Clive is tall, with a smooth mane of white hair and very expensive clothing. I have to admit, he's larger than life. When you see him in a room, you can't help but keep looking at him.

"Ah! The brother I've heard all about."

I'm not anti-church. I grew up going on Sundays with my mom, who was the head of the ladies' auxiliary. After she died, though, I stopped going regularly. And when I married Zoe, I stopped going at all. She wasn't—as she put it—a Jesus person. She said religion preached unconditional love by God, but there were always conditions: you had to believe what you were told, in order to get everything you ever wanted. She didn't like it when religious folks looked down on her for being an atheist; but to be honest, I didn't see how this was any different from the way she looked down on people for being Christians.

When Clive shakes my hand, a shock of electricity jumps between us. "I didn't

know we were having guests for dinner," I say, looking at Reid.

"The pastor's not a guest," Reid replies. "He's family."

"A brother in Christ," Clive says, smiling.

I shift from one foot to the other.
"Well. I'll see if Liddy needs some help
in the kitchen—"

"I'll do that," Reid interrupts. "Why
don't you stay here with Pastor Clive?"

That's when I realize that my drinking—which I thought I'd been so secret
and clever about—has not been secret
and clever at all. That this dinner is not
some friendly meal with a clergyman
but a setup.

Uncomfortable, I sit down where Reid
was a moment before. "I don't know
what my brother's told you," I begin.

"Just that he's been praying for you,"
Pastor Clive says. "He asked me to
pray for you, too, to find your way."

"I think my sense of direction's pretty
good," I mutter.

Clive sits forward. "Max," he asks,
"do you have a personal relationship
with Jesus Christ?"

"We're . . . more like acquaintances."

He doesn't smile. "You know, Max, I never expected to become a pastor."

"No?" I say politely.

"I came from a family that didn't have two nickels to rub together, and I had five younger brothers and sisters. My dad got laid off when I was twelve, and my mom got sick and was in the hospital. It fell to me to feed the household, and we didn't have any money in the bank. One day, I went to the local food store and told the cashier that I would pay her back as soon as I could, but the cashier said she couldn't give me the food in my basket unless I paid. Well, a man behind me—all dressed up in a suit and tie—said he'd take care of my expenses. 'You need a shopping list, boy,' he said, and he scribbled something on his business card and set it on one side of the cashier's scale. Even though it was only a piece of paper, the scale started to sink. Then he took the milk, bread, eggs, cheese, and hamburger out of my cart and stacked them on the other side of the scale. The scale didn't budge—even though, clearly, all those items should have tipped the balance. With a weight of zero pounds, the cashier had no choice but to give me the food for free—but the man handed her over a twenty-dollar bill, just the same. When I got home, I found the business card in my grocery bag, along with all the food. I took it out to read the list the man had written, but there was no list. On the back of the card it just said, *Dear God, please help this boy.* On the front was his name: Reverend Billy Graham."

"I suppose you're going to tell me that was a miracle."

"Of course not . . . the scale was broken. Grocer had to buy himself a new one," Clive says. "The miracle part came from the way God broke the scale at just the right moment. The point, Max, is that Jesus has a plan for your life. That's a funny thing about him: He loves you now, even while you're sinning. But He also loves you too much to leave you this way."

Now I'm starting to get angry. This isn't my home, granted, but isn't it a little rude to try to convert someone in his own living room?

"The only way to please God is to do what He says you have to do," Pastor Clive continues. "If your job is baking pies at the Nothing-but-Pies Bakery, you don't go to work and decide to bake cookies. You'll never get your promotion that way. Even if your cookies are the most delicious ones in the world, they're still not what your boss wants you to bake."

"I don't bake pies *or* cookies," I say. "And with all due respect, I don't need to get religion."

Pastor Clive smiles and sits back, his fingers strumming on the armrest of the couch. "That's the other funny thing about Jesus," he says. "He's got a way of showing you you're wrong."

The storm comes out of nowhere. It's not completely unexpected, in late November, but it is not the light dusting that the weathermen have forecast. Instead, when I open the bar door and slip on the ice that's built up on the threshold, the snow is falling like a white curtain.

I duck back inside and tell the bartender to give me another beer. There's no point in heading out now; I might as well ride out the storm.

There's no one else at the bar tonight; on a Tuesday when the roads are slick, most people choose to stay in. The bartender gives me the television remote, and I find a basketball game on ESPN. We cheer on the Celtics, and they go into overtime, and eventually choke. "Boston teams," the bartender says, "they'll break your heart every time."

"Think I'm gonna pack it in early tonight," the bartender says. By now, there's nearly eight inches on the ground. "You all right getting home?"

"I'm the plow guy," I say. "So I'd better be."

My Dodge Ram's got an Access plow, and thanks to flyers I've printed up on Reid's Mac, I have a handful of clients who expect me to come and make the driveway passable before it's time to leave for work in the morning. During a good storm, like this one, I won't sleep at night—I'll just plow till it's over. This is the first big nor'easter of the season, and I could use the influx of cash it will bring.

My breath fogs the windshield of the truck when I get inside. I turn up the defroster and see the red devil lights of the bartender's Prius skidding out of the parking lot. Then I put the truck into gear and head in the direction of my first client.

It's slippery, but it's nothing I haven't driven in before. I turn on the radio—the voice of John freaking Tesh fills the truck cab. *Did you know that it takes twenty minutes for your stomach to relay the message to your brain that you're full?*

"No, I didn't," I say out loud.

I can't use my high beams because of the volume of snow, so I almost miss the bend in the road. My back wheels start to spin, and I turn in to the skid. With my heart still pounding, I take my foot off the accelerator and move slower, my tires cutting into the accumulation and packing it down beneath the truck.

After a few minutes, the world looks different. Whitewashed, with humps and towers that look like sleeping giants. The landmarks are missing. I'm not sure I'm in the right place. I'm not sure I really know *where* I am, actually.

I blink and rub my eyes, flick on my high beams . . . but nothing changes.

Now, I'm starting to panic. I reach for my phone, which has a GPS application on it somewhere, to see where I've taken a wrong turn. But while I'm fumbling around in the console, the truck hits a patch of black ice and starts to do a 360.

There's someone standing in the road.

Her dark hair is flying around her face, and she's hunched over against the cold. I manage to jam my foot on the brake and steer hard to the right, desperately trying to turn the truck before it hits her. But the tires aren't responding on the ice, and I look up, panicked, at the same time she makes eye contact with me.

It's Zoe.

"Nooooo," I scream. I lift up my arm as if I can brace myself for the inevitable crash, and then there is a sickening shriek of metal and the wallop of the air bag as the truck somersaults through the very spot where she was standing.

When I come to, I'm covered in the diamond dust of crushed glass, I'm hanging upside down, and I can't move my legs.

God help me. Please, God. Help. Me.

It is perfectly silent, except for the soft strike of snow against the upholstery. I don't know how long I've been knocked out, but it doesn't look like dawn's coming anytime soon. I could freeze to death, trapped here. I could become another one of those snowy white mounds, an accident no one even knows happened until it's too late.

Oh, God, I think. *I'm going to die.*

And right after that: *No one will miss me.*

The truth hurts, more than the burning in my left leg and the throb of my skull and the metal digging into my shoulder. I could disappear from this world, and it would probably be a better place.

I hear the crunch of tires, and see a beam of headlights illuminating the road above me. "Hey!" I yell, as loud as I can. "Hey, I'm here! Help!"

The headlights pass by me, and then I hear a car door slam. The policeman's boots kick up snow as he runs down the embankment toward the overturned truck. "I've called for an ambulance," he says.

"The girl," I rasp. "Where is she?"

"Was there another passenger in this truck?"

"Not . . . inside. Truck hit her . . ."

He runs up the embankment, and I watch him shine a floodlight. I want to speak. But I am wicked dizzy, and when I try to talk, I throw up.

Maybe it's hours and maybe it's minutes, but a fireman is sawing through the seat belt that's kept me alive, and another one is using the Jaws of Life to cut the truck into pieces. There are voices all around me:

Get him onto a backboard . . .
Compound fracture . . .
. . . tachycardic . . .

The policeman is suddenly in front of me again. "We looked all over. The truck didn't hit anyone," he says. "Just a tree. And if you hadn't turned where you did and gone off the road, you'd be at the bottom of a cliff right now. You're a lucky guy."

The rush of relief I feel comes in sobs. I start crying so hard that I cannot breathe; I cannot stop. Did I hallucinate Zoe because I was drunk? Or was I drunk because I keep hallucinating Zoe?

The snow strikes me in the face, a thousand tiny needles, as I am moved from the wreckage to an ambulance. My nose is running and there is blood in my eyes.

Suddenly, I don't want to be this person anymore. I don't want to pretend I'm fooling the world when I'm not. I want someone else to have a plan for me, because I'm not doing a very good job myself.

The ambulance grumbles to life as

the EMT hooks me up to another monitor and then starts an IV. My leg feels like it is on fire every time the driver brakes.

"My leg . . ."

"Is probably broken, Mr. Baxter," the EMT says. I wonder how she knows my name, and then realize she is reading it off my license. "We're taking you to the hospital. Is there someone you want me to call?"

Not Zoe, not anymore. Reid will need to know, but right now, I don't want to think about the look in his eyes when he realizes I've been drinking and driving. And I probably need a lawyer, too.

"My pastor," I say. "Clive Lincoln."

I am nervous, but Liddy and Reid stand on either side of me with smiles so wide on their faces that you'd think I'd cured cancer, or figured out world peace, instead of just coming to the Eternal Glory Church to give my testimony about finding Jesus.

It couldn't have been more transparent for me if the answers had been tattooed on my face: the lowest of lows for me was that crash. Zoe's apparition had been Jesus's way of coming into my life. If I hadn't seen her there, I'd be dead now. But instead I swerved. I swerved right into His open arms.

When Clive had come to me at the hospital, I was drugged with painkillers and had a brand-new cast on my left leg and stitches in my scalp and my shoulder. I hadn't stopped crying since they'd loaded me into that ambulance. The pastor sat down on the edge of my bed and reached for my hand. "Let the Devil out, son," Clive said. "Make room for Christ."

I don't think I can explain what happened after that. It was simply as if someone flipped a switch in me, and there wasn't any hurt anymore. I felt like I was floating off the bed, and would have, if that cotton blanket hadn't been holding me down. When I looked at my body—at the spaces between my fingers and the edges of my fingernails, I swear I could see light shining out.

For anyone who hasn't accepted Jesus into his heart, this is what it feels like: as if you've resisted the fact that your vision's gone blurry, and you need glasses. But eventually you can't see a foot in front of you without knocking things over and bumping into dead ends, so you go to the optometrist. You walk out of that office with a new pair of glasses, and the world looks sharper, brighter, more colorful. Crisp. You can't understand why you waited so long to make the appointment.

When Jesus is with you, nothing seems particularly scary. Not the thought of never having another drink; not the moment you sit in court during your DUI charge. And not right now, when I will be baptized in the name of the Father, the Son, and the Holy Spirit.

After leaving the hospital, I started attending the Eternal Glory Church. I met with Pastor Clive, who sent out a prayer chain letter so that all these people I didn't even know were praying for me. It's a feeling I've never had before—strangers who didn't judge me for the mistakes I'd made but just seemed happy I'd showed up. I didn't have to be embarrassed about dropping out of college or getting divorced or drinking myself into a ditch. I didn't have to measure up at all, actually. The fact that Jesus had placed me in their lives meant I was already worthy.

The Eternal Glory Church hasn't got its own building, so it rents out the auditorium from a local school. We are standing in the back, waiting for Pastor Clive to give us the signal. Clive's wife is playing the piano, and his three little daughters are singing. "They sound like angels," I murmur.

"Yeah," Reid agrees. "There's a fourth kid, too, who doesn't perform."

"Like the Bonus Jonas," I say.

The hymn ends, and Pastor Clive stands on the stage, his hands clasped. "Today," he bellows, "is all about Jesus."

There is a chorus of agreement from the congregation.

"Which is why, today, our newest brother in Christ is going to tell us his story. Max, can you come on up here?"

With Reid's and Liddy's help, I make my way down the aisle on crutches. I don't like being the center of attention, usually, but this is different. Today, I'll tell them the story of how I came to Christ. I will publicly announce my faith, so that all these people can hold me accountable.

Welcome, I hear.

Hello, Brother Max.

Clive leads me to a chair on the stage. It must come from a classroom; there are tennis balls on the feet of the chair to keep it from scratching up the linoleum. Beside it is what looks like a meat freezer, filled with water, with a set of steps leading up to it. I sit down on the chair, and Clive steps between Liddy and Reid, holding their hands. "Jesus, help Max grow closer to You. Let Max know God, love God, and spend quality time with His word."

As he prays over me, I close my eyes. The lights from the stage are warm on my face; it makes me think of when I was little, and would ride my bike with my face turned up to the sun and my eyes closed, knowing that I was invincible and couldn't crash, couldn't get hurt.

Voices join Pastor Clive's. It feels like

a thousand kisses, like being filled to bursting with all the good in the world, so that there isn't any room for the bad. It's love, and it is unconditional acceptance, and not only *haven't* I failed Jesus but He says I never will. His love pours into me, until I can't keep it inside anymore. It spills out of my open throat—syllables that aren't really any language, but still, I get the message. It's crystal clear, to me.

	TRACK 1	SING YOU HOME
	TRACK 2	THE HOUSE ON HOPE STREET
✓	**TRACK 3**	**REFUGEE**
	TRACK 4	THE LAST
	TRACK 5	MARRY ME
	TRACK 6	FAITH
	TRACK 7	THE MERMAID
	TRACK 8	ORDINARY LIFE
	TRACK 9	WHERE YOU ARE
	TRACK 10	SAMMY'S SONG

VANESSA

I haven't given much thought to Zoe Baxter until I find her drowning at the bottom of the YMCA pool.

I don't know who it is, at first. I am swimming my laps at 6:30 A.M.—just about the only exercise I can drag myself out of bed for—and am midstroke doing the crawl when I see a woman slowly floating down to the bottom, with her hair fanning out around her head. Her arms are outstretched, and she doesn't look like she is sinking as much as just letting go.

I jackknife and dive, grab her hand, and yank her through the water. She starts fighting me as we approach the surface, but by then the adrenaline has kicked in and I haul her out of the pool and kneel over her, dripping on her face as she coughs and rolls to her side. "What the hell," she gasps, "are you *doing*?"

"What the hell were *you* doing?" I reply, and as she sits up, I realize whom I've saved. *"Zoe?"*

It is quiet at the Y. Pre-Christmas, the lap lane occupants have dwindled down to me, a few elderly swimmers, and the occasional physical therapy/rehab patient. Zoe and I are playing out this little scene on the tile edge of the pool without anyone really paying attention.

"I was staring up at the lights," Zoe says.

"Here's a news flash: you don't have to drown to do that." Now that we're both out of the water, I'm shivering. I grab my towel and wrap it around my shoulders.

I heard, of course, about the baby. It was horrible, to say the least, to have the guest of honor at a baby shower rushed to the hospital to deliver a stillborn. I wasn't even planning on going to the shower, but I'd felt bad for her—

what kind of woman has so few friends that she has to invite people who've contracted her music therapy services? Afterward, naturally, I felt even worse for her. I'd helped her bookkeeper clean up the restaurant, after the ambulance screamed away. There had been little baby-bottle bubble wands at each place setting; and I'd collected them on the way out, figuring that I'd give them back to Zoe at some point in the future. They were still somewhere in my trunk.

I don't know what to say to her. *How are you?* seems superfluous. *I'm sorry* seems even worse.

"You should try it," Zoe says.

"Suicide?"

"Once a school counselor always a school counselor," she answers. "I told you, I wasn't trying to kill myself. Just the opposite, actually. You can feel your heart beat, all the way to your fingers, when you're down there."

She slips back into the pool like an otter and looks up at me. Waiting. With a sigh, I throw down my towel and dive back in. I open my eyes underwater and see Zoe sinking to the bottom again, so I mimic her. Twisting onto my back, I look up at the quivery Morse code dashes of the fluorescent lights, and exhale through my nose so that I sink.

My first instinct is to panic—I've run out of air, after all. But then my pulse starts beating under my fingernails, in my throat, between my legs. It's as if my heart has swelled to fill up all the space beneath my skin.

I could see why, for someone who's lost so much, feeling this full could be a comfort.

When I can't stand it anymore, I kick to the surface. Zoe splashes up beside me and treads water. "When I was little, I wanted to be a mermaid when I grew up," she says. "I used to practice by tying my ankles together and swimming in the town pool."

"What happened?"

"Well, obviously I didn't become a mermaid."

"Classic underachiever . . ."

"It's never too late, right?" Zoe pulls

herself out of the pool and sits on the edge.

"I just don't know what the job market's like these days for sirens at sea," I say. "Now, on the other hand, vampires are absolutely to die for. There's a huge demand for the undead."

"It figures." Zoe sighs. "Just when I've rejoined the world of the living."

I stand up, and hold out a hand to pull Zoe to her feet. "Welcome back," I say.

Because it is a YMCA, there's no fancy juice bar, so instead we get coffee at a Dunkin' Donuts, which are scattered so frequently through Wilmington that you can stand in the doorway of one and spit into the doorway of another. Zoe follows me in her car and parks in the spot beside me. "Quite the license plate," she says, as I get out of the car.

Mine reads VS-66. It's a Rhode Island thing to have a low-numbered license plate. There are people who bequeath two- and three-digit plates to relatives in their wills; at one point a former governor made fighting plate-number corruption part of his electoral platform. If you have your initials and a low number—like me—you're probably a mob boss. I'm not a mob boss, but I know how to get things done. The day I had to register my new car, I brought each of the clerks a six-pack and asked them what they could do for me.

"Friends in high places," I reply, as we go into the coffee shop. We both order vanilla lattes and sit at a table in the back of the store.

"What time do you have to be at work?" Zoe asks.

"Eight. You?"

"Same." She takes a sip of her drink. "I'm at the hospital today."

The mention of that place feels like a net thrown over us, a memory of her being whisked away by ambulance from her own party. I fiddle with the lid of my cup. Even though I counsel kids every day, I am uncomfortable here with her. I'm not sure why I asked her to grab a cup of coffee, in fact. It's not like we know each other very well.

I had hired Zoe to work with an autistic boy several months ago. He had been in our school district for six years and had never, as far as I knew, said a word to a single teacher. It was his mother who'd heard about music therapy, and asked me to try to find someone local who could work with her son. I am the first to admit I wasn't expecting much when I met Zoe. She looked a little misplaced, a seventies child who'd been dropped into the new millennium. But within a month, Zoe had the boy playing improvised symphonies with her. The parents thought Zoe was a genius, and my principal thought I was brilliant for finding her.

"Look," I begin, after a long, weird silence, "I don't really know what to say about the baby."

Zoe looks up at me. "No one does." She traces the edge of her fingertip around the plastic lid of the coffee cup. I think that is just going to be that, and I'm about to look at my wristwatch and exclaim over the time when she speaks again. "There was a death coordinator at the hospital," she says. "She came into the room—afterward—and asked

Max and me about where we wanted the body to go. If we wanted an autopsy. If we knew what kind of coffin we wanted. If we were going with cremation instead. She said we could take him home, too. Bury him, I don't know, in the backyard." Zoe looks up at me. "Sometimes I still have nightmares about that. About burying him, and then the snow melting in March, and I'd walk outside and find bones sitting there." She blots her eyes with a napkin. "I'm sorry. I don't talk about this. I've *never* talked about this."

I know why she is opening up to me. It's the same reason kids come into my office and confess that, after every meal, they make themselves throw up; or cut themselves in the privacy of the shower with a straight-edge razor blade. Sometimes it's easier to speak to a stranger. The problem is that, once you turn your heart inside out for someone to see, the other person loses her anonymity.

Once, when Zoe was working with the autistic student, I'd observed their session. *You have to come into music therapy at the place where the patient is,* she explained, and when he arrived she didn't make eye contact with him or force an interaction. Instead she took out her guitar and started playing and singing to herself. The boy sat down at the piano and began racing his hands over the keys in angry arpeggios. Gradually, every time he paused, she would play an equally forceful chord on her guitar. At first, he didn't connect what she was doing, and then he began to pause more frequently, waiting for her to musically interact. I realized they were having a conversation: first his sentence, then hers. They just were speaking a different language.

Maybe that was all Zoe Baxter needed—a new method of communication. So she'd stop sinking to the bottoms of pools. So she'd smile.

Full disclosure here: I am the person who buys the broken piece of furniture, sure I can repair it. I used to have a rescued greyhound. I am a pathological fixer, which accounts for my career as a school counselor, since God knows it's not about the money or job satisfaction. So it's not really a surprise to me that my immediate instinct, with Zoe Baxter, is to put her back together again.

"Death coordinator," I say, shaking my head. "And I thought *my* job sucked."

Zoe glances up, and then a snort bubbles out of her. She covers her mouth with her hand.

"It's okay to laugh," I say gently.

"I feel like it's not. Like it means none of this mattered to me." She shakes her head, and suddenly her eyes are full of tears. "I'm sorry. You didn't come to the Y this morning to listen to this. Some date *I* am."

Immediately, I freeze. What does she know? What has she heard?

Why does it matter?

You'd think that by now, at age thirty-four, I'd be less worried about what people think. I suppose it's just that when you've been burned before, you're less likely to dip a toe into the lake of fire.

"It's a good thing we ran into each other," I hear myself say. "I was thinking of calling you."

Really? I think, wondering where I'm going with this.

"Really?" Zoe replies.

"There's a kid who's been suffering from depression," I say. "She's been in and out of hospitals, and she's failing school. I was going to ask you to come in and work with her." In truth, I haven't really been thinking of Zoe and her music therapy, at least not in conjunction with Lucy DuBois. But now that I've said it, it makes sense. Nothing else has worked for the girl, who's attempted suicide twice. Her parents—so conservative that they wouldn't let Lucy talk to a shrink—would just need to be convinced that music therapy isn't modern voodoo.

Zoe hesitates, but I can tell she's considering the offer. "Vanessa, I already told you that I don't need to be rescued."

"I'm not saving you," I say. "I'm asking you to save someone else."

At the time, I think I mean Lucy. I don't realize I'm talking about me.

———

When I was growing up in the southern suburbs of Boston, I used to ride my banana bike with glitter streamers up and down the streets of my neighborhood, silently marking the homes of the girls I thought were pretty. At age six, I fully believed that Katie Whittaker, with her sunshine hair and constellation of freckles, would one day marry me and we'd live happily ever after.

I can't really remember when I realized that wasn't what all the other girls were thinking, and so I started saying along with the rest of the female second graders that I had a crush on Jared Tischbaum, who was cool enough to play on the travel soccer team and who wore the same jean jacket to school every single day because, once, the actor Robin Williams had touched it in an airport baggage terminal.

I lost my virginity one night in the guest team's baseball dugout on school grounds with my first boyfriend, Ike. He was sweet and tender and told me I was beautiful—in other words, he did everything right—and yet I remember going home afterward and wondering what all the fuss was about when it came to sex. It had been sweaty and mechanical, and, even though I really did love Ike, something had been missing.

My best friend, Molly, was the person I confided this to. I'd find myself on the phone with her after midnight, dissecting the sinew and skeleton of my relationship with Ike. I'd study with her for a history test and not want to leave. I would make plans to go shopping with her at the mall on Saturday and would breathlessly count down the school days until the weekend came. We'd criticize the shallow girls who started dating guys and no longer had time for their female friends. We vowed to be inseparable.

In October 1998, during my junior year of college, Matthew Shepard—a young, gay University of Wyoming student—was severely beaten and left for dead. I didn't know Matthew Shepard. I wasn't a political activist. But my boyfriend at the time and I got on a Greyhound bus and traveled to Laramie to participate in the candlelight vigil at the university. It was when I was surrounded by all those points of light that I could confess what I had been terrified to admit to myself: it could have been me. That I was, and always had been, gay.

And here's the amazing thing: even after I said it out loud, the world did not stop turning.

I was still a college student majoring in education, with a 3.8 average. I still weighed 121 pounds and preferred chocolate to vanilla and sang with an a cappella group called Son of a Pitch. I swam at the school pool at least twice a week, and I was still much more likely to be found watching *Cheers* than getting wasted at a frat party. Admitting I was gay changed nothing about who I had been, or who I was going to be.

Part of me worried that I didn't fit into either camp. I'd never *been* with a woman, and was afraid that it would be as uneventful for me as fooling around with a guy. What if I wasn't *really* gay— just totally, functionally asexual? Plus, there was an added wrinkle to this new social world that I hadn't considered: the default assumption, when you meet a woman, is that she's heterosexual (unless you happen to be at an Indigo Girls concert . . . or a WNBA basketball game). It wasn't like certain girls sported an *L* on the forehead, and my gaydar had not yet been finely tuned.

In the end, though, I shouldn't have worried. The girl who was my lab partner in biochemistry invited me to her dorm room for a study session, and pretty soon we were spending all of our free time together. When I wasn't with her, I wanted to be. When a professor said something ridiculous or sexist or hilarious, she was the first one I wanted to tell. One Saturday at a football game we shivered in the stands underneath a wool tartan blanket, passing a thermos of hot cocoa laced with Baileys back and forth. The score was close, and during one really important fourth down, she grabbed on to my hand, and even after the touchdown, she didn't let go. The first time she kissed me, I truly thought I'd had an aneurysm—my pulse was thundering so loud and my senses were exploding. *This,* I remember thinking, the only word I could hold on to in a sea of feelings.

After that, I could look back with twenty-twenty vision and see that I never had boundaries with my female friends. I wanted to see their baby pictures and listen to their favorite songs and fix my hair the same way they fixed theirs. I would hang up the phone and think of one more thing I had to say. I wouldn't have defined it as a physical attraction—it was more of an emotional attachment. I could never quite get enough, but I never let myself ask what "enough" really was.

Believe me, being gay is not a choice. No one would choose to make life harder than it has to be, and no matter how confident and comfortable a gay person is, he or she can't control the thoughts of others. I've had people move out of my row in a movie theater if they see me holding hands with a woman—apparently disgusted by our public display of affection when, one row behind us, a teenage couple is practically undressing each other. I've had the word DYKE written on my car in spray paint. I've had parents request that their child be moved to a different school counselor's jurisdiction, parents who, when asked for a reason why, say that my "educational philosophy" doesn't match theirs.

You can argue that it's a different world now than the one when Matthew Shepard was killed, but there is a subtle difference between tolerance and acceptance. It's the distance between moving into the cul-de-sac and having your next-door neighbor trust you to keep an eye on her preschool daughter for a few minutes while she runs out to the post office. It's the chasm between being invited to a colleague's wedding with your same-sex partner and being able to slow-dance without the other guests whispering.

I remember my mother telling me that, when she was a little girl in Catholic school, the nuns used to hit her left hand every time she wrote with it. Nowadays, if a teacher did that, she'd probably be arrested for child abuse. The optimist in me wants to believe sexuality will eventually become like handwriting: there's no right way and wrong way to do it. We're all just wired differently.

It's also worth noting that, when you meet someone, you never bother to ask if he's right- or left-handed.

After all: Does it really matter to anyone other than the person holding the pen?

The longest relationship I've ever had with a woman is with Rajasi, my hairdresser. Every four weeks I go to her to get my roots dyed blond and my hair trimmed into its shaggy pixie cut. But today Rajasi is furious and punctuating her sentences with angry snips of the scissors. "Um," I say, squinting at my bangs in the mirror. "Isn't that a little short?"

"An arranged marriage!" Rajasi says. "Can you believe it? We came here from India twenty years ago. We're as American as it comes. My parents eat at McDonald's once a week, for God's sake."

"Maybe if you told them—"

A hunk of hair flies past my eyes.

"They had my *boyfriend* over for dinner last Friday," Rajasi huffs. "Did they honestly think I'd ditch the guy I've been dating for three years because some decrepit old Punjabi is willing to give them a bunch of chickens for a dowry?"

"Chickens?" I say. "Really?"

"I don't know. That's not the point." She is still cutting, lost in her rant. "Is it or is it not 2011?" Rajasi says. "Shouldn't I be allowed to marry whomever I want?"

"Honey," I reply, "you are preaching to the choir."

I live in Rhode Island, one of the only states in New England to *not* have recognized same-sex marriage. For this reason, couples who want to get hitched cross the border into Fall River, Massachusetts. It seems simple enough, but it actually creates a thicket of issues. I have friends, two gay men, who tied the knot in Massachusetts and then, five years later, split up. Their property and assets were all in Rhode Island, where they lived. But because their marriage was never legal in the state, they couldn't actually *get* divorced.

Rajasi stops. "And?" she says.

"And what?"

"Here I am going on about my love life when you haven't mentioned a single thing about yours . . ."

I laugh. "Rajasi, I have a better chance of hooking up with your Punjabi than anyone else right now. I think my romantic pool has gone bone-dry."

"You make it sound like you're sixty," Rajasi says. "Like you're going to sit home all weekend crocheting with a hundred cats."

"Don't be silly. Cats are much better at cross-stitching. Besides, I have big plans for the weekend. I'm headed to Boston to see a ballet."

"Isn't it supposed to snow?"

"Not enough to stop us from going," I say.

"*Us,*" Rajasi repeats. "Do tell . . ."

"She's just a friend. We're celebrating her anniversary."

"Without her husband?"

"It's a divorce thing," I say. "I'm trying to get her through a rough spot."

Zoe and I had become pretty good friends in the weeks since our encounter at the Y. I must have called her first, since I was the one who had her home number. I was going to be picking up a painting from a frame shop near her house, and did she want to meet for lunch? Over deli sandwiches, we talked about the research she was doing on depression and music therapy; I told her about broaching the topic with Lucy's parents. The next weekend, she won two tickets to a movie preview on a radio giveaway, and asked me if I wanted to go. We began spending time together, and in that bizarre exponential way that new friendships seem to snowball, it grew hard to imagine a time when I didn't know her.

We've talked about how she found out about music therapy (as a kid, she broke her arm and needed a pin put in surgically, and there was a music therapist in the pediatrics wing of the hospital). We've talked about her mother (who calls Zoe three times a day, often to discuss something completely unnecessary, like last night's Anderson

Cooper report or what day Christmas falls on three years from now). We've talked about Max, his drinking, and the rumor mill that now puts him at the right hand of the pastor of the Eternal Glory Church.

Here's what I hadn't expected about Zoe: she was funny. She had a way of looking at the world that was just off-kilter enough to surprise me into laughing:

If someone with multiple personality disorder tries to kill himself, is it attempted homicide?

Isn't it a little upsetting that doctors call what they do "practice"?

Why are you in a movie but on TV?

Isn't a smoking section in a restaurant a little like a peeing section in a pool?

We had a lot in common. We'd grown up in households with single parents (her father deceased, mine running off with his secretary); we had always wanted to travel and never had enough money to do it; we both were freaked out by clowns. We had a secret fascination with reality TV. We loved the smell of gasoline, hated the smell of bleach, and wished we knew how to use fondant, like pastry chefs. We preferred white wine to red, extreme cold to extreme heat, and Goobers to Raisinets. We both had no problem using a men's room at a public venue if the line for the ladies' room was too long.

Tomorrow would have been her tenth wedding anniversary, and I could tell she was dreading it. Zoe's mom, Dara, was away in San Diego this weekend at a life coaching conference, so I suggested that we do something Max would never in a million years have wanted to do. Immediately, Zoe picked the ballet at the Wang Theatre in Boston. It was *Romeo and Juliet,* Prokofiev. Max, she had told me, never could handle classical dance. If he wasn't remarking on the men's tights, he was fast asleep.

"Maybe that's what I should do," Rajasi muses. "Take this fool my parents are flying in to a place he'll absolutely detest." She glances up. "What would a Brahmin hate the most?"

"All-you-can-eat barbecue?" I suggest.

"A heavy metal rave."

Then we look at each other. "NAS-CAR," we say at the same time.

"Well, I'd better go," I say. "I'm supposed to pick Zoe up in fifteen minutes."

Rajasi pivots the hairdressing chair toward the mirror again and winces.

When your hairdresser winces, it's never good. My hair is so short that it sticks up in small, grasslike clumps on the top of my head. Rajasi opens her mouth, and I shoot a dagger look in her direction. "Don't you dare tell me it'll grow out . . ."

"I was going to say the good news is that the military look is in this spring . . ."

I rub my hands through my hair, trying to mess it up a little, not that it helps. "I would kill you," I say, "but I actually think you'll suffer more by being alive to meet the Punjabi guy."

"See? You're already starting to like this look. If you didn't, you'd be too busy crying to make jokes." She takes the money I hold out to her. "Be careful driving," Rajasi warns. "It's already starting to snow."

"A dusting," I say, waving good-bye. "No worries."

Another thing, it turns out, that we have in common: *Romeo and Juliet.* "It's always been my favorite Shakespeare play," Zoe says, once the company has taken its bows and she rejoins me in the sumptuous renovated lobby of the Wang Theatre after a trip to the restroom. "I always wanted a guy to walk up to me and start a conversation that naturally became a sonnet."

"Max didn't do that?" I ask, smiling.

She snorts. "Max thought a sonnet was something you ask for in the plumbing section of Home Depot."

"I once told the head of the English department at school that I liked *Romeo and Juliet* the best," I say, "and she told me I was a philistine."

"What! Why?"

"Because it's not as complex as *King Lear* or *Hamlet,* I guess."

"But it's dreamier. It's everyone's fantasy, right?"

"To die with your lover?"

Zoe laughs. "No. To die before you start making lists of all the things about him that drive you crazy."

"Yeah, imagine the sequel, if it had ended differently," I reply. "Romeo and Juliet are disowned by their families and move into a trailer park. Romeo grows a mullet and becomes addicted to online poker while Juliet has an affair with Friar Lawrence."

"Who, it turns out," Zoe adds, "runs a meth lab in his basement."

"Totally. Why else would he have known what drug to give her in the first place?" I loop my scarf around my neck as we brace ourselves to walk into the cold.

"Now what?" Zoe asks. "You think it's too late to grab dinner some . . ." Her voice trails off as we step outside. In the three hours we have been in the theater, the storm has thickened into a blizzard. I cannot see even a foot in front of me, the snow is whirling that fiercely. I start to step into the street, and my shoe sinks into nearly eight inches of accumulation.

"Wow," I say. "This sort of sucks."

"Maybe we should wait it out before driving home," Zoe replies.

A limo driver who's leaning against his vehicle glances over at us. "Settle in for a nice long wait, then, ladies," he says. "AccuWeather says we're getting two feet before this is all over."

"Sleepover," Zoe announces. "There are plenty of hotels around—"

"Which cost a fortune—"

"Not if we split the cost of a room." She shrugs. "Besides. That's what credit cards are for." She links her arm through mine and drags me into the wild breath of the storm. On the other side of the street is a CVS. "Toothbrushes, toothpaste, and I need to get some tampons," she says, as the sliding doors close behind us. "We can get nail polish, too, and curlers, and make each other up and stay up late and talk about boys . . ."

Not gonna happen, I think. But she is right—to drive home in this would be stupid, reckless.

"I have two words for you," she says, cajoling. "Room service."

I hesitate. "I pick the pay-per-view movie?"

"Deal." Zoe holds out her hand to shake.

There is no real reason for me to fight an impromptu hotel stay. I can afford the luxury of a room for one night, or at least justify it to myself. But all the same, as we check in and carry our CVS bags upstairs, my heart is racing. It's not that I've been dishonest to Zoe by not talking about my sexual orientation, but it hasn't exactly been a topic of discussion, either. Had she asked, I would have told her the truth. And just because I am a lesbian doesn't mean that I will ravish any female in close proximity, in spite of what homophobes think. Yet there's an extra wrinkle here: it would be ludicrous to think that a straight woman would not be able to maintain a platonic friendship with a man . . . and yet, if she found herself in this situation, she probably wouldn't be sharing a room with that male buddy.

When I told my mother, finally, that I

was gay, the first thing she said was "But you're so pretty!" as if the two were mutually exclusive. Then she got quiet and went into the kitchen. A few minutes later she came back into the living room and sat down across from me. "When you go to the Y," she asked, "do you still use the ladies' locker room?"

"Of course I do," I said, exasperated. "I'm not a transsexual, Ma."

"But Vanessa," she asked, "when you're in there . . . do you peek?"

The answer, by the way, is no. I change in a stall, and I spend most of my time in there staring down at the floor. In fact, I probably am more un-comfortable and hyperaware being in there than anyone else would be if she knew the woman in the purple Tyr suit was gay.

But it's just one more thing I have to worry about that most people never do.

"Oooh," Zoe says, when she steps into the room. "Swank-o-la!"

It is one of those hotels that is being redone to accommodate the metro-sexual businessman, who apparently

likes tweedy black comforters, chrome
lighting, and margarita mix on the mini-
bar. Zoe opens the curtains and looks
down on the Boston Common. Then
she takes off her boots and jumps on
one of the beds. Finally, she reaches
for the CVS bag. "Well," she says, "I
guess I'll unpack." She holds out two
toothbrushes, one blue and one purple.
"Got a preference?"

"Zoe . . . you know I'm a lesbian,
right?"

"I was talking about the toothbrushes," she says.

"I know." I run my hand through my
ridiculous, spiky hair. "I just . . . I don't
want you to think I'm hiding anything."

She sits down across from me on her
own bed. "I'm a Pisces."

"What difference does that make?"

"What difference does it make to me
if you're gay?" Zoe says.

I let out the breath I didn't realize I
have been holding. "Thanks."

"For what?"

"For . . . I don't know. Being who you
are, I guess."

She grins. "Yeah. We Pisces, we're a

special breed." Rummaging in the pharmacy bag again, she comes out with the box of tampons. "Be right back."

"You all right?" I ask. "That's the fifth time you've gone to the bathroom this hour." I reach for the television remote while Zoe's in the bathroom. There are forty movies playing. "Listen up," I call out. "Here are our choices . . ." I recite each title while an Adam Sandler clip plays on endless loud repeat. "I need a comedy," I say. "Did you ever see the Jennifer Aniston one in theaters?"

Zoe doesn't answer. I can hear water running.

"Thoughts?" I yell. "Comments?" I flick through the titles again. "I'm going to make an executive decision . . ." I pause at the Purchase screen, because I don't want Zoe to miss the beginning of the film. While I wait, I pore through the room service menu. I could practically buy a small car for the cost of a T-bone, and I don't see why the ice cream is sold only in pints instead of scoops, but it looks decidedly more gourmet than what I might have cooked myself at home.

"Zoe! My stomach is starting to eat its own lining!" I glance at the clock. It's been ten minutes since I paused the screen, fifteen since she went into the bathroom.

What if the things she said about me aren't really what she feels? If she's regretting staying over, if she's worried I'm going to crawl into her bed in the middle of the night. Getting up, I knock on the bathroom door. "Zoe?" I call out. "Are you okay?"

No answer.

"Zoe?"

Now, I'm getting nervous.

I rattle the knob and yell her name again and then throw all my weight against the door so that the lock pops open.

The faucet is running. The tampon box is unopened. And Zoe is lying unconscious on the floor, her jeans around her ankles, her panties completely drenched in blood.

I ride with Zoe on the short ambulance trip to Brigham and Women's Hospital.

If there is a silver lining in any of this, it's that being stranded in Boston has put us in spitting distance of some of the best medical facilities in the world. The EMT asks me questions: *Is she usually this pale? Has this happened before?*

I don't really know the answer to either question.

By then Zoe has regained consciousness, even if she's so weak she can't sit up. "Don't worry . . . ," she murmurs. "Happens . . . a lot."

Just like that I realize that, no matter how much I think I already know about Zoe Baxter, there is a great deal more I don't.

While she is examined by a doctor and given a transfusion, I sit and wait. There's a television playing a *Friends* rerun, and the hospital is deathly quiet, almost like a ghost town. I wonder if the doctors have all been stranded here by the storm, like us. Finally, a nurse calls for me, and I go into the room where Zoe is lying on the bed with her eyes closed.

"Hey," I say softly. "How do you feel?"

She swivels her head toward me and glances up at the bag of blood hanging, the transfusion she's being given. "Vampiric."

"B positive," I answer, trying to make a joke, but neither of us smiles. "What did the doctor say?"

"That I should have come to a hospital the last time this happened."

My eyes widen. "You've passed out before from having your period?"

"It's not really a period. I'm not ovulating, not regularly anyway. I never have. But since the . . . baby . . . this is what a period looks like, for me. The doctor did an ultrasound. She said I have a fluffy endometrial stripe."

I blink at her. "Is that good?"

"No. I need a D & C." Zoe's eyes fill with tears. "It's like a bad flashback."

I sit down on the edge of the bed. "It's completely different," I say, "and you're going to be fine."

It *is* different—not just because a stillborn isn't involved. The last time Zoe had a health crisis her husband and her mother were at her side. Now, all she's got nearby is me—and what

do I know about taking care of someone other than myself? I don't have a
dog anymore. I don't even have a gold-
fish. I killed the orchid my principal
bought me for Christmas.

"Vanessa?" she asks. "Can you give
me the phone so I can call my mom?"

I nod and take her cell phone out of
her purse just as two nurses come in to
prep Zoe for her surgery. "I'll call her
for you," I promise as Zoe is wheeled
down the hallway. After a moment I flip
open her cell phone.

I can't help it. It's a little like being
invited to someone's home for dinner
and you go to the bathroom and peek
in the medicine cabinet—I scroll through
her contacts to see if I can get a better
picture of Zoe from the people she
knows. Most of the people listed I have
never heard of, predictably. Then there
are the old staples: AAA, the local pizza
place, the numbers of the hospitals and
schools where she is contracted.

I find myself wondering, though.
Who's Jane? Alice? Are they friends of
hers from college, or professional col-

leagues? Has she ever mentioned them to me?

Has she ever mentioned me to *them*?

Max is still listed. I wonder if I should call him. I wonder if Zoe would want me to.

Well, that's not what she asked. Scrolling up, I find Dara listed, predictably, under MOM.

I dial, but it rolls right into voice mail, and I hang up. I just don't think it's right to leave an alarmist message on someone's phone when she's three thousand miles away and can't really do anything to help Zoe right now. I'll keep trying.

An hour and a half after Zoe is wheeled into surgery, she is brought back to the room. "She'll be groggy for a while," the nurse tells me. "But she's going to be fine."

I nod and watch the nurse close the door behind her. "Zoe?" I whisper.

She's fast asleep, drugged, with her eyelashes casting blue shadows on her cheeks. Her hand lies uncurled on top of the cotton blanket, as if she is offering me something I cannot see. Another pint of blood hangs on an IV pole to her left, its contents snaking through the crazy straw tubing into the crook of her elbow.

The last time I was in a hospital, my mother was dying by degrees. Pancreatic cancer was the diagnosis, but it was no secret that her morphine doses grew higher and higher, until the sleep permanently outdistanced the pain. I know Zoe is not my mother, does not have the same illness, and yet there's something about the way she is lying so still and silent in this bed that makes me feel like I'm living my life over again, reading a chapter that I wish had never been printed.

"Vanessa," Zoe says, and I jump. She licks her lips, dry and white.

I reach for her hand. It's the first time I've held Zoe's hand, which feels small, birdlike. There are calluses on the tips of her fingers, from her guitar strings. "I tried your mother. I haven't been able to reach her. I can leave a message, but I thought maybe—"

"I can't . . . ," Zoe murmurs, interrupting.

"You can't what?" I whisper, leaning closer, straining to hear.

"I can't believe . . ."

There are so many things I can't believe. That people deserve what they get, both bad and good. That one day I'll live in a world where people are judged by what they do instead of who they are. That happy endings don't have contingencies and conditions.

"I can't believe," Zoe repeats, her voice small enough to slip into my pocket, "that we wasted money on a hotel room . . ."

I look down at her, to see if she is kidding, but Zoe has already drifted back to sleep.

We've come a long way from the days when being gay and being an educator were incompatible, but there's still a don't-ask-don't-tell policy in place at my high school. I don't actively hide my sexual orientation from my colleagues, but I don't go out of my way to broadcast it, either. I am one of the two adult advisers for the students' Rainbow Alliance, but the other one—Jack Kumanis—is as straight as they come. He's got five kids, competes in triathlons, is prone to quoting *Fight Club*—and he happened to be raised by two moms.

Still, I'm careful. Although most school counselors would think nothing of closing their office doors for a private session with a student, I never do. My door is always just the tiniest bit ajar, so that there can't be any doubt that whatever is happening is completely legitimate and interruptible.

My job runs the gamut from listening to students who just need to be heard through networking with admissions counselors at colleges so that they put our school on their virtual maps and supporting the kid too shy to find her own voice to logistically juggling the schedules of three hundred students who all want their first-choice English electives. Today I have on my couch Michaela Berrywick's mother—parent of a ninth grader who just received a B plus in her social studies class. "Mrs. Berrywick," I say, "this isn't the end of the world."

"I don't think you understand, Ms. Shaw. Michaela has been dying to go to Harvard since she was tiny."

Somehow I doubt that. No child comes out of the womb planning her high school résumé; that comes courtesy of zealous parenting. When I was in school, the term *helicopter parent* didn't even exist. Now parents hover so much that their kids forget how to be kids.

"She can't let a history teacher with a grudge against her make a permanent blot on her record," Mrs. Berrywick stresses. "Michaela is more than willing to do any extra credit necessary to get Mr. Levine to reconsider his grading policy . . ."

"Harvard doesn't care if Michaela got a B plus in social studies. Harvard wants to know that she spent her freshman year learning more about who she really is. Finding something that she liked doing."

"Exactly," Mrs. Berrywick says. "Which is why she joined the SAT study prep class."

Michaela will not be taking the SATs

for another two years. I sigh. "I'll talk to Mr. Levine," I say, "but I can't make any promises."

Mrs. Berrywick opens her purse and takes out a fifty-dollar bill. "I appreciate you seeing my side of things."

"I can't take your money. You can't buy a better grade for Michaela—"

"I'm not," the woman interrupts, smiling tightly. "Michaela earned the grade. I'm just . . . offering my gratitude."

"Thanks," I say, pressing the bill back at her. "But I truly can't accept this."

She looks me up and down. "No offense," she whispers, conspiratorial, "but you could use a little wardrobe update."

I'm thinking of going to Alec Levine and asking him to lower Michaela Berrywick's grade when I hear someone crying in the outer office. "Excuse me," I say, certain that it's the tenth grader I saw an hour ago who was twelve days late for her period, and whose boyfriend had dumped her after they had sex. I grab my box of tissues—school counselors ought to do product endorsements for Kleenex—and walk out.

It's not the tenth grader, though. It's Zoe.

"Hey," she says, and she tries to smile but fails miserably.

It's been three days since our disastrous trip to Boston. After Zoe's D & C, I finally got in touch with her mother, who flew home from her conference and met me at Zoe's place. I'd called Zoe multiple times since then to see how she was feeling, until she finally told me that if I called again and asked her how she was feeling she'd hang up on me. In fact, today she was supposed to go back to work.

"What's wrong?" I ask, as I lead her into my office.

And close the door.

She wipes her eyes with a tissue. "I don't get it. I'm not a bad person," Zoe says, her mouth twisting. "I try to be nice and I compost and I give money to homeless people. I say please and thank you and I floss every day and I volunteer in a soup kitchen at Thanksgiving. I work with people who have Alzheimer's and depression and who are scarred and I try to give them some-

thing good in their day, one little thing
to take with them." She looks up at me.
"And what do I get? Infertility. Miscarriages. A stillborn. A goddamned embolism. A divorce."

"It's *not* fair," I say simply.

"Well, neither's the phone call I got
today. The doctor—the one from
Brigham and Women's? She said they
did some tests." Zoe shakes her head.
"I have cancer. Endometrial cancer. And
wait—I'm not finished yet—it's a *good*
thing. They caught it early enough, so I
can have a little hysterectomy, and I'll
be just fine and dandy. Isn't that just
fabulous? Shouldn't I be thanking my
lucky stars? I mean, what's next? An
anvil falling on my head from the second story? My landlord evicting me?"
She stands up, whirling in a circle. "You
can come out now," she shouts to the
walls, the floor, the ceiling. "Whatever
shitty version of *Candid Camera* this is;
whoever decided I was this year's Job—
I'm done. I'm *done.* I'm—"

I stand up and hug her tight, cutting
off whatever she was about to say. Zoe
freezes for a moment, and then she

starts sobbing against my silk blouse. "Zoe," I say. "I'm—"

"Don't you dare," Zoe interrupts. "Don't you dare tell me you're sorry."

"I'm not," I say, straight-faced. "I mean, if you look at sheer probability— the fact that all these things are happening to you means it's much more likely I'm safe. I'm positively charmed, in fact. You're good luck for me."

Zoe blinks, stunned, and then a laugh barks out of her. "I can't believe you said that."

"I can't believe I made you laugh, when you clearly ought to be railing against the heavens or renouncing God or something. Let me tell you, Zoe, you make a lousy cancer sufferer."

Another laugh. "I have cancer," she says, incredulous. "I actually have cancer."

"Maybe you can get gangrene, too, before sunset."

"I wouldn't want to be greedy," Zoe answers. "I mean, surely someone else needs a plague of locusts or the swine flu—"

"Termites!" I add. "Dry rot!"

"Gingivitis . . ."

"A leaky muffler," I say.

Zoe pauses. "Metaphorically," she points out, "that was the problem in the first place."

This makes us laugh even harder, so much so that the guidance department secretary pokes her head in to make sure we're all right. By then, my eyes are tearing, my abdominal muscles actually ache. "I need a hysterectomy," Zoe says, bent over to catch her breath, "and I can't stop laughing. What's wrong with me?"

I stare at her as soberly as I can. "Well . . . I believe you have cancer," I say.

When I came out to Teddy, my college boyfriend, at the Matthew Shepard vigil, the most remarkable thing happened: he came out to me, too. There we were, two gays who had tried to act as straight as possible for the rest of the college community—and now, happily, were coming clean. We still cuddled and hugged but with the utter relief of know-

ing that we no longer had to try (unsuc-
cessfully) to arouse each other, or to
fake attraction. (When I've told heterosexual people in the past that I had a
boyfriend in college, slept with him, the
whole nine yards, they are always surprised. But just because I'm gay doesn't
mean I *can't* have sex with a guy—only
that it's not at the top of my to-do list.)
In the wake of our newfound same-
sexual awakening, Teddy and I went to
Provincetown over Memorial Day weekend. We ogled drag queens racing
down Commercial Street in high heels
and bronze-oiled men in butt floss walking the beach. We went to a tea dance
at the Boatslip and afterward went to
the PiedBar—where I'd never seen so
many lesbians in one room in my life.
That weekend, it was as if the world
had been turned upside down, and
straight folks were the anomaly rather
than the norm. And yet, I didn't feel like
I fit in there, either. I have never been
one of those gay people who hangs out
exclusively with gay people, or parties
all the time, or lives a wild and deca-
dent lifestyle. I'm not butch. I wouldn't

know how to ride a motorcycle if my life depended on it. No, I'm much more likely to be in my pajamas by 8:00 P.M., watching reruns of *House* on the USA network. Which means that the women I run across most of the time are more likely to be straight than to be lesbian.

Everyone who's gay has had the unfortunate circumstance of falling for someone who's not. The first time it happens, you think: *I can change her. I know her better than she knows herself.* And invariably, you are left with a broken relationship and an even more broken heart. The straight equivalent, in a way, is the woman who's sure that the guy she loves—the one who beats her every night—will eventually stop. The bottom line in both cases is that people don't change; that no matter how charming you are and how fiercely you love, you cannot turn a person into someone she's not.

I had crushes on straight girls my whole childhood, even if I couldn't put a name to the feeling—but my first grown-up mistake was Janine Durfee, who played first base on a college intramural softball team. I knew she had a boyfriend—one who was continuously cheating on her. One night when she came to my dorm room in tears because she'd walked in on him with someone else, I invited her inside while she calmed down. Somehow listening to her cry morphed into me kissing her and ten phenomenal days as a couple before she went back to the guy who treated her like dirt. *It was fun, Vanessa,* she said apologetically. *It's just not me.*

It's important to point out that I have plenty of straight friends, women I've never been attracted to but still like to meet for lunch, movies, whatever. But over the years there have been a few who made a tiny flame fan inside me, a *what if.* They are the ones I have to actively keep my distance from, because I'm not a masochist. There are only so many times you can hear: *It's not you. It's me.*

I am not a proving ground. I don't want to be the experiment. I have no interest in seeing if my personal charms can overpower the wiring of someone's brain.

I believe I was born the way I am, and so I have to believe that someone straight is born that way, too. But I also believe you fall in love with a *person;* it stands to reason sometimes that could be a guy, and sometimes that could be a girl. I've often asked myself what I'd do if the greatest love of my life turned out to be male. Are you attracted to someone because of *who* they are, or *what* they are?

I don't know. But I *do* know that I'm at the stage of my life where I want *forever,* not *right now.*

I know that the first person I kissed won't be nearly as important as the last person I kiss.

And I also know better than to dream about things that can't happen.

I am sitting at my desk getting nothing done.

Every two minutes I check the clock in the corner of the computer. It's 12:45, which means that Zoe should be long out of surgery.

Her mom is at the hospital. I thought

about going there, too, but didn't know if that would seem weird. It's not like Zoe *asked* me to come, after all. And I didn't want to impose, if she just felt like being alone with her mom.

But I wonder if the reason she didn't ask is because she didn't want me to feel obligated to come.

Which I wouldn't have, at all.

12:46.

Last weekend Zoe and I had gone to the art museum at RISD. The current exhibition was an empty room, with cardboard boxes on the perimeter. I'd sat down on one and been shooed out by a museum guard before realizing that I was inadvertently making myself part of the art. "Maybe I'm a philistine," I had said, "but I like my art on canvas."

"Blame Duchamp," Zoe had answered. "The guy took a urinal, signed it, and put it on display in 1917 as a work of art called *Fountain*."

"You're kidding . . ."

"No," Zoe had said. "It was recently voted the most influential art by, like, five hundred experts."

"I suppose that's because you're supposed to realize anything can be art—like a urinal or a cardboard box—if you stick it in a museum?"

"Yes. Which is why," Zoe had said, straight-faced, "I'm donating my uterus to RISD."

"Make sure you have cardboard boxes, too. And a window. Then it can be called *Womb with a View.*"

She had laughed, a little wistfully. "More like *Empty Womb,*" Zoe said, and before she got tangled in her own thoughts, I had pulled her down the street to a place where they make the most amazing lattes, with foam designs on top that truly *are* art.

12:50.

I wonder if Dara will call me when Zoe's out of surgery. I mean, it's perfectly normal that I'd want to make sure she sailed through it. I tell myself that just because I haven't heard from her doesn't mean anything's wrong.

I am the kind of person who imagines the worst. When friends fly somewhere, I check the arrivals online, just to make sure there wasn't a crash.

When I go out of town, I unplug all my appliances in case there is a power surge.

On my computer browser, I pull up the main page of the hospital where Zoe's having her surgery. I type in the words "laparoscopic hysterectomy" on Google and look on the tab for a list of possible complications.

When the phone rings I pounce on it. "Hello?"

But it's not Dara, and it's not Zoe. The voice is tiny, so faint that it's gone before it even registers. "Just calling to say good-bye," Lucy DuBois murmurs.

It's the girl—a junior—whom I mentioned to Zoe weeks ago, the one who has suffered from depression for some time now. This isn't the first time she's called me in the middle of a crisis.

But it's the first time she's sounded like this. Like she's underwater and sinking fast.

"Lucy?" I yell into the phone. "Where are you?" In the background, I hear a train whistle, and what sounds like church bells.

"Tell the world," Lucy slurs, "that I said *fuck you*."

I grab the daily attendance sheet, where, prophetically, Lucy DuBois has already been marked absent.

It's a pretty remarkable thing, to save someone's life.

Based on the train whistle and the bells I heard, the police were able to focus their search near an old wooden bridge that backs up against a specific Catholic church with a 1:00 P.M. Mass. Lucy was found lying under a trestle with a liter of Gatorade and an empty bottle of Tylenol beside her.

I met her mother at the hospital. Now, after being given an activated charcoal solution to drink, Lucy has been brought up to the inpatient psych ward on suicide watch. It remains to be seen how much damage she's done to her liver and kidneys.

Sandra DuBois sits beside me on a chair in the waiting room. "They need to keep her under observation for a few days," she says, and she forces herself to meet my eye. "Ms. Shaw, I don't know how to thank you."

"Please, it's Vanessa," I say. "And I do: Let me help your daughter."

I have tried, for the past month, to convince Lucy's parents that music therapy is a valid scientific tool to try to break through to their increasingly isolated daughter. So far, I haven't gotten them to agree. Sandra and her husband are heavily involved in the Eternal Glory Church—and they don't treat mental illness on a par with physical illness. If Lucy was diagnosed with appendicitis, they would understand the need for treatment. But depression, to them, is something a good night's sleep and a Bible study meeting can cure.

I kind of wonder how many suicide attempts it will take before that changes.

"My husband doesn't believe in psychiatrists . . ."

"So you've told me." He's not even here, in spite of Lucy's close call—he is traveling for business, apparently. "Your husband wouldn't necessarily have to know. We could keep this a secret, just between you and me."

She shakes her head. "I don't really see how singing songs can make a difference—"

"Make a joyful noise unto the Lord," I quote, and she blinks at me, as if I have finally spoken her language. "Look, Mrs. DuBois. I don't know what will help Lucy, but whatever you and I have done so far doesn't seem to be working. And you might have a whole congregation praying for your daughter, but if I were in your shoes, I'd have a backup plan just in case."

The woman's nostrils flare, and I'm certain that I've crossed that unwritten line where professionalism and personal belief bleed together. "This music therapist," Sandra says finally, "she's worked with adolescents before?"

"Yes." I hesitate. "She is a friend of mine."

"But is she a good Christian?"

I realize I have no idea what religious affiliation, if any, Zoe is. If she asked for a priest at the hospital, or even checked off a box on her intake form for any given denomination. Stumped, I watch as Sandra DuBois stands up and starts down the hall, toward Lucy.

And then I remember Max. "I believe she has relatives who attend your church," I call out.

Lucy's mother hesitates. Then, before she turns the corner, she looks back at me, and nods.

On the first day I visited Zoe, she was unconscious. Dara and I played gin rummy, and she asked me probing questions about my childhood before offering to read the dregs of my green tea.

On the second day I visited Zoe, I brought a flower that I'd made by sticking three dozen guitar picks into a piece of floral foam in the shape of a daisy. And let me just say I am not crafty, and in fact have a gag reaction when confronted by a glue gun or crochet hook.

On the third day, she is waiting for me at the front door. "Kidnap me," she begs. "Please."

I look over her shoulder, toward the kitchen, where I can hear Dara banging pots and pans for dinner preparations. "Seriously, Vanessa. There is only so much conversation about the positive effects of copper bracelets on a body that a normal human can take."

"She's going to kill me," I murmur.

"No," Zoe says. "She's going to kill *me*."

"You're not even supposed to be walking . . ."

"The doctor didn't have any restrictions against going for a little ride. Fresh air," she says. "You've got a convertible . . ."

"It's *January*," I point out.

Still, I know that I'm going to do what she asks; Zoe could probably convince me that it's a fantastic idea to take a vacation to Antarctica in the middle of winter. Hell, I'd probably book a ticket, if she was going, too.

She directs me to a golf course that is covered in snow, a local haunt for elementary school kids who drag their inflatable tubes up the hill and then grab each other's legs and arms before sledding down, linked like atoms in a giant molecule. Zoe rolls down the window, so that we can hear their voices.

Man, that was awesome.

You almost hit that tree!

Did you see how much air I got on that jump?

Next time, I get to go first.

"Do you remember," I ask, "when the most tragic part of your day was finding out that the cafeteria was serving meat loaf for hot lunch?"

"Or what it felt like to wake up and find out it was a snow day?"

"Actually," I admit, "I still get to do that."

Zoe watches the kids make another run. "When I was in the hospital, I had a dream about a little girl. We were on a Flexible Flyer and I was holding her in front of me. It was the first time she'd ever been sledding. It was so, so real. I mean, my eyes were tearing up because of the wind, and my cheeks were chapped, and that little girl—I could smell the shampoo in her hair. I could feel her heart beating."

So this is why she directed me to the hill, why she is watching these children as if she's going to be tested later on their features. "I'm guessing she wasn't someone you knew?"

"No. And now I never will."

"Zoe—" I put my hand on her arm.

"I always wanted to be a mother," she says. "I thought it was because I wanted to read bedtime stories or see my child singing in the school chorus or shop for her prom dress—you know, the things I remember making my own mom so happy. But the real reason turned out to be selfish. I wanted someone who would grow up to be my anchor, you know?" she says. "The one who calls every day to check in. The one who runs out to the pharmacy in the middle of the night if you're sick. The one who misses you, when you're away. The one who *has* to love you, no matter what."

I could be that person.

It hits me like a hurricane: the realization that what I've labeled friendship is—on my end, anyway—more than that. And the understanding that what I want from Zoe is something I will never have.

I've been here before, so I know how to act, how to pretend. After all, I'd much rather have a piece of her than nothing at all.

So I move away from Zoe, letting my arm drop, intentionally putting space between us. "Well," I say, forcing a smile. "I guess you're stuck with me."

	TRACK 1	SING YOU HOME
	TRACK 2	THE HOUSE ON HOPE STREET
	TRACK 3	REFUGEE
✓	**TRACK 4**	**THE LAST**
	TRACK 5	MARRY ME
	TRACK 6	FAITH
	TRACK 7	THE MERMAID
	TRACK 8	ORDINARY LIFE
	TRACK 9	WHERE YOU ARE
	TRACK 10	SAMMY'S SONG

ZOE

My very first best friendship was grounded in proximity. Ellie lived across the street in a house that always looked a little tired at the edges, with its droopy window wells and frayed clapboards. Her mother was single, like mine, although by choice and not by fate. She worked in an insurance company and wore low heels and boxy suits to the office, but I remember her glamorously affixing fake eyelashes and ratting her hair before heading out to a dance club on weekends.

I was completely unlike Ellie, who—at age eleven—was a stunning girl with sunshine twined in the curls of her hair, and long colt legs with a perpetual summer tan. Her room was always a mess, and she'd have to dump piles of clothes and books and stuffed animals on the floor in order for us to have a place to sit on the bed. She thought nothing of stealing into her mother's closet to "borrow" clothes for dress up or sprays of perfume. She read magazines, never books.

But the one thing Ellie and I had in common was that, of all the kids in our class, we were the two without fathers. Even kids whose parents were divorced saw the missing parent for weekends or holidays, but not Ellie and me. I couldn't, obviously. And Ellie had never met her dad. Ellie's mother referred to him as the One, in a reverent tone that made me think he must have died young, like my own father. Years later I learned that this wasn't the case at all; that the One was a married guy who'd been cheating on his wife but wouldn't leave her.

Ellie's older sister, Lila, was supposed to watch us on the nights when her mom went out, but Lila spent all her time in her bedroom with the door closed. We weren't allowed to bother her, and most of the time we didn't, even though she had the coolest fluorescent posters that glowed under a black light behind her bed. Instead we cooked ourselves Campbell's soup and watched scary movies on the premium cable channels, shielding our eyes from the screen.

I could tell Ellie anything. Like how, sometimes, I woke up screaming because I had a nightmare that my mother had died, too. Or that I worried I would never be brilliant at anything, and who wanted to be average her whole life? I confessed that I faked a stomachache to get out of taking a math quiz and that I had once seen a boy's penis at camp when his bathing suit slid off during a jackknife dive. On school nights I called her before I went to sleep, and in the morning, she phoned me to ask what color shirt I was wearing, so that we would match.

One weekend, during a sleepover at Ellie's house, I climbed out of the bed we shared and crept down the hallway. The door to her mother's room was open, and inside, the room was empty, even though it was after 3:00 A.M. Lila's door, as usual, was closed, but there was a purple line of light bleeding out from beneath it. I turned the knob, wondering if she was still awake. Inside, the room was magical—cloudy with incense and lavender streams of light, those ultraviolet posters coming alive in 3-D. One, a skull with rosette eyes, seemed to be moving toward me. Lila was lying on the bed with her eyes wide open and a rubber hose tied around her arm, like the kind I'd seen at the doctor's office when I had to have a blood test, once. A syringe was in the palm of her open hand.

I was quite sure she was dead.

I took a step forward. Lila was incredibly still, and faintly blue in the eerie light. I thought of my father, and how he collapsed on the lawn. I was gathering the loose threads of a scream in my throat, when suddenly Lila rolled over in one languid move, scaring the hell out of me. "Get lost, you little shit," she said, her words as round and thin as bubbles, popping as soon as they hit the air.

I do not remember the rest of that night. Except that I ran home, even though it was three in the morning.

And that, after what happened, Ellie and I were never really friends anymore.

When I was in high school, my mother used to make up alternate names for the kids I invited over to our house. Robin became Bonnie, Alice became Elise, Suzy became Julie. No matter how many times I corrected her, she preferred to call these girls by names that felt comfortable to her, instead of what was accurate. After a while, my friends even started answering to whatever she called them.

Which is why it's so extraordinary to me that my mother has never—not once—messed up Vanessa's name. The two of them hit it off the moment they first met. There is no end to the things they have in common; and they seem to think it's funny that it drives me crazy.

It's been two months since Vanessa and I bumped into each other at the Y, and she has slipped seamlessly into the role of my closest friend at a time when I desperately needed it—since my former closest friend happened to have recently divorced me. So much of a friendship is like a love affair—the novelty and sparkle wearing down at the edges to become something comfortable and predictable, like the cardigan you take out of your drawer on a rainy Sunday because you need to surround yourself with something cozy and familiar. Vanessa is the one I call when I am procrastinating on organizing my taxes; when I am channel surfing and find *Dirty Dancing* on TNT and cannot stop watching; when the homeless guy in front of Dunkin' Donuts looks at the five-dollar bill I've given him and asks if he can have it in ones. She's the one I call when I'm bored in traffic on I-95, and when I'm crying because a two-year-old patient with burns over eighty percent of his body dies in the middle of the night. I've programmed her cell number into my phone, on the speed-dial key that used to belong to Max.

It is easy, with twenty-twenty hindsight, to see how I got to a point where I didn't really have any friends. There's that necessary shift that comes with marriage, when your best confidant is now the one you're sleeping with at night. But then the other women I knew all started having babies, and I distanced myself from them out of self-preservation and jealousy. Max was the only one who understood what I so badly wanted and needed. Or so I'd told myself.

Here's what girlfriends do for you: they provide the reality check. They are the ones who tell you when you have spinach between your teeth or when your ass looks fat in a pair of jeans or when you're being a bitch. They tell you, and there's no drama or agenda, like there would be if the message had come from your husband. They tell you the truth because you need to hear it, but it doesn't alter the bond between you. I don't think I realized how much I missed that, until now.

Right now, Vanessa and I are about to be late to a movie because my mother is talking about a breakthrough with one of her clients. "So, I bought two dozen bricks and loaded them in the back of my car," my mother is saying. "And then, when we got to the cliff, I had Deanna write on each of the bricks with a Sharpie marker—keywords, you know, that signified her emotional baggage."

"Brilliant," Vanessa says.

"You think? So she writes *My Ex* on one. And *Never made peace with my sister* on another. And *Didn't lose last 20 pounds after having kids,* and so on. I'm telling you, Vanessa, she went through three markers alone. And then I got her on the edge of the cliff and had her hurl the bricks, one at a time. I told her that the minute they hit the water, that weight was going to be off her shoulders for good."

"Sure hope there wasn't a humpback migration going on below the cliff," I murmur, tapping my foot impatiently. "Look, I hate to break up the professional development session, but we're about to miss the early showing—"

Vanessa stands up. "I think it's a terrific idea, Dara," she says. "You ought to write it up and submit it to a professional journal."

My mother's cheeks pinken. "Honestly?"

I grab my purse and my jacket. "Are you going to let yourself out?" I ask my mother.

"No, no," she says, getting to her feet. "I'll just go home."

"Are you sure you don't want to come along?" Vanessa asks.

"I'm sure my mother's got better things to do," I say quickly, and give her a quick hug. "I'll call you in the morning," I say, and I drag Vanessa out of the apartment.

Halfway to the car, Vanessa turns around. "I forgot something," she says, tossing me the keys. "I'll be right back." So I let myself into the convertible and turn the ignition. I am surfing the channels of her radio when she slips into the driver's seat. "Okay," Vanessa says, backing out of the driveway. "Who spit in your Cheerios?"

"Well, what were you thinking, inviting my mom to come with us?"

"That she's all alone on a Saturday night?"

"I'm forty, Vanessa—I don't want to hang out with my mother!"

"You would if you couldn't," Vanessa says.

I look at her. In the dark, the reflection from the rearview mirror casts a yellow mask around her eyes. "If you miss your mother so much, you can have mine," I say.

"I'm just saying you don't have to be so mean."

"Well, you don't have to enable her, either. Did you seriously think her brick exercise was a good one?"

"Sure. I'd use it myself, except the kids would probably write the names of their teachers on the bricks they're tossing, and that wouldn't be very constructive." She pulls up to a stop sign and turns to me. "You know, Zoe, my mother used to tell me the same story five times. Without fail. I was constantly saying, *Ma, yes, I know,* and rolling my eyes. And now—I can't even really remember her voice. I think sometimes I've got it, in my head, but then it fades before I can ever really hear it. Sometimes, I put on old videotapes just so I don't completely forget how she sounds, and I listen to her telling me to get a serving spoon for the potatoes, or singing 'Happy Birthday.' Right now, I'd *kill* to have her tell me a story five times. I'd settle for even once."

I know, halfway through her story, that I am going to cave in. "Is this what you do with the kids in school?" I sigh. "Make them see themselves for the petty, nasty people they really are?"

"If I think it's going to work," she says, smiling.

I turn on my cell phone. "I'll tell my mother to meet us at the theater."

"She's already coming. That's why I ran back into the house—to invite her."

"Were you really so sure I'd change my mind?"

"Give me a break." Vanessa laughs. "I even know what you're going to order at the concession counter."

She probably does. Vanessa is like that—if you say or do something once, it sticks in her memory so that she will be able to reference it the next time it's necessary. Like how I once mentioned I don't like olives, and then, a month later at a restaurant when we were given a basket of olive bread, she asked for crackers instead before I could even make a comment.

"Just for the record," I say, "there's still a lot about me you *don't* know."

"Popcorn, no butter," Vanessa says. "Sprite." She purses her lips. "And Goobers, because this is a romantic comedy and those are never quite as good without chocolate."

She's right. Down to the candy.

I think, not for the first time, that if Max had been even half as observant and attentive as Vanessa, I'd probably still be married.

When we pull up to the theater, I'm amazed to find a crowd. The movie has been out for a few weeks now—it's a silly, fizzy romantic comedy. The other movie playing is an independent film called *July* that's gotten a lot of press, because a very popular preteen singing sensation is starring in it, and because of the subject matter: instead of being a Romeo and Juliet tragedy . . . the love story is about Juliet and Juliet.

Vanessa spots my mother on the other side of the throng and waves her over. "Can you believe this?" she says, looking around.

I've seen a few articles written about the film and the controversy surrounding it. I begin to wonder if we should go see *that* movie instead, just based on its popular appeal. But as we get closer to the theater, I realize that the people milling around are not in the ticket line. They're flanking it, and they're carrying signs:

GOD HATES FAGS
GAY: <u>G</u>OD <u>A</u>BHORS <u>Y</u>OU
ADAM AND EVE, NOT ADAM AND STEVE

They are not militant, crazy people. The protesters are calm and organized, and wearing black suits with skinny ties, or modest floral print dresses. They look like your neighbor, your grand-mother, your history teacher. In this, I suppose, they have something in com-mon with the people they are slander-ing.

Beside me, I feel Vanessa's spine go rigid. "We can leave," I murmur. "Let's just rent a video and watch it at home."

But before I can pull away, I hear my name being called. "Zoe?"

At first, I don't recognize Max. The last time I saw him, after all, he was drunk and disheveled, and trying to ex-plain to a judge why we should be granted a divorce. I'd heard that he started going to Reid and Liddy's church, but I hadn't quite expected a transformation this . . . radical.

Max is wearing a fitted dark suit with a charcoal tie. His hair has been trimmed neatly, and he's clean-shaven. On the lapel of his suit is a pin: a small gold cross.

"Wow," I say. "You look great, Max."

We do an awkward dance, where we move toward each other for a kiss on the cheek, but then I pull away, and he pulls away, and we both look down at the ground.

"So do you," he says.

He is wearing a walking cast. "What happened?" I ask. It seems crazy that I wouldn't know. That Max would have gotten hurt, and no one relayed the message to me.

"It's nothing. An accident," Max says.

I wonder who took care of him, when he was first hurt.

Behind me, I am incredibly conscious of my mother and Vanessa. I can feel their presence like heat thrown from a fireplace. Someone in the front of the line buys a ticket to *July,* and the protest starts up in earnest, with chanting and yelling and sign waving. "I heard you were part of Eternal Glory, now," I say.

"Actually, it's a part of *me,*" Max replies. "I let Jesus into my heart."

He says this with a brilliant white smile, the same way he'd say, *I got my car waxed this afternoon* or *I think I'll have Chinese food for dinner*—as if this is part of normal everyday conversation instead of a statement that might give

you pause. I wait for Max to snicker—
we used to make fun of Reid and Liddy
sometimes for the glory-be snippets
that fell out of their mouths—but he
doesn't.

"Have you been drinking again?" I
ask, the only explanation I can come
up with to reconcile the man I know
with the one standing in front of me.

"No," Max says. "Not a drop."

Maybe not of alcohol, but it's pretty
clear to me that Max has been chug-
ging whatever Kool-Aid the Eternal
Glory Church is offering. There's something just *off* about him—something
Stepford-like. I preferred Max with all
his complicated imperfections. I preferred Max when we used to make fun
of Liddy for saying "Jeezum Crow"
when she was frustrated, for being gull-
ible enough to believe him when he told
her that Rick Warren was mounting a
presidential campaign.

Full disclosure: I'm not a religious
person. I don't begrudge people the
right to believe in whatever they believe, but I don't like having those same
beliefs forced on me. So when Max

says, "I've been praying for you, Zoe,"
I have absolutely no idea what to say. I
mean, it's nice to be prayed for, I suppose, even if I've never asked for it.

But do I really want to be prayed for
by a bunch of people who are using
God to camouflage a message of hate?
There are beautiful, wholesome teenage girls standing in front of the ticket
booth handing out flyers that say: I WAS
BORN BLOND. YOU CHOOSE TO BE GAY. Their
clean-cut attentiveness, their claim of
being "Good Christians" are the icing, I
realize, on a cake that's laced with ar-
senic. "Why would you want to do this
kind of thing?" I ask Max. "Why does a
movie even matter to you?"

"Perhaps I can answer that," a man
says. He has a cascade of white hair
and stands nearly six inches taller than
Max; I think I recognize him from news
clips as the pastor of this church. "We
wouldn't be here if the homosexuals
weren't promoting their own agenda,
their own activism. If we sit back, who's
going to speak for the rights of the traditional family? If we sit back, who's
going to make sure our great country

doesn't become a place where Johnny has two mommies and where marriage is as God intended it to be—between a man and woman?" His voice has escalated. "Brothers and sisters—we are here because Christians have *become* the minority! Homosexuals claim they have a right to be heard? Well, *so do Christians*!"

There is a roar from his congregants, who push their placards higher in the air.

"Max," the pastor says, tossing him a set of keys, "we need another box of pamphlets from the van."

Max nods and then turns to me. "I'm really glad you're doing well," he says, and for the first time since we've started talking I believe him.

"I'm glad you're doing well, too." I mean it, even if he's on a road I'd never walk myself. But in a way, this is the ultimate vindication for me, the proof that our relationship could never have been mended. If this is where Max was headed, it was not somewhere I'd ever have wanted to go.

"You're not going to see *July*, I hope?"

Max says, and he offers up that half smile that made me fall in love with him.

"No. The Sandra Bullock movie."

"Wise choice," Max replies. Impulsively, he leans forward and kisses me on the cheek. I breathe in the scent of his shampoo and am viscerally hit with an image of the bottle in the shower, with its blue cap and its little sticker about tea tree oil and its health properties. "I think about you every day . . . ," Max says.

Drawing back, I am suddenly dizzy; I wonder if this is the ghost of old love.

". . . I think of how much happier you could be, if you let the Lord in," Max finishes.

And just like that, I am firmly rooted in reality again. "Who *are* you?" I murmur, but Max has already turned his back, headed to the parking lot to do his pastor's bidding.

The bar is called Atlantis and is tragically hip, set in a new boutique hotel in Providence. On the walls a projector ripples color, to simulate being under the sea. The drinks are all served in cobalt glassware, and the booths are carved out of fake coral, with cushions fashioned to look like bright sea anemone. The centerpiece of the room is a huge water tank, where tropical fish swim with a woman squeezed into a silicone mermaid tail and shell bra.

Fortunately, my mother has decided to go home after the movie, leaving Vanessa and me to have a drink by ourselves. I am fascinated by the woman in the tank. "How does she breathe?" I ask out loud, and then see her surreptitiously sneak a gulp of oxygen from a scubalike device that she's concealing in her hand, which is attached to an apparatus at the top of the tank.

"I stand corrected," Vanessa says. "There *is* a career path for women who dreamed of being mermaids when they were girls."

A waitress brings us our drinks and nuts served, predictably, in a large shell. "I could see where this would get old very fast," I say.

"I don't know. I was reading about how, in China, theme restaurants are all the rage right now. There's one that serves only TV dinners. And another that only has medieval food, plus you have to eat with your hands." She looks up at me. "The one I'm itching to go to, though, is the prehistoric restaurant. They serve raw meat."

"Do you have to kill it yourself?"

Vanessa laughs. "Maybe. Imagine being the hostess: 'Uh, miss, we reserved a table with the hunters, but we were seated with the gatherers instead.'" She lifts her drink—a dirty martini, which tastes like paint thinner to me (when I told Vanessa this, she said, "When did you last drink paint thinner?"), and toasts. "To Eternal Glory. May they one day succeed in separating Church and Hate."

I lift my glass, too, but I don't drink from it. I'm thinking about Max.

"I don't understand people who complain about the mysterious 'homosexual agenda,'" Vanessa muses. "You know what's on that agenda, for my gay friends? To spend time with family, to pay their bills, and to buy milk on the way home from work."

"Max was an alcoholic," I say abruptly. "He had to drop out of college because of his drinking. He used to surf whenever the conditions were right. We'd fight because he was supposed to be running a business, and then I'd find out that he ditched his clients for the day because of some ten-foot swells."

Vanessa sets down her drink and looks at me.

"My point is," I continue, "that he wasn't always like this. Even that suit . . . I don't think he owned more than a sports jacket the entire time we were married."

"He looked a little like a CIA operative," Vanessa says.

My lips twitch. "All he needs is an earpiece."

"I'm pretty sure the hotline to God is wireless."

"People must see through all that rhetoric," I say. "Does anyone really take Clive Lincoln seriously?"

Vanessa runs her finger around the lip of her martini glass. "I was at the grocery store yesterday and there was a bumper sticker on the pickup truck

next to my car. It said, SAVE A DEER . . .
SHOOT A QUEER." She glances up. "So
yeah. I think some people take him seriously."

"But I never expected Max to be one
of them." I hesitate. "Do you think this
is my fault?"

I expect Vanessa to immediately dismiss the idea, but instead, she thinks
for a moment. "If you hadn't been pulling yourself together after you lost the
baby, then maybe you would have been
able to help Max when he needed it.
Sounds to me, though, like Max was
already broken when you met him. And
if that's the case, no matter how much
you patched him up, sooner or later he
was going to fall apart again." She picks
up her glass and drains it. "You know
what you need? You need to let go."

"Of what?"

"Max, obviously."

I can feel my cheeks burn. "I'm not
holding on to him."

"Hey, I get it. It's only natural, since
you two—"

"He wasn't even my type," I blurt out,
and I realize after I say it that it is true.

"Max was—well, he was just completely different from the kinds of guys who were usually interested in me."

"You mean big and brawny and sexy?"

"You think?" I ask, surprised.

"Just because I don't hang modern art in my house doesn't mean I can't appreciate it," Vanessa says.

"Max was always trying to teach me about football, and I hated football. All those guys piling on top of each other on Astroturf. And basketball is pointless. You don't even have to watch a whole game—it always comes down to the last two minutes. And he was messy. He'd leave a melon on the counter after he cut himself a slice, and by nighttime, the kitchen would be crawling with ants. And he could hold a grudge like nobody's business. I wouldn't even know he was upset until six months went by and he brought it up during an argument about something totally different."

"But you married him," Vanessa points out.

"Well," I answer. "Yeah."

"Why?"

I don't even know how to answer that. "Because," I say finally, "when you love someone, you don't see the parts of him you don't like."

"Seems to me you need to do a better job next time of getting what you really want."

"Next time!" I repeat. "I don't think so. I'm through with relationships."

"Oh really. You're putting yourself on the shelf at forty?"

"Shut up," I say. "Get back to me after you're divorced."

"Zo, I'd take you up on that, if only because it means I'd have the right to be married. Seriously, look around. There's got to be someone attractive in here for you . . ."

"I am *not* letting you set me up, Vanessa."

"Then just tell me. As an academic exercise, of course . . ."

"Tell you what?"

"What you're looking for."

"For God's sake, Vanessa, I have no idea. I'm not thinking about any of that yet."

I glance at the mermaid. She is on

break, emerging from the tank by hopping up a ladder. When she gets to the top, where there is a ledge she can sit on, she reaches for a towel and dries herself off before checking her Black-Berry.

"Someone real," I hear myself saying. "Someone who never has to pretend, and who I never have to pretend around. Someone who's smart, but knows how to laugh at himself. Someone who would listen to a symphony and start to cry, because he understands that music can be too big for words. Someone who knows me better than I know myself. Someone I want to talk to first thing in the morning and last thing at night. Someone I feel like I've known my whole life, even if I haven't."

When I'm done, I look up to find Vanessa smirking at me. "Gee," she says. "I'm certainly glad you aren't thinking about this yet."

I finish my wine. "Well, *you* asked."

"I did. So that when I bump into your future spouse on the street, I can give out your number."

"What's *your* perfect date?" I ask.

Vanessa tosses a twenty-dollar bill on the table. "Oh, I'm not nearly as discriminating. Female, desperate, willing." She glances up at the mermaid, now drinking sullenly from a whiskey glass. "Human."

"You're so picky," I say, laughing. "How are you ever going to find someone?"

"Story of my life," she replies. "Story of my life."

It is not until I am home and lying in bed that I realize Vanessa never seriously answered my question, at least not nearly as seriously as I'd answered hers.

And that—with the exception of the pronoun I'd used—the verbal sketch I gave of my perfect match had actually described Vanessa.

What songs would be on a mix tape that describes you?

It's a question I've used my whole life, as a foolproof test of character. It grew out of the old "Witch Doctor" record that reminded my mother so much of my missing dad. There's no question that, for her, this would be one of the tracks. And "Always and Forever"—the song she and my dad danced to at their wedding—which, when heard in its elevator Muzak incarnation, always made them circle around in each other's arms no matter where they were or how large the crowd, which to me was magical and mortifying all at once. And a Beatles song—she tells a story about sleeping outside a hotel where the Fab Four were camped for a press junket, just so that she could get a glimpse of them as they left for the airport. And Enya and Yanni, which she uses now for mindful breathing. Seriously, if you looked through the Favorites list on my mother's iPod, you could probably sketch her out as thoroughly as if you'd met her in person.

This is true of anyone: the music we choose is a clear reflection of who we really are. There is a lot you can tell about a person who lists Bon Jovi among his favorites. Or, for that matter, Weezer. Or the original cast recording of *Bye Bye Birdie*.

I first used the mix tape test to check romantic compatibility in high school, when my boyfriend insisted on playing one Journey track over and over again on his car stereo whenever we were steaming up the windows. He'd stop in the middle of whatever we were doing to belt out the chorus. I should have known better than to trust a man who loved power ballads.

After that, I asked all my potential love interests about the fictional mix tape. I told them there was no right answer, which is true. There are, however, some blatantly wrong answers:

"Crazy."
"I'm Too Sexy."
"Mmmbop."
"The Streak."
"All My Ex's Live in Texas."

Max's list was a collection of country music, a genre of which I've never been a fan. Somehow the songs always seem to talk about drinking and having your wife leave you, or else they compare women to large pieces of farm equipment, like tractors and trucks. You know that old joke about the cowboy and the biker who are on death row, set to be executed on the same day? The prison guard asks the cowboy for his last request, and he begs to hear the song "Achy Breaky Heart" before he dies. The guard then asks the biker for *his* last request. "To be killed before you play that song," he says.

The most interesting people I've ever met are the ones who answer the question with music I have never experienced before: South African a cappella groups, Peruvian drummers, up-and-coming alt rockers from Seattle, Jane Birkin, the Postelles. When I was at Berklee I dated a boy whose list was all rap. I had grown up in the suburbs listening to Casey Kasem and didn't know much about hip-hop music. But he explained how its roots grew from the griots of West Africa—traveling singers and poets who were keeping a centuries-old oral storytelling tradition. He played me rap songs that were social commentary. He taught me how to write my own flow, how to feel poetry in syl-

lables and rhythm in the spaces between the words. He taught me that
what wasn't said was just as important
as what was.

I fell pretty hard for him, actually.

I stopped using the question to learn
more about potential dates once I met
Max, of course, but I didn't retire the
inquiry. Now, I ask my clients. I've met
people whose lists are all classical; I've
met people who choose only heavy
metal. I've met burly, tattooed motorcy-
clists who love opera and grandmoth-
ers who know Eminem's lyrics by heart.

The music we listen to may not de-
fine who we are.

But it's a damn good start.

In February, Vanessa and I sign up for
a Bikram yoga class, the kind that's
done in an abnormally hot room. We go
to one session and leave at the halfway
point five-minute break, certain we are
both about to have strokes.

So the next week I call her up and
tell her that maybe belly dancing is
more our thing. We are pretty good at

it, actually, but our classmates are not. We get booted by the instructor because we can't stop laughing when we are supposed to be focusing.

On Saturdays, we fall into a habit. Vanessa comes to my house with coffee and bagels, and we read the paper at the kitchen table. Then we make a list of all the errands we need to accomplish during the weekend. Like me, she is too busy during business hours to get to the cleaners or the grocery store or the post office, so we pool our destinations. Instead of going alone, it is a lot more fun to wander the aisles of Walmart together debating whether plus-size Tinker Bell lingerie is serving a niche market or creating an aberrant one.

We go to the farmers' market—which is mostly jars of honey and beeswax candles and crafts made from homespun wool, at this time of year—and we wander from booth to booth, trying free samples. Sometimes we get inspired and pick a recipe out of *Cooking Light,* then cobble together the ingredients and spend the afternoon making the soufflé or the ragout or the beef Wellington.

One Saturday in early March, I am left to my own devices. Vanessa's gone to San Francisco to a friend's wedding, which is actually a good thing—since I have more to do than usual. The student Vanessa spoke with me about months ago—Lucy DuBois—has just been released from a six-week inpatient program for depressed adolescents at McLean Hospital. She is coming back to school, and I'm going to start working with her. I have been poring over books about teens and depression, and music therapy for mood disorders.

I've promised Vanessa I'll pick up her dry cleaning along with mine, so I make a quick run downtown before settling in to reread Lucy's school file. The woman who runs the cleaner is tiny, with a quickness to her movements that always makes me think of a hummingbird. "You're all alone today," she says, taking the tickets from me and running the wonderful maze of mechanized hangers. Last week, when Vanessa said they looked like something out of a Tim Burton movie, the owner took us behind the counter to see how they snaked around back, like a giant zipper running the perimeter of the ceiling.

"Yeah. Flying solo this weekend," I reply.

She hands me my trousers, and a bright bouquet of Vanessa's button-down shirts. I trade her this week's dry cleaning and tuck the pink slips into my purse. "Thanks," I say. "See you next week."

"Tell your partner I said hello!"

I freeze in the act of zipping my wallet. "She's not—*I'm* not—" I shake my head. "Mrs. Chin, Vanessa and I— We're just friends."

It is, I suppose, an honest mistake. She has seen me with Vanessa for weeks now; it's actually wonderful to think the world has changed enough that a storekeeper might assume two people of the same sex are a couple.

So why am I blushing?

As I carry the dry cleaning back to my car, I think that, actually, this is funny. That when I tell Vanessa, she'll think so, too.

The last teens I worked with were part of a diversion program meant to bring together warring adolescent gangs in the inner city. Previously, they'd been on the streets trying to kill each other. When I told them we'd be doing a drum circle together, they nearly charged for each other's throats, but their resource officers forced them to sit down on the perimeter of the pile of percussion instruments I'd assembled: a djembe and a tubano, a conga drum, an ashiko, and a djun-djun. One by one, I handed out the instruments, and, believe me, if you are an adolescent boy with a drum in your hands, you're going to beat it. We started with a simple hand rhythm: clap-clap-lap; clap-clap-lap. Then we moved to the drums. Eventually, we went around the circle so each kid could have a spotlighted solo with a unique rhythm.

Here's what's great about a drum circle: no one ever has to play alone. And

all the inappropriate ways of express-
ing anger can be channeled into the
movement of beating that drum instead
in a safe, controlled setting. Before the
group could even realize it, they were
creating a piece of music, and they
were doing it together.

So I have to admit, I'm feeling pretty
confident about my first session with
Lucy DuBois. One of the fantastic things
about music is that it accesses both
sides of the brain—the analytical left
side and the emotional right side—and
forces a connection. This is how a
stroke victim who can't speak a sentence might be able to sing a lyric; how
a patient frozen by severe Parkinson's
disease can use the sequence and in-
herent rhythm in music in order to move
and dance again. If music has the ability to bypass the part of the brain that
isn't working correctly in order to facili-
tate a link to the rest of the brain in
these other situations, it must be able
to do the same for a mind crippled by
clinical depression.

In school, Vanessa's different than
she is when we're just hanging out to-

gether. She wears tailored pantsuits and silk blouses in bright jewel colors, and she walks briskly, as if she is already five minutes late. When she comes across two teens groping in the hall, she breaks them apart with efficiency. "People," she sighs, with a quietly unassuming authority, "is this really how you want to waste my time?"

"No, Miz Shaw," the girl murmurs, and she and her boyfriend slink down opposite sides of the hallway, like two magnets repelled by the same polarity.

"Sorry about that," Vanessa says, as I hurry to keep pace with her. "In my job, hormones are an occupational hazard." She smiles at me. "So what's the game plan for today?"

"An assessment," I tell her. "The whole point of therapy is to come into the process where Lucy is."

"I'm psyched. I've never really seen you in action before," Vanessa says.

I stop walking. "I don't know if that's a good idea . . ."

"Oh, I'm sure you're going to be great—"

"It's not that," I interrupt. "Vanessa,

it's *therapy.* If you referred Lucy to a psychiatrist, you wouldn't expect to sit in on the session, would you?"

"Right. Got it," she says, but I can tell she's still miffed. "Anyway," Vanessa starts moving at breakneck speed again, "I got you a room to use in the special needs wing."

"Look, I don't want you to—"

"Zoe," Vanessa says brusquely, "I understand."

I tell myself that I will explain it to her later. Because we turn the corner into the reserved room, and Lucy DuBois is slumped in a chair.

She has long ropes of red hair, some of which are caught beneath her checked flannel shirt. Her eyes are a hooded, angry brown. Her sleeves are rolled up to show faint red scars on her wrists, as if she's daring the rest of us to comment. She's chewing gum, which is banned on the school grounds.

"Lucy," Vanessa says. "Get rid of the gum."

She takes it out of her mouth and mashes it onto the surface of the desk.

"Lucy, this is Ms. Baxter."

I toyed with going back to my maiden name, Weeks, but that made me think of my mother. Max had taken a lot away from me, but legally, I could still use that name if I wanted to. And a girl who's grown up at the end of the alphabet doesn't lightly decide to toss away a last name that begins with a *B*. "You can call me Zoe," I say.

Everything about this girl screams *defensive*—from her hunched shoulders to her studious refusal to look me in the eye. I notice that she's got a nose ring—one tiny, thin gold hoop that looks like a trick of the light until you do a second glance—and what seem to be tattoos on the knuckles of one hand.

They're letters, actually.

F.U.C.K.

I remember Vanessa telling me that Lucy's family attends Eternal Glory— Max's ultraconservative church. I try to imagine Lucy handing out pamphlets in front of the movie theater with the bright, sparkly teenage girls who'd been there the night Pastor Clive & Co. set up their protest.

I wonder if Max knows her.

"I'm really looking forward to working with you, Lucy," I say.

She doesn't move a muscle.

"I'll expect you to give Zoe your full attention," Vanessa adds. "Do you have any questions before you two start?"

"Yeah." Lucy's head falls backward, like a dandelion too heavy for its stem. "If I don't show up for these sessions, do I get a cut on my record?"

Vanessa looks at me and raises her brows. "Good luck," she says, and she closes the door behind her as she leaves.

"So." I pull a chair in front of Lucy's so that she cannot help but see me, and sit down. "I'm really glad that I'll be getting to work with you. Did anyone explain what music therapy is, exactly?"

"Bullshit?" Lucy offers.

"It's a way to use music to access feelings that are sometimes locked in-side," I say, as if she hasn't even spo-ken. "In fact, you're probably doing a little of this on your own already. Every-one does. You know how, when you have a bad day and you only want to put on your sweats and eat a pint of chocolate ice cream and sob to the song 'All by Myself'? That's music therapy. Or when it finally gets warm enough to roll down the windows of you car, so you crank up the stereo and sing along? That's music therapy, too."

As I speak, I take out a notebook, so that I can begin to do my assessment. The plan is to write down comments a client gives, and my own impressions, and later to cobble them into a more formal clinical document. When I do this in the hospital, it's easy—I assess the pain level of the client, her state of anxiety, her facial expressions.

Lucy, however, is a blank slate.

Her eyes stare straight over my shoulder; her thumb absently scratches at the carvings on the desk made by ball-point pens and bored students.

"So," I say brightly. "I thought that, today, maybe you could help me learn a little more about you. Like, for example, have you ever played an instrument?"

Lucy yawns.

"I guess that's a no. Well, have you ever *wanted* to play one?"

When she doesn't answer, I move my chair forward a little.

"Lucy, I asked if you ever wanted to play an instrument . . ."

She pillows her head on her arms, closing her eyes.

"That's okay. A lot of people never learn to play instruments. But, you know, if that's something you become interested in when we're working together, I could help you. I know how to play everything—woodwinds, percussion, brass, keyboard, guitar . . ." I look down at my notebook. So far I've written Lucy's name and nothing else.

"Everything," Lucy repeats softly.

I am so excited to hear her sandpaper voice that I nearly fall forward out of my seat. "Yes," I reply. "Everything."

"Do you play the accordion?"

"Well. No." I hesitate. "But I could learn it with you, if you wanted."

"Didgeridoo?"

I tried, once, but couldn't master the round breathing. "No."

"So basically," Lucy says, "you're a fucking liar, like everyone else I've ever met."

I learned a long time ago that en-
gagement—any at all, even anger—is a
step above complete indifference.
"What kind of music do you like? What
would I find on your iPod?"

Lucy has slipped back into silence.
She takes out a pen and colors an
elaborate pattern on the inside of her
palm, a Maori knot of twists and swirls.

Maybe she doesn't have an iPod. I
bite the inside of my lip, angry at myself for making a socioeconomic assumption about a client. "I know your
family is pretty religious," I say. "Do you
listen to Christian rock? Maybe there's
one particular band you really like?"

Silence.

"How about the first pop song whose
lyrics you memorized? When I was little, my best friend's older sister had a
record player, and she used to play
'Billy, Don't Be a Hero' on repeat. It was
1974, and Paper Lace was singing it. I
saved up my allowance to buy my own
copy. Even now when I hear that song
I get teary at the end when the girl gets
the memo about her boyfriend's death,"
I say. "It's funny—if I could pick one

song to bring to a desert island, I'd take that one. Believe me, I've heard a lot more complex and deserving music since then, but for sheer nostalgia, that would have to get my vote." I look at Lucy. "How about you? What music would you want to bring if you were stranded on a desert island?"

Lucy smiles sweetly at me. *"The Very Best of David Hasselhoff,"* she says, and then she stands up. "Can I go to the bathroom?"

I just stare at her for a moment; Vanessa and I haven't really talked about whether that's allowed. But this is therapy, not jail—and besides, keeping her from going would be cruel and unusual punishment. "Sure," I say. "I'll wait here."

"I bet you will," Lucy murmurs, and she slips out the door.

I tap my fingers against the desk, and then pick up my pen. *Client is very resistant to providing personal details,* I write.

Likes Hasselhoff.

Then I cross off that last bit. Lucy only said that to see my reaction.

I think.

I had been so certain that I could break through to Lucy; I'd never doubted my skills as a therapist. But then again, the work I'd been doing lately involved either a captive audience (the nursing home residents) or those in so much physical distress that music could only help, not hurt (the burn victims). The factor of the equation I had left out was that, although I may have been looking forward to this session, Lucy DuBois wanted to be anywhere *but* here.

After a few minutes I start looking around the room.

Although most special needs kids are mainstreamed, this small conference room has the facilities for those whose Individualized Education Programs mandate them: bouncy balls to sit on instead of chairs; mini workstations where kids can stand behind the desks or work with others; shelves of books; tubs of Kooshes and rice and sandpaper. On the whiteboard is a single written phrase: *Hi, Ian!*

Who's Ian? I wonder. *And what did*

they do with him so that Lucy and I could meet?

I realize that about fifteen minutes have passed since Lucy left to go to the bathroom. Walking out of the classroom, I spy the girls' restroom just across the hall. I push through the door to find a girl leaning toward the mirror, applying black eyeliner.

I duck down, but there are no feet beneath any of the stalls.

"Do you know Lucy DuBois?"

"Uh, *yeah,*" the girl says. "Total freak."

"Did she come into the bathroom?"

The girl shakes her head.

"Dammit," I mutter, walking back into the hallway. I glance into the room where we have been meeting, but I'm not naïve enough to think Lucy will be waiting.

I will have to go back to the main office, and report the fact that Lucy left the session.

I'll have to tell Vanessa.

And then I'll do exactly what Lucy did: cut my losses, and leave.

After failing miserably with Lucy, the last thing I want to do is go home. I know there will be messages waiting from Vanessa—she wasn't in her office when I signed out, and so I had to leave an explanatory and apologetic note about the abortive first music therapy session. I turn off my cell phone and drive to the most anonymous place I could think of: Walmart. You'd be surprised at how much time you can spend wandering through the aisles; looking at Corelle dinnerware with lemon and lime patterns, and comparing the prices of generic vitamins to those of brand names. I fill up a cart with things I do not need: dish towels and a camping lantern and a BeDazzler; three Jim Carrey DVDs packaged together for ten dollars, Crest Whitestrips. Then I abandon the cart somewhere in the fishing and hunting section and unfold a lawn chair. I sit down and try to read the latest *People.*

I don't quite know why my failure with Lucy DuBois is so crushing. I've had plenty of other clients whose initial meetings were not dynamic successes.

The autistic boy I worked with at the same high school a year ago, for example, did nothing but rock in a corner for the first four visits. I know that, in spite of what happened today, Vanessa will trust my judgment if I say that next time will be better. She'll forgive me for letting Lucy slip away; she'll probably even blame the girl instead of me.

I'm not afraid of her being disappointed.

It's just that I don't want to be the one to disappoint her.

"Excuse me," an employee says. I look up to see his big Walmart badge, his thinning hair. He speaks slowly, as if I am a toddler unable to understand him. "The chairs are not for sitting."

Then what are *they for?* I wonder. But I just smile politely, get up, refold the chair, and stick it back on the shelf.

I drive mindlessly for a half hour before finding myself in the parking lot of a bar that's only a mile from my house. I used to work there—first as a waitress, then as a singer—before Max and I started in vitro. Then, I was tired all the time, or stressed, or both. Playing acoustic guitar at 10:00 P.M. twice a week lost its appeal.

It's nearly empty, because it's a Wednesday, and it's only just past dinnertime.

Also because there is a big sign out front that says, WEDNESDAY IS KARAOKE NIGHT.

Karaoke, in my opinion, is right up there on the list of the greatest mistakes ever invented, along with Windows Vista and spray-on hair for balding men. It allows people who would normally only have the courage to sing in the confines of their own showers with the water running loudly to instead get on a stage and have fifteen minutes of dubious fame. For every truly remarkable karaoke performance you've ever heard, you've probably heard twenty horrendous ones.

Then again, by the time I've had my fourth drink in two hours, I am nearly ripping the microphone out of the hands of a middle-aged lady with a bad perm. I tell myself that this is because if she sings one more Celine Dion song I will have to strangle her with the hose that's hooked up to the soda keg underneath the bar. But it is equally likely that the reason I need to sing is because I know it's the one thing that will make me feel better.

The difference between people who become musicians and people who become music therapists is simple: a change in focus from what you personally can get out of music and what you can encourage someone else to get out of it. Music therapy is music without the ego—although most of us still hone our skills by playing in community bands and performing in choirs.

Or, in my case right now, karaoke.

I know I have a good voice. And on a day when my other abilities are being called into question, it's downright restorative to have the patrons of the bar clapping and asking for an encore, to have the bartender handing me a glass to use as a tip jar.

I sing a little Ronstadt. A bit of Aretha. Some Eva Cassidy. At some point, I go out to my car to grab a guitar. I sing a few songs I've written, and sprinkle them with a little Melissa Etheridge and an acoustic version of Springsteen's "Glory Days." By the time I sing "American Pie," I've got the whole bar doing the chorus with me, and I am not thinking about Lucy DuBois at all.

I'm not thinking, period. I'm just letting the music carry me, *be* me. I'm a thread of sound that slips like a stitch through every single person in this room, binding us tightly together.

When I finish, everyone applauds. The bartender pushes another gin and tonic down the bar toward me. "Zoe," he says, "it's about time you came back."

Maybe I should do more of this. "I don't know, Jack. I'll think about it."

"Do you take requests?"

I turn around to find Vanessa standing beside the barstool.

"I'm sorry," she says.

"Which version? Brenda Lee or Buckcherry?" I wait until she's climbed onto the stool beside mine and ordered a drink. "I'm not going to ask how you found me."

"You have the only bright yellow Jeep in this entire town. Even the traffic helicopters can find you." Vanessa shakes her head. "You're not the first one Lucy's run away from, you know. She did the same thing to the school shrink, the first time they met."

"You could have *told* me . . ."

"I was hoping it would be different this time," Vanessa says. "Are you going to come back?"

"Do you *want* me to come back?" I ask. "I mean, if you just want a warm body for Lucy to ditch, you could hire some teenager at minimum wage."

"I'll tie her down to the chair next time," Vanessa promises. "And maybe we can make her listen to that lady sing Celine Dion."

She points to the middle-aged woman whose karaoke career I intercepted. "You've been here that long?"

"Yeah. Why didn't you tell me you could sing like that?"

"You've heard me sing a hundred times—"

"Somehow when you chime in with the Hot Pockets jingle, it doesn't really convey the full range of your voice."

"I used to play here a couple times a

week," I tell her. "I forgot how much I liked it."

"Then you should do it again. I'll even come be your audience so you never have to play to an empty room."

Hearing her talk about an empty room reminds me of the music therapy session my client abandoned. I wrap my arms around the neck of my guitar case, as if creating a shield for myself. "I really thought I could get Lucy to open up. I feel like such a loser."

"I don't think you're a loser."

"What *do* you think of me?" The words slip out, before I have even meant for them to fly away.

"Well," Vanessa says slowly, "I think you're the most interesting person I've ever met. Every time I think I have you pegged, I learn something else about you that totally surprises me. Like last weekend when you said that you keep a list of all the places you wish you'd gone to when you were younger. Or that you used to watch *Star Trek* and memorized the dialogue from every episode. Or that, I now realize, you are the next Sheryl Crow."

There is a buttery glow to the room now; my cheeks are flushed, and I'm dizzy even though I'm sitting down. I did not drink very much when I was married to Max—out of solidarity, and then intended pregnancy—and for this reason the alcohol I'm not accustomed to has even more sway over my system. I reach across Vanessa to the stack of napkins beside the olive tray, and the fine hairs on my wrist brush against the silk sleeve of her blouse. It makes me shiver.

"Jack," I call out. "I need a pen."

The bartender tosses me one, and I unfold the cocktail napkin and write the numbers one through eight in a list. "What songs," I ask, "would be on the mix tape that describes you?"

I hold my breath, thinking that she's going to start laughing or just crumple the napkin, but instead Vanessa takes the pen out of my hand. When she bows her head toward the bar, her bangs cover one eye.

Did you ever notice how other people's houses have a smell? I had asked, the first time I went over to Vanessa's.

Please tell me mine isn't something awful like bratwurst.

No, I said. *It's clean. Like sunlight on sheets.* Then I asked her what my apartment smelled like.

Don't you know?

No, I'd explained. *I can't tell because I live there. I'm too close to it.*

It smells like you, Vanessa had said. *Like a place nobody ever wants to leave.*

Vanessa bites her lip as she writes down her list. Sometimes, she squints, or looks over at the bartender, or asks me a rhetorical question about the name of a band before she finds the answer herself.

A few weeks ago we were watching a documentary that said people lie on an average of four times a day. *That's 1,460 times a year,* Vanessa had pointed out.

I did the math, too. *Almost eighty-eight thousand times by the time you're sixty.*

I bet I know what the most common lie is, Vanessa had said: *I'm fine.*

I had told myself the reason I'd left the school without waiting for Vanessa to return to her office was because she was busy. I was afraid she'd think I was an abysmal music therapist. But the other reason I'd run was because I wanted (*wished for?*) her to come after me.

"Ta da," Vanessa says, and she pushes the cocktail napkin back toward me. It lifts, like a butterfly, and then settles on the bar.

Aimee Mann. Ani DiFranco. Damien Rice. Howie Day.

Tori Amos, Charlotte Martin, Garbage, Elvis Costello.

Wilco. The Indigo Girls. Alison Krauss.

Van Morrison, Anna Nalick, Etta James.

I can't speak for a moment.

"I know, it's weird, right? Pairing Wilco and Etta James on the same CD is like sitting Jesse Helms and Adam Lambert next to each other at a dinner party . . . but I felt guilty getting rid of one." Vanessa leans closer, pointing to the list again. "I couldn't pick individual songs, either. Isn't that like asking a mom which kid she loves the most?"

Every single artist she has put on her

list is one I would have put on my list.
And yet I know I've never shared that
information with her. I couldn't have,
because I've never formally made my
own CD playlist. I've tried but could
never finish, not with all the possible
songs in this world.

In music, perfect pitch is the ability
to reproduce a tone without any reference to an external standard. In other
words—there's no need to label or
name notes, you can just start singing
a C-sharp, or you can listen to an A
and know what it is. You can hear a car
horn and know that it is an F.

In life, perfect pitch is the ability to
know someone from the inside out,
even better maybe than she knows herself.

When Max and I were married, we
fought over the car radio all the time.
He liked NPR; I liked music. I realize
that, in all the months I've been friends
with Vanessa, in all the car rides we've
taken—from a quick run to the local
bakery to a trip to Franconia Notch,
New Hampshire—I have never changed
the station. Not once. I've never even

wanted to fast-forward through a CD she's picked.

Whatever Vanessa plays, I just want to keep listening to.

Maybe I gasp, and maybe I don't, but Vanessa turns, and for a moment we are frozen by our own proximity.

"I have to go," I mutter, tearing myself away. I dig out all the money I have in my pocket and leave it crumpled on the bar, then grab my guitar case and hurry into the parking lot. Even as I unlock my car, with my hands still shaking, I can see Vanessa standing in the doorway. Even when the door is closed and I rev the engine, I know she's calling my name.

On the night that Lila was shooting up heroin, there was a reason I'd been wandering through Ellie's house.

I had awakened in the middle of the night to find Ellie staring at me. "What's the matter?" I asked, rubbing sleep from my eyes.

"Can you hear that?" she whispered.

"Hear what?"

"Ssh," Ellie said, holding a finger up to her lips. Then she moved the same finger to my lips.

But I didn't hear anything. "I think—"

Before I could finish, Ellie put both of her hands on my cheeks and kissed me.

At that moment, I heard everything. From the bass in my blood to the sound of the house settling, to luna moths beating their heavy wings against the glass of the windows, to a baby crying somewhere down the block.

I leaped out of the bed and started running down the hallway. I knew Ellie wouldn't call after me, because she'd wake up the whole household. But Ellie's mother, as it turned out, wasn't home yet. And Lila, Ellie's sister, was OD'ing in her bedroom when I burst through the door.

Back then I thought that I was running away from Ellie, but now I wonder if I was actually running away from myself.

I wasn't upset because my best friend unexpectedly kissed me.

I was upset because I started to kiss her back.

For two hours I drive aimlessly, but I think I know where I'm headed even before I get there. There is a light on upstairs at Vanessa's house, so when she opens the door I don't feel guilty about waking her.

"Where have you been?" she bursts out. "You're not answering your phone. Dara and I have both been trying to reach you. You never went home tonight—"

"We have to talk," I interrupt.

Vanessa steps back so that I can come into the entryway. She is still wearing the clothes she was wearing today at school, and she looks like hell—her hair's a mess; there are faint purple circles beneath her eyes. "I'm sorry," she says. "I didn't mean for you—for me to—" She breaks off, shaking her head. "The thing is, Zoe, nothing happened. And I can promise you nothing *will* happen, because it's way too important for me to have you as a friend than to risk losing you because—"

"Nothing happened? *Nothing* happened?" I can barely breathe. "You're my best friend," I say. "I want to be with you all the time, and when I'm not, I'm thinking about being with you. I don't know anyone—including my mother, and my ex-husband—who *gets* me the way you do. I don't even have to speak a sentence out loud for you to finish it." I stare at Vanessa until she looks me in the eye. "So when you tell me *Nothing happened*? You're dead wrong, Vanessa, because I love you. And that means *everything* happened. *Everything.*"

Vanessa's jaw drops. She doesn't move a muscle. "I . . . I don't understand."

"That makes two of us," I admit.

We never know people as well as we think we do—including ourselves. I don't believe you can wake up and suddenly be gay. But I do believe you can wake up and realize that you cannot spend the rest of your life without a certain individual.

She is taller than I am, so I have to come up on my toes. I put my hands on her shoulders.

It is not like kissing a man. It's softer. More intuitive. More equal.

She puts her hands on either side of my face, and the room falls away. I have never gotten so lost in a kiss before.

And then, the space between us explodes. My heart keeps missing beats and my hands cannot bring her close enough to me. I taste her and realize I have been starving.

I have loved before, but it didn't feel like this.

I have kissed before, but it didn't burn me alive.

Maybe it lasts a minute, and maybe it's an hour. All I know is that kiss, and how soft her skin is when it brushes against mine, and that, even if I did not know it until now, I have been waiting for this person forever.

VANESSA

When I was little, I became obsessed
with the prizes offered on Bazooka Joe
comics. A gold-plated ring with my initial, a chemical magic set, a telescope,
a genuine compass. You remember
those wax papers, wrapped around the
nuggets of gum? A fine white dust
coated the Bazooka and would rub off
on your fingers as you read the joke,
which was rarely if ever funny.

Each prize sounded more exotic than
the last, and could be mine for a pit-
tance and a ridiculous number of Bazooka comics. But nothing captured
my fancy as much as the one I found
on a gum wrapper in the spring of 1985.
If I could just manage to amass $1.10

and sixty-five Bazooka comics, I could have my own pair of X-ray vision glasses.

For a full week I would go to sleep at night wondering what you could see with X-ray vision. I pictured people in their underwear, the skeletons of dogs walking in the street, the insides of jewelry boxes and violin cases. I wondered if I would be able to peer through walls, if I would know what was going on in the teachers' lounge, if I could read through the manila folder on Ms. Watkins's desk and see the answer key for the math test. There was a world of possibility in X-ray vision, and I knew I could not live another day without it.

So I began to save. It didn't take long to scrape together $1.10, but the Bazooka comics were another story entirely. I bought twenty pieces of gum that week with my allowance. I traded my best Topps baseball card—a Roger Clemens Red Sox rookie—to Joey Palliazo for ten Bazooka comics (he had been saving up for the decoder rings). I let Adam Waldman touch my boob for another five (believe me, it didn't do anything for either one of us). Eventually, within a few weeks, I had enough comics and change to mail off to the address listed. In four to six weeks, those X-ray vision glasses would be mine.

I spent the time imagining a world where I could see beneath the surface. Where I could eavesdrop on the conversations of my parents about my Christmas gifts, could see what leftovers were in the fridge before I opened it, could read my best friend's diary to see if she felt about me the same way I felt about her. Then one day, a plain brown box arrived with my name on it. I ripped it open, unraveled the Bubble Wrap, and pulled out a pair of white plastic glasses.

They were too big for my face and slid down my nose. They had slightly opaque lenses with a fuzzy white bone etched in the center of each one. When I put them on, everything I looked at was printed with that stupid fake bone.

I couldn't see through anything at all.

I tell you this as a cautionary tale:

beware of getting what you want. It's bound to disappoint you.

You would think, after that first kiss, there would have been some kind of apology, an awkward pause between us. And in fact the next day, after eight hours at school analyzing every moment of that kiss (Was Zoe drunk, or just a little buzzed? Did I encourage her, or was that entirely her own idea? Was it really as magical as I thought it had been, or was that twenty-twenty hindsight?), I met Zoe at the hospital where she was working with burn victims. She told the nurses she was taking a ten-minute break, and we walked down a long hallway, close enough to hold hands, except we didn't.

"Listen," I said, as soon as we were outside and out of earshot of anyone who happened to be eavesdropping.

That was as far as I got before Zoe launched herself at me. Her kiss was blistering. "God, yes," she breathed against my lips, when we broke apart. "That's *exactly* how I remembered it."

Then she looked up at me, her eyes bright. "Is it always like this?"

How was I supposed to answer that? The first time I'd kissed a woman, I felt like I had been shot into space. It was unfamiliar and exciting and felt so incredibly right that I couldn't believe I'd never done it before. There was an evenness of the playing field that was different from the kisses I'd shared with guys—and yet somehow it wasn't soft and delicate. It was surround-sound, earthshaking, *intense.*

But that said, it *wasn't* always like this.

I wanted to tell Zoe that, yes, the reason it felt like her skin was on fire was because she was kissing a woman. But more than that, I wanted to tell Zoe that the reason it felt like her skin was on fire was because she was kissing *me.*

So I didn't actually answer. I just reached for her, cradled her head in my hands, and kissed her again.

In the three days since then, we have spent hours in her car, on my couch, and in the supply room at the hospital making out like we are teenagers. I know every inch of her mouth. I know what spot on her jaw, when brushed, makes her shudder. I know that the hollow behind her ear smells of lemons and that she has a birthmark shaped like Massachusetts at the nape of her neck.

Last night when we stopped, flushed and breathing hard, Zoe said, "What happens next?"

Which is how I've ended up where I am right now: lying on my bed, fully clothed, with the curtain of Zoe's hair covering my face as she kisses me. With her hands moving tentatively over the terrain of my body.

I think we both knew tonight would end up like this—in spite of its humble beginnings of an Italian dinner and a bad movie. How does sex ever happen between couples, except as an electrical storm that's been gathering in the space between the two people, which finally combusts?

But this is different. Because even though it's Zoe's first time, I'm the one who has everything to lose if it's not perfect.

Namely, Zoe.

So I tell myself that I'm going to let her go at her own pace, which means the most incredible torture, as her hands move from my shoulders to my ribs to my waist. But then she stops. "What's the matter?" I whisper, imagining the worst: she is disgusted by this; she is feeling nothing; she knows she has made a mistake.

"I think I'm scared," Zoe confesses.

"We don't have to do anything," I say.

"I want to. I'm just afraid I'm going to do it wrong."

"Zoe," I tell her, "there is no *wrong*."

I slip her hands beneath the hem of my shirt. Her palms brand my stomach; I am sure I will wake up with her initials seared into my skin. Slowly, her hands inch up, until they are touching the lace of my bra.

Here is the thing about lesbian sex: it doesn't matter if your body isn't perfect, because your partner feels the same way. It doesn't matter if you've never touched a woman, because you *are* one, and you already know what you like. When Zoe finally takes off my blouse, I think I cry out, because she covers my mouth with hers and swallows the sound. And then her shirt comes off, too, and the rest. We are a tangle of smooth legs and peaks and valleys, of sighs and pleas. She grabs for me, and I try to slow us down, and somehow we meet in the glorious middle.

Afterward, we curl together on top of the covers. I can smell her skin and her sweat and her hair, and I love the thought that, even when she is gone, my sheets will still retain that memory. But things that are this perfect don't last very long. I have been down this path before with a straight woman, so I know that having a fantasy come true doesn't always mean it will be permanent. I can believe Zoe wanted this to happen between us. I just can't believe she'll want it to continue.

She shifts in her sleep and rolls over, so that she is facing me. Her leg slides between mine. I pull her closer, and wonder when the novelty of me will wear off.

Two weeks later, I am still waiting for the other proverbial shoe to drop. Zoe and I have spent every night together—it's gotten to the point where I don't even ask if she wants to come over after work, because I know she'll already be there waiting with Chinese takeout or a DVD we had been talking about watching or a fresh-baked pie she insists she can't eat by herself.

There are moments I cannot believe how happy I am. But there are just as many moments when I remember that, to Zoe, this is still just the bright, shiny new toy. In private, Zoe is so, so gay. She reads all my back issues of *Curve*. She calls her cable company and gets Logo. She starts talking to me about Provincetown: if I've ever been, if I'd ever go again. She acts the way I did when I first embraced who I really was—like I'd been let out of my cage for the first time in twenty years. However, she's never told anyone—not even me—that she's fallen for a woman. She's never been in a relationship before that causes people on the street to whisper when she walks by. She's never been called a dyke. This isn't real yet, for her. And when it is, she will come back to me and tell me it's all been a wonderful, fun mistake.

And yet . . . I'm too weak to turn her away now, when she wants me. When it just feels so damn good to be with her.

Which is why, when she asks me to observe her second session with Lucy, I immediately agree. I had asked to be there last time, but now I wonder if that was only so that I'd get to see Zoe working, and not because I was thinking of Lucy's welfare. Zoe had refused anyway, and she was right—but she's changed her tune this week, after Lucy's abandonment. I think, frankly, she wants me there to bar the door if Lucy tries to run again.

Today I help her lug in a bunch of instruments from her car. "Lucy plays this?" I ask, as I set down a small marimba.

"No. She doesn't play any musical instruments. But the thing about the ones I've brought today is that you don't have to play an instrument to sound good. They're all tuned to the pentatonic scale."

"What's that?"

"A scale with five pitches. It's different from a heptatonic scale, which is seven notes, like the major scale—*do re mi fa so la ti.* You find them all over the world—in jazz, blues, Celtic folk music, Japanese folk music. The thing about it is that you just can't play a wrong note—whatever key you hit, it's going to sound good."

"I don't get it."

"You know the song 'My Girl'? By the Temptations?"

"Yeah."

Zoe lifts the lap harp she's holding and plays the instrumental intro, those six familiar rising notes that repeat. "That's a pentatonic scale. So is the melody that the aliens understood in *Close Encounters of the Third Kind.* And a blues scale is based on a minor pentatonic scale." She puts down the harp and hands me a mallet. "Try it."

"Thanks but no thanks. My last experience with an instrument was violin, when I was eight. The neighbors called the fire department because they thought an animal was dying inside my house."

"Just *try* it."

I take a mallet and tentatively strike a bar. And another. And a third. Then I hit the same pattern. Before I know it I'm striking different bars, making up a song as I go. "That," I say, "is pretty cool."

"I know, right? It takes all the stress out of music."

Imagine if there was a pentatonic scale for life: if no matter what step you took, you could not strike a wrong note.

I hand her back the mallet just as Lucy sulks through the door. That's really the only way to describe it—she takes a look at Zoe and then glances at me and realizes she is not going to escape as easily this time around. She throws herself into a chair and starts gnawing on her thumbnail.

"Hi, Lucy," Zoe says. "It's good to see you again."

Lucy snaps her gum. I stand up, grab the trash can, and hold it under her jaw until she spits it out. Then I close the door of the special needs room, so that the noise in the hall doesn't interrupt Zoe's session.

"So, you can see that Ms. Shaw is with us today. That's because we want to make sure you haven't got a pressing appointment somewhere else again," Zoe tells her.

"You mean you don't want me to ditch," Lucy says.

"That too," I agree.

"I was thinking, Lucy, that maybe you could tell me one thing you liked about our last session, so that I could make sure we get to do it again . . ."

"That I cut it short," Lucy replies.

If I were Zoe, I'd probably want to throttle the kid. But Zoe just smiles at her. "Okay," she says. "I'll make sure we keep things moving along then." She takes the lap harp and puts it on the desk in front of Lucy. "Have you ever seen one of these?" When Lucy shakes her head, Zoe plucks a few strings. The notes are sporadic at first, and then rearrange themselves into a lullaby.

"Hush, little baby, don't say a word," Zoe sings softly, *"Mama's gonna buy you a mockingbird. And if that mockingbird don't sing, Mama's gonna buy you a diamond ring."* She puts down the harp. "I never really understood those lyrics. I mean, wouldn't you rather have a mockingbird that could say everything you taught it to say? That's so much cooler than a piece of jewelry." She strums the harp a few more times. "Maybe you'd like to try this?"

Lucy makes no move to touch it. "I'd rather have the diamond ring," she says finally. "I'd pawn it and use the money for a bus ticket and get the hell out of here."

In the year I've known Lucy, I have never heard her string so many words together in a response. Stunned—maybe music does work wonders—I lean forward to see what Zoe will do next.

"Really?" she says. "Where would you go?"

"Where *wouldn't* I go?"

Zoe pulls the marimba closer. She begins to tap out a rhythm that feels vaguely African, or Caribbean. "I used to think of traveling around the world. I was going to do that after graduating from college. Work in one place, you know, waiting tables or something, until I got enough cash to travel somewhere else. I told myself I never wanted to be the kind of person who had more stuff than she could carry in a knapsack."

For the first time, I see Lucy actively look at Zoe. "Why didn't you do it?"

She shrugs. "Life got in the way."

Where, I wonder, did she dream about going? A pristine beach? A blue glacier rising from the center of an ice field? The crowded bookstalls on the banks of the Seine?

Zoe begins to play another melody with the mallet. This one sounds like a polka. "One of the really cool things about these two instruments is that they're tuned on a pentatonic scale. Lots of world folk music is based off that. I love the way you can hear a piece of music, and it brings a snapshot from another part of the world into your mind. Next best thing to being there, if you can't hop a plane because you've got math next period, for example." She taps the mallet, and the tune sounds Asian, the notes jumping up and down the scale. I close my eyes and see cherry blossoms, paper houses. "Here," Zoe says, handing the mallet to Lucy. "How about if you play me a song that sounds like where you wish you were?"

Lucy takes the mallet in her fist and stares at it. She strikes the highest bar, just once. It sounds like a high-pitched cry. Lucy strikes it one more time, and then lets the mallet roll from her fingers. "This is so unbelievably gay," she says.

I can't help it, I flinch.

Zoe doesn't even look in my direction. "If by 'gay' you mean happy, which you must, because I can't imagine you'd find anything about playing a marimba that points to sexual orientation—well, then, I would have to disagree. I think Japanese folk songs are pretty melancholy, actually."

"What if that's not what I meant?" Lucy challenges.

"Then I suppose I'd ask myself why a kid who hates being labeled by everyone else, including therapists, is so willing to label other people."

At that, Lucy folds back into herself. Gone is the girl willing to talk about running away. In her place is the familiar drawstring purse of a mouth, the angry eyes, the folded arms. One step forward, two steps back. "Would you like to try the marimba?" Zoe asks again.

She is met by a stony wall of silence.

"How about the harp?"

When Lucy ignores her again, Zoe pulls the instruments aside. "Every songwriter uses music to express something she can't have. Maybe that's a place, and maybe that's a feeling. You know how sometimes you feel like if you don't let go of some of the pressure that's inside you, you're going to explode? A song can be that release. How about you pick a song, and we talk about the place it takes us when we listen to it?"

Lucy closes her eyes.

"I'll give you some choices," Zoe says. " 'Amazing Grace.' 'Wake Me Up

When September Ends.' Or, 'Goodbye
Yellow Brick Road.'"

She could not have picked three
more diverse options: a spiritual, a
Green Day song, and an Elton John
oldie.

"Okay, then," Zoe says, when Lucy
doesn't respond. "I'll pick." She begins
to play the lap harp. Her voice starts
out on a husky low note, and swings
upward:

> *Amazing grace, how sweet the
>   sound . . .*
> *That saved a wretch like me.*
> *I once was lost, but now I'm found.*
> *Was blind, but now I see.*

There is a richness to Zoe's singing
that feels like tea on a rainy day, like a
blanket over your shoulders while you're
shivering. Lots of women have pretty
voices, but hers has a soul. I love how,
when she wakes up in the morning, it
sounds as if her throat is coated in
sand. I love how, when she gets frustrated, she doesn't yell but instead belts
one high, operatic note of anger.

When I look over at Lucy, she has tears in her eyes. She furtively glances at me, and wipes them away as Zoe finishes the song with a few strokes plucked on the harp. "Every time I hear that hymn I imagine a girl in a white dress, standing barefoot on a swing," Zoe says. "And the swing's on a big old elm tree." She laughs, shaking her head. "I have no idea why. It's actually about a slave trader who was struggling with his life, and how some divine power got him to see the person he was meant to be instead. How about you? What does the song make you think of?"

"Lies."

"Really!" Zoe says. "That's interesting. What sorts of lies?"

Suddenly Lucy stands so abruptly that she knocks over her chair. "I hate that song. I hate it!"

Zoe moves quickly so that she is only inches away from the girl. "That's great. The music made you feel something. What did you hate about it?"

Lucy narrows her eyes. "That you were singing it," she says, and she shoves Zoe out of the way. "I'm fucking done." She kicks the marimba as she passes. It sounds a low good-bye.

Zoe turns to me as the door slams behind Lucy. "Well," Zoe says, beaming. "At least this time, she stayed twice as long."

"The dead man on the train," I say.

"I beg your pardon?"

"That's what the song makes me think of," I say. "I was in college and I was going home for Thanksgiving. The trains were full, and I wound up sitting next to an old man who asked me what my name was. *Vanessa,* I told him, and he said *Vanessa What?* I didn't know him, and I was afraid to give out my last name in case he was a serial killer or something, so I told him my middle name instead: *Vanessa Grace.* And he started singing to me, substituting my name for *Amazing grace.* He had a really beautiful, deep voice, and people clapped. I was embarrassed, and he wouldn't quit talking, so I pretended to fall asleep. When we got to South Station, the last stop, he was leaning against the window with his eyes closed. I shook him, to tell him that it was time to get off the train, but he didn't wake up. I got a conductor, and the police and ambulance came, and I had to tell them everything I knew—which was almost nothing." I hesitate. "His name was Murray Wasserman, and he was a stranger, and I was the last person he sang to before he died."

When I finish speaking, I find Zoe staring at me. She glances at the door of the room, which is still closed, and then she hugs me. "I think he was probably a pretty lucky guy."

I look at her dubiously. "To drop dead? On Amtrak? The day before Thanksgiving?"

"No," Zoe says. "To have you sitting next to him, on the last ride of his life."

I duck my head. I'm not a praying woman, but I pray at that moment that, when it's my turn, Zoe and I will still be traveling together.

The day after I told my mother that I was a lesbian, the shock had worn off and she was full of questions. She asked me if this was some phase I was going through, like the time I'd been hell-bent on dyeing my hair purple and getting an eyebrow ring. When I told her I was convinced of my attraction to women, she burst into tears and asked me how she had failed me as a mother. She told me she'd pray for me. Every night, when I went to bed, she slipped a new pamphlet under the door. Many trees have died so that the Catholic Church can preach against homosexuality.

I started to wage a counterattack. On every pamphlet, I took a thick marker and wrote the name of someone famous who had an LGBT child: Cher. Barbra Streisand. Dick Gephardt. Michael Landon. I'd slip these under *her* bedroom door.

Finally, at a stalemate, I agreed to meet with her priest. He asked me how I could do this to the woman who'd raised me, as if my sexuality was a personal attack on her. He asked if I'd considered becoming a nun instead. Not once was I asked if I was afraid, or lonely, or worried about my future.

On the way home from the church, I asked my mother if she still loved me.

"I'm trying," she said.

It took my first long-term girlfriend (whose own mother, when she came out to her, shrugged and said, *Tell me something I* don't *know*) to make me understand why *my* mother was the complete opposite. "You're dead to her," my girlfriend had told me. "Everything she's dreamed of for you, everything she figured you'd be and have, it's not going to happen. She's been seeing you in suburbia with a cookie cutter husband and your two point four kids and a dog, and now you've gone and ruined that by being with me."

So I gave my mother time to grieve. I never flaunted my girlfriends in front of her, or brought one home to a holiday meal, or signed her name on a Christmas card. Not because I was ashamed but simply because I loved my mother, and I knew that was what she needed from me. When my mother got sick and went into the hospital, I took care of her. I like to think that, before the morphine took over her mind—

before she died—she realized that my being a lesbian mattered far less than the fact that I was a good daughter.

I'm telling you this as a means of explaining that I have been through the coming-out ringer, and wish to repeat it about as much as a person wants a second root canal. But when Zoe begs me to come with her when she tells Dara about us, I know I will. Because it's the first proof I have that—maybe—Zoe isn't just trying this new gay persona on for size, and planning to return it and go back to her old, straight self.

"Are you nervous?" I ask, as we stand side by side in front of Zoe's mother's front door.

"No. Well, yeah. A little." She looks at me. "It feels big. It's big, right?"

"Your mother is one of the most open-minded people I've ever met."

"But she considers herself an expert on me," Zoe says. "It was just the two of us, when I was growing up."

"Well, I grew up with a single mom, too."

"This is different, Vanessa. On my birthday, my mother still calls me at

10:03 A.M. and screams and pants into the phone to relive the birth experience."

I blink at her. "That's just plain strange."

Zoe smiles. "I know. She's one in a million. It's a blessing and a curse all at once." With a deep breath, she rings the doorbell.

Dara opens it with a mangled coat hanger in her hands. "Zoe!" she says, delighted to see her daughter. "I didn't know you were coming out here!"

Zoe's laugh is strangled. "You have no idea . . ."

Dara wraps her arms around me for a quick hug, too. "How are you, Vanessa?"

"Great," I say. "I've never been better."

In the background there is a man's voice, deep and soothing. *Sense the water. Sense it rising beneath you . . .*

"Oh," Dara says. "Let me go shut that off. Come in, you two." She hustles toward the stereo and turns off the CD player, taking the disc out of the machine and slipping it into its plastic sleeve. "It's my homework for my dowsing class. That's what the coat hanger's for."

"You're looking for water?"

"Yes," Dara says. "When I find it, the rods will move by themselves and cross in my hands."

"Let me save you some trouble," Zoe replies. "I'm pretty sure the water comes out of the faucets."

"O ye of little faith. For your information, my practical girl, dowsing is a very lucrative skill. Say you're going to invest in a piece of land. Don't you want to know what's under the surface?"

"I'd probably hire an artesian well company," I say, "but that's just me."

"Maybe so, Vanessa, but who's going to tell the well company where to dig, eh?" She smiles at me. "You two hungry? I've got a nice coffeecake in the fridge. One of my clients is trying to visualize becoming a pastry chef . . ."

"You know, Ma, actually, I came to tell you something really important," Zoe says. "Something really good, I think."

Dara's eyes widen. "I had a dream

about this, just last night. Let me guess—you're going back to school!"

"What? No!" Zoe says. "What are you talking about? I have a master's degree!"

"But you *could* have majored in classical voice. Vanessa, have you ever heard her sing . . ."

"Um, yes—"

"Mom," Zoe interrupts. "I'm not going back to school for classical voice. I'm perfectly happy as a music therapist—"

Dara looks up at her. "For jazz piano, then?"

"For God's sake, I'm not going back to school. I came here to tell you I'm a lesbian!"

The word cleaves the room in half.

"But," Dara says after a moment. "But you were married."

"I know. I was with Max. But now . . . now I'm with Vanessa."

When Dara turns to me, her eyes seem wounded—as if I've betrayed her by pretending to be Zoe's good friend when, in truth, that's what I *have* been. "I know this is unexpected," I say.

"This isn't you, Zoe. I know you. I know who you are . . ."

"So do I. And if you think this means I'm going to start riding a Harley and wearing leather, you don't know me at all. Believe me, I was surprised, too. This isn't what I thought was going to happen to me."

Dara starts to cry. She cups Zoe's cheeks in her hands. "You could get married again."

"I could, but I don't want to, Ma."

"What about grandchildren?"

"I couldn't seem to make that happen even *with* a man," Zoe points out. She reaches for her mother's hand. "I found someone I want to be with. I'm happy. Can't you be happy for me?"

Dara sits very still for a moment, looking down at their intertwined fingers. Then she pulls away. "I need a minute," she says, and she picks up her dowsing rods and walks into the kitchen.

When she leaves, Zoe looks up at me, teary. "So much for her open-mindedness."

I put my arm around her. "Give her a break. You're still getting used to these feelings, and it's been weeks. You can't expect her to get over the shock in five seconds."

"Do you think she's okay?"

See, this is why I love Zoe. In the middle of her own freak-out moment, she's worried about her mother. "I'll go check," I say, and I head into the kitchen.

Dara is leaning against the kitchen counter, the dowsing rods beside her on the granite. "Was it something I did?" she asks. "I should have gotten married again, maybe. Just so there was a man in the house—"

"I don't think it makes a difference. You have been a wonderful mother. Which is why Zoe is so afraid you'll want to disown her."

"Disown her? Don't be ridiculous. She said she was a lesbian, not a Republican." Dara draws in her breath. "It's just . . . I have to get used to it."

"You should tell her that. She'll understand."

Dara looks at me, then nods. She pushes back through the swinging door into the living room. I think about following her, but I want to give Zoe a minute alone with her mother. I want them to have the shift and redistribution of their relationship that I never got to have with my own mom, that acrobatic feat of love where everything is turned upside down and yet they are both still able to keep their balance.

So instead, I eavesdrop. I push the door open a crack in time to hear Dara speaking. "I couldn't love you any more if you told me right now that you were straight," she says. "And I don't love you any less because you told me you aren't."

I gently close the door. In the kitchen, I turn around, surveying the bowl of fruit on the counter, the cobalt blue toaster, the Cuisinart. Dara has left behind her dowsing rods. I pick them up, hold them lightly in my hands. In spite of the fact that the faucet and the pipes are less than a foot away, the rods do not jump in my hands or twitch or cross. I imagine having that sixth sense, the certainty that what I'm looking for is within reach, even if it's still hidden.

––––––––

Movie theaters are wonderful places to be gay. Once the lights go down, there's no one to stare at you if you hold your girlfriend's hand or snuggle closer to her. Attention at the movies, by definition, is focused on the spectacle on the screen and not in the seats.

I'm not a PDA kind of person. I've never started kissing someone in public; I just don't have the kind of selfless abandon that you see in teenage couples who are forever making out or walking down a street with their hands tucked halfway down each other's pants. So I'm not saying that I'd necessarily walk down the street with my arm around the woman I love—but I'd sure like to know that, if I were so inclined, I wouldn't attract a trail of shocked, uncomfortable stares. We're conditioned to seeing men holding guns but not men holding hands.

When the movie credits roll, people begin to get out of their seats. As the lights come up, Zoe's head is on my shoulder. Then I hear, "Zoe? Hey!"

She leaps up as if she's been caught in the act of doing something wrong and pastes a huge smile on her face. "Wanda!" she says, to a woman who looks vaguely familiar. "Did you like the movie?"

"I'm not a big Tarantino fan, but actually, it wasn't bad," she says. She slips her arm through a man's elbow. "Zoe, I don't think you've ever met my husband, Stan? Zoe's a music therapist who comes to the nursing home," Wanda explains.

Zoe turns to me. "This is Vanessa," she says. "My . . . my friend."

Last night Zoe and I had celebrated a month together. We had champagne and strawberries, and she beat me at Scrabble. We made love, and when we woke up in the morning she was wrapped around me like a heliotrope vine.

Friend.

"We've met," I say to Wanda, although I am not about to point out that it was at the baby shower for the baby who died.

We walk out of the movie theater with Wanda and her husband, making small talk about the plot and whether this will be an Oscar contender. Zoe is careful to keep a good foot of distance away from me. She doesn't even make eye contact with me again until we're in my car, driving back to my place.

Zoe fills the silence with a story about Wanda and Stan's daughter, who wanted to join the army because she had a boyfriend who had already shipped out. I don't think she notices that I haven't said a word to her. When we reach the house, I unlock the door and walk inside and strip off my coat. "You want some tea?" Zoe asks, heading into the kitchen. "I'm going to put up the kettle."

I don't answer her. I am a thousand shades of hurt right now, and I don't trust myself to speak.

Instead I sit down on the couch and pick up the newspaper I never got a chance to read today. I can hear Zoe in my kitchen, taking mugs out of the dishwasher, filling the kettle, turning on the stove. She knows where everything is, in which drawer to find the spoons, in which cabinet I keep the tea bags.

She moves around my house as if she belongs here.

I am staring blankly at editorials when she comes into the living room, leans over the back of the couch, and wraps her arms around me. "Any more letters about the police chief scandal?"

I push her away. "Don't."

She backs off. "Guess the movie really got to you."

"Not the movie." I turn around to look at her. *"You."*

"Me? What did *I* do?"

"It's what you didn't do, Zoe," I say. "What is it? You only want me when no one else is around? You're more than happy to come on to me when nobody's watching?"

"Okay. Clearly you're in a crappy mood—"

"You didn't want Wanda to know we're together. That was obvious . . ."

"My business associates don't have to know the details of my personal life—"

"Oh, yeah? Did you tell her when you got pregnant last time?" I ask.

"Of course I did—"

"There you go." I swallow, trying really hard to not cry. "You told her I was your friend."

"You *are* my friend," Zoe says, exasperated.

"Is that *all* I am?"

"What am I supposed to call you? My lover? That sounds like a bad seventies movie. My partner? I don't even know if that's what we are. But the difference between you and me is that I don't care what it's called. I don't have to label it for everyone else. So why do *you*?" In the kitchen the teakettle starts to scream. "Look," Zoe says, taking a deep breath. "You're overreacting. I'm going to turn off the stove and just go home. We can talk about this tomorrow, when we've both slept on it."

She walks into the kitchen, but instead of letting her go, I follow her. I watch her movements, efficient and graceful, as she takes the kettle off the burner. When she turns to me, her features are smooth, expressionless. "Good night."

She walks past me, but just as she

reaches the kitchen doorway, I speak. "I'm afraid."

Zoe hesitates, her hands framing the door, as if she is caught between two moments.

"I'm afraid that you're going to get sick of me," I admit. "That you're going to get tired of living a life that still isn't a hundred percent accepted by society. I'm afraid that, if I let myself feel ecstatic about being with you, then when you leave me, I won't be able to pull myself back together."

In one move, Zoe is across the kitchen again, facing me. "Why do you think I'd leave?"

"My track record," I say. "That, and the fact that you have no idea how hard it is. I still worry every day that some parent is going to out me, and convince the school board I should lose my job. I listen to the news and hear politicians who know nothing about me making decisions about what I should and shouldn't be allowed to do. I don't understand why the most intriguing thing about my identity is always that I'm gay—not that I'm a Leo or know how

to tap dance or that I majored in zool-
ogy."

"You can tap dance?" Zoe asks.

"The point is," I say, "you spent forty
years straight. Why *wouldn't* you return
to the path of least resistance?"

Zoe looks at me as if I am incredibly thick-headed. "Because, Vanessa.
You're not a guy."

That night, we don't make love. We
drink the tea Zoe brews, and we talk
about the first time I was called a dyke,
how I came home and cried. We talk
about how I hate when the mechanic
always assumes that I know what he's
talking about when he works on my car,
just because I'm a lesbian. I even do a
little tap routine for her: step-ball-
change, step-ball-change. We spoon
on the couch.

The last thing I remember thinking
before I fall asleep in her arms is *This is
good, too.*

In spite of my disappointment over the
X-ray vision glasses from the Bazooka
comics prize cache, I wound up saving

up for one more item that I simply had to have. It was a whale's tooth good-luck charm, on a key chain. What intrigued me was the description of the item:

Guaranteed to bring the owner a lifetime of good fortune.

I knew better, after my X-ray glasses, than to expect the whale's tooth to be either real whale or real tooth. Probably it would be plastic, with a hole punched through the top for the metal key ring attached to it. But I still found myself saving up my allowance again to buy Bazooka gum. I hunted on the floor of my mother's car for spare change, so that I could gather the $1.10 for shipping and handling.

Three months later, I had my sixty-five Bazooka comics and sent off my envelope for my prize. When the charm arrived, I was a little surprised to see that the tooth seemed to be legitimate (although I couldn't really tell you if it came from a whale) and that the silver key ring attached to it was heavy, shiny.

I slipped it into the front pocket of my backpack and started wishing.

The next day was Valentine's Day in school. We had each made little "mailboxes" out of shoe boxes and construction paper. This was in the era of transactional analysis, when no one was allowed to feel left out, so the teacher had a foolproof plan: every girl in the class would send a card to every boy, and vice versa. I was guaranteed, this way, to receive fourteen Valentines in return for the fourteen Tweety and Sylvester cards I had addressed to the boys in class—even Luke, unfortunately, who picked his nose and ate it. At the end of the school day, I carried home my shoe box and sat on my bed and sorted the cards. To my surprise, there was one extra. Yes, every boy had given me a Valentine, as expected. But the fifteenth came from Eileen Connelly, who had sparkly blue eyes and hair as black as night and who once, in gym class, had put her arms around me to show me how to properly hold a bat. HAPPY VALENTINE'S DAY, the card said, FROM, EILEEN. It didn't matter that it wasn't signed with "Love." It didn't matter that she might have given a card to every girl in the class in addition to me. All I knew at that moment—all I cared about—was that she had been thinking of me, however briefly. I was convinced that the only reason I'd gotten this bonus Valentine was that whale's tooth charm—which was fast acting indeed.

Over the years, every time I moved—from my home to my college dorm, from my college dorm to my apartment in the city, from my apartment to this house—I have gone through my belongings and sorted the wheat from the chaff. And every time, in my nightstand, I have come across that whale's tooth good-luck charm. I can never quite bear the thought of getting rid of it.

Apparently, it's still working.

MAX

There are four white marble disks at the far eastern corner of my brother's back-yard. Too small to be stepping-stones, some are even covered with a tangle of brush—rosebushes that, as far as I can tell, have never been pruned. They are memorials, one for each baby that Reid and Liddy have lost.

Today, I'm putting down a fifth stone.

Liddy wasn't very far along this time, but the house is full of crying. I'd like to tell you I came out here so that my brother and his wife could grieve in private, but the truth is it brings back too many memories for me. So instead, I went to the plant nursery and found the matching marble disk. And I'm thinking that—as a thank-you for all Reid's done for me—I'm going to fix up this little area of the lawn into a garden, when the ground thaws. I'm thinking about adding a flowering quince and some pussy willows, some variegated weigela. I'll put a small granite bench in the center, with the stones in a half-moon shape around it—a place Liddy could come out to just sit and think and pray. And I'll stagger the flowers so that there is always something in bloom—purples and blues, like grape hyacinth and cornflowers, heliotrope and purple verbena; and the whitest of whites: star magnolias, Callery pear, Queen Anne's lace.

I have just started making a sketch of this angels' garden when I hear footsteps behind me. Reid stands with his hands in the pockets of his jacket. "Hey," he says.

I turn around and squint into the sun. "How is she?"

Reid shrugs. "You know."

I do. I've never felt so lost as the times when Zoe miscarried. In this, all prospective parents have something in common with the Eternal Glory Church: to them, a life is a life, no matter how small. These aren't cells, they're your future.

"Pastor Clive's in there with her now," Reid adds.

"I'm really sorry, Reid," I say. "For whatever that's worth." Zoe and I had both gone to the clinic to be tested for infertility problems. I can't remember much about the condition that caused my sperm count to be low, and made the ones that did show up for the party less motile, but I do remember that it was genetic. Which means Reid's probably in the same boat.

He suddenly bends down and picks up the marble disk I've bought. I haven't been able to chip at the frozen ground enough to set it in place. I watch him turn it over in his hands, and then he cradles it like a discus and sends it flying into the brick wall of the built-in barbecue. The marble breaks in half and falls to the ground. Reid kneels, burying his face in his hands.

You've got to understand—my big brother is one of the most unflappable people I've ever met. In my life history, when I'm falling apart at the seams, he is the constant I can count on to hold me together. Seeing him losing control like this paralyzes me.

I grab his shoulders. "Reid, man, you gotta calm down."

He looks up at me, his breath hanging in the frigid air. "Pastor Clive's in there talking about God, *praying* to God, but you know what I think, Max? I think God checked out a long time ago. I don't think God gives a rat's ass about my wife wanting a baby."

In the months since my baptism, I have come to believe that God has a reason for everything. It makes sense when the bad guys get their due, then, but it's harder to understand why a savior who loves us would make awful things happen to good people. I've prayed long and hard about this stuff, trying to figure it all out, and it seems to me that most of the time, if God gives us something bad, it's supposed to be a wake-up call—a way to let us know not so subtly that we're messing up our lives. Maybe it's because we're with the wrong girl, or because we've grown too big in our own heads, or maybe it is just because we've gotten so greedy about the here and now we've forgotten that what matters the most isn't self but selflessness. Just think of those folks you meet who have survived an incurable disease—how many of them start thanking Jesus right and left? Well, all I'm saying is: maybe the reason they got sick in the first place was because that illness was the only way He could get their attention.

I can tell you—although it hurts me to say this—I see now that I am the reason why Zoe and I couldn't have a baby. That was Jesus, hitting me in the head with a two-by-four over and over until I understood that I wasn't worthy enough to be a father until I welcomed the Son. But Reid and Liddy—they are another story. They've been doing everything right, for so long. They don't deserve this kind of heartbreak.

We both look up as Pastor Clive comes out of the house. He stands in front of Reid, casting a shadow. "She threw you out, too," Reid guesses.

"Liddy just needs a little time," the pastor says. "I'll come check on her tonight, Reid."

As Pastor Clive lets himself out the gate, Reid rubs his hand over his face. "She won't talk to me. She won't eat anything. She won't take the pills the doctor gave us. She won't even pray." He looks at me, his eyes bloodshot. "Is it a sin to say that, sure, I loved that baby, but I love my wife more?"

I shake my head. After all the times I found myself boxed into a corner and couldn't find a way out, only to notice my brother's hand reaching out for me, I can finally be the one to reach out to *him.* "Reid," I tell him, "I think I know what to do."

It takes me ten hours to drive round-trip to Jersey and back. When I pull into Reid's driveway, the light in their bedroom is off. I find my brother in the kitchen washing dishes. He's wearing Liddy's pink apron, the one that says I'M THE COOK, THAT'S WHY, and has a frill of ruffles around the edge. "Hey," I say, and he turns around. "How is she?"

"Same," Reid replies. He looks dubiously at the paper bag in my hands.

"Trust me." I take out the box of Orville Redenbacher's Movie Theater Butter popcorn and stick one bag in the microwave. "Did Pastor Clive come back?"

"Yeah, but she still wouldn't talk to him."

That's because she doesn't want to talk, I think. Talking only brings her right back to this nightmare. Right now, she needs to escape.

"Liddy doesn't eat microwave popcorn," Reid says.

Actually, my brother doesn't *let* Liddy eat microwave popcorn. He's a big fan of organic stuff, although I'm not sure if it's because there's a health benefit or because he just likes having the priciest items, no matter what the category. "There's a first time for everything," I answer. The microwave dings, and I take out the bloated bag, rip it open into a big blue ceramic bowl.

The bedroom is pitch dark and smells

like lavender. Liddy is lying on her side under the covers of her big four-poster bed, facing away from me. I'm not sure if she's asleep, and then I hear her voice. "Go away," she murmurs. The words sound like she's at the bottom of a tunnel.

I ignore her and eat a handful of popcorn.

The sound, and the smell of the butter, make her roll over. She squints at me. "Max," she says. "I'm not really in the mood for company."

"That's cool," I tell her. "I'm just here to borrow your DVD player." I reach into the paper bag and pull out the movie. Then I load it and turn on the TV.

Bullets won't kill it! the promo promises.

Flames can't hurt it!
Nothing can stop it!
The SPIDER . . . will eat you alive!

Liddy sits up against her pillows. Her eyes drift to the screen, to the incredibly fake giant tarantula that is terrorizing a bunch of teens. "Where did you get this?"

"Just a place I know." It's a head

shop in Elizabeth, New Jersey, that has a mail-order cult B-movie business. I've ordered online from them. But because I couldn't wait long enough for a DVD to be shipped to me, and because this was Liddy we were talking about, I drove to the store instead.

"This is a good one," I tell Liddy. "1958."

"I don't want to watch a movie right now," Liddy says.

"Okay." I shrug. "I'll turn the sound down low."

So I pretend to watch the television, where the teenage girl and her boy-friend go looking for her missing dad and find instead a massive web from a giant spider. But in reality, I'm stealing glances at Liddy. In spite of herself, she can't help but watch, too. After a few minutes, she reaches for the popcorn in my lap, and I give her the whole bowl.

Just about the time the teenagers drag the lifeless body of the spider back to the high school gym to study it—only to learn it's actually still alive—Reid pokes his head into the bedroom. By then, I'm lounging back on his side of the bed. I give Reid a thumbs-up, and I can see the relief on his face when he sees Liddy sitting up, engaged in the world of the living again. He backs out and closes the door behind him.

A half hour later, we've almost finished the popcorn. When the tarantula is finally electrocuted and falls, I turn to find tears running down Liddy's face.

I'm pretty sure she doesn't even know she's crying.

"Max," she asks. "Can we watch it again?"

There's the obvious benefit to joining a church like Eternal Glory—being saved. But there's another advantage, too, and that's being rescued. Unlike finding Jesus, which is like a strike of lightning, this is much more subtle. It's the elderly lady who shows up at Reid's door the week after I go to church for the first time, with a banana bread to welcome me into the congregation. It's my name on a prayer list when I have the flu. It's putting up my plowing flyer on the church message board and finding all the little tags with my phone number ripped off within days by Eternal Glory folks who like to support their own. I wasn't just born again, I was given a large, extended family.

Pastor Clive is the father I wish I'd had growing up—one who understands that I may have stumbled in the past but who sees endless possibility. Instead of focusing on everything I've done wrong in my life, he celebrates the things I've done right. He took me out to an Italian restaurant last week to celebrate my third month of sobriety; he has gradually given me more and more responsibility in the church—from being called on to do a reading during a Sunday service to this afternoon's shopping adventure for our annual church chicken pie supper.

It is just past three-thirty, and Elkin and I are each manning a grocery cart at the Stop & Shop. This isn't where I usually get my food, but the owner is a member of Eternal Glory and gives Pastor Clive a discount and, even more important, has agreed to donate the chicken for free.

We have loaded our carts with piecrust mix and frozen peas and carrots, and we are waiting in line at the butcher counter to get the chicken that's been reserved for us when I hear a familiar voice. When I turn, I see Zoe reading the label on a jar of Caesar salad dressing. "I think there should be new nutrition guidelines," she says to another woman. "No fat; low fat; reduced fat; and fat, but with a great personality."

The woman she's with plucks the Caesar dressing from Zoe's hand. She puts it back on the shelf and picks up a vinaigrette instead. "And *I* think pudding should be its own food group," she says, "but we can't always get what we want."

"I'll be right back," I tell Elkin, and I walk toward Zoe. Her back is to me, so I tap her on the shoulder. "Hey."

She turns and breaks into a wide smile. She looks relaxed and happy, as if she's spent a lot of time laughing lately. "Max!" She gives me a hug.

I pat her awkwardly. I mean, are you supposed to hug back the woman you divorced? The woman she's shopping with—who's taller, a little younger, with a boyish haircut—has her lips pressed tightly together in what's supposed to be a smile. I hold out my hand. "I'm Max Baxter."

"Oh!" Zoe says. "Max, this is . . . Vanessa."

"Nice to meet you."

"Look at you, all dressed up with no-where to go." Zoe playfully pulls on my black tie. "And you got rid of your cast."

"Yeah," I say. "Just a brace now."

"What are you doing here?" Zoe asks, and then she rolls her eyes. "Well, obvi-ously I know what you're doing here . . . there's only one reason to come to the grocery store . . ."

"You'll have to excuse her," Vanessa says. "She gets this way when she's had too many cups of coffee in the morning . . ."

"Yeah," I say quietly. "I know."

Vanessa looks from Zoe to me and then back to Zoe again. I'm not sure why, but she looks a little pissed off. If she's Zoe's friend, surely she knows I'm her ex-husband; I can't imagine why anything I've said might have upset her. "I'm just going to grab the produce," Vanessa says, backing away. "It's very nice to meet you."

"Same here." Zoe and I watch her walk away toward the organic section. "Remember the time you decided to go a hundred percent organic and our grocery bill quadrupled for the week?" I ask.

"Yeah. I stick to the organic grapes and lettuce now," she replies. "Live and learn, right?"

It's a weird thing, divorce. Zoe and I were together for almost a decade. I fell in love with her, I slept with her, I wanted a family with her. There was a time—albeit long ago—when she knew me better than anyone else in the world. I don't want to talk to her about food. I want to ask her how we got from dancing at our own wedding to standing three feet apart from each other in a grocery aisle making small talk.

But Elkin appears with his cart. "Man, we're good to go." He jerks his chin at Zoe. "Hi."

"Zoe, this is Elkin. Elkin, Zoe." I look

at her. "We're having a church supper tonight—chicken pie. All homemade. You ought to come."

Something freezes behind her features. "Yeah. Maybe."

"Well then." I smile at her. "It's good to see you."

"You, too, Max." She pushes her cart past me and goes to join Vanessa near the Swiss chard. I see them arguing, but I am too far away to hear anything they are saying.

"Let's go," Elkin says. "The ladies' auxiliary gets really steamed when we don't get the ingredients back on time."

The whole time Elkin is loading the items onto the conveyor belt of the checkout counter, I am trying to figure out what didn't seem quite right about Zoe. I mean, she looked great, and she sounded happy. She obviously had found friends to hang out with, just like I had. And yet there was something off the mark, something that I could not put my finger on. As the cashier scans the items, I find myself glancing at the aisles behind us, for another glimpse of Zoe.

We head to my truck and start loading the groceries into the flatbed. It's
started to pour. "I'll bring the cart back,"
Elkin yells, and he pushes it toward one
of the receptacle cages two rows behind us. I am about to get into my truck
when I am stopped by Zoe.

"Max!" She's run out of the grocery
store, her hair flying out behind her like
the tail of a kite. Rain pelts her face,
her sweater. "There's something I need
to tell you."

On our fifth date, we had gone camping in the White Mountains with a tent
I'd borrowed from a guy whose lawn I
cared for. But it was dark by the time
we arrived and we wound up missing
the campsite and just going off into the
woods to pitch our tent. We'd crawled
into our little space, zipped it shut, and
had just about managed to get undressed when the tent collapsed on us.

Zoe had burst into tears. She'd curled
up in a ball on the muddy ground, and
I'd put my hand on her shoulder. *It's
okay,* I'd said, although that was a lie. I
couldn't make the rain stop. I couldn't
fix this. She'd rolled over and looked at

me, and that's when I realized that she was laughing, not crying. She was laughing so hard she couldn't catch her breath.

I think that was the moment I really knew I wanted to be with her for the rest my life.

Every time Zoe cried after she found out she wasn't pregnant, I always looked twice, hoping it would turn out to be something other than tears. Except it wasn't.

I don't know why I'm thinking of that right now, as the rain straightens her hair and sets off the light in her eyes. "That woman I'm with," Zoe says, "Vanessa. She's my new partner."

When we were married, Zoe was always talking about how hard it was to find people who understood that music therapy is a valid tool for healing, how nice it would have been to have a community of therapists like she'd known when she was studying at Berklee. "That's great," I say, because it seems to be what she needs to hear. "You always wanted someone to go into business with."

"You don't understand. Vanessa is my *partner.*" She hesitates. "We're *together.*"

In that instant I realize what wasn't quite adding up for me inside the store. Zoe and this woman had been shopping with the same cart. Who goes grocery shopping together unless they share a refrigerator?

I stare at Zoe, not sure what I am supposed to say. Building behind my eyes is a headache, and it comes with words:

The wicked will not inherit the kingdom of God. Do not be deceived: Neither the sexually immoral, nor idolaters, nor adulterers, nor male prostitutes, nor homosexual offenders, nor thieves, nor the greedy, nor drunkards, nor slanderers, nor swindlers, will inherit the kingdom of God.

It's from 1 Corinthians 6:9–10, and to me it's a pretty clear comment on God's opinion of a gay lifestyle. I open my mouth to tell Zoe this, but instead, what I say is "But you were with *me.*" Because the two must be, *have* to be, mutually exclusive.

Elkin pounds on his side of the pickup, so that I will unlock it and let him get out of the rain. I push the button on the keypad and hear his door open and close, but I still stand there, stunned by Zoe's revelation.

There are so many layers to the paralysis I feel that I can barely begin to count them. Shock, for what she's told me. Disbelief, because I cannot believe she was faking her relationship with me for nine years. And pain, because even though we are not married now, I can't stand the thought of her being left behind when Christ comes back. I wouldn't wish that horror on anyone.

Elkin honks the horn, startling me. "Well," Zoe says with a little half smile, the kind that used to make me fall for her on a daily basis. She turns and sprints back toward the awning of the grocery store, where Vanessa is waiting with the cart.

As she runs, her pocketbook slips off her shoulder and catches in the hook of her elbow. As Zoe starts to push their cart into the parking lot, Vanessa adjusts the purse, so it sits where it belongs.

It's a casual, intimate gesture. The same kind of thing, once, I would have done for Zoe.

I can't tear my eyes away as they unload the groceries into the back of an unfamiliar car—a vintage convertible. I keep staring at my newly gay ex-wife although I am getting drenched to the core, although this rain keeps me from seeing her clearly.

Because the Eternal Glory Church makes its home in the auditorium of a middle school, the actual offices are in a different location. It's a small former law office in a strip mall that adjoins a Dunkin' Donuts. There is a waiting area with a receptionist, a copy machine/ break room with a small table and a minifridge and coffeemaker, a chapel, and Pastor Clive's office.

"You can go in now," says Alva, his secretary. She is small and bent like a question mark, with a sparse dusting of white pin curls on her scalp. Reid jokes that she's been here since the Flood, but there's a part of me that thinks he might be right.

Pastor Clive's office is warm and worn, with floral couches and an abundance of plants and a bookshelf filled with inspirational texts. A lectern holds an oversize, open Bible. Behind the desk is a huge painting of Jesus riding a phoenix as it rises from the ashes. Pastor Clive once told me that Christ had come to him in a dream and told him that his ministry would be like that of the mythical bird, that it would soar from a cesspool of immorality into grace. The next morning he'd gone out and had the artwork commissioned.

The pastor is bent over a spider plant that has seen better days. The tips of all the leaves are brown and brittle. "No matter how much I take care of this little baby," he says, "she always seems to be dying."

I step up to the plant and stick my finger into the soil to check the hydration. "Does Alva water it?"

"Faithfully."

"With tap water, I'm guessing. Spider

plants are sensitive to the chemicals in tap water. If you switch to distilled water, and trim off the tips of the leaves, everything will go back to a healthy, normal green."

Pastor Clive smiles at me. "You, Max, are a true gift."

At his words, I feel like there's a fire glowing inside me. I've screwed up so much in my life that hearing praise is still a rarity. He leads me to the couch on the far side of the room and offers me a seat and then a bowl of licorice. "Now," he says, "Alva tells me you were pretty upset on the phone."

I don't know how to say what I need to say—I only know that I have to say it. And the person I'd normally confide in, Reid, has got his own problems right now. Liddy's better, but she's by no means a hundred percent.

"I can assure you," Pastor Clive says gently, "your brother and Liddy are going to come through this latest challenge even stronger than they were before. God's got a plan for them, even if He hasn't seen fit to let us in on the secret yet."

Hearing the pastor talk about the miscarriage makes me squirm—I should be praying for my brother, not wallowing in my own confusion about a woman I willingly divorced. "This isn't about Reid," I say. "I saw my ex-wife yesterday, and she told me she's gay."

Pastor Clive sinks back against the cushions of his chair. "Ah."

"She was at the grocery store with a woman—her *partner.* That's what she called it." I look down at my lap. "How *could* she? She loved me, I know she did. She married me. She and I—we— well, *you know*. I would have been able to tell if she was just going through the motions. I would have known." I stop to catch my breath. "Wouldn't I?"

"Maybe you did," Pastor Clive muses, "and that's ultimately what made you realize that your marriage was over."

Is that possible? Could I have gotten vibes from Zoe, could I have known about her even before she knew herself?

"I imagine you're feeling . . . inadequate," the pastor says. "Like maybe if you had been more of a man, this would never have happened."

I can't look him in the eye, but my cheeks are flaming.

"And I imagine you're angry. You probably feel as if everyone who hears about her new lifestyle is going to be judging you, for being played the fool."

"Yes!" I explode. "I just don't—I can't—" The words jam in my throat. "I don't understand why she's doing this."

"It's not her choice," Pastor Clive says.

"But . . . no one's born gay. You say that all the time."

"You're right. And I'm right, too. There are no biological homosexuals—we're all heterosexual. But some of us, for a variety of reasons, find ourselves struggling with a homosexual problem. No one *chooses* to be attracted to someone of the same sex, Max. But we *do* choose how we'll act on those feelings." He leans forward, his hands between his knees. "Little boys aren't born gay—they're made queer, by mothers who are too smothering, or who rely on their sons for their own emotional satisfaction; or by fathers who are too distant—which leads the boy to find male acceptance in another, incorrect way. Likewise, little girls whose mothers are too detached might never get the model they need to develop their femininity; and their fathers were usually absent as well."

"Zoe's dad died when she was little . . . ," I say.

Pastor Clive looks at me. "What I'm saying, Max, is don't be angry at her. She doesn't need your anger. What she needs—what she *deserves*—is your grace."

"I . . . I don't understand."

"When I was a young man, I served in the ministry of a pastor who was as conservative as they come. It was during the AIDS crisis, and Pastor Wallace started visiting gay patients who were hospitalized. He'd pray with them if they felt comfortable, and he'd just hang out with them if they didn't. Well, eventually, a local homosexual radio station got wind of what Pastor Wallace was doing, and they asked him to come on the air. When he was asked for his opinion on homosexuality, he said flat out that it was a sin. The DJ admitted he didn't like that—but he liked Pastor Wallace himself. The next weekend, a few gay men came to his church service. The week after that, the number had doubled. The congregation got skittish, and asked what they were supposed to do with all these homosexuals around. And Pastor Wallace replied, 'Why, let them sit on down.' The homosexuals, he said, could join the gossips and the fornicators and the adulterers and all the other sinners among us."

He stands up and walks toward his desk. "It's a strange world, Max. We have megachurches. We have Christian satellite television and Christian bands on the pop charts. We have *The Shack,* for goodness' sake. Christ is more visible than He's ever been, with even more influence than ever before. So why do abortion clinics still thrive? Why is the divorce rate climbing? Why is pornography rampant?" He pauses, but I don't think he's waiting for an answer from me. "I'll tell you why, Max.

It's because the moral weakness we see outside the church has invaded it as well. Look no further than Ted Haggard or Paul Barnes—there are sex scandals in our own leadership. The reason we can't speak to the most critical issue of our time is because, morally, we've given up our authority."

I frown, a little confused. I don't really get what this has to do with Zoe.

"At prayer meeting we hear people say that they have cancer, or that they need a job. We never hear someone confess to looking up Internet porn, or to having gay fantasies. Why *is* that? Why is church not a safe place to come if you're tempted by sin—any sin? If we can't be that safe place, we share the responsibility when those people fall. You know, Max, of all people, how it feels to sit at a bar and not be judged— to just have a drink and let it all hang out. Why can't the church be more like that? Why can't you walk in and say, *Oh, God, it's just you. Cool. I can be myself, now.* Not in a way that ignores our sins—but in a way that makes us accountable for them. You see where I'm headed with this, Max?"

"No, sir," I admit. "Not really . . ."

"You know what brought you to me today?" Pastor Clive says.

"Zoe?"

"No. Jesus Christ." A smile breaks over Pastor Clive's face. "You were sent here to remind me that we can't get so wrapped up in the battle we forget the war. Alcoholics get recovery medallions to commemorate the time they've been sober. We in the church need to *be* that token for the homosexual who wants to change."

"I don't know if Zoe wants to change—"

"We've already learned that you can't tell a pregnant woman not to have an abortion—you have to help her do what's right, by offering counseling and support and adoption possibilities. So we can't just say that being gay is wrong. We have to also be willing to bring these people into the church, to *show* them how to do the right thing."

What the pastor is talking about, I realize, is becoming a guide. It is as if

Zoe's been lost in the woods. I may not be able to get her to come with me right away, but I can offer her a map. "You think I should talk to her?"

"Exactly, Max."

Except we have a history.

And I have hardly been at this born-alive-in-Christ thing long enough to be persuasive.

And.

(*Even if it hurts me*)

(*Even if it makes me feel like less of a man*)

(*Who am I to say that she's wrong?*)

But I can't even admit this last thought to myself, much less to Pastor Clive.

"I don't think she really wants to hear what the church has to say."

"I never said it would be an easy conversation, Max. But this isn't about sexual ethics. We're not anti-gay," Pastor Clive says. "We're pro-Christ."

When it's put that way, everything becomes clear. I'm not going after Zoe because she hurt me or because I'm angry. I'm just trying to save her soul. "So what do I do?"

"You pray. Zoe has to confess her

sin. And if she can't, you pray for that to happen. You can't drag her to us, you can't force counseling. But you *can* make her see that there's an alternative." He sits down at his desk and starts flipping through a Rolodex. "There are some of our members who've struggled with unwanted same-sex attraction but who hold to a Christian worldview instead."

I think about the congregation—the happy families, the bright faces, the glow in their eyes that I know comes from the Holy Spirit. These people are my friends, my family. I try to figure out who has lived a gay lifestyle. Maybe Patrick, the hairdresser whose Sunday ties always match his wife's blouse? Or Neal, who is a pastry chef at a five-star restaurant downtown?

"You've met Pauline Bridgman, I assume?" Pastor Clive says.

Pauline?

Really?

Pauline and I were cutting carrots just yesterday while preparing the chicken pies for the church supper. She is tiny, with a nose that turns up at the end and eyebrows plucked too thin. When she talks, she uses her hands a lot. I don't think I've ever seen her not wearing pink.

When I think of lesbians, I picture women who look tough and scrappy, with spiked hair and baggy jeans and flannel shirts. Sure, this is a stereotype . . . but still, there's nothing about Pauline Bridgman that suggests she used to be gay.

Then again, nothing about Zoe tipped me off, either.

"Pauline sought the help of Exodus International. She used to speak at Love Won Out conferences about her experience becoming ex-gay. I think, if we asked, she'd be more than happy to share her story with Zoe."

Pastor Clive writes Pauline's number down on a Post-it note. "I'll think about it," I hedge.

"I would say, *What do you have to lose?* Except that's not what's important here." Pastor Clive waits until I am looking directly at him. "It's all about what *Zoe* has to lose."

Eternal salvation.

Even if she's not my wife anymore.

Even if she never really loved me.

I take the Post-it note from Pastor Clive, fold it in half, and slip it into my wallet.

That night I dream that I am still married to Zoe, and she is in my bed, and we are making love. I slide my hand up her hip, into the curve of her waist. I bury my face in her hair. I kiss her mouth, her throat, her neck, her breast. Then I look down at my hand, splayed across her belly.

It is not my hand.

For one thing, there is a ring on the thumb—a thin gold band.

And there's red nail polish.

What's the matter? Zoe asks.

There's something wrong, I tell her.

She grabs my wrist and pulls me closer. *There's nothing wrong.*

But I stumble into the bathroom, turn on the lights. I look into the mirror, and find Vanessa staring back at me.

When I wake up, the sheets are drenched with sweat. I get out of Reid's guest room bed, and in the bathroom (careful not to look into the mirror) I wash my face and dunk my head under the faucet. There's no way I'll fall back asleep now, so I head to the kitchen for a snack.

To my surprise, though, I'm not the only one awake at three in the morning.

Liddy is sitting at the kitchen table, shredding a napkin. She's wearing a thin white cotton robe over her nightgown. Liddy actually wears nightgowns, the kind made out of fine cotton with tiny embroidered roses at the collar and the hem. Zoe usually slept naked, and if she wore anything at all, it was one of my T-shirts and a pair of my boxers.

"Liddy," I say, and she jumps at the sound of my voice. "Are you all right?"

"You scared me, Max."

She's always seemed fragile to me—sort of like the way I picture angels, gauzy and delicate and too pretty to look at for long periods of time. But right now, she looks broken. There are blue half-moons under her eyes; her lips are chapped. Her hands, when they're not tearing the paper napkin, are shaking. "You need help getting back to bed?" I ask gently.

"No . . . I'm fine."

"You want a cup of tea?" I ask. "Or I could make you some soup . . . ?"

She shakes her head. Her waterfall of gold hair ripples.

It just doesn't seem right to sit down when Liddy's in her own kitchen, and when she's obviously come here to be by herself. But it doesn't seem right to leave her here, either. "I could get Reid," I suggest.

"Let him sleep." She sighs, and when she does the small pile of shredded paper she's created is blown all around her, onto the floor. Liddy bends down to pick up the pieces.

"Oh," I say, grateful for something to do. "Let me."

I kneel before she can get there, but she pushes me out of the way. "Stop," she says. "Just *stop*." She covers her face with her hands. I cannot hear her, but I see her shoulders shaking. I know she's crying.

At a loss, I hesitantly pat her on her back. "Liddy?" I whisper.

"Will everyone just stop being so fucking nice to me!"

My jaw drops. In all the years I've known Liddy, I've never heard her swear, much less drop the F-bomb.

Immediately she blushes. "I'm sorry," she says. "I don't know . . . I don't know what's wrong with me."

"I do." I slide into the seat across from her. "Your life. It isn't turning out the way you figured it would."

Liddy stares at me for a long moment, as if she's never really looked at me before. She covers my hand with both of hers. "Yes," she whispers. "That's it exactly." Then she frowns a little. "How come you're awake, anyway?"

I slide my hand free. "Got thirsty," I say, and I shrug.

"Remember," Pauline says, before we get out of her VW Bug, "today is all about love. We're going to pull the rug out from beneath her because she's going to be expecting hate and judgment, but that's not what we're going to give her."

I nod. To be honest, even getting Zoe to agree to meet with me had been more of an ordeal than I thought. It didn't seem right to set up a time under false pretenses—to say that I had paperwork for her to sign, or a financial issue to discuss that had something to do with the divorce. Instead, with Pastor Clive standing next to me and praying for me to find the right words, I called her cell and said that it had been really nice to run into her at the grocery store. That I was pretty surprised by her news about Vanessa. And that, if she could spare a few minutes, I'd really like to just sit down and talk.

Granted, I didn't mention anything about Pauline being there, too.

Which is why, when Zoe opens the door to this unfamiliar house (red Cape on a cul-de-sac, with an impressively landscaped front yard), she looks from me to Pauline and frowns. "Max," Zoe says, "I thought you were coming alone."

It's weird to see Zoe in someone

else's home, holding a mug that I bought her one Christmas that says I'M IN TRE-BLE. Behind her, on the floor, is a jumble of shoes—some of which I recognize and some of which I don't. It makes my ribs feel too tight.

"This is a friend of mine from the church," I explain. "Pauline, this is Zoe."

I believe Pauline when she says she's not homosexual anymore, but there's something that makes me watch her shake hands with Zoe all the same. To see if there is a flicker in her eye, or if she holds on to Zoe a moment too long. There's none of that, though.

"Max," Zoe asks, "what's going on here?"

She folds her arms, the way she used to do when a door-to-door salesman came around and she wanted to make it clear she did not have the time to listen to his spiel. I open my mouth to explain but then snap it shut without saying anything. "This is a really lovely home," Pauline says.

"Thanks," Zoe replies. "It's my girlfriend's."

The word explodes into the room,

but Pauline acts like she never heard it. She points to a photo on the wall behind Zoe. "Is that Block Island?"

"I think so." Zoe turns. "Vanessa's parents had a summer home there when she was growing up."

"So did my aunt," Pauline says. "I keep telling myself I'll go back, and then I never do."

Zoe faces me. "Look, Max, you two can drop the act. I'm going to be honest with you. We have nothing to talk about. If you want to get sucked into the mindwarp of the Eternal Glory Church, that's your prerogative. But if you and your missionary friend here came to convert me, it just isn't going to happen."

"I'm not here to convert you. Whatever happened between us, you have to know I care about you. And I want to make sure you're making the right choices."

Zoe's eyes flash. "*You* are preaching to *me* about making the right choices? That's pretty funny, Max."

"I've made mistakes," I admit. "I make them every day. I'm not perfect by any means. But none of us are. And that's exactly why you should listen to me when I say that the way you feel— it's not your fault. It's something that's happened to you. But it's not who you *are.*"

She blinks at me for a moment, trying to puzzle out my words. The moment she understands, I can see it. "You're talking about Vanessa. Oh, my God. You've taken your little anti-gay crusade right into my living room." Panicking, I look at Pauline as Zoe throws open her arms. "Come on in, Max," she says sarcastically. "I can't wait to hear what you have to say about my degenerate lifestyle. After all, I spent the day with dying children at the hospital. I could use a little comic relief."

"Maybe we should go," I murmur to Pauline, but she moves past me and takes a seat on the living room couch.

"I used to be exactly like you," she tells Zoe. "I lived with a woman and loved her and considered myself to be a homosexual. We were on vacation, eating dinner at a restaurant, and the waitress took my girlfriend's order and then turned to me. 'Sir,' she said, 'what can I get you?' I have to tell you, I didn't look the way I do now. I dressed like a boy, I walked like a boy. I wanted to be mistaken for a boy, so that girls would fall for me. I completely believed that I had been born this way, because feeling different from everyone else was all I could ever remember. That night I did something I had not done since I was a child—I took the Bible out of the hotel nightstand and started to read it. By pure accident, I had landed on Leviticus: *Do not lie with a man as one lies with a woman; that is detestable.* I wasn't a man, but I knew that God was talking about me."

Zoe rolls her eyes. "I'm a little rusty on my Scripture, but I'm pretty sure that divorce isn't allowed. And yet I didn't show up at your doorstep after we got the final decree from the court, Max."

Pauline continues as if Zoe hasn't spoken. "I started realizing I could separate the *who* from the *do*. I wasn't gay—I was gay-identified. I reread the studies that allegedly proved I was born this way, and I found flaws and gaps big enough to drive a truck through. I had fallen for a lie. And once I realized that, I also realized that things could change."

"You mean . . . ," Zoe says breathlessly, "it's that easy? I name it and I claim it? I say I believe in God, and I'm magically saved. I say I'm not gay, and hallelujah! I must be cured. I'm sure if Vanessa walked through that door right now, I wouldn't find her attractive at all."

As if Zoe has conjured her, Vanessa walks into the living room, still unbuttoning her jacket. "Did I just hear my name?" she asks. Zoe walks up to her and gives her a fast peck on the lips, a hello.

As if it's something they do all the time.

As if it doesn't make my stomach turn.

As if it's perfectly natural.

Zoe looks at Pauline. "Drat. Guess I'm not cured after all."

By now, Vanessa has noticed us. "I didn't know we were having company."

"This is Pauline, and of course you know Max," Zoe says. "They're here to keep us from going to Hell."

"Zoe," Vanessa says, pulling her aside, "can we talk for a minute?" She leads Zoe into the adjacent kitchen. I have to strain to listen, but I manage to catch most of what she's saying. "I'm not going to tell you you can't invite someone into our house, but what the hell are you thinking?"

"That they're insane," Zoe says. "Seriously, Vanessa, if no one ever tells them they're delusional, then how are they going to find out?"

There is a little more conversation, but it's muffled. I look at Pauline nervously. "Don't worry," she says, patting my arm. "Denial is normal. Christ calls on us to spread His word, even when it seems like it's falling on deaf ears. But I always think of a talk like this as if I'm spreading mahogany stain on a natural wood floor. Even if you wipe away the color, it's seeped in a little bit, and you can't get rid of it. Long after we leave, Zoe will still be thinking about what we've said."

Then again, putting mahogany stain on a piece of pine only changes the way it looks on the outside. It doesn't turn it into real mahogany. I wonder if Pauline's ever thought about that.

Zoe comes through the door, trailed by Vanessa. "Don't do this," Vanessa pleads. "If you started dating someone black, would you invite the KKK over to discuss it?"

"Honestly, Vanessa," Zoe says dismissively, and she turns to Pauline. "I'm sorry. You were saying?"

Pauline folds her hands in her lap. "Well, I think we were talking about my own moment of discovery," she says, and Vanessa snorts. "I realized I was vulnerable to same-sex attraction for several reasons. My mother was an Iowa farm girl—the kind of woman who got up at four A.M. and had already changed the world before breakfast. She believed hands were made for working and that, if you fell down and cried, you were weak. My dad traveled a lot and just wasn't around. I was always a tomboy, and wanted to play football with my brothers more than I wanted to sit inside and play with my dolls. And of course, there was a cousin who sexually abused me."

"Of course," Vanessa murmurs.

"Well," Pauline says, looking at her, "everyone I've ever met who's gay-identified has experienced some kind of abuse."

I look at Zoe, uncomfortable. She hasn't been abused. She would have told me.

Of course, she didn't tell me she liked women, either.

"Let me guess," Vanessa says. "Your parents didn't exactly welcome you with open arms when you told them you were gay."

Pauline smiles. "My parents and I have the best relationship now—we've been through so much, my gracious . . . It wasn't *their* fault I was gay-identified. It was a host of factors—from that abuse to not being secure in my own gender to feeling like women were sec-ond-class citizens. For all these rea-sons, I began to behave a certain way. A way that took me away from Christ. I wonder," she asks Zoe, "why do you think you were open to pursuing a same-sex relationship? Clearly you weren't born that way, since you were happily married—"

"So happily married," Vanessa points out, "that she got divorced."

"It's true," I agree. "I wasn't there for you, Zoe, when you needed me. And I can't ever make that up to you. But I can keep the same mistake from happening twice. I can help you meet people who understand you, who won't judge you, and who will love you for who you are, not for what you do."

Zoe slides her arm through Vanessa's. "I've already got that right here."

"You can't—you're not—" I find myself stumbling over the words. "You are not gay, Zoe. You're not."

"Maybe that's true," Zoe says. "Maybe I'm not gay. Maybe this is a one-time deal. But here's what I know: I want that one-time deal to last a lifetime. I love Vanessa. And she happens to be a woman. If that makes me a lesbian, now, so be it."

I start praying silently. I pray that I will not stand up and start screaming. I pray that Zoe will become as miserable as possible, as quickly as possible, so that she can see Christ standing right in front of her.

"I'm not a fan of labels, either," Pauline says. "Goodness, look at me now. I don't even like to call myself ex-gay, because that suggests I was born a homosexual. No way—I'm a heterosexual, evangelical, Christian woman, that's all. I wear skirts more than I wear slacks. I never leave the house without makeup. And if you happen to see Hugh Jackman walking down the street, could you just hang on to him until—"

"Have you ever slept with a man?" Vanessa's voice sounds like a gunshot.

"No," Pauline admits, blushing. "That would go against the core beliefs of the church, since I'm not married."

"How incredibly convenient." Vanessa turns to Zoe. "Twenty bucks says Megan Fox could seduce her in the time it takes to say an Our Father."

Pauline won't rise to the bait. She faces Vanessa, and her eyes are full of pity. "You can say whatever you want about me. I know where that anger's coming from. See, I *was* you, once. I know what it's like to be living the way you do, and to be looking at a woman like me and thinking I'm a total fruit-cake. Believe me, I had books left on my dresser and articles slipped beneath my coffee cup on the kitchen table— my parents did everything they could to try to push me to give up my gay identity, and it only made me more certain I was absolutely right. But Vanessa, I'm not here to be that person. I'm not going to give you literature and make follow-up phone calls or try to pretend I'm your new best friend. I'm simply here to say that when you and Zoe are ready—and I do believe one day you will be—I can give you the resources you're looking for to put Christ's needs above your own."

"So, let me get this right," Zoe says. "I don't have to change right now. I can take a rain check . . ."

"Absolutely," I reply. I mean, it's a step in the right direction, isn't it?

". . . but you still think our relation-ship is wrong."

"Jesus does," Pauline says. "If you

look at Scripture and think differently, you're reading it wrong."

"You know, I went to catechism for ten years," Vanessa says. "I'm pretty sure the Bible also says polygamy's a good idea. And that we shouldn't eat scallops."

"Just because something's written in the Bible doesn't mean it was God's created intent—"

"You just said that if it's Scripture, it's fact!" Vanessa argues.

Pauline raises her chin a notch. "I didn't come here to dissect semantics. The opposite of homosexuality isn't heterosexuality. It's holiness. That's why I'm here—as living proof that there's another path. A better path."

"And how exactly does that jibe with turning the other cheek?"

"I'm not judging you," Pauline explains. "I'm just offering my biblical worldview."

"Well," Vanessa says, getting to her feet. "I guess I'm blind then, because that's far too subtle a distinction for me to see. How dare you tell me that what makes me *me* is wrong? How dare you say that you're tolerant, as long as I'm just like you? How dare you suggest that I shouldn't be allowed to get married to someone I love, or adopt a child, or that gay rights don't qualify as civil rights because, unlike skin color or disabilities, you think that sexual orientation can be changed? But you know what? Even *that* argument doesn't hold water, because you can change your religion, and religious affiliation is still protected by law. Which is the *only* reason I'm going to ask you politely to leave my home, instead of throwing you out on your hypocritical evangelical asses."

Zoe stands up, too. "Don't let the door hit you on the way out," she says.

On the way back home, it starts to rain. I listen to the windshield wipers keeping time and think about how Zoe, in the passenger seat, used to drum on the glove compartment along with the beat.

"Can I ask you something personal?" I say, turning to Pauline.

"Sure."

"Do you . . . you know . . . ever miss it?"

Pauline glances at me. "Some people do. They struggle for years. It's like any other addiction—they figure out that this is their drug, and they make the decision to not let that be part of their lives. If they're lucky, they may consider themselves completely cured and have a true identity change. But even if they aren't that lucky, they still get up in the morning and pray to God to get through one more day without acting on those attractions."

I realize that she did not really answer my question.

"Christians have been called upon to struggle for ages," Pauline says. "This isn't any different."

Once, Zoe and I went to a wedding of one of her clients. It was a Jewish wedding, and it was really beautiful— with trappings and traditions I had never seen before. The bride and groom stood under a canopy, and the prayers were in an unfamiliar language. At the end, the rabbi had the groom stomp on a wineglass wrapped in a napkin. *May your marriage last as long as it would take to put these pieces back together,* he said. Afterward, when everyone was congratulating the couple, I sneaked underneath the canopy and took a tiny shard of glass from the napkin where it still lay on the grass. I threw it into the ocean on the way home, so that, no matter what, that glass could never be reconstructed, so the couple would stay together forever.

When Zoe asked what I was doing and I told her, she said she thought she loved me more in that moment than she ever had before.

My heart, it kind of feels like that wineglass these days. Like something that's supposed to be whole but— thanks to some idiot who thought he knew better—doesn't stand a freaking chance.

	TRACK 1	SING YOU HOME
	TRACK 2	THE HOUSE ON HOPE STREET
	TRACK 3	REFUGEE
	TRACK 4	THE LAST
✓	**TRACK 5**	**MARRY ME**
	TRACK 6	FAITH
	TRACK 7	THE MERMAID
	TRACK 8	ORDINARY LIFE
	TRACK 9	WHERE YOU ARE
	TRACK 10	SAMMY'S SONG

ZOE

Everyone wants to know what the sex is like.

It's different from being with a man, for all the obvious reasons, and many more that you'd never imagine. For one thing, it's more emotional, and there's less to prove. There are moments that are soft and tender, and others that are raw and intense—but it's not as if there's a guy to play the dominant role and a girl to play the passive one. We take turns being protected, and being the protector.

Sex with a woman is what you wish it was with a man but it rarely seems to be: all about the journey, and not the destination. It's foreplay forever. It is the freedom to not have to suck in your stomach or think about cellulite. It is being able to say, *that feels good* and, more important, *that doesn't.* I will admit that, at first, it was strange to curl up in Vanessa's arms when I was used to resting against a muscular chest— but the strangeness wasn't unpleasant. Just unfamiliar, as if I'd suddenly moved to the rainforest after living in the desert. It is another kind of beautiful.

Sometimes when a male colleague finds out I am with Vanessa, I can see it in his eyes—the expectation that every night is a girl-on-girl porn video. My current sex life is no more like that than my former one was like a love scene with Brad Pitt. I could sleep with a man again, but I don't think I'd enjoy it, or feel as safe, or as daring. So if I am not filled by Vanessa—in the literal sense, anyway—I am fulfilled by her, which is way better.

The real difference between my marriage to Max and my relationship with Vanessa has nothing to do with the sex, actually. It's about balance. When Max would come home, I'd wonder if he was in a good mood, or if he'd had a good day—and I would become the person he needed me to be accordingly. With Vanessa, I get to come home and just be me.

With Vanessa, I wake up and think: *This is my best friend. This is the most brilliant person in my life.* I wake up and think, *I have so much more to lose.*

Every day is a negotiation. Vanessa and I sit down over coffee, and, instead of her burying herself in the newspaper— like Max used to do—we discuss what needs to be done. Now that I've moved in with her, we have a household to run. There's no man who's expected to change the lightbulbs that burn out, or take out the trash. If something heavy has to be moved, we do it together. One of us has to mow the lawn, do the bills, clean out the gutters.

When I was married, Max would ask what was for dinner; I'd ask if he picked up the dry cleaning. Now, Vanessa and I map out our chores. If Vanessa needs to run an errand on the way home from school, she might pick up takeout. If I'm headed into town, I'll take her car for the day, so that I can fill it up with gas. There is a lot of talking, a lot of give-and-take, when it's just two women in a kitchen.

It's funny—when I used to hear gay people using the term *partner* for their significant other, it seemed strange to me. Weren't heterosexual spouses partners, too? But now I see that this isn't the case, that there is a difference between someone you call your "other half" at a cocktail party and someone who truly completes you. Vanessa and I have to invent the dynamic between us, because it's not the traditional husband-wife deal. The result is that we're constantly making decisions together. We're always asking each other for opinions. We assume nothing. And that way, we're a lot less likely to get our feelings bruised.

You'd think that by now, a month into this relationship, some of the blush has worn off, that I might love Vanessa but not be quite as in love with her—but it's not true. She's still the one I can't wait to talk to after something phenomenal happens at work. She's the one I want to celebrate with when, three months after my hysterectomy, I'm still cancer-free. She's the one I want to lounge around with on a lazy Sunday. For this reason, a lot of chores that we could divide and conquer on weekends take twice as long, because we do them together. Since we want to be together anyway, why not?

Which is why we find ourselves in the grocery store on a Saturday afternoon in March, reading the labels on salad dressing, when Max walks up to me. I hug him, a reflexive habit—and try not to look at his black suit and skinny tie. He looks like the kid from high school who thought if he dressed like the cool guys he'd become one by default, except it never really works that way.

I can feel Vanessa, burning behind me, waiting for an introduction. But the words get stuck in my throat.

Max holds out his hand; Vanessa shakes it. This is hell, I think. The man I used to love and the woman I cannot live without. I know what Vanessa wants, what she expects. For all the protesting I've done to convince her that I'm not leaving her anytime soon, here is the perfect proof. All I have to do is tell Max that, now, Vanessa and I are a couple.

So why can't I?

Vanessa stares at me, and then her mouth tightens. "I'm just going to grab the produce," she says, but as she moves away, I feel something snap inside my chest, like a string too tightly wound.

Max's friend appears, a clone in a similar suit, with an Adam's apple that bobs like the plumb bubble in a level. I mumble through a hello, but I am trying to see over his shoulder to the root vegetable bins, where Vanessa stands with her back to me. Then I hear Max inviting me to his church.

Fat chance, I think. I imagine showing up in front of that homophobic group and holding hands with Vanessa. We'd probably be tarred and feathered. I mumble a response and make a bee-line for her.

"You're pissed at me," I say.

Vanessa is squeezing mangoes. "Not pissed. Just kind of disappointed." She looks up. "Why didn't you tell him?"

"Why did I *have* to? It's nobody's business but yours and mine. I just met Max's friend, and he didn't say, *Oh, by the way, I'm straight.*"

She sets down the fruit. "I am the last person in the world who wants to wave a banner or march in a Pride parade," Vanessa says. "And I get that it's not easy to tell someone you used to love that you love someone else. But when you *don't* say it out loud, that's when people fill in the silence with their own stupid assumptions. Don't you believe that, if Max knew you were in a same-sex relationship, he might think twice before he pickets against gays again? Because all of a sudden it's not some faceless queer in a crowd, Zoe, it's someone he *knows*." She looks away. "And me. When I see you working over-time to *not* call me your girlfriend, it makes me think that, no matter what you say to me, you're lying. That you're still looking for that escape hatch."

"That's not why I—"

"Then why not? Are you ashamed of me?" Vanessa asks. "Or are you ashamed of *yourself*?"

I am standing in front of the cartons of strawberries. I once had a client who, before she was in hospice with ovarian cancer, had been a botanist. She couldn't eat solid food anymore but told me she missed strawberries the most. They were the only fruit in the world with seeds on the outside, and because of this, they weren't even really berries. They were part of the rose family, not that you could tell by looking.

"Meet me outside," I say to Vanessa.

It is raining by the time I catch up to Max at his truck. "That woman I'm with. Vanessa," I say. "She's my new partner."

Max looks at me like I'm crazy. Why would I run out in the rain to tell him this? Then he starts talking about my work, and I realize Vanessa is right— he's misunderstood, because I haven't told him the simple truth. "Vanessa is my *partner,*" I repeat. "We're *together.*"

I can tell the moment that he understands what I am saying. Not because of the invisible shutters that close over his eyes but because something bursts inside me, sweet and free. I don't know why I thought I needed Max's approval in the first place. I may not be the woman he thought he knew, but that goes both ways.

Before I know it I am headed back to Vanessa, who's waiting with the grocery cart under the dry overhang of the store. I find myself running. "What did you say to him?" Vanessa asks.

"That I kind of want to be with you forever. Except forever's not long enough," I tell her. "I may be paraphrasing a bit."

The expression on her face makes me feel the way I do when, after months of winter, I see that first crocus. *Finally.*

We duck our heads in the rain and hurry to Vanessa's car to load the groceries. As she puts the bags into the trunk, I watch two children pass by. They are preteens, a boy with peach fuzz on his face and a girl who is smacking her bubble gum. Their arms are locked around each other, one hand in the other's back jeans pocket.

They don't look old enough to watch PG movies, much less date, but no one even blinks as they walk by. "Hey," I say, and Vanessa turns, still holding a bag of groceries. I put my hands on either side of her face and I kiss her, long and lovely and slow. I hope Max is watching. I hope the whole world is.

When most people hear screaming, they run in the opposite direction. Me, I grab my guitar and run toward it.

"Hi," I say, bursting into one of the pediatric rooms at the hospital. "Can I help?"

The nurse, who is valiantly trying to take an IV out of a little boy, sighs with relief. "Be my guest, Zoe."

The boy's mother, who's been holding him down while he struggles, nods at me. "All he knows is that it hurt going in, so he thinks it's going to hurt coming out, too."

I make eye contact with her son. "Hi," I say. "I'm Zoe. What's your name?"

His lower lip trembles. "C-Carl."

"Carl, do you like to sing?"

Adamantly, he shakes his head. I glance around the room and notice a pile of Power Ranger figurines on the nightstand. Pulling my guitar in front of me, I begin to play the chords for "The Wheels on the Bus," except I change the words. "The Power Rangers . . . they kick kick kick," I sing. "Kick kick kick . . . kick kick kick. The Power Rangers they kick kick kick . . . all day long."

Somewhere in the middle of the verse, he stops fighting and looks at me. "They also jump," he says.

So the next verse we sing together. He spends ten minutes telling me everything else the Power Rangers do—the red one, and the pink one, and the black one. Then he looks up at the nurse. "When are you going to start?" Carl asks.

She grins. "I already finished."

Carl's mother looks up at me with utter relief. "Thank you *so* much . . ."

"No problem," I say. "Carl, thanks for singing with me."

I have no sooner exited the room and turned the corner than another nurse runs up to me. "I've been looking all over for you. It's Marisa."

She doesn't have to tell me what's the matter. Marisa is a three-year-old who's been in and out of the hospital for a year with leukemia. Her father, a bluegrass musician, loves the idea of music therapy for his daughter, because he knows how much music can transport a person. Sometimes I go in when she is alert and happy, and we'll do a sing-along of her favorites—"Old Mac-Donald" and "I'm a Little Teapot" and "John Jacob Jingleheimer Schmidt" and "My Bonnie Lies over the Ocean." Sometimes I'll go in during her chemo treatments, which make her feel like her hands are burning, and I'll create songs about dipping her hands in ice water, about building igloos. Lately, though, Marisa's been so ill that it's been her family and me just singing for her, while she sleeps through a drugged haze.

"Her doctor says within the hour," the nurse murmurs to me.

I quietly open the door to her room. The lights are off, and the gray light of late afternoon is caught in the folds of

the hospital blanket that covers the little girl. She is still and pale, a pink knit
cap covering her bald head, glittery silver nail polish on her fingers. I was here
last week when Marisa's big sister ap-
plied it. We sang "Girls Just Wanna
Have Fun," even though Marisa slept
through it. Even though Marisa wasn't
conscious to know that someone cared
enough to make her look pretty.

Marisa's mother is crying softly in her
husband's arms. "Michael, Louisa," I
say. "I'm so sorry."

They don't answer, but they don't
have to. Illness can make family of
strangers.

A hospital worker sits beside the bed,
making a plaster cast of Marisa's handprint before she passes, something that
is offered to the parents of any terminal
pediatric patient. The air feels heavier,
as if we are all breathing in lead.

I step back, beside Marisa's sister,
Anya. She looks at me, her eyes red
and swollen. I squeeze her hand, and
then, in keeping with the mood, I begin
to improvise on my guitar, instrumental
riffs that are somber and in minor keys.

Suddenly Michael turns to me. "We don't want you playing that in here."

Heat rushes to my cheeks. "I-I'm sorry. I'll go."

Michael shakes his head. "No—we want you to play the songs you always play for her. The ones she loves."

So I do. I play "Old MacDonald," and one by one, her family join in. The hospital worker presses Marisa's hand to the plaster, wipes it clean.

When the machines connected to Marisa begin to flatline, I keep singing.

My Bonnie lies over the ocean.
My Bonnie lies over the sea.

I watch Michael kneel down at his daughter's bedside. Louisa curls her hand over Marisa's. Anya jackknifes at the waist, an origami of grief.

My Bonnie lies over the ocean.
Oh, bring back my Bonnie to me.

There is a high-pitched hum, and then a nurse comes in to turn off the monitor, to rest her hand gently on

Marisa's forehead as she offers her condolences.

Bring back.
Bring back.
Bring back my Bonnie to me.

When I finish, the only sound in the room is the absence of a little girl.

"I'm so sorry," I say again.

Michael holds out his hand. I do not know what he wants, but my body seems to. I hand him the pick I've been using to strum the guitar. He presses it into the plaster, just above the spread of Marisa's handprint.

I hold myself together until I walk out of the room. Then I lean against the wall and slide down until I am sitting, sobbing. I cradle my guitar in my arms, the way Louisa was cradling the body of her daughter.

And then.

I hear a baby crying—that high, hitched shriek that grows more and more hysterical. Heavily I get to my feet and trace the sound two doors down from Marisa's room, where an infant is being held down by her tearful mother and a nurse while a phlebotomist attempts to draw blood. They all look up when I enter. "Maybe I can help," I say.

It has been a hellish, busy day at the hospital, and my drive home is consumed by the thought of a large glass of wine and collapsing on the couch, which is why I almost don't pick up my cell phone when I see Max's name flash onto the screen. But then I sigh and answer, and he asks me for just a few moments of my time. He doesn't say what it's for, but I'm assuming it has to do with paperwork being signed. There is, even after a divorce, no shortage of paperwork.

So I am completely surprised when he arrives with a woman in tow. And I'm even more shocked when I realize that the reason he's brought her is to save me from the newly degenerate life I'm living.

I'd laugh, if I didn't feel like crying quite so much. Today I watched a three-year-old die, but my ex-husband thinks that *I* am what's wrong with this world. Maybe if his God wasn't so busy paying attention to the lives of people like Vanessa and me, he could have saved Marisa.

But life isn't fair. It's why little girls don't make it to their fourth birthdays. It's why I lost so many babies. It's why people like Max and my governor seem to think they can tell me who to love. If life isn't fair, I don't have to be, either. And so I channel all the anger I'm feeling at things I cannot change or control, and direct it at the man and woman sitting on the couch across from me.

I wonder if Pastor Clive, who runs the largest gay-bashing fraternity in these parts, has ever considered what Jesus would think of his tactics. Something tells me that a progressive rabbi who ministered to lepers and prostitutes and everyone else society had marginalized—someone who recommended treating people the way you wanted to be treated—wouldn't exactly admire the Eternal Glory Church's position. But I have to give them this: they are smooth. They have circular rhetoric for everything. I find myself fascinated by Pauline, who won't even call herself a former lesbian, because she sees herself as so blatantly heterosexual now. Is it really that easy to believe what you tell yourself? If I had said, in the middle of all those failed pregnancies and miscarriages, that I was happy, *would* I have been?

If only the world were as simple as Pauline seems to think.

I am trying to trap her in her own circular logic when Vanessa gets home. I give her a kiss hello. I would have anyway, but I'm particularly happy that Pauline and Max have to watch. "This is Pauline, and of course you know Max," I say. "They're here to keep us from going to Hell."

Vanessa looks at me like I've lost my mind. "Zoe, can we talk for a minute?" she says, and drags me into the kitchen. "I'm not going to tell you you can't invite someone into our house," she says, "but what the hell are you thinking?"

"Did you know you're not a lesbian?" I say. "You just have a lesbian *problem.*"

"The only problem I have right now is getting these two people out of my living room," Vanessa replies, but she follows me back inside. I see her getting more and more tightly wound as Pauline tells us that everyone gay has been sexually abused and that femininity means wearing panty hose and makeup. Finally, Vanessa reaches her limit. She throws Max and Pauline out and closes the door behind them. "I love you," she tells me, "but if you ever have your ex-husband over again with that poor man's Anita Bryant, I'd like enough advance notice to get away first. Three thousand miles or so."

"Max said he had to talk to me," I explain. "I figured it was about the divorce. I didn't know he was bringing backup."

Vanessa snorts. She steps out of her high heels. "I don't even like the fact that they were on my couch, frankly. I feel like we ought to fumigate. Or hold an exorcism or something—"

"Vanessa!"

"I just didn't expect to see him in my

house. Especially tonight, when I . . ." Her voice trails off into silence.

"When you what?"

"Nothing." She shakes her head.

"I guess you can't blame them for wishing that, one day, we'll wake up and realize how wrong we've been."

"Can't I?"

"No," I say, "because that's exactly what we wish about *them*."

Vanessa offers me a half smile. "Leave it to you to find the only thing I have in common with Pastor Clive and his band of merry heterosexuals."

She walks into the kitchen, and I assume she's getting the wine out of the fridge. It is a tradition for us to unwind and tell each other about our days over a nice glass of Pinot Grigio. "I think we still have some of the Midlife Crisis," I call out. It's a wine from California that Vanessa and I bought just because of the name on the label. While I wait, I sit down on the couch, in the spot Max vacated. I flip through the channels on the television, pausing on *Ellen*.

Max and I sometimes watched her, when he got home from landscaping.

He liked her Converse sneakers and her blue eyes. He used to say that he wouldn't want to be stuck in a room with Oprah, because she was intimidating—but Ellen DeGeneres, she was someone you'd take out for a beer.

What I like about Ellen is that (yep) she's gay, but that's the least interesting thing about her. You remember her because she's good at what she does on TV, not because she goes home to Portia de Rossi.

Vanessa walks into the living room, but instead of bringing a glass of wine, she is carrying two champagne flutes. "It's Dom Pérignon," she says. "Because you and I are celebrating."

I look at the bubbles rising in the pale liquid. "I had a patient die today," I blurt out. "She was only three."

Vanessa sets both glasses on the floor and hugs me. She doesn't say anything. She doesn't have to.

You know someone's right for you when the things they don't *have* to say are even more important than the things they do.

Crying won't bring Marisa back. It

won't stop people like Max and Pauline from judging me. But it makes me feel better, all the same. I stay this way for a while, with Vanessa stroking my hair, until I am dry-eyed and feeling only empty inside. Then I look up at her. "I'm sorry. You wanted to celebrate something . . ."

Color rises to Vanessa's face. "Some other time."

"I'm not letting my crap day trump your good one—"

"Really, Zo. It can wait—"

"No." I turn on the couch so that I am cross-legged, facing her. "Tell me."

She looks pained. "It's stupid. I can ask you later—"

"Ask me what?"

Vanessa takes a deep breath. "If you meant what you said yesterday. After we ran into Max at the grocery store."

I had told her that I wanted to be with her forever. That forever wasn't long enough.

And in spite of the fact that this is never how I imagined my life—

In spite of the fact that there are people I have never even met who will hate me for it—

In spite of the fact that it has been only months, not years—

The first thing I do every morning is panic. And then I look at Vanessa and think, *Don't worry; she's still here.*

"Yes," I tell her. "Every word."

Vanessa uncurls her fist. Inside is a gold ring with a constellation of diamonds dotting its surface. "If forever's not long enough, how about the rest of my life?"

For a moment I cannot move, cannot breathe. I am not thinking of logistics, of how people will react to this news. All I am thinking is: *I get Vanessa. Me, and no one else.*

I start crying again, but for a different reason. "A lifetime," I say, "is a decent start."

I am surrounded by clouds. They brush the toes of my sneakers. They litter the floor. I might go so far as to say I've landed in Heaven—except that I've been dragging my feet to avoid shopping for a bridal gown, which makes this whole experience a little more like Hell.

My mother is holding out a gown with a sweetheart neckline that dissolves into a skirt of feathers. It looks like a chicken that ran into a combine. "No," I say. "Emphatically no."

"There's one over there with Swarovski crystals on the bodice," my mother says.

"You can wear it," I mutter.

It was not my idea to come to the bridal salon in Boston. My mother had a dream that revealed us shopping here, in the Priscilla showroom, and after that there was no escaping a trip. She is a big believer in the predictive power of the subconscious.

My mother—who took a week to adjust to the fact that Vanessa and I were a couple—is even more excited about the wedding than we are. I secretly think she loves Vanessa more than she loves me, since Vanessa is the grounded, good-head-on-her-shoulders daughter she never had—the one who can talk about IRAs and retirement planning and who keeps a birthday book so she never forgets to send a card. I think my mother truly believes Vanessa will take care of me forever; whereas with Max, she had her doubts.

But I'm itchy, in this place that's full of other brides who have weddings without complications. I feel like I'm being smothered by tulle and lace and satin, and I haven't even tried on a single dress yet.

When the salesclerk approaches us and asks if she can help, my mother steps forward with a bright smile. "My gay daughter's getting married," she announces.

I can feel my cheeks burn. "Why am I suddenly your *gay* daughter?"

"Well, I'd think, of all people, *you'd* know the answer to that."

"You never introduced me before as your straight daughter."

My mother's face falls. "I thought you *wanted* me to be proud of you."

"Don't make this *my* fault," I say.

The salesclerk looks from me to my mother. "Why don't I give you a few more minutes?" she asks, and she slinks away.

"Now look at what you've done. You've made her uncomfortable," my mother sighs.

"Are you *kidding*?" I grab a sequined pump from a rack. "'Hi,'" I mimic. "'Do you have this shoe for my mother the sadomasochist? She wears a seven and a half.'"

"First of all, I'm not into S and M. And second of all, that shoe is absolutely hideous." She looks at me. "You know, not everyone is out to attack you. Just because you're a new member of a minority group doesn't mean you have to assume the worst about everyone else."

I sit down on the white couch, in the middle of a mountain of tulle. "That's easy for you to say. You aren't getting pamphlets, daily, from the Eternal Glory Church. 'Ten Tiny Steps to Jesus.' 'Straight≠Hate.'" I look up at her. "You may feel like trumpeting my relationship status, but I don't. It's not worth making someone squirm." I glance at the salesclerk, who is wrapping a gown in plastic. "For all we know, she sings in the Eternal Glory Church choir."

"For all we know," my mother counters, "she's gay, too." She sits down next to me, and the dresses pouf up around us, a tiny explosion. "Honey . . . what's wrong?"

To my great embarrassment, my eyes well up with tears. "I don't know what to wear to my own wedding," I admit.

My mother takes one look at me, then grabs my hand and pulls me up from the couch and downstairs onto Boylston Street. "What on earth are you talking about?"

"The bride's supposed to be the focus of all the attention," I sob. "But what happens when there are two brides?"

"Well, what's Vanessa wearing?"

"A suit." A beautiful white suit she found at Marshalls that fits like it was tailored to her. But I have never worn a suit in my life.

"Then I'd think you can wear anything you want . . ."

"Not white," I blurt out.

My mother purses her lips. "Because you were already married?"

"No. Because—" Before I can say what has been lying smooth and heavy on my heart, like a fresh layer of asphalt, I snap my mouth shut.

"Because what?" my mother urges.

"Because it's a *gay* wedding," I whisper.

When Vanessa proposed, I never even thought twice about saying yes. But I would have been entirely happy to get married at a courthouse in Massachusetts, instead of having a big ceremony and reception. "Come on, Zo," she had said. "There are two times in your life everyone you love comes together—your wedding and your funeral—and I know I won't have nearly as much fun at the second one." But even as I sat down every night with Vanessa at the computer to research bands and venues for the reception, I kept thinking I would find the escape hatch, the way to convince Vanessa to just take a vacation to Turks and Caicos instead.

And yet.

Unlike me, she'd never walked down an aisle. She'd never been fed wedding cake or danced until there were blisters on her feet. If that was what she wanted, then I wasn't going to deny her the experience.

I wanted everyone to know how happy I was with Vanessa, but I didn't need a wedding to do it. I just wasn't sure if that was because this was still new to me or because I had heard loud and clear what Max thought—that a gay marriage isn't a *real* one.

I cannot explain why this even mattered. We weren't going to be asking Pastor Clive to officiate, after all. The people who would be invited to our wedding loved us and wouldn't be judging the fact that there were two tiny brides on the cake, instead of a bride and a groom.

But to get married, we had to cross the Rhode Island border. We had to find a minister who was supportive of gay marriage. Eventually we would have to hire a lawyer to draw up papers to give each other power of attorney for medical decisions, to become beneficiaries on each other's life insurance policies. I wasn't ashamed of wanting a lifetime with Vanessa. But I *was* ashamed that the steps I had to take in order to do it made me feel like a second-class citizen.

"I'm happy," I tell my mother, although I am bawling.

My mother looks at me. "What you need," she says, waving her hand dismissively at the bridal salon behind us, "is none of this. What you need is elegant and understated. Just like you and Vanessa."

We try three stores before we find it—a simple ivory, knee-length sheath that doesn't make me look like Cinderella. "I fell in love with your father during a fire drill," my mother says idly, as she fastens the buttons on the back. "We were both working at a law firm— he was an accountant and I was a secretary—and they evacuated the building. We met next to a chain-link fence, and he offered me half a Twinkie. When the building got the all clear, we didn't go back inside." She shrugs. "At his funeral, a lot of my friends said it was just bad luck that I fell for a guy who died in his forties, but you know, I never saw it that way. I thought it was *good* luck. I mean, what if there hadn't been a fire drill? Then we never would have met. And I'd much rather have had a few great years with him than none at all." She turns me so that I am facing her. "Don't let anyone tell you who you should and shouldn't love, Zoe. Yes, it's a gay wedding . . . but it's *your* wedding."

She turns me again so that I can see myself in the mirror. From the front, this could be any pretty, simple dress. But from the back, everything is different. A row of satin buttons gives way, at the waist, to a fan of pleats. It's as if the dress is opening like a rose.

As if someone watching me walk away might think, *That's not what I expected.*

I stare at myself. "What do you think?"

Maybe my mother is talking about the dress, and maybe she's talking about my future. "I think," she says, "you've found the perfect one."

———

When Lucy walks into our conference room, I am already picking out a melody on my guitar and humming along. "Hey there," I say, glancing up at her. Today her red hair is matted and twisted. "Trying for dreadlocks?"

She shrugs.

"I had a roommate in college who wanted dreads. She chickened out at the last minute because the only way to get rid of dreadlocks is to cut them all off."

"Well, maybe I'll just shave my head," Lucy says.

"You could do that," I agree, delighted that we are having what could almost be called a conversation. "You could be the next Sinéad O'Connor."

"Who?"

I realize that, when the bald musician ripped up a picture of the Pope on *Saturday Night Live* in 1992, Lucy wasn't even alive yet. "Or Melissa Etheridge. Did you see her perform at the Grammys when she was bald from chemo? She sang Janis Joplin."

I take out my pick and begin the chord progressions for "Piece of My

Heart." From the corner of my eye, I watch Lucy staring at my fingers as they move up and down the frets. "I remember hearing that performance and thinking how brave she was, as a cancer survivor . . . and how it was the perfect song. Suddenly it wasn't about a woman standing up to a guy—it was about beating anything that thought it could take you down." I play a thread of melody and then sing the next line: *"I'm gonna show you, baby, that a woman can be tough."*

With a strong chord I finish. "You know," I say, as if this thought has just occurred to me, instead of being a lesson I've planned all along, "the thing about lyrics is that they work really well when they connect personally to the musician—or the listener." I start playing the same melody again, but this time I improvise the words:

Didn't you ever feel like you were
    all alone, well yeah,
And didn't you ever feel that you
    were on your own.
Honey, you know you do.

Each time you tell yourself that
    you're out of luck
You wonder how you ever, ever
    got so stuck.
I want you to listen, listen, listen,
    listen already
Gotta know that I am ready to
    help you, Lucy.
Gonna show you I am ready to help
    you, Lucy—

Just as I am beginning to really rock out, Lucy snorts. "That is the lamest crap I've ever heard," she murmurs.

"Maybe you want to take a stab at it," I suggest, and I put the guitar down and reach for a pad and a pen instead. I write out the lyrics mad lib style, leaving gaps and spaces where Lucy can instead substitute her own thoughts and feelings.

Sometimes you make me feel like

_____.
Don't you know that I _____?

I do a fill-in-the-blank pattern like this for the entire song, and then set it on

the table between us. For a few minutes Lucy just ignores it, focusing instead on a tangled strand of her hair.
And then, slowly, her hand reaches out
and pulls the paper closer.

I try not to get too excited about the
fact that she's taken an active step toward participation. Instead, I pick up
my guitar and pretend to tune it, even
though I did this before Lucy arrived
today.

When she writes, she hunches over
the paper, as if she's protecting a secret. She's a lefty; I wonder why I haven't
noticed that before. Her hair falls over
her face like a curtain. Each of her fingernails is painted a different color.

At one point, her sleeve inches up
and I see the scars on her wrist.

Finally, she shoves the paper in my
direction. "Great," I say brightly. "Let's
take a look!"

In every blank, Lucy has written a
string of expletives. She waits for me to
look at her, and she raises her eyebrows
and smirks.

"Well." I pick up my guitar. "All right,
then." I put the paper on the table where

I can see it, and I begin to sing, certain that if anyone would understand anger and anguish it would be Janis Joplin, and that she won't be rolling over in her grave. *"Sometimes you make me feel like a motherfucking asshole,"* I sing, as loud as I can. *"Don't you know that I . . . cocksucker—"* I break off, pointing to the page. "I can't quite read that . . ."

Lucy blushes. "Uh . . . fucktard."

"Don't you know that I . . . cocksucker fucktard," I sing.

The door to the hallway is wide open. A teacher walks by and does a double take.

"Come on, come on, come on, come on and take it . . . Take a motherfucking shithole asswipe . . ."

I sing as if this is any song, as if the swear words mean nothing to me. I sing my heart out. And eventually, by the time I finish the chorus, Lucy is staring at me with the ghost of a smile playing over her lips.

Unfortunately, there is also a small crowd of students standing in the open doorway, caught on the tightrope between shocked and delighted. When I finish, they start clapping and hollering, and then the bell rings.

"Guess that's all the time we have," I say. Lucy slings her backpack over her shoulder and, like usual, makes a beeline to get as far away from me as possible. I reach for my guitar case, resigned.

But at the threshold of the door, she turns around. "See you next week," Lucy says, the first time she's acknowledged to me that she has any plan to return.

I know it's supposed to be good luck if it rains on your wedding, but I'm not sure what it means when there's a blizzard. It is the day of my wedding to Vanessa, and the freak April snowstorm the weathermen have predicted has taken a turn for the worse. The Department of Transportation has even closed patches of the highway.

We came to Fall River the night before, to get everything sorted out, but the majority of our guests were driving up today for the evening ceremony. After all, Massachusetts is less than an hour away. But today, even that seems too far.

And now, if a weather disaster isn't enough, there's a plumbing snafu, too. The pipes burst at the restaurant where we were planning to hold our reception. I watch Vanessa try to calm down her friend Joel—a wedding planner who took on our nuptials as his gift to us. "They've got three inches of standing water," Joel wails, sinking his head into his hands. "I think I'm hyperventilating."

"I'm sure there's somewhere that can hold a party on short notice," Vanessa says.

"Yeah. And maybe Ronald McDonald will even agree to officiate." Joel looks up sharply at Vanessa. "I have a repu-tation, you know. I will not, I repeat, *not* have French fries as an hors d'oeuvre."

"Maybe we should reschedule," Van-essa says.

"Or," I suggest, "we could just go to a justice of the peace and be done with it."

"Honey," Joel says. "You are not wasting that gorgeous peau de soie dress on a city hall wham-bam-stamp-you-ma'am wedding."

Vanessa ignores him and walks toward me. "Go on."

"Well," I say. "The party's the least important thing, isn't it?"

Behind me, Joel gasps. "I did not hear that," he says.

"I don't want everyone to drive up here and risk their lives," I say. "We've got Joel as a witness, and I'm sure we can drag in someone else off the street."

Vanessa looks at me. "But don't you want your mother here?"

"Sure I do. But more than that, I just want to get married. We've got the license. We've got each other. The rest, it's just gravy."

"Do me a favor," Joel begs. "Call your guests and leave it up to them."

"Should we tell them to bring their bathing suits for the reception?" Vanessa asks.

"Leave that part up to me," he says. "If David Tutera can fix a wedding catastrophe, so can I."

"Who the hell is David Tutera?" Vanessa asks.

He rolls his eyes. "Sometimes you are *such* a dyke." He takes her cell phone off the table and presses it into her hand. "Start calling, sister."

"The good news," my mother says, as she closes the bathroom door behind her, "is that you're still walking down an aisle."

It took her five hours, but she managed to make it to Massachusetts in the storm of the century. Now, she is keeping me company until it's show-time. It smells of popcorn in here. I look at myself in the wide industrial mirror. My dress looks perfect; my makeup seems too dramatic in this dim light. My hair, in this humidity, doesn't have a prayer of holding a curl.

"The minister's here," my mother tells me.

I know, because she already popped in to say hello to me. Maggie MacMillan is a humanist minister we found in the yellow pages. She's not gay, but she performs same-sex marriages all the time, and both Vanessa and I liked the fact that there wasn't a religious component to her ceremony. Frankly, after Max's visit, we'd both had about as much religion as we could stand. But she really sold us in her office by whooping with delight when we'd told her we'd be crossing the border to Massachusetts to get married. "I wish Rhode Island would get with the program," she'd said with a smirk. "But I suppose the legislature thinks if they give gays and lesbians civil rights, *everyone* in the state is going to want them . . ."

Joel sticks his head inside the door. "You ready?" he asks.

I take a deep breath. "Guess so."

"You know I tried to get you a gay magician for the reception, but it didn't work out," Joel says. "He vanished with a poof." He waits for me to get the punch line and then grins. "Works every time with a nervous bride."

"How's Vanessa doing?" I ask.

"Gorgeous," he says. "Almost as gorgeous as you."

My mom gives me a kiss on the cheek. "See you out there."

Vanessa and I made the decision to

walk down the aisle together. Neither of us has a father around to escort the bride, and this time, I didn't feel like I was being given away into someone's safekeeping. I felt like we were there to balance each other. So I follow Joel out of the women's room and wait while he gets Vanessa out of the men's room. She is wearing her white suit, and her eyes are bright and focused. "Wow," she says, staring at me. I see her throat working, as she tries to find words that are big enough for what we are feeling. Finally she reaches for my hands, and rests her forehead against mine. "I'm afraid that, any second now, I'm going to wake up," she whispers.

"Okay, lovebirds," Joel says, clapping his hands to interrupt us. "Save it for the guests."

"All four of them?" I murmur, and Vanessa snorts.

"I thought of another one," she says. "Rajasi."

We have been trading, for the past four hours, the names of people we think will brave the elements to celebrate our wedding with us. Possibly

Wanda, from the nursing home—she grew up in Montana and is used to blizzards. And Alexa, my office assistant—whose husband works for the DOT, and who could probably hijack a snowplow to get her here. It stands to reason that Vanessa's longtime hairdresser will probably be one of the guests waiting for us, too.

With my mom, that makes a whopping four people at our party.

Joel leads us through a tangle of gears and pulleys and equipment, past stacks of boxes and through a doorway. A short curtain has been set up, and Joel hisses a command: "Just follow the runner and be careful not to trip over the gutters . . . and, ladies, remember, you are *fabulous*." He kisses us on our cheeks, and then Vanessa reaches for my hand.

A string quartet begins to play. Together, Vanessa and I step onto the white runner and make the hard right turn at the edge of the curtain—the place where we step onto the aisle of the bowling alley we will be walking down, the place where the guests can see us.

Except there aren't four of them. There are nearly eighty. From what I can see, everyone we called earlier today—everyone we advised not to come in this treacherous weather—has made the trip to be here with us.

That's the first thing I notice. The second is that this AMC Lanes & Games bowling alley—the only spot in town that Joel could rent out completely on such short notice—doesn't even look like a bowling alley anymore. There are vines woven with lilies lining the gutters on either side of the aisle we're walking down. There are fairy lights strung overhead and on the walls. The automatic ball return is draped with white silk, and on it are frames with the faces of my father and both of Vanessa's parents. The pinball machines are draped in velvet and covered with appetizers and heaping bowls of fresh shrimp. The air hockey table sports a champagne fountain.

"What a quintessentially lesbian wedding," Vanessa says to me. "Who else would tie the knot in a room full of balls?"

We are still laughing when we reach the end of the makeshift aisle. Maggie's waiting, wearing a purple shawl edged with a rainbow of beading. "Welcome," she says, "to the blizzard of 2011 *and* the marriage of Vanessa and Zoe. I'm going to refrain from making any jokes about lucky strikes, and instead I'm going to tell you that they've come to honor their commitment to each other not only today but for all the tomorrows to come. We rejoice with them . . . and for them."

Maggie's words fade as I look at my mother's face, my friends' faces, and, yes, even the face of Vanessa's hairdresser. Then Vanessa clears her throat and begins to recite a Rumi poem:

The moment I heard my first love
    story I began seeking you, not
    realizing the search was useless.
Lovers don't meet somewhere
    along the way.
They're in one another's souls
    from the beginning.

When she is through, I can hear my mother sniffling. I pull out of my mind the ribbon of words I've memorized for Vanessa, an E. E. Cummings poem with syllables full of music.

> i carry your heart with me(i carry it
>   in
> my heart)i am never without
>   it(anywhere
> i go you go,my dear;and whatever
>   is done
> by only me is your doing,my
>   darling)
>   i fear
> no fate(for you are my fate,my
>   sweet)i want
> no world(for beautiful you are my
>   world,my true)
> and it's you are whatever a moon
>   has always meant
> and whatever a sun will always
>   sing is you

There are rings, and we are both crying, and laughing.

"Vanessa and Zoe," the minister says, "may you avoid splits and always play a perfect game. As you've pledged in this ceremony, in front of family and friends, to be partners for life, I can only say what's been said thousands of times before, at thousands of weddings . . ."

Vanessa and I both grin. It took us a long time to figure out how to end our ceremony. You can't very well say *I now pronounce you husband and wife.* By the same token, *I now pronounce you partners* sounds somehow lesser-than, not a true marriage.

Our minister smiles at us.

"Zoe? Vanessa?" she says. "You may kiss the bride."

Just in case you aren't sure that the Highlands Inn is lesbian-friendly after you call its phone number (877-LES-B-INN), there is a row of Adirondack chairs in all the colors of the rainbow set on a hilltop. It hasn't escaped my sense of irony that this little corner of open-minded paradise is set in Bethlehem, New Hampshire, that maybe this sleepy namesake town at the edge of the White

Mountains could be the birthplace of a new way of thinking.

After our wedding ceremony—which may have been the only ceremony in the world that has included both a chocolate–Grand Marnier ganache cake with real gold leaf *and* a midnight game of cosmic bowling in the dark— Vanessa and I wait out the storm to drive to our honeymoon destination. We have plans to cross-country ski, to go antiquing. But we spend nearly the first twenty-four hours of our honeymoon in our room—not fooling around, although there are lovely interludes of just that. Instead, we sit in front of the fireplace, drinking the champagne the inn owner has given us, and we talk. It seems impossible to me that we haven't exhausted our stories, but each one unfolds into another. I tell Vanessa things I have never even told my mother: about what my father looked like the morning he died; how I'd stolen his deodorant from the bathroom and kept it hidden in my underwear drawer for the next few years so that, when I needed his smell for comfort, I'd have it. I tell her how, five years ago, I found a bottle of gin in the toilet tank and I threw it out but never told Max I'd stumbled across it, as if not speaking of it would mean it hadn't really happened.

I sing the alphabet for her, backward.

And in return, Vanessa tells me about her first year of school counseling, about a sixth grader who confessed that her father was raping her, who ultimately was moved out of the school and the state by the same father, and who—periodically—Vanessa still tries to Google to see if she survived. She tells me about how, when she buried her mother, there was still a bitter, hard nut in her heart that hated this woman for never accepting Vanessa the way she was.

She tells me about the one and only time she tried pot in college, and wound up eating an entire large pepperoni pizza and a loaf of bread.

She tells me that she used to have nightmares about dying alone on the floor of her living room, and it being weeks before some neighbor noticed she hadn't left the house.

She tells me that her first pet was a hamster, which escaped in the middle of the night and ran into the radiator vent and was never seen again.

Sometimes, when we're talking, my head is on her shoulder. Sometimes her arms are around me. Sometimes we are at opposite ends of a couch, our legs tangled. When Vanessa had first given me the brochure for this place, I had balked—did we have to hide out with the other quarantined lesbian couples during our honeymoon? Why couldn't we just go to New York City, or the Poconos, or Paris, like any other newlyweds?

"Well," Vanessa had said, "we could. But there we *wouldn't* be like any other newlyweds."

Here, we *are*. Here, no one bats an eye if we're holding hands or checking into a room with a queen-size bed. We take a few excursions—to the Mount Washington Hotel for dinner, and to a movie theater—and each time we leave the grounds of this inn, I find us automatically putting a foot of space between us. And yet, the minute we come back home, we are glued at the hip.

"It's like tracking," Vanessa says, when we are sitting in the inn's dining room at a breakfast table one morning, watching a squirrel dance across a lip of ice on a stone wall. "I nearly got kicked out of graduate school for writing a paper that advocated separating students by ability. But you know what? Ask a kid who's struggling in math if he likes being in a mixed-level class, and he'll tell you he feels like a moron. Ask the math genius if he likes being in a mixed-level class, and he'll tell you he's sick of doing all the work during group projects. Sometimes, it's better to sort like with like."

I glance at her. "Careful, Ness. If GLAAD could hear you now, they'd strip you of your rainbow status."

She laughs. "I'm not advocating gay internment camps. It's just—well, you know, you grow up Catholic, and it's kind of nice when you make a joke about the Pope or talk about the Stations of the Cross and you don't get a blank stare back in return. There's something really nice about being with your *people.*"

"Full disclosure," I say. "I didn't know the cross had stations."

"I want my ring back," she jokes.

We are interrupted by the shriek of a toddler who has run into the breakfast room, nearly crashing into a waitress. His mothers are in hot pursuit. "Travis!" The boy giggles and looks over his shoulder before he ducks under our tablecloth, a human puppy.

"I'm sorry," one of the women says. She fishes him out, nuzzles his belly, and then swings him onto her back.

Her partner looks at us and grins. "We're still looking for his off switch."

As the family walks off toward the reception area, I watch that little boy, Travis, and I imagine what my own son would have looked like at his age. Would he have smelled of cocoa and peppermint; would his laugh sound like a cascade of bubbles? I wonder if he would be afraid of the monsters that live beneath his mattress, if I could sing him the courage to sleep through the night.

"Maybe," Vanessa says, "that will be us someday."

Immediately I feel it—that flush of utter failure. "You told me it didn't matter to you. That you have your students." Somehow I choke out the words. "You know I can't have kids."

"It didn't matter to me before because I never wanted to be a single mom. I saw enough of that when I was a kid. And of course I know you can't have babies." Vanessa threads her fingers through mine. "But Zoe," she says. "*I* can."

An embryo is frozen at the blastocyst stage, when it is approximately five days old. In a sealed straw filled with cryoprotectant fluid—a human antifreeze—it is gradually cooled to −196 degrees Celsius. The straw is then attached to an aluminum cane and stored in a canister of liquid nitrogen. It costs eight hundred dollars a year to keep the embryo frozen. When thawed at room temperature, the cryoprotectant fluid is diluted so that the embryo can be restored to its culture medium. It's assessed for damage to see if it's suitable for transfer. If the embryo survives mostly intact, it has a good chance of leading to a successful pregnancy. Cellular damage, if not extensive, is not a deal breaker. Some embryos have been frozen for a decade and still gone on to produce healthy children.

When I was undergoing in vitro, I always thought of the extra embryos we froze as snowflakes. Tiny, potential babies—each one a little different from the next.

According to a 2008 study in the journal *Fertility and Sterility,* when patients who didn't want more children were asked about their frozen embryos, fifty-three percent didn't want to donate them to others because they didn't want their children finding an unknown brother or sister one day; and they didn't want other parents raising their child. Sixty-six percent said they'd donate the embryos for research, but that option wasn't always available at clinics. Twenty percent said they'd keep the embryos frozen forever. Often, the husband and wife are not in agreement.

I have three frozen embryos, swimming in liquid nitrogen in a clinic in Wilmington, Rhode Island. And now that Vanessa has mentioned it, I cannot eat or drink or sleep or concentrate. All I can do is think of these babies, who are waiting for me.

Heads-up for all those activists out there trying so hard to prevent a constitutional amendment allowing gay marriage: nothing changes. Yes, Vanessa and I have a piece of paper that is now in a small fireproof safe in an envelope with our passports and social security cards, but that's about all that is different. We are still best friends. We still read each other the editorials in the morning paper, and we kiss good night before we turn out the lights. Or in other words, you can stop law, but you can't stop love.

The wedding was anticlimactic, a speed bump in the road of real life. But now that we are back home, it's life as usual. We get up, we get dressed, we go to work. Which for me proves a necessary distraction, because when I am alone I find myself staring at the paperwork from the fertility clinic that was a second home to me for five years, trying to gather the courage to make the call.

I know there is no logical reason to believe that all the medical complications I faced will affect Vanessa as well. She's younger than me; she's healthy. But the thought of putting her through what I went through—not the physical worries but the mental ones—is almost too much for me to handle. In this, I have a newfound respect for Max. The only thing harder than losing a baby, I think, is watching the person you love most in the world lose one.

So I am actually looking forward to occupying my thoughts with something else today—my next session with Lucy. After all, at our last meeting, when I belted out a string of curses, I got her smiling.

When she walks into our classroom, however, she isn't happy at all. Her burgeoning dreadlocks have been brushed out, and her hair is lank and unwashed. She has dark circles under her eyes, which are bloodshot. She is wearing black leggings and a ripped T-shirt and two different-colored Converse sneakers.

On her right wrist is a gauze pad, wrapped with what looks like duct tape.

Lucy doesn't make eye contact. She slings herself into a chair, pivots it so that it is facing away from me, and puts her head down on the desk.

I get up and close the door to the room. "You want to talk about it?" I ask.

She shakes her head, but doesn't lift it up.

"How did you get hurt?"

Lucy brings her knees up, curling into herself, the smallest ball.

"You know," I say, mentally ditching my lesson plan, "maybe we should just listen to some music together. And if you feel like it, you can talk." I walk toward my iPod, which is hooked up to a portable speaker, and scan through my playlists.

The first song I play is "Hate on Me,"

by Jill Scott. I want to find something that matches Lucy's mood, that brings her back to me.

She doesn't even twitch a response.

I move on to frenetic songs—the Bangles, Karen O. Spirituals. Even Metallica. When we reach our sixth song— "Love Is a Battlefield" by Pat Benatar— I finally admit defeat. "All right, Lucy. Let's call it a day." I hit the Pause button on the iPod.

"Don't."

Her voice is thin, thready. Her head is still tucked against her knees, her face hidden.

"What did you say?"

"Don't," Lucy repeats.

I kneel beside her and wait until she turns and looks at me. "Why not?"

Her tongue darts out, wets her lips. "That song. It's how my blood sounds."

With its driving bass and insistent percussion, I can see why she'd feel this way. "When I'm pissed off," I tell her, "this is what I play. Really loud. And I drum along to the beat."

"I hate coming here."

Her words cut through me. "I'm really sorry to hear—"

"The special ed room? Seriously? I'm already the school's biggest freak, and now everyone thinks I'm retarded, too."

"Mentally challenged," I correct automatically, and Lucy gives me the look of death.

"I think you need to play some percussion," I announce.

"And I think you need to go f——."

"That's enough." I grab her wrist—the one that isn't injured—and tug her to a standing position. "We're going on a field trip."

At first I am dragging her, but by the time we are headed down the hallway, she is tagging along willingly. We pass couples plastered to lockers, making out; we skirt four giggling girls who are bent over a phone, staring at the screen; we weave between the overstuffed lacrosse players in their team jerseys.

The only reason I even know where the cafeteria is, is because Vanessa's taken me there for coffee other times when I've been at the school. It looks like every other school cafeteria I've ever seen—a life-size petri dish breeding social discontent, students sorting themselves into individual genuses: the Popular Kids, the Geeks, the Jocks, the Emos. At Wilmington High the hot lunch line and kitchen are tucked behind the tables, so we march right down the center of the caf and up to the woman who is slinging mashed potatoes onto plates. "I'm going to need you to clear this area," I announce.

"Oh, you are," she says, and she raises a brow. "Who died and left you queen?"

"I'm one of the school therapists." This is not exactly true. I have no affiliation with the school. Which is why, when I get into trouble for doing this, it won't really be devastating. "Just a little ten-minute break."

"I didn't get a memo about this—"

"Look." I pull her aside and, in my best educator voice, say, "I have a suicidal girl here, and I'm doing some esteem building. Now, last time I checked, this school and every other school in the country had a suicide prevention initiative on the docket. Do you really want the superintendent to find out that you were impeding progress?"

I am completely bluffing. I don't even know the name of the superintendent. And Vanessa will either kill me when she hears I did this or congratulate me—I'm just not sure which.

"I'm going to get the principal," the woman huffs. Ignoring her, I move behind the counter and begin to grab hanging pots and pans and turn them over on the work surfaces. I gather ladles, spoons, spatulas.

"You're going to get reamed," Lucy says.

"I don't work for the school," I reply, shrugging. "I'm an outsider, too." I set up two drumming stations—one makeshift high hat (an overturned skillet), a snare (an overturned pot), and leave the metal server door at our feet to be the bass drum. "We're going to play the drums," I announce.

Lucy looks at the kids in the cafeteria—some of whom are watching us, most of whom are simply ignoring us. "Or not."

"Lucy, did you or did you not want to

get out of that awful special ed room? Get over here and stop arguing with me."

To my surprise, she actually does. "On the floor is our kick drum. Four beats, even. Kick it with your left foot, because you're a lefty." As I count off, I hit my boot against the metal doors of the serving table. "You try it."

"This is really stupid," Lucy says, but she tentatively kicks the metal, too.

"Great. That's four-four time," I tell her. "Now your snare is at your right hand." I hand her a metal spoon and point to the overturned pot. "Hit on beats two and four."

"For real?" Lucy asks.

As an answer, I play the next beat— eighth notes on the high hat: one-and-two-and-three-and-four. Lucy keeps up her rhythm, and with her left hand copies what I'm doing. "Don't stop," I tell her. "That's a basic backbeat." Over the cacophony I pick up two wooden spatulas and do a drum solo.

By now, the entire cafeteria is watching. A group of kids groove to a make-shift rap.

Lucy doesn't notice. She's pouring herself into the rhythm as it shimmies through her arms and her spine. I start singing "Love Is a Battlefield," the words raw, like flags ripping in a wind. Lucy can't take her eyes off me. I sing through one chorus, and then on the second, she joins in.

No promises. No demands.

She's grinning like mad, and I think that surely this breakthrough will be written up in the annals of music therapy—and then the principal walks into the cafeteria, flanked by the lunch lady on one side and Vanessa on the other.

My spouse doesn't look particularly happy, I might add.

I stop singing, stop banging the pots and pans.

"Zoe," Vanessa says, "what on earth are you *doing*?"

"My job." I take Lucy's hand and pull her in front of the serving station. She is absolutely mortified to be caught in the act. I hand the principal the spatula I've been drumming with and push past him without saying a word, until Lucy and I are facing the entire room of students. Quickly I raise our joined hands in a rock-band victory moment. "Thank you, Wilmington High!" I yell. "Peace out!"

Without another word—and with the stares of the principal and Vanessa boring into my back—Lucy and I ride out of the cafeteria to a round of applause and high fives. "Zoe," she says.

I drag her through unfamiliar halls of the school, intent on getting as far away from the administration as possible.

"Zoe—"

"I'm going to get fired," I mutter.

"Zoe," Lucy says. "Stop."

With a sigh, I turn to apologize. "I shouldn't have put you on the spot like that."

But then I see that the flush in her cheeks wasn't shame but excitement. Her eyes are sparkling, her smile infectious. "Zoe," she breathes. "Can we do that again?"

In spite of Wanda's warning, I am still a little taken aback to open the door of Mr. Docker's room at Shady Acres and find him shrunken and faded in his bed. Even when he was in one of his quiet, catatonic states before, he was able to be moved to a rocking chair or to the common room, but, according to Wanda, he hasn't left his bed in the two weeks since I've seen him. He hasn't spoken, either.

"Morning, Mr. Docker," I say, taking my guitar out of its case. "Remember me? Zoe? I'm here to play some music with you."

I have seen this before with some of my patients—especially those in hospice care. There's a cliff at the end point of a person's life; most of us peer over the edge of it, hanging on. That's why, when someone chooses to let go, it's so dramatically visible. The body will seem almost transparent. The eyes will be looking at something the rest of us can't see.

I start finger picking and humming, an impromptu lullaby. Today isn't the day to get Mr. Docker to engage. Today, music therapy is all about being the Pied Piper, taking him peacefully to the point where he can close his eyes and leave us all behind.

As I play wordlessly for Mr. Docker, I find myself tearing up. The old man was a cranky, bitter bastard, but it's the thorn in your side that leaves the biggest hole. I put down my guitar and reach for his hand. It feels like a bundle of sticks. His eyes, a rheumy blue, remain focused on the blank, black screen of the dormant television.

"I got married," I tell him, although I am sure he's not listening.

Mr. Docker doesn't budge.

"It's strange, isn't it, how we wind up in places we never would have imagined. I bet you never thought, when you were in your big corner office, that one day you'd be stuck here, in a room that overlooks a parking lot. You never imagined, when you were ordering everyone around, that one day there might not be someone to hear you. Well, I know what that's like, Mr. Docker." I look down at him, but he continues to stare straight ahead at nothing. "You fell in love once. I know you did, because you've got a daughter. So you know what I mean when I say that I don't think anyone who falls in love has a choice. You're just pulled to that person like true north, whether it's good for you or bound to break your heart."

When I was married to Max, I mistook being a lifeline for being in love. I was the one who could save him; I was the one who could keep him sober. But there is a difference between mending someone who's broken and finding someone who makes you complete.

I don't say it out loud, but this is how I know that Vanessa will not hurt me: she cares more about my well-being than she does about her own. She'd break her *own* heart before causing even the smallest hairline fracture in mine.

This time when I glance down, Mr. Docker is looking right at me. "We're going to have a baby," I tell him.

The smile starts deep inside of me, like a pilot light, and fans the flames of possibility.

Saying it out loud, it's suddenly real.

————————

Vanessa and I are standing at the reception window of the fertility clinic. "Baxter," I say. "We've got a meeting to discuss a frozen embryo transfer?"

The nurse finds my name on her computer. "There you are. Did you bring your husband today, too?"

I feel my face flush. "I'm remarried. When I called, you said I needed to come in with my spouse."

The nurse looks up at me, and then at Vanessa. If she's surprised, her face doesn't register it at all. "Just wait here," she says.

Vanessa looks at me as soon as she leaves her desk. "What's the problem?"

"I don't know. I hope there's nothing wrong with the embryos . . ."

"Did you read that article about the family that was given the wrong embryos?" Vanessa asks. "I mean, God, can you imagine?"

I shoot her a pointed look. "*Not* helping."

"Zoe?" At the sound of my name, I turn to find Dr. Anne Fourchette, the clinic director, walking toward me. "Why don't you two come into my office?"

We follow her down the hall to the paneled, posh space that I must have been in before but have no recollection of seeing prior to this. Most of my visits were in treatment rooms. "Is there a problem, Dr. Fourchette? Did you lose them?"

She is a striking woman with a fall of prematurely white hair, a bone-crushing handshake, and a drawl that extends my name by three or four extra syllables. "I'm afraid there was a misunderstanding," she says. "Your ex-husband has to sign off on the release of the embryos. Once he does that, we can schedule a transfer."

"But Max doesn't want them. He *divorced* me because he didn't want to be a father."

"Then it's really all academic," Dr. Fourchette replies brightly. "It's a legal technicality we need to cover before we can schedule your appointment with a social worker."

"Social worker," Vanessa repeats.

"It's something we routinely do with same-sex couples, to address some of the issues that you might not have considered. If your partner has the baby, for example, Zoe, then once he's born, you'll have to formally adopt him."

"But we're married—"

"Not according to the state of Rhode Island." She shakes her head. "Again, it's nothing to worry about. We just have to get the ball rolling."

That familiar wave of disappointment floods me; once again this baby track is full of hurdles.

"All right," Vanessa says briskly. "Is there something Max has to sign? Some form?"

Dr. Fourchette hands her a sheet of paper. "Just have him send it back to us, and as soon as we get it, we'll call you." She smiles at us. "And I'm really happy for you, Zoe. Congratulations to you both."

Vanessa and I don't speak until we are outside the clinic, riding down together in an otherwise empty elevator. "You have to talk to him," she says.

"And say what? *Hey, I'm married to Vanessa and we'd like you to be our sperm donor?*"

"It's not like that," Vanessa points

out. "The embryos already exist. What plans does *he* have for them?"

The doors slide open on the ground floor. A woman is waiting, with a baby in a stroller. The baby is wearing a white, hooded sweater with little bear ears sticking up.

"I'll try," I say.

I find Max at a client's house, raking out mulch and twigs from the flower beds in preparation for spring landscaping. The snow has melted as quickly as it arrived, and it smells like spring. Max is wearing a shirt and tie, and he's sweating. "Nice place," I say appreciatively, looking around the grounds of this McMansion.

Max wheels at the sound of my voice. "Zoe? What are you doing here?"

"Liddy told me where to find you," I say. "I was wondering if you've got a minute to talk?"

He leans on the rake and wipes the perspiration from his forehead, nods. "Sure. You want to, uh, sit down?" He gestures to a stone bench in the center of a hibernating garden. The granite is cold through the fabric of my jeans.

"What's it like?" I ask. "When it's blooming, I mean?"

"Oh, it's pretty awesome, actually. Tiger lilies. They should be up by the end of April, if I can keep the beetles off of them."

"I'm glad you're still doing landscaping. I wasn't sure."

"Why wouldn't I be doing it?"

"I don't know." I shrug. "I thought you might be working for your church."

"Well, on Mondays I do," he says. "They're one of my clients." He rubs his jaw with his fist. "I saw a sign outside a bar, saying you'd be singing. You haven't performed since before we got . . . well, for a long time."

"I know—I sort of fell back into it." I hesitate. "You weren't *at* the bar . . . ?"

"No." Max laughs. "I'm cleaner than soap these days."

"Good. I mean, that's really good. And, yeah, I've been doing a little singing here and there. Acoustically. It keeps me on my toes for my therapy sessions."

"So you're still doing that."

"Why wouldn't I be?"

He shakes his head. "I don't know. A lot about you has . . . changed."

It is so strange, to encounter an ex. It's as if you're in a foreign film, and what you're saying face-to-face has nothing to do with the subtitles flowing beneath you. We are so careful not to touch, although once upon a time, I slept plastered to him in our bed, like lichen on a rock. We are two strangers who know every shameful secret, every hidden freckle, every fatal flaw in each other.

"I got married," I blurt out.

Since Max hasn't been paying me alimony, there's really no reason he would have known. For a second he looks completely baffled. Then his eyes widen. "You mean, you and . . . ?"

"Vanessa," I say. "Yes."

"Wow." Max shifts, sliding centimeters away from me on the stone bench. "I, uh, didn't realize it was so . . . real."

"Real?"

"Serious, I mean. I figured it was

some fling you had to get out of your system."

"You mean the same way you were a casual drinker?" As soon as I say the words, I regret them. I'm supposed to be here to win Max over to my side, not to antagonize him. "I'm sorry. That was uncalled for."

Max looks like he's about to be sick. "I'm glad you told me face-to-face. It would have been really tough to hear that through the grapevine."

For a moment, I almost feel sorry for him. I can only imagine the flak he'll get from his new church buddies about me. "There's more," I say, swallowing. "Vanessa and I want to start a family. Vanessa's young and healthy, and there's no reason she can't have a baby."

"I can think of a pretty major one," Max says.

"Well, actually, that's why I'm here." I take a deep breath. "It would mean a lot to us if the baby Vanessa had was biologically mine. And there are three embryos left over from when you and I were trying. I'd like your permission to use them."

Max's head snaps up. "What?"

"I know this is a lot to take in at once—"

"I told you I don't want to be a father . . ."

"And I'm not asking you to. No strings attached, Max. We'll sign anything you want to guarantee that. We're not expecting you to support a baby in any way—not with money, or with your name, nothing. You won't have any obligations or responsibilities to the baby, if we're lucky enough to have one." I meet his gaze. "These embryos—they already exist. They're just waiting. For how long? Five years? Ten? Fifty? Neither of us wants them destroyed, and you've already said you don't want kids. But I do. I want them so bad that it hurts."

"Zoe—"

"This is my last chance. I'm too old to go through in vitro again to harvest more eggs with an anonymous sperm donor." With a shaking hand I pull the form from the clinic out of my purse. "Please, Max? I'm begging you."

He takes the piece of paper but

doesn't look at it. He doesn't look at *me.* "I . . . I don't know what I'm supposed to say."

You do, I realize. *You just won't say it.*

"Think about it?" I ask.

He nods, and I stand up. "I really appreciate this, Max. I know this wasn't what you expected." I take a step back. "I, um, guess I'll call you. Or you call me."

He nods, then folds the paper in half and half again, and tucks it into his back pocket. I wonder if he will even look at it. If he'll tear it up in little pieces and rake it into the dirt. If he'll send it through the wash in his jeans so that he cannot read the words anymore.

I start walking down to the curb, where I've left my car, but I am stopped by Max's voice. "Zoe," he calls out. "I still pray for you, you know."

I face him. "I don't need your prayers, Max," I say. "Just your consent."

	TRACK 1	SING YOU HOME
	TRACK 2	THE HOUSE ON HOPE STREET
	TRACK 3	REFUGEE
	TRACK 4	THE LAST
	TRACK 5	MARRY ME
✓	**TRACK 6**	**FAITH**
	TRACK 7	THE MERMAID
	TRACK 8	ORDINARY LIFE
	TRACK 9	WHERE YOU ARE
	TRACK 10	SAMMY'S SONG

MAX

Sometimes God just plain pisses me off.

I am the first to tell you that I'm not always the brightest crayon in the box, and that I would never assume I could know what the Lord has up His sleeve, but there are situations where it's really hard to figure out what He's thinking at all.

Like when you hear about a bunch of kids being killed in a school shooting.

Or when there's a hurricane that wipes out an entire community.

Or when Alison Gerhart, a sweet twenty-something who went to Bob Jones University and who had the prettiest soprano in the church choir and who never smoked a day in her life was diagnosed with lung cancer and dead in a month.

Or when Ed Emmerly, a deacon at Eternal Glory, lost his job just when his son needed a pricey spinal surgery.

Since Zoe's unexpected visit, I've been praying over what's the right thing to do here, but it's not a matter of black or white. We're in agreement about one thing: to us, those are not just frozen cells in that clinic; they're potential children. Maybe we both believe this for very different reasons—mine religious and hers personal—but either way, we don't want to see those embryos flushed down a drain. I've been putting off the inevitable by agreeing to keep them frozen, suspended in limbo. Zoe wants to give them the chance at life every baby deserves.

Even Pastor Clive would side with her on that.

But he'd probably go ballistic if I told him that this future baby was going to spend its life with two lesbian mothers.

On the one hand, I have God remind-ing me that I can't destroy a potential life. But what kind of life is it to subject an innocent child to a gay household? I mean, I've read the literature that Pastor Clive's given me, and it's clear to me (and to the scientists who are quoted) that being gay is not biological but environmental. You know how gays reproduce, don't you? Since they can't very well do it the biblical way, they recruit. It's why the Eternal Glory Church fights so hard against allowing gay teachers in schools—those poor kids don't have a snowball's chance in Hell at not being corrupted.

"Afternoon, Max," I hear, and I look up to see Pastor Clive coming in from the parking lot, carrying a bakery box. He doesn't smoke or drink, but he has a real weakness for cannoli. "Care to share a piece of gustatory paradise from Federal Hill?"

"No thanks." The sun, behind his head, gives him a halo. "Pastor Clive, have you got a minute?"

"Sure. Come on inside," he says.

I follow him past the church secretary, who offers me a Hershey's Kiss from a bowl on her desk, and into his office. Pastor Clive cuts the strings tied around the bakery box with a hunting knife he keeps on a loop of his belt and lifts one of the pastries. "Still can't be tempted?" he asks, and, when I shake my head, he licks the cream from one end. "This," he says, his mouth full, "is how I know there's a God."

"But God didn't make those cannoli. Big Mike did, down at Scialo Brothers."

"And God made Big Mike. It's all a matter of perspective." Pastor Clive wipes his mouth with a napkin. "What's weighing you down today, Max?"

"My ex-wife just told me that she's married to a woman and she wants to use *our* embryos to have a baby." I want to rinse my mouth out. Shame tastes bitter.

Pastor Clive slowly puts down his cannoli. "I see," he says.

"I've been praying. I know the baby deserves to live. But not . . . not like that." I look down at the ground. "I may not be able to keep Zoe from going to Hell on Judgment Day, but I'm not going to let my kid be dragged down with her."

"Your kid," Pastor Clive repeats. "Max, don't you see? You said it yourself—this is *your* baby. This may be Jesus's way of telling you it's time for you to take responsibility for those embryos, lest they wind up in your ex-wife's control."

"Pastor Clive," I say, panicking. "I'm not cut out to be a father. Look at me. I'm a work in progress."

"We're *all* works in progress. But being responsible for that baby's life doesn't necessarily mean what you think. What would you wish most for that child?"

"To grow up with a mom and a dad who love him, I guess. And who can give him everything he needs . . ."

"And who are good Christians," Pastor Clive adds.

"Well, yeah." I look up at him. "A couple like Reid and Liddy."

Pastor Clive comes around the desk and sits on the edge of it. "Who have been trying for years to be blessed with a child of their own. You've been praying for your brother and sister-in-law, haven't you?"

"Of course I have—"

"You've been asking God to bless them with a baby." I nod. "Well, Max. When God closes a door, it's only because He's opened a window."

Only once in my life have I had the same kind of parting-of-the-clouds-so-the-sun-shines-through moment as I have right now—and that was when I was in the hospital and Pastor Clive helped me clear away the smoke and bullshit to see Jesus, close enough for me to touch if I reached out. But now I see that the reason Zoe came to me today was because God has a plan for me. If I am not capable of raising this baby on my own, at least I know he'll be cared for by my own flesh and blood.

This baby is my family, and that's where he belongs.

"There's something I need to talk to you two about," I say at dinner that night, as Reid passes me a platter of scalloped potatoes. "I want to give you something."

Reid shakes his head. "Max, I've told you. You don't owe us anything."

"I do. I owe you my life, if you want to get technical about it, but that's not what I'm talking about," I say.

I turn to Liddy. Weeks after the miscarriage, she still looks like a ghost. Just the other day I found her sitting in her parked car in the garage, staring out the windshield at a row of shelves that held power tools and paint. I asked her where she was going, and she jumped a foot, she was so surprised to see me. *I have no idea,* she said, and she looked down at herself as if she was wondering how she got there in the first place.

"You can't have a baby," I state.

Liddy's eyes fill with tears, and Reid is quick to interrupt. "We can, and we will, have a baby. We've just been expecting it to happen on *our* timeline instead of God's. Isn't that right, honey?"

"And I've got a baby I can't have," I continue. "When Zoe and I got divorced, there were still three frozen embryos left at the clinic. Zoe wants to use them.

But I think . . . I think they should go to you two."

"What?" Liddy breathes.

"I'm not father material. I can barely take care of myself, much less some- one else. But you guys—you deserve to have a family. I can't imagine a bet- ter life for a kid than living here with you." I hesitate. "In fact, I've experi- enced it."

Reid shakes his head. "No. Five years from now, you'll be back on your feet. Maybe even married—"

"You wouldn't be taking my kid away from me," I say. "I'd still be Uncle Max. I'd still get to take him out surfing. Teach him how to drive. All that stuff."

"Max, this is crazy—"

"No it's not. You're already looking into adoption," I say. "I saw the bro- chures on the kitchen counter. This is the same thing—Pastor Clive says that embryo adoption happens all the time. But this embryo, it's related to you."

I can tell, that gets to my brother. We both look at Liddy at the same time.

There's a piece of me that's selfish here, I've got to admit. A woman like

Liddy—pretty, smart, religious—she's everything a guy could want, everything I'll probably never have. She's stuck by me throughout the years, even when Reid got frustrated with me for not living up to my potential, or for just plain ruining my life. If Liddy gets pregnant after the embryos are transferred, it will be her baby—hers and Reid's—but I have to confess that I like the thought of being the one who can bring a smile back to her face.

God knows I wasn't able to do that with my own wife.

Liddy, though, doesn't look happy. She looks terrified. "What if I lose this one, too?"

It's a possibility; it always is when you are doing in vitro. But there are no guarantees in life, period. The baby who's born completely healthy could sleep the wrong way and suffocate. The triathlete could drop dead because of a congenital heart defect he never knew about. The girl you thought you loved could fall in love with someone else. Yeah, Liddy might miscarry. But what are the alternatives here? That the baby

remains an ice cube for the next decade or two? That it's born to two
women who choose to live in sin?

Reid looks at Liddy with so much
hope in his eyes that I turn away, embarrassed. "What if you don't?" he
says.

Suddenly I'm on the outside of a window looking in. A Peeping Tom, an ob-
server instead of a player.

But that baby. That baby, he won't
be.

That night I am brushing my teeth in
the guest bathroom when Reid comes
to stand in the doorway. "You can
change your mind," he says, and I don't
pretend to not know what he's talking
about.

I spit out the toothpaste, wipe my
mouth. "I'm not going to."

Reid looks uncomfortable, shifting
from one foot to the other. His hands
are in his trouser pockets. He barely
even looks like the man I know—the
one who is always in control of a situation, the one whose charm is matched

only by his brains. I realize, with a start, that, although Reid is a golden boy who seems to do everything right the first time around, I've just found something he's not good at.

Gratitude.

He'll give you the shirt off his back, but when it comes to accepting some good old-fashioned assistance for himself, he is at a loss.

"I don't know what to say," Reid admits.

When we were little, Reid made up a secret language, with a vocabulary book and everything. Then he taught it to me. At the dinner table, he'd say, *Mumu rabba wollabang,* and I would burst out laughing. My mother and father would just look at each other, baffled, because they didn't know that Reid had just said that the meat loaf smelled like monkey butt. It drove my parents crazy, the way we could communicate outside the boundaries of normal conversation.

"You don't have to say anything," I tell him. "I already know."

Reid nods, and pulls me into an embrace. He's fighting tears, I can tell by his breathing. "I love you, little brother," he murmurs.

I close my eyes. *I believe in you. I'm praying for you. I want to help you.* Reid has said many things to me over the years, but it's only now that I realize how long I've waited to hear him say this.

"I already know that, too," I reply.

Mrs. O'Connor's made doughnuts. She does it the old-fashioned way, frying them up, and sprinkling a little bit of sugar over them. I always look for her name on the church office bulletin board sign-up sheet, to see when she's bringing a snack to the fellowship coffee after the service. You can bet I'm the first one out of the auditorium sanctuary, so that I get to that platter before the Sunday School kids do.

I've loaded up my plate with more than is my fair share when I hear Pastor Clive's voice. "Max," he says, "I should have known we'd find you here."

I turn around, a doughnut already

stuffing my mouth. The pastor is stand-ing next to a newcomer, or at least I think he is a newcomer. He's taller than Pastor Clive and has black hair slicked back with some kind of oil or mousse. His tie is the same color as his pocket square—pinkish, like smoked salmon. I have never seen teeth so white in my life.

"Ah," he says, reaching for my hand. "The infamous Max Baxter."

Infamous? What have I done now?

"Max," the pastor says, "this is Wade Preston. Maybe you recognize him from TV?"

I shake my head. "Sorry."

Wade laughs big and loud. "Gotta get me a better publicist! I'm an old friend of Clive's. We went to seminary together."

He has a Southern accent that makes his words sound like they're swimming underwater. "So you're a pastor, too?"

"I'm a lawyer and a good Christian," Wade says. "As much as that sounds like an oxymoron."

"Wade's being modest," Pastor Clive explains. "He's a voice for the pre-born.

In fact, he's made it his life's mission to ensure their rights and to protect them. He's very interested in your case, Max."

What case?

I don't realize I've said that out loud until Wade Preston answers. "Clive tells me you're going to file to keep your lesbian ex-wife from getting her hands on your child."

I look at Pastor Clive, and then around the room to see if Reid and Liddy have entered yet, but I'm on my own here.

"What you need to know, Max, is that you're not alone," Wade says. "It's the *gay-by boom:* homosexuals are trying to pervert the notion of a family as being anything other than a mother and a father in a loving Christian household. My goal is to do for adoptions what the Defense of Marriage Act does for the sanctity of *that* sacrament—namely, to keep innocent children from being victimized." He puts his arm around my shoulders, steering me away from a clot of church hens who have come to the coffee urn. "You know how I found Jesus, Max? I was ten years old and stuck in summer school because I failed

fourth grade. And my teacher, Mrs. Percival, asked if anyone wanted to stay
with her during recess to pray. Well, let
me tell you, I couldn't have cared less
about religion at the time. All I wanted
was to be the teacher's pet so that I
could be the first one in line for snack
that day, because we got served cookies, and there were never enough chocolate ones to go around, and the vanilla
ones tasted like—pardon my French—
ass. I figured I'd say a few silly prayers
with her and I'd cut to the front of that
snack line.

"Sure enough, I listened to her Je-
sus-this and Jesus-that. I pretended to
go along with it, but the whole time I
was thinking of those cookies. When it
came time for snack, Mrs. Percival let
me be the line leader. I raced to the
snack table, but I might as well have
been flying there, I was so light on my
feet. And I looked at the tray, and there
wasn't a single chocolate cookie on it."

I glance down at my plate of doughnuts.

"Here's the incredible part, Max. I
picked up one of those vanilla cookies,

which were probably baked out of cardboard and donkey crap, and I took a big ol' bite, and it was the most delicious thing I'd ever eaten. It tasted like chocolate and Christmas morning and winning the World Series, all wrapped up into one little dollop of dough. And that's the moment I realized that Jesus was with me, even when I didn't expect it."

"You got saved over a cookie?" I ask.

"Yes, I did. And you know how I know for sure? Because since that moment in Mrs. Percival's remedial summer class, I have been in a car accident that killed every other passenger but myself. I've survived spinal meningitis. I've graduated at the top of my law school class at Ole Miss. I've sailed through life, Max, and I am smart enough to know I'm not the captain of my own ship, if you get my drift. And because God's been looking out for me, I believe it's my Christian duty to look out for those who can't look out for themselves. I've been admitted to practice law in nineteen states," Wade says. "I'm active with the Snowflakes Frozen

Embryo Adoption program—you've heard of it?"

Only because Pastor Clive told Reid and Liddy about it, after the last miscarriage. It's a Christian adoption agency that starts before the baby is born and lets people who've been through IVF match their extra embryos with families who need them.

"What I'm trying to tell you," he says smoothly, "is that I've got the experience local counsel might not have. There are men all over the country—men like you—who try to do everything right and who still find themselves in this horrible situation. You've been saved. Now it's up to you to save your children." He looks directly into my eyes. "And I'm here to help."

I don't know what to say. I got a voice mail on my phone from Zoe yesterday. She just wanted to know if I'd signed the paper yet. If I wanted to talk more, meet for coffee, ask her any questions.

I kept her message. Not because of what she was asking but because of her voice. She wasn't singing, but there

was a rise and fall to her words that
made me think of music.

The thing is, I've already fucked up
again. I don't really want to tell Zoe I've
come to a decision, but I have to. And
something tells me she'll be about as
thrilled to have her babies raised by
Liddy and Reid as I am to have mine
raised by two dykes.

Wade Preston reaches into the pocket
inside his suit jacket and pulls out his
card. "Why don't we meet next week?"
he suggests. "We have a lot to discuss
to get this ball rolling." As Pastor Clive
leads him away to meet some of the
other congregants, he flashes that mil-
lion-dollar smile at me again.

I have six doughnuts on my plate,
and I don't even want to eat one anymore. I feel sick, actually.

Because the truth is: the ball's been
set in motion.

It's halfway down the hill already.

The night before I am supposed to meet
Wade Preston at Pastor Clive's office—
he thought we might appreciate the

privacy—I have a dream. Liddy is pregnant already, and, instead of just Reid
being in the delivery room, there are
dozens of people, all wearing hospital
scrubs and blue masks. You can't make
out who anyone is, except for their
eyes.

Pastor Clive is sitting between Liddy's
legs and acting as the doctor. He
reaches down to catch the baby. "You're
doing great," he tells her as she
screams, pushing this bloody mess of
baby into the world.

A nurse takes the baby and swaddles
it, and when she does she gasps. She
calls over Pastor Clive, who looks into
the folds of the blue blanket and says,
"Sweet Jesus."

"What's wrong?" I ask, pushing
through the crowd. "What's the matter?"

But they don't hear me. "Maybe she
won't notice," the nurse whispers, and
she hands Liddy the baby. "Here's your
son," she coos.

Liddy lifts up the corner of the blanket draping the newborn and starts to

shriek. She nearly drops the baby, and I rush forward to pick him up.

That's when I see it: he has no face.

Instead there's just a mottled oval of lumps and boils, a seam where a mouth should have been.

"I don't want it!" Liddy cries. "He's not really mine!"

One of the masked observers steps forward. She takes the baby from me and begins to pinch the flesh into false features—a hill of a nose, two thumb-print eyes—as if the baby is made of clay. She gazes down as if it is the most beautiful thing she has ever seen. "There," she says. She pulls off her mask and smiles, and that's when I see it is Zoe.

I'm sweating when I walk into Pastor Clive's office to meet with Wade, so much that I've nearly soaked through my shirt, and I'm figuring he'll think either I'm a freak or I have some weird metabolic disorder, when in fact I'm just a little scared to tell him what I've been thinking all morning.

Namely, that I may be making a mistake. Sure, I want to help Liddy and Reid . . . but I don't want to hurt Zoe.

Wade's wearing another perfectly tailored suit, this one with a faint silver shine to it that makes him look the way Jesus always does in paintings—glowing, a little brighter than everyone else around Him.

"It's good to see you, Max," Wade says, pumping my hand up and down. "I gotta tell you, since I talked with you on Sunday, you've been at the forefront of my mind."

"Oh," I say. "Well."

"Now, we've got a lot of background to cover, so I'm just going to ask you questions, and you do your best to answer them."

"Can I ask you one first?" I say.

He looks up, nods. "Absolutely."

"It's not so much of a question, really. It's more of a statement. I mean, I know I have a right to decide what happens to these embryos. But Zoe does, too."

Wade sits down on the edge of Pastor Clive's desk. "You are a hundred percent right, at least when you look at this issue superficially. You and Zoe both have an equal gametic claim to these embryos. But let me ask you this: Did you intend to raise these pre-born children in a heterosexual relationship with your ex-wife?"

"Yeah."

"Yet, unfortunately, your marriage didn't last."

"That's exactly it," I burst out. "Nothing worked out the way we planned. And finally, she seems to be happy. It may not be what *I'd* do, or what *you'd* do, but why should I ruin that for her? I always believed she'd be a good mom. And she's said that I don't have to pay child support—"

"Whoa." Wade holds up a hand. "Let's unpack this a bit. First of all, if you did give Zoe the pre-born children, you're still the father. These little people, they already exist, Max. You can't remove your biological responsibility to them. So even if they're raised in this lesbian household, you're going to be on the hook for child support. And even if your ex-wife doesn't ask for it now, at any point in that child's life he can come back to you saying he needs financial or emotional support. Zoe may say you don't have to have a relationship with this baby, but that's not her decision to make." He folds his arms. "Now you say your ex-wife would make a good parent—and I have no doubt that's true. What about your brother and sister-in-law?"

I look at Pastor Clive. "They'd be the best parents I could ever imagine."

"And what about your wife's lesbian lover?"

"I don't know very much about her—"

"Except for the fact that she wants to take your children away from you," Wade points out.

Here's all I know about Vanessa: I had a wife, a wife who loved me and made love with me, and now all of a sudden she's sleeping with some woman who seduced her.

Pastor Clive walks toward an over-size Bible on a lectern and starts reading aloud:

"Because of this, God gave them over to shameful lusts. Even their women exchanged natural relations for

unnatural ones. In the same way the men also abandoned natural relations with women and were inflamed with lust for one another. Men committed indecent acts with other men and received in themselves the due penalty for their perversion.

"That's what God has to say about homosexuals in Romans 1:26–27," the pastor says. "Homosexuality—it's a perversion. Something to be punished for."

"What if that pre-born child is a little boy, Max?" Wade asks. "You realize he has an overwhelming chance of becoming homosexual himself if you let him be raised by two lesbians. Frankly, even if Zoe is the Mother of the Year, who's going to be the daddy in that household? How's your son going to learn how to be a man?"

I shake my head. I don't have an answer for that. If the baby goes to Reid and Liddy, he'll have a great father figure. The same one I've looked up to my whole life.

"The best parental decision you can make," Wade says, "even if it's the *only* parental decision you make—is to ask yourself what's really best for your child."

I close my eyes.

"I understand from Pastor Clive that you and Zoe lost a number of babies while you were trying to get pregnant," Wade says. "Including one that was nearly at term."

I can feel my throat tighten. "Yes."

"How did you feel when he died?"

I press my thumbs into the corners of my eyes. I don't want to cry. I don't want them to see me crying. "It hurt like hell."

"If you felt that way about losing one child," Wade asks, "how are you going to feel about losing three more?"

I'm sorry, I think, and I don't even know who I'm apologizing to anymore. "Okay," I mutter.

"I beg your pardon?"

"Okay," I repeat, looking up at Wade. "What do we do next?"

Liddy is in the kitchen when I come home from my meeting. She's baking a blueberry pie, even though blueberries are totally out of season. It's my favorite.

She's making her own crust, too. Zoe never made her own crust. She said it was pointless, when Pillsbury had already put all that hard work into it.

"It's called *pro hac vice,*" I explain. "It means that Wade Preston is an out-of-state attorney who's allowed to represent me because of the experience he has in the field."

"So you have *two* lawyers?" Liddy asks.

"I guess. I haven't met this Ben Benjamin guy yet, but Wade says he knows the judges in the state and can help come up with the best strategy. He used to clerk for Judge O'Neill, and there's a chance he can even get the case in front of him."

Liddy leans into the countertop, rolling the dough between two sheets of plastic wrap. The ball flattens into a perfect circle, which she flips into a ceramic pie plate. "It sounds complicated."

"Yeah, but they know what they're

doing." I don't want her worrying about this. I want her to believe it's all going to happen just the way she wants. A positive frame of mind is just as important as any reproductive plumbing when it comes to pregnancy. At least that's what Zoe's OB used to say.

Liddy spoons the filling—there are berries in there, which she's tried to keep me from swiping—and some sugar and that white powdery crap that's not flour—into the crust. She puts a few pats of butter on top. Then she takes the second ball of dough out of the fridge so that she can roll the top crust.

She lifts up the Saran Wrap and pulls the sheet out. But instead of rolling, she jackknifes, leaning on the counter and covering her face with her hands.

She's sobbing.

"Liddy? What's wrong?"

She shakes her head, waving me off.

I start to panic. I ought to call Reid. I ought to call 911.

"I'm fine, Max," she chokes. "Honestly."

"You're *crying*!"

She looks up at me. Her eyes are the color of sea glass, the kind you find on the beach and keep in your pocket. "Because I'm happy. You've made me so unbelievably happy."

It doesn't make sense to me, but neither does the way I feel when she leans against me for a second. She gives me a quick hug and then moves back to the pie, rolling the pastry dough as if the world has not just shifted on its axis.

Ben Benjamin has little round glasses and a mouth pursed like a funnel. He's sitting across from me in the church office conference room writing down everything I say, as if there's going to be a quiz later. "How did you divide your assets?" he asks.

"We just kind of split everything."

"What do you mean?"

"Well, Zoe took the musical instruments, and I took my landscaping equipment. We said we'd each take care of our own debt. We didn't have a house or anything."

"Did you address the issue of the embryos in your final judgment?"

"Well, no. It wasn't like they were property."

Wade leans forward, hands clasped. "Of course not. They're *people*."

Ben makes a note on his pad. "So while you were representing yourselves during the divorce, the two of you just made an honest mistake. You forgot to talk about those little . . . people . . . in their frozen time capsules during the divorce decree. Right?"

"I guess so," I say.

"No, you *know* so," Ben corrects. "Because that's how we're going to open this up. You didn't realize this needed to be addressed during the divorce, so we bring it back to family court again by filing an action."

"What if Zoe files one first?" I ask.

"Believe me," Wade says, "the clinic isn't going to make a single move without having consent from both of you— or a court order. In fact, I'm going to give counsel for the clinic a call just to make sure of it."

"But even if we go to court, won't the

judge think I'm scum for wanting to give my babies away? I mean, Zoe wants them for herself."

"That's a compelling argument," Ben agrees, "except you both have an equal biological claim to the embryos—"

"Pre-born children," Wade interrupts.

Ben glances up. "Right. The children. You have just as much right to say what happens to them as your ex-wife does. Even if you wanted to have them destroyed—"

"Which he doesn't," Pastor Clive says.

"No, but if you did, the court would have to consider your legal right to do so."

"The court cares about *the best interests of the children*," Wade adds. "You've heard that term. And the choices here are a traditional Christian family or a unit that doesn't even come close to approximating that definition."

"We'll have your brother and sister-in-law testify. They're going to be a very central part of this trial," Ben says.

I run my thumbnail along a groove in the table. Last night, Liddy and Reid had been online looking up baby names. *Joshua's nice,* Reid had said, and Liddy had said maybe *Mason.*

Too trendy, Reid had said.

And Liddy had said, *Well, what does Max think? He ought to have a say in this, too.*

I flatten my hands on the table. "About this trial . . . I probably should have brought this up before. But I can't afford one lawyer, much less two of you."

Pastor Clive puts his hand on my shoulder. "Don't you worry about that, son. The church is taking care of it. After all, this is going to bring us a lot of attention."

Wade leans back, a smile unraveling across his face. "Attention," he says, "is what I do best."

ZOE

I like Emma. And Ella. And Hannah.

"Does every baby name have to be a palindrome?" Vanessa asks.

"No," I tell her, as we sprawl across the living room floor, surrounded by every single baby name book stocked by the local bookstore.

"Florals?" Vanessa says. "Rose? Lily? Or Daisy. I've always liked Daisy."

"Amanda Lynn?" I wait to see if she'll get the joke.

Vanessa smirks. "Well, it's better than Tuba or Banjo . . ."

"How about girl names that are also boy names?" I say. "Like Stevie. Or Alex."

"It would save us half the work here," Vanessa admits.

I have been pregnant three times and have avoided doing just this: hoping. It's a lot easier to not be disappointed when you have no expectations. And yet this time I almost can't help myself. There was something about the way I left things with Max that makes me believe this might actually happen.

After all, he didn't say no right away, which is what I expected.

Which means he's still thinking.

And that has to be good, right?

"Joey," Vanessa suggests. "That's kind of cute."

"If you're a kangaroo . . ." I roll over onto my back and look up at the ceiling. "Clouds."

"No way. I'm not doing the hippie thing. No Clouds or Rain or Meadow. I mean, imagine the poor kid when she's ninety and in a nursing home."

"I wasn't talking about a name," I say. "I was thinking about the nursery. I've always thought it would be peaceful to fall asleep staring up at clouds painted on your ceiling."

"That's cool. You think Michelangelo is listed in the yellow pages?"

The doorbell rings as I toss a pillow at her. "You expecting anyone?" I ask.

Vanessa shakes her head. "Are you?"

A man is standing on the porch, smiling. He's wearing a red baseball cap and a Red Sox sweatshirt and doesn't strike me as a serial killer, so I open the door. "Are you Zoe Baxter?" he asks.

"Yes . . ."

He pulls a sheaf of blue papers out of his back pocket. "These papers are for you," he says. "You've been served."

I open the folded document and words leap off the page at me:

Pray this Honorable Court . . .
. . . award him full possession and custody of his pre-born children . . .
. . . wishes to provide them with an appropriate two-parent family . . .

I sink to the floor and read.

In support thereof, it is hereby stated:
1. The plaintiff is the biological fa-

ther of these pre-born children, which were conceived during a heterosexual, God-condoned, constitutional marriage for the purposes of being raised in a heterosexual, God-condoned, constitutional marriage.

2. *Since these pre-born children were conceived the parties have divorced.*

3. *Since the final judgment the defendant has engaged in a meretricious, deviant, homosexual lifestyle.*

4. *The defendant has contacted the clinic for possession of the pre-born children for the purpose of having them transferred to her lesbian lover.*

"Zoe?"

Vanessa sounds like she is a thousand miles away. I hear her, but I cannot move.

"Zoe?" she says again, and she grabs the paper out of my hand. I open my mouth, but nothing comes out. There is no language to describe a betrayal this big.

Vanessa starts flipping through the pages so quickly I expect them to burst into flame. "What *is* this garbage?"

Equilibrium is nothing more than smoke and mirrors. You can be punched without ever fielding a blow. "It's from Max," I say. "He's trying to take away our baby."

VANESSA

Just after Thanksgiving 2008, a woman on her deathbed confessed to killing two girls forty-two years earlier, who had bullied her for being a lesbian. Sharron Smith had gone into the ice cream shop in Staunton, Virginia, where they all were employed to say she couldn't work the next day. According to the police transcript, one thing led to another, and she shot them.

I don't know why she was packing a .25-caliber automatic handgun when she went into the ice cream store, but I understand her motivation. Especially while I am standing here, holding this ridiculous legal allegation from Zoe's ex-husband.

One that calls me meretricious and deviant.

I am flooded with a feeling I thought I left behind in college, when I was called a freak by girls in the locker room, who would move away from my changing area because they were sure I was staring at them; when I was pinned into a dark corner at a dance and groped by some asshole on the football team, who had bet his friends he could turn me into a real girl. I was punished just because I was me, and what I wanted to say—what I never *did* say, until my throat was sore with the effort of silence—was *Why do I matter to you? Why can't you just worry about yourselves instead?*

So although I don't condone violence any more than I am truly meretricious and deviant, in that moment I sort of wish I had Sharron Smith's balls.

"I'm calling that son of a bitch," Zoe announces.

I don't know if I've ever seen her this upset. Her face is flushed a dark red; she is crying and spitting mad all at once. She punches the buttons so hard on the telephone handset that it tumbles out of her hands. I pick it up, hit the speakerphone button, and set it on the counter so that we can both listen.

To be honest, I'm surprised Max even picks up.

"I can't talk to you. My lawyer told me not to—"

"Why?" Zoe interrupts. "Why would you do this to me?"

There is a long pause—so long that I think Max may have disconnected the call. "I'm not doing this to you, Zoe. I'm doing it *for* our kids."

When we hear the dial tone on the other end of the line, Zoe picks up the phone and throws it across the kitchen. "He doesn't even *want* kids," she cries. "What is he going to do with the embryos?"

"I don't know." But it's clear to me that this might not be about the babies, to Max. That it's about Zoe, and the lifestyle she's living.

Or in other words, punishment for just being herself.

I have a sudden flashback of my mother bursting into tears, once, when she took me to the doctor's office for vaccinations. I was five or so, and clearly I was terrified of needles. I'd practically been hyperventilating the whole morning in anticipation of how painful this would be, and, sure enough, I was twisting my tiny body into knots to get away from the nurse practitioner. The sound of my mother's sobbing, though, immediately made me stop. It wasn't as if *she* was getting the shot, after all.

It hurts me, she tried to explain, *when you hurt.*

I was too young and too literal to understand it at the time, and, until now, I hadn't loved someone enough to know what she meant. But seeing Zoe like this, knowing that what she wants most in the world is being yanked out of her grasp—well, I can't breathe. I can't see anything but fire.

So I leave her standing in the kitchen, and I walk into the bedroom. I fall to my knees in front of my nightstand and start rummaging through past issues of unread *School Counselor* magazines and recipes I've clipped from the

Wednesday newspaper that I keep meaning to cook and never quite get around to. Buried several layers down is an issue of the *Options Newsletter,* a publication for the transgender, lesbian, gay, bi, and questioning. In the back are all the classified ads.

GLAD. Gay & Lesbian Advocates & Defenders. Winter Street, Boston.

I grab the newsletter and carry it back into the kitchen, where Zoe has wilted at the table. I pick up the telephone from where it's landed beneath a windowsill and dial the number in the advertisement.

"Hi," I say brusquely. "My name's Vanessa Shaw. My wife has just been served with a lawsuit by her ex-husband. He's trying to gain custody and control of frozen embryos we had hoped to use to start a family, and he's making it into an evangelical, right-wing, gay-bashing, precedent-setting case. Can you help us?" The words come out in a furious flood, until Zoe has lifted her head from the table and is staring at me, wide-eyed. "Yes," I tell the receptionist. "I'll hold."

Muzak fills my ear. Zoe was the one who told me that the company that invented all that awful elevator music went bankrupt in 2009. She called it musical karma.

She walks toward me, taking the newsletter out of my hand and glancing down at the ad for legal services.

"If Max wants a fight," I tell her, "then that's what he's going to get."

When I was twenty-four I broke my ankle playing pond hockey the day after Christmas. I snapped clear through the fibula, and a surgeon affixed a metal plate to my bone (the last time, I like to say, that a man will ever screw me). Although my teammates got me to the ER, my mother had to come stay in my apartment because I was completely incapacitated. I could hobble around on my crutches but couldn't get on and off the toilet. I couldn't hoist myself out of the bathtub. I couldn't go anywhere at all, because my crutches slipped and skidded on the ice outside.

If not for my mother, I probably would

have wasted away on saltines, tap water, and bad soap operas.

Instead, my mother stoically helped me in and out of the bathroom. She washed my hair in the tub so I wouldn't lose my balance. She drove me to and from the doctor's appointments and stocked my fridge and cleaned my house.

In return I bitched and moaned at her because I was really furious at myself. Finally, I hit a nerve. She threw down the plate of food she'd made me—it was a grilled cheese sandwich, I remember, because I complained about it being American cheese and not Swiss—and walked out the door.

Fine, I told myself. *I don't need her.*

And I didn't. Not for the first three hours, anyway. And then I really had to pee.

At first I hobbled on my crutches to the bathroom. But I couldn't lever myself down off them onto the toilet without the fear of falling. I wound up balancing on one foot and urinating into an empty coffee mug, and then I collapsed back on the bed and called my mother.

I'm sorry, I sobbed. *I'm helpless.*

That's where you're wrong, she told me. *You're not helpless. You need help. There's a big difference.*

On Angela Moretti's desk is a sealed glass jar, and swimming inside is what looks like a dried prune.

"Oh," she says, when she sees me looking at it. "That's from my last case."

Zoe and I have taken the day off from work to meet with Angela at her office in downtown Boston. She reminds me of Tinker Bell on speed—tiny, talking a mile a minute. Her black curls bounce as she lifts the jar and moves it closer to me.

"What is it?"

"A testicle," Angela says.

No wonder I didn't recognize it. Beside me, Zoe chokes and starts coughing.

"Some asshole got it bitten off in a barroom brawl."

"And he *saved* it?" I say.

"In formaldehyde." Angela shrugs. "He's a guy," she replies, by way of explanation. "I represented his ex-wife. She's got a same-sex spouse now, and the jerk wouldn't let her see her kids. She brought it to me for safekeeping because she said this is the most important thing in the world to him and she wanted it as collateral. I kept it because I liked the idea of having the plaintiff by the balls."

I like Angela Moretti already—and not just because she keeps a reproductive organ on her desk. I like her because Zoe and I walked into this office and nobody batted an eye to see us holding hands—out of solidarity and nerves, I suppose. I like Angela because she's on our side, and I didn't even have to try to convince her.

"I'm really scared," Zoe says. "I just can't believe Max is doing this."

Angela whips out a pad of paper and an expensive-looking fountain pen. "You know, life changes people sometimes. My cousin Eddie, he was the biggest bastard north of New Jersey until he shipped out during the Gulf

War. I don't just mean cranky—he was the kind of guy who *tried* to hit the squirrel with his car when it ran across the road. I don't know what he saw in that desert, but when Eddie came home, he became a monk. God's honest truth."

"Can you help us?" I ask.

Zoe bites her lip. "And can you tell us what it's going to cost?"

"Not a dime," Angela says. "And by that I mean, not a dime. GLAD is a nonprofit organization. We've been in New England for over thirty years protecting the civil rights of people who are gay, lesbian, transgender, bisexual, and questioning. We brought to court the precedent-setting case of *Goodridge v. Department of Public Health,* which said it was unconstitutional to not allow gay people to marry—and as a result Massachusetts became the first state in the country to allow gay marriage, back in 2004. We've fought for gay adoption rights, so that the unmarried partner of a child's biological parent can adopt that child and become a second legal parent—without the biological parent having to relinquish her rights. We have challenged the federal Defense of Marriage Act. Your case fits into our agenda completely," Angela says, "just like your ex-husband's case fits in with Wade Preston's agenda."

"You know his lawyer?" I ask.

She snorts. "You know the difference between Wade Preston and a vulture? Frequent flier miles. He's a homophobic nutbag who travels around the country trying to get states to amend their constitutions so that gay couples can't marry. He's this millennium's Anita Bryant and Jesse Helms all rolled up into one and stuffed in an Armani suit. But he also plays hard and tough, and it's going to get ugly. He's going to drag in the media and put the courthouse in an uproar because he'll want to get the public on his side. He's going to make you the poster children for unmarried heathens who aren't fit to raise a baby." Angela looks from me to Zoe. "I need to know that you two are in this for the long haul."

I reach for Zoe's hand. "Absolutely."

"But we *are* married," Zoe points out.

"Not according to the great state of Rhode Island. If your case was being brought to a Massachusetts court, you'd have a much stronger position than you do in your home state."

"What about the millions of straight couples who aren't married but have babies? Why isn't anyone questioning *their* ability to raise a child?"

"Because Wade Preston is going to make sure this is viewed as a custody case even though we're not talking about children, we're talking about property. And anytime there's a custody case, the morality of your relationship is going to be on the hot seat."

Zoe shakes her head. "Biologically, it's my baby."

"By that argument, it's also Max's baby. He has as much legal right to the embryos as you do—and Preston is going to say he has a better moral plan for that unborn child."

"Well, he's not exactly the model Christian daddy," I say. "He isn't married. He's a recovering alcoholic—"

"Good," Angela mutters, writing on her pad. "That might help. But we don't know yet what Max wants to do with the embryos. Our position is going to be to paint you as a loving, committed couple with strong roots in the community and respect in your individual professions."

"Will that be enough?" Zoe asks.

"I don't know. We aren't going to be able to control the wild ride that Wade Preston's about to launch, but we've got a strong case, and we're not going to let him roll right over us. Now, let me get some background information from you. You were married when?"

"In April, in Fall River," I say.

"And you're presently living where?"

"Wilmington, Rhode Island."

Angela writes this down. "You live in the same house?"

"Yes," I say. "Zoe moved in with me."

"Do you own the home?"

I nod. "It's a three bedroom. We have plenty of room for kids."

"Zoe," Angela says, "I know you've struggled with infertility and don't have any children—but Vanessa, what about you? Have you ever been pregnant?"

"No . . ."

"But she doesn't have any fertility problems," Zoe adds.

"Well, I *assume* I don't. Lesbians are always shooting blanks, so you never really know."

Angela grins. "Let's talk about Max for a second. When you were married to him, did he drink?"

Zoe looks into her lap. "There were times I found alcohol hidden, but I'd throw it out. He knew—after all, he took the empty bottles out in the recycling. But we never talked about it. If I found a stash and emptied it down the sink, he'd start acting like the perfect husband, offering back rubs, taking me out to dinner. That would last until I found the next bottle hidden under the vacuum cleaner bags or behind the lightbulbs in the closet. It was almost as if we could have a whole conversation about him toeing the line without ever speaking a word."

"Was Max ever abusive?"

"No," Zoe says. "We went through hell trying to have a baby, but I never doubted that he loved me. The things coming out of his mouth now don't even sound like Max. They sound like something his brother would say."

"His brother?"

"Reid took care of Max before I met him, and got him into AA. He's a member of the Eternal Glory Church, which Max goes to, now; and Max lives with him."

"You know what you call a nun who's passed her bar exam?" Angela says, idly scanning the legal complaint that I faxed to the office after my initial phone call. "A sister-in-law."

Beside me, Zoe laughs.

"There you go," Angela says. "As long as you can make a good lawyer joke, there's still hope in the world. And I got a million of them." She sets down the fax. "There's a lot of religious language in here. Could Reid be a part of Max's decision to file the lawsuit?"

"Or Clive Lincoln," Zoe says. "He's the pastor who runs it."

"Lovely man," Angela replies, rolling her eyes. "He threw a bucket of paint at me once on the steps of the Massachusetts State House. Was Max always religious?"

"No. When we got married, we even stopped going to Reid and Liddy's house because we felt like we were being preached to."

"What was Max's attitude about homosexuality back then?" Angela asks.

Zoe blinks. "I don't think we ever really talked about it. I mean, he wasn't openly intolerant, but he wasn't advocating for gay rights, either."

"Does Max have a girlfriend now?"

"I don't know."

"When you told him that you wanted to use the embryos, did he say anything about wanting to use them himself?"

"No. He said he'd think about it," Zoe says. "I came home and told Vanessa I thought we'd be good to go."

"Well, we never know people as well as we think we do." Angela puts down her pad. "Let's talk a little about how this case is going to proceed. Zoe, you know you're going to have to testify— and you, too, Vanessa. You'll have to speak very openly and honestly about your relationship, though you might get flak for it even in this day and age. I called the clerk this morning and learned that the case has been assigned to Judge O'Neill."

"Is that good?" I ask.

"No," Angela replies flatly. "You know what you call a lawyer with an IQ of fifty, right? Your Honor." She frowns. "Padraic O'Neill is about to retire— something I've personally been praying for for the past decade. He has a very traditional, conservative outlook."

"Can we switch?" Zoe says.

"Unfortunately, no. If courts let us switch judges just because we don't like who we've drawn, we'd be switching judges all the time. However, as conservative as O'Neill is, he still has to abide by the law. And legally, you have a strong case."

"What's happened before in Rhode Island with cases like this?"

Angela looks at me. "There are none. We'll be making law."

"So," Zoe murmurs. "It could really go either way."

"Look," Angela says. "Judge O'Neill's not the guy I would have picked, but it's who we have, and we'll tailor our case in a way that lets him see how you two are the best solution for the disposition of the embryos. Wade Preston's entire argument is based on the protocol of the best traditional family, yet Max is single. He doesn't even have his own home to raise a kid in. On the other hand, you two present the image of a committed, loving, intelligent couple. You were the first one to broach the subject of using the embryos with the clinic. Ultimately, this case will come down to you two versus Max—and even a judge like Padraic O'Neill will see the writing on the wall."

There is a soft knock behind us, and a secretary opens the door. "Ange? Your eleven o'clock is here."

"Great kid, you ought to meet him. He's transgendered and wants to join the high school's traveling soccer team, but he hasn't had his surgery yet, and the coach says they can't afford an extra separate hotel room. I am *so* gonna win this one." She stands up. "I'll let you know what's next," Angela says. "Unless you have any questions?"

"I do," Zoe says, "but it's sort of personal."

"You want to know if I'm a lesbian."

Zoe blushes. "Well. Yeah. But you don't have to answer."

"I'm straight as a two-by-four. My husband and I have three rugrats and a house full of constant chaos."

"But you . . ." Zoe hesitates. "You work here?"

"I eat kung pao chicken like it's going out of style, but I'm pretty sure I don't have an Asian cell in my body. I love Toni Morrison novels and Tyler Perry movies although I'm not black." Angela smiles. "I'm straight, Zoe, and I'm happily married. The reason I work here is because I think you deserve that, too."

I'm not really sure when I began telling myself I'd never have kids. I'm still young, sure, but options are different when you're a lesbian. The dating pool is smaller; chances are you will wind up going out with someone who already knows the last person who broke your heart. Plus, unlike straight people, who are almost expected to fall onto a track that leads to marriage and kids, a gay couple has to make a serious, expensive, invested effort to have a baby. Lesbians need a sperm donor, gays need a surrogate mother, or else we have to forge into the rough waters of adoption, where same-sex couples are often turned away.

I was never the kind of girl who dreamed of babies and who practiced swaddling my teddy bears. As an only child, I didn't have a chance to help care for a younger sibling. I hadn't had a serious relationship, before Zoe, for several years. I would have happily settled for love, without offspring, if that was my trade-off.

Besides, I told myself, I already had children. About six hundred of them, at Wilmington High School. I listened to them, and cried with them, and told them that tomorrow was always going to look a little better than today. Even the ones who have graduated I still think about, connect with on Facebook.

I enjoy knowing that, like I promised, everything worked out okay.

But lately, I've been doing a lot of thinking.

What if I wasn't just everyone's substitute mother during the hours of eight and three but an actual one? What if there was an open school night I got to attend as an audience member instead of a speaker? What if I found myself on the other side of the school counselor's desk one day, advocating for my daughter, who was desperate to be placed in an English class that was already overcrowded?

I have not experienced that butterfly beat of life inside me, not yet. But I bet it's a little like hope. Once you feel it, you know the absence of it as well.

Zoe and I haven't had our baby, but we've allowed ourselves to wish. And I'll tell you—from that moment, I was a goner.

It has been a hellish morning. A sophomore was suspended for robotripping, drinking Robitussin cough syrup in order to get high. But right now, everything's quiet. I would call Zoe, but I know she's in the weeds. Taking time off to visit the GLAD offices meant missing a day at the hospital for her; because of that, she's postponed her music therapy lesson with Lucy so that she can spend a few hours on the pediatric burn unit. It is May, and I have no shortage of work I could do, but instead of doing my job, I turn on my computer and Google "Pregnancy."

I click on the first website. *Weeks 3 and 4,* I read. *Your baby is the size of a poppy seed.*

> *Week 7. Your baby is the size of a blueberry.*
> *Week 9. Your baby is the size of a green olive.*
> *Week 19. Your baby is the size of a mango.*
> *Week 26. Your baby is the size of an eggplant.*
> *Delivery: Your baby is the size of a watermelon.*

I press my hand against my abdomen. It seems inconceivable (pun intended) that this might be a home to someone, soon. Someone the size of a green olive, nonetheless. Why do they describe everything in terms of food? No wonder pregnant women are always starving.

Suddenly Lucy bursts into my office. "What the fuck?" she says.

"Language," I reply.

She rolls her eyes. "You know, if I'm taking the time from my day to meet with her, she could at least have the courtesy to show up."

I can easily translate Lucy's anger— what she really means is that she's dis- appointed her session's been post- poned. That—even if she'd rather die than admit it—she likes meeting with Zoe.

"I left a note on your locker," I say. "Didn't you get it?" It is the way we communicate in this school—by taping onto lockers notes for school counselor appointments and academic counsel- ing sessions and even notices of field hockey championships.

"I don't go near my locker. Last year someone put a dead mouse inside just to see what I'd do."

That's pretty appalling, but not surprising. Teenagers never fail to amaze me with the ingenuity of their cruelty. "Zoe's work schedule was a little crazy this week, and she had to reschedule. She'll be here for your next appointment."

Lucy doesn't ask me how I know this. She doesn't know that I'm married to her music therapist. But hearing that Zoe hasn't left for good seems to mollify her. "So she's coming back," Lucy repeats.

I tilt my head. "Is that what you want?"

"Well, if she ditches me, it sure as hell would fit the pattern of my life. Depend on someone, and they fuck you over." Lucy looks up at me. *"Language,"* she says, at the exact same moment that I do.

"Your drumming session was pretty interesting," I say, remembering the impromptu rock concert in the cafeteria. I had spent an hour in a closed session with my principal after that fiasco, trying to explain the merits of music therapy with suicidal kids, and why having to sterilize the pots and pans and soup ladles once more was a small trade-off for mental health.

"I've never had anyone do that for me before," Lucy admits.

"What do you mean?"

"She knew she was going to get in trouble. But she didn't care. Instead of making me do what I'm supposed to do, or be what everyone wants me to be, she did something totally crazy. It was . . ." Lucy stumbles, trying to find her words. "It was fucking brave, is what it was."

"Maybe Zoe's getting you to feel more comfortable being yourself."

"Maybe you're using the hour I would have spent in music therapy to play Freud."

I grin. "You know all my tricks."

"You're about as hard to read as Elmo."

"You know, Lucy," I say. "School's out in less than two months."

"Tell me about it—I'm counting the days."

"Well—if you have any plans to con-tinue music therapy over the summer, it's something we'll need to arrange in advance."

Lucy's gaze flies up to meet mine. I can tell she hasn't considered this— when school breaks in June, so do all school activities, including school-based counseling sessions.

"I'm sure Zoe would agree to meet with you over the summer," I say smoothly. "And I'm happy to use my key to let you guys into the school for your sessions."

She jerks her chin up. "We'll see. It's not like I really care one way or the other."

But she does, desperately. She just won't say so out loud. "You have to admit, Lucy," I tell her, "you've already come a long way. You couldn't wait to get out of the room during that first session with Zoe, and, well, look at you now. You're angry because she had to reschedule."

Lucy's eyes flash, and I think she's going to tell me to go do something anatomically impossible, but then she shrugs. "She kind of crept up on me. But . . . not like in a bad way. Like when you're standing on the beach right down by the ocean, and you think you've got a handle on it, and then when you look down again you've sunk so far that the water's up to your hips. And before you can get freaked out, you realize you actually don't mind going swimming."

Beneath the barrier of my desk, my hand steals to my belly again. Our baby will be the size of a plum, a nectarine, a tangelo. A harvest of the sweetest things. Suddenly I want to hear Zoe's voice asking me for the thousandth time whether or not yogurt containers can be recycled, or whether I wore her blue silk blouse last week and took it to the cleaners. I want ten thousand ordinary days with her; and I want this baby as proof that we loved each other so fiercely that magic happened. "Yes," I agree. "That's exactly what she's like."

Angela Moretti had said she'd call us when she had more news, but we didn't expect it to be just days after our first meeting. This time, she said, she was willing to drive to us, so Zoe and I made a vegetable lasagna and started drinking the wine before Angela even arrived, out of sheer nervousness. "What if she doesn't like lasagna?" Zoe asks, as she's tossing the salad.

"With a name like Moretti?"

"That doesn't mean anything . . ."

"Well, who doesn't like lasagna?" I ask.

"I don't know. Lots of people."

"Zo. Whether or not she likes pasta is not going to make or break this case."

She turns, her arms crossed. "I don't like this. If it was something simple, she would have just told us over the phone."

"Or maybe she's heard you make a hell of a lasagna."

Zoe drops the salad tongs. "I'm a wreck," she says. "I can't handle this."

"It's going to get a lot worse before it gets better."

She moves into my arms, and, for a moment, we just hold each other in the kitchen. "Today at the nursing home during group session we were playing the handbells and Mrs. Greaves got up and went to the bathroom and forgot to come back," Zoe says. "She was my F. Do you have any idea how hard it is to play 'Amazing Grace' without an F?"

"Where did she go?"

"The staff found her in the garage, sitting in the van that takes the residents to the grocery store on Thursdays. They found the bell in the oven about an hour later."

"Was it on?"

"The van?" Zoe asks.

"The oven."

"No. Thank goodness."

"And the moral of this story is that you and I might have a massive lawsuit to fight, but we haven't lost our handbells."

I can feel her smile against my collarbone. "I knew you'd help me find that silver lining," Zoe says.

There's a knock at the front door. Angela's already talking by the time I open it. "You know what Wade Preston and a sperm have in common? A one in three million chance of becoming human." She hands me a thick sheaf of papers. "Mystery solved. Now we know

what Max wants to do with the embryos—give them to his brother."

"What?" It's Zoe's voice, but it sounds
like a punch.

"I don't get it." I skim through the pa-
pers, but they are written in legalese.
"He can't give them away like they're a
Yankee swap."

"Well, he's sure as hell gonna try,"
Angela says. "Today I received a motion from Ben Benjamin, the local lawyer who's working with Wade Preston.
He wants to implead Reid and Liddy
Baxter as third-party plaintiffs. Max
joins them in the petition and says his
brother and sister-in-law are the intended recipients of the embryos." She
snorts. "Ten guesses who's paying
Wade's fat bill."

"So they're buying the embryos?"

"They'll never call it that, but, in effect, that's exactly what's happening.
Reid and Liddy fund the lawsuit; they
position themselves as the recipient
potential parents, and suddenly Wade's
got his retainer *and* a traditional Christian couple to wave like a banner in
front of Judge O'Neill."

Very slowly, I'm piecing this together. "You mean Liddy's going to have Zoe's baby?"

"That," Angela says, "is their plan."

I'm so angry I am literally shaking. "*I'm* having Zoe's baby."

But Angela isn't listening. She's looking at Zoe, who seems to be paralyzed. "Zoe? You okay?"

I know this much about my spouse: when she yells, it will blow over quickly. It's when her voice is just above a whisper that she's furious; and right now, Zoe's words are virtually inaudible. "You're telling me that my child, the one I want my wife to carry and that I want to raise myself . . . is going to be carried and raised by someone I cannot *stand*? That I have no say in this?"

Angela takes my glass of wine out of my hand and drains it in one swallow. "They're going to ask the judge to give the embryos to Max. Then he'll be able to do whatever he wants with them— but they're telling the judge that he plans to give them to Reid and Liddy, because they know damn well it will sway the court's decision."

"Why can't Reid and Liddy have their own freaking children?" I ask.

Zoe turns. "Because Reid's got the same infertility issues that Max did. It's genetic. We went to a clinic for answers—and they went to Clive Lincoln."

"The embryos were created during Max and Zoe's *marriage.* If she still wants them, how could any judge give them away to a stranger?"

"From their viewpoint, Max believes that the best future for these potential children is a two-parent, heterosexual, rich Christian family. And Reid and Liddy aren't strangers. They're genetically related to those embryos. Too related, if you ask me. Reid is the embryos' uncle, and his wife is going to give birth to his niece or nephew. Sounds like the *Deliverance* family reunion."

"But Reid and Liddy could use a sperm donor. Or go through in vitro, like Max and Zoe did. This is Zoe's last set of viable eggs. It's the last chance we have to both be biologically connected to a child," I say.

"And that's what I'm going to tell the

judge," Angela says. "Zoe, as the biological mom, has the clearest, strongest
right to the embryos, and plans to raise
the resulting child or children in a stable, strong family. Far from the future
full of hell and brimstone that Wade
Preston's touting."

"So what do we do?" Zoe asks.

"Tonight we're going to sit down and
you're going to tell me everything you
know about Reid and Liddy Baxter. I'm
going to file a motion to try to keep
them out of this case, but I have a sinking feeling that they're going to worm
themselves into it," Angela says. "We're
still going to fight. The fight just got a
little bit harder."

At that moment, the timer on the
oven goes off. We have lasagna with
homemade sauce; we have fresh garlic
bread and a salad topped with pear
and Brie and candied walnuts. Five
minutes ago, Zoe and I were trying to
create a memorable meal, so that, in
case there was any karmic holdover in
the legal world, Angela Moretti would
learn firsthand how nurturing this home
was, and would subsequently throw a

hundred and ten percent of her heart and soul into the battle. Five minutes ago, dinner smelled delicious.

Now, no one's hungry.

MAX

Imagine if you were the positive pole of a magnet, and you were told that under no circumstances were you allowed to touch that negative pole that was sucking you in like a black hole. Or if you crawled out of the desert and found a woman standing with a pitcher of ice water, but she held it out of your reach. Imagine jumping off a building, and then being told not to fall.

That's what it feels like to want a drink.

And that's how I feel when Zoe calls me, after she's been served the legal papers.

Pastor Clive knew that she'd call— which is why he'd told Reid to stick by me like glue on the day the process server was headed to her house. Reid took the day off work, and we went out fishing for tautog on his boat. He's got a sweet Boston Whaler and takes his clients out to catch blues or mackerel. Tautog, though, are different. They live in the places your line is bound to get snagged. And you can't set the hook as soon as you feel a hit, either. You have to wait for the tog to swallow the whole green crab you're using for bait, or you're bound to reel in empty.

So far we've been out here for hours and we haven't caught anything.

It's warm enough in early May for us to strip off our sweatshirts and get sunburns—my face feels tight and uncomfortable, although that may have less to do with the sun than with me imagining what it's like when Zoe opens that door.

Reid reaches into the cooler and takes out two cold Canada Dry ginger ales. "These fish sure don't want to be caught," he says.

"Guess not."

"We may have to make up a story for

Liddy," Reid says. "To spare ourselves excessive male humiliation."

I squint up at him. "I don't think she cares if we bring home tog or not."

"Still, who wants to admit he's been outsmarted by a rock dweller?"

Reid reels in his line and baits another green crab. He is the one who taught me how to string a hook through a worm for the first time, even though, when I tried, I threw up. He was with me when I caught my first lake trout, and from the way he carried on, you would have thought I'd won the lottery.

He'll be a really good dad.

As if he can read my mind, he looks up with a huge smile on his face. "Remember when I taught you how to cast? How you got your hook caught on Mom's straw sunhat and sent it sailing into the middle of the lake?"

I haven't thought of that in years. I shake my head. "Maybe you'll do a better job teaching your son."

"Or daughter," Reid says. "No reason she can't be a Bassmaster, too." He is so excited about the possibility. All I have to do is look at his face, and I can practically see his future: a first ballet recital, a prom photo, a father-daughter dance at a wedding. I've underestimated him, all this time. I thought he only got jazzed up about his business deals, but now I think maybe the reason he threw himself into his work was because he wanted a family he couldn't have, and it hurt too much to be reminded of that day in and day out.

"Hey, Max?" Reid asks, and I glance up. "You think my kid . . . you think he or she will like me?"

I've rarely seen Reid less than completely sure of himself. "What do you mean?" I say. "Of course."

Reid rubs the nape of his neck. His vulnerability makes him, well, more human. "You say that," he points out, "but we didn't think so highly of our old man."

"That was different," I tell him. "Dad wasn't you."

"How so?"

I have to think about that for a second. "You never stop caring," I say. "He never started."

Reid lets the words sink in, and

flashes me a smile. "Thanks," he says. "It means a lot, knowing you trust me to do this."

Well, of course I do. On paper, no one looks like a better set of parents than Reid and Liddy. I have a sudden flashback memory of sitting up in bed with a calculator, trying to figure out how far in debt Zoe and I would be if we not only used in vitro to conceive but then actually had to pay for the baby's doctor's visits and diapers and food and clothing. Zoe had crumpled my calculations. *Just because it doesn't work on paper,* she had said, *doesn't mean we won't find a way to make it work in real life.*

"It's normal, right? To be a little freaked out about becoming a father?"

"You don't become someone's role model because you're smart enough to have all the right answers," I say slowly. I'm thinking of Reid, and why I always looked up to him. "You become someone's role model because you're smart enough to keep asking the right questions."

Reid looks at me. "You're different,

you know. The way you talk, the decisions you make. I mean it, Max. You're not who you used to be."

I have wanted Reid's approval all my life. So why do I feel like I'm going to be sick?

When the phone rings, it's bizarre. Not just because we're floating off the shore of Rhode Island but because we both already know who it is. "Remember what Wade said," Reid tells me, as I hold the ringing cell phone in my hand.

Zoe starts yelling before I even have it pressed to my ear. "I can't talk to you," I interrupt. "My lawyer told me not to—"

"Why would you do this to me?" Zoe's crying. I know, because when she cries, her voice sounds like it's wrapped in flannel. Lord knows I've heard it enough times over the telephone lines, when she called to report another miscarriage, and tried to convince me that, really, she was fine, when clearly she wasn't.

Reid puts his hand on my shoulder. For solidarity, support. I close my eyes.

"I'm not doing this to you, Zoe. I'm doing it *for* our kids."

I feel Reid reach for the phone, push the button to end the call.

"You're doing the right thing," he says.

If I'm really so different, now, why do I need Reid to tell me that?

Next to my foot is the bucket of green crabs we're using as bait. No one likes green crabs; they're at the bottom of the food chain. They're moving in circles, getting in each other's way. I have an uncontrollable urge to toss them all overboard so they have a second chance.

"You all right?" Reid asks, peering up at me. "How do you feel?"

Thirsty.

"Kind of seasick, believe it or not. I think maybe we should just pack it in." And when we reach the dock, fifteen minutes later, I tell him that I promised Pastor Clive I'd help clear some brush at his place.

"Sorry about the fishing," Reid says. "Better luck next time?"

"Couldn't get much worse."

I help him get the boat on the trailer and hose it down and then wave to him as he drives home to Liddy.

The thing is, I never promised Pastor Clive anything about clearing brush. I get into my truck and start driving. I'd throw myself on a board and surf to beat all the thoughts out of my head, but the water's dead flat today—my curse. Meanwhile, my tongue feels like it's swollen twice its size, and my throat's gone so narrow I can barely whistle my next breath through it.

Thirsty.

It's not like one little drink would really hurt. After all, like Reid said, I'm different now. I've found Jesus; together I know we can walk away from the second one. And to be honest, I think if Jesus were in my shoes right now, he would want a cold one, too.

I don't want to go to a bar, because the walls have eyes and you never know what's going to get back to someone. Now that Reid's paying the bulk of Wade Preston's fee (*Anything for my little brother,* he had said), and with the church pitching in the rest—well, the last thing I need is for some member of the congregation to go tattling about me stumbling off the straight and narrow. So instead I drive to a liquor store all the way in Woonsocket, where I don't know anyone and nobody knows me.

Speaking of legal evidence—which is apparently what I'm going to be doing a lot of in the near future—here is some:

1. I only buy one bottle of J.D.
2. I plan to have a few sips and toss the rest.
3. As further proof that I am thinking clearly and not falling off the wagon (or being run over by it, for that matter), I don't even crack the seal until I reach Newport again. That way, when I drive home, it's only a matter of miles.

All of the above is presented, Your Honor, as proof that Max Baxter is in full control of himself and his life and his drinking.

But when I pull into a parking lot and open the bottle, my hands are shaking. And when that first golden lick hits my throat, I swear I see the face of God.

The first time I was introduced to Liddy, I didn't like her. Reid had met her while he was doing business down in Mississippi; she was the daughter of one of his investment portfolio clients. She held out a limp hand and dimpled her cheeks and said, "I am just *so* delighted to meet Reid's baby brother." She looked like a doll, with her blond curls and her tiny waist and hands and feet. She wore a purity ring.

Reid and I had actually talked about that little detail. I knew Reid was no saint and had had his share of relationships in the past—and I myself couldn't imagine buying a lifetime supply of ice cream without tasting the flavor first— but it was my brother's life, and I was far from qualified to tell him how to live it. If he wanted to hold (limp) hands with his fiancée until his wedding night, that was his problem, not mine.

Liddy's only job, although she had been out of Bible college for three years, was teaching Sunday School at her daddy's church. She'd never gotten her driver's license. Sometimes, I'd pick fights with her just because it was so easy. "What did you do when you had to buy something?" I'd ask. "What if you wanted to go out to a bar one night?"

"Daddy pays," she told me. "And I don't go out to bars."

She wasn't just sweet, she was saccharine, and for the life of me I didn't see why Reid was blind to the fact that Liddy was too good to be true. No one was that pure and sweet; no one actually read the Bible from cover to cover or burst into tears when Peter Jennings reported on starving children in Ethiopia. I figured she was hiding something, like that she used to be a biker chick or that she had ten kids stashed away in Arkansas, but Reid just laughed at me. "Sometimes, Max," he said, "a cigar really is just a cigar."

Liddy had grown up as the only spoiled child of an evangelical minister, and because she was making a major life change by moving north of the Mason-Dixon Line, her father insisted she give it a trial run. So she and her cousin Martine moved to Providence, in a tiny apartment on College Hill that Reid had found for her. Martine was eighteen and thrilled to be away from home. She started wearing short skirts and heels and spent a lot of time flirting with Brown students on Thayer Street. Liddy, on the other hand, began volun-teering at the soup kitchen at Amos House. "I'm telling you, she's an angel," Reid would say.

But I didn't answer. And because he knew I didn't like his fiancée—and he didn't want that kind of strain in his family—he decided that the best way for me to get to like her more was to spend more time with her. He started making excuses, working late, and asked me to drive Liddy each day from downtown Providence to Newport, where he'd then take her out to dinner or a movie.

I'd get her in my pickup, and she'd immediately change the radio station to a classical one. Liddy was the one who told me that composers used to always end their pieces in a major chord—even when the piece was mostly written in a minor one—because ending with a minor chord had some connotation of the Devil. It turned out that she was a flutist who'd played with all-state symphonies and had been first chair at her Bible college.

I'd swear a blue streak at a driver who cut into my lane, and she would flinch as if I'd hit her.

When she asked me questions, I tried to shock her. I told her I sometimes surfed in the darkness just to see if I could make it through riding a curl without smashing my head against the rocks. I told her my last girlfriend had been a stripper (which was true, but it didn't involve a pole—just wallpaper. Yet I didn't mention this to Liddy).

One freezing cold day, when we were stuck in traffic, she asked me to turn up the heat in the truck. I did, and three seconds later she complained because it was too hot. "For God's sake," I said, "make up your mind!"

I figured she'd lay into me for taking the Lord's name in vain, but instead Liddy turned to me. "How come you don't like me?"

"You're marrying my brother," I replied. "I think it matters more if *he* likes you."

"You didn't answer my question."

I rolled my eyes. "We're just different, is all."

She pursed her lips. "Well, *I* don't think so."

"Oh really," I said. "Have you ever gotten drunk?"

Liddy shook her head.

"Ever bummed a cigarette?"

She hadn't.

"Have you ever stolen a pack of gum?"

Not even once.

"Ever cheated on a guy?"

No.

"I bet you've never even gotten to third base," I muttered, and she blushed so bright that I felt like my own face was on fire.

"Waiting for marriage isn't a crime," Liddy said. "It's the best gift you can give someone you love. Besides, I'm not the first girl to do it."

But you may be the first one to actually carry through with it, I thought. "Have you ever lied?"

"Well. Yes. But only so I could keep Daddy's birthday surprise party a secret."

"Have you ever done *anything* you regretted later?"

"No," she said, just like I expected.

I rested my wrist on the steering wheel and glanced at her profile. "Have you ever *wanted* to?"

We were stopped at a red light. Liddy looked at me, and, maybe for the first time, I really, really looked at her. Those blue eyes, which I'd thought were so empty and glassy, like those of a toy doll, were full of hunger. "Of course," she whispered.

Behind us, a driver honked; the light had turned. I looked out the windshield and realized that it had started snowing; that meant my chauffeur services would take even longer. "Hold your horses," I said to the driver under my breath, at the same time that Liddy realized the weather had turned.

"Oh my," she cried (who in this millennium says *Oh my?*), and before I could stop her she jumped out of the truck. She ran into the middle of the intersection, her arms outstretched and her eyes closed, as the snowflakes landed on her hair and her face.

I honked, but she didn't respond. She was going to cause a massive pileup. Cursing under my breath, I got out of the pickup. "Liddy," I yelled. "Get into the fucking car!"

She was still spinning. "I've never seen snow before!" she said. "This never happens in Mississippi! It's so pretty!"

It wasn't pretty. Not on a grimy Providence street where a guy was doing a drug deal on the corner. But cynics always assume the worst, and I guess I was the biggest cynic of them all. Because, at that moment, I realized why I distrusted Liddy on principle. I was afraid that maybe someone like Liddy had to exist in the universe in order to balance someone like me. A woman who couldn't do anything wrong surely canceled out a guy who never did anything right.

Together, we were two halves of a whole.

I knew then why Reid had fallen for her. Not in spite of the fact that she was so sheltered but because of it. He would be there for all these firsts—her first bank account, her first sexual encounter, her first job. I'd never been someone's first *anything,* unless you counted *mistake.*

By now, other cars had started honking. Liddy grabbed my hand and twirled me around while she laughed.

I managed to get her back into the car, but I sort of wished I hadn't. I wished we'd just stayed in the middle of that street.

When we started driving again, her cheeks were pink and she was out of breath.

Reid might have everything else, I remember thinking, but that first snow? That was mine.

One sip, when you measure it, is practically nothing. A teaspoonful. A taste. Certainly not enough to really help you quench a thirst, which is why that first sip leads to just a tiny second one, and then really just enough to wet my lips. And then I start thinking about Zoe's voice and Liddy's and they blend together and I take another swallow because I think that may split them apart again.

I really haven't drunk very much. It's just that it's been so long, the buzz starts fast and spreads through me. There is a rush like a tide in my head every time my foot hits the brake, which manages to wash away whatever I was thinking at that moment.

Which feels awfully good.

I reach for the bottle again, and, to my surprise, there's nothing in it.

It must have spilled, because there's no way I drank a fifth of whiskey.

I mean, I couldn't have, right?

In my rearview mirror is a lit Christmas tree. It takes me by surprise when I happen to glance at it, and then I can't stop staring, even though I know my eyes should be on the road. Then the tree lets out a siren.

It's May; there are no Christmas tree lights. The cop raps against my window.

I have to unroll it, because if I don't he'll arrest me. I tell myself to get a grip, to be polite and charming. I can convince him I haven't been drinking. I did that for years, with the rest of the world.

I think I recognize him. I think he may even go to my church. "Don't tell me," I say, offering up a gummy, sheepish grin. "I was going forty in a thirty-mile-an-hour zone?"

"Sorry, Max, but I'm gonna have to ask you to step out of the—"

"Max!" We both turn at the sound of another voice, followed by the slam of a car door.

The cop falls back as Liddy leans into my open window. "What were you *thinking,* driving yourself to the emergency room?" She turns to the policeman. "Oh, Grant, thank goodness you found him—"

"But I didn't—"

"He fell off a ladder while he was

cleaning out the gutters, and conked his head, and I go off to get an ice pack and by the time I get back I see him zooming off in his truck." She frowns at me. "You could have killed yourself! Or worse—you could have killed someone else! Didn't you just tell me you were seeing double?"

I honestly don't know what to say. I'm wondering if *she* conked her head.

Liddy opens the driver's side door. "Move over, Max," she says, and I unbuckle and slide across the bench into the truck's passenger seat. "Grant, I just cannot thank you enough. We are so blessed to have you as a public safety officer, not to mention as a member of our congregation." She looks up at him and smiles. "Will you be a darling and make sure my car gets back home?"

She gives a little wave as she drives off.

"I didn't bang my head—"

"Don't you think I know that?" Liddy snaps. "I was out looking for you. Reid told me you left him at the dock to go help Pastor Clive."

"I did."

She glances at me. "That's funny. Because *I* was with Pastor Clive all afternoon, and I never saw you."

"Did you tell Reid?"

Liddy sighs. "No."

"I can explain—"

She holds up one small hand. "Don't, Max. Just . . . don't." Wrinkling her nose, she says, "Whiskey."

I close my eyes. Stupid idiot I am, believing I can pull a fast one. I look drunk. I smell drunk. "How would you know, if you've never had it?"

"Because my daddy did, every day of my childhood," Liddy says.

There is something about the way she says it that makes me wonder if her father, the preacher, was trying to drown his own demons, too.

She drives past the turn that would have led to our house. "Lord knows I can't take you home in this state."

"You could hit me over the head and take me to the hospital," I mutter.

Liddy purses her lips. "Don't think I haven't considered it," she says.

The biggest knock-down fight I ever had with Zoe was after Christmas Eve at Reid and Liddy's house. We'd been married about five years by then and had already had our share of fertility nightmares. Anyway, it's not a secret that Zoe wasn't a big fan of my brother and his wife. She had been watching the Weather Channel all day, hoping to convince me that the snow we were going to be getting that night was enough to keep us from driving from our place to theirs.

Liddy loved Christmas. She decorated—not in a cheesy inflatable Santa way but with real garlands wrapped around the banister and mistletoe hanging from the chandeliers. She had a collection of antique wooden St. Nicholas dolls, which were propped up on windowsills and tables. She switched out her everyday dishes for a set with holly around the edges. Reid told me it took her an entire day to prepare the house for the holidays, and looking around, I totally believed it.

"Wow," Zoe murmured, as we waited in the foyer for Liddy to take our coats and hang them up in the closet. "It's like we've fallen into a Thomas Kinkade painting."

That's when Reid appeared, holding mugs of hot cider. He never drank when I was around. "Merry Christmas," he said, clapping me on the back and kissing Zoe on the cheek. "How are the roads?"

"Nasty," I told him. "Getting worse."

"We may not be able to stay long," Zoe added.

"We saw a car slide off the road on the way back from church," Reid said. "Luckily, no one got hurt."

Every Christmas Eve, Liddy directed the children's Nativity play. "So how did it go?" I asked her. "You guys taking it to Broadway?"

"It was pretty unforgettable," Reid said, and Liddy swatted him.

"We had an animal control issue," she said. "One of the little girls in Sunday School has an uncle who runs a petting zoo, and he loaned us a donkey."

"A donkey," I repeated. "A real one?"

"He was very tame. He didn't even move when the girl playing Mary climbed onto his back. But then"—she shuddered—"he stopped halfway down the aisle and . . . did his business."

I burst out laughing. "He took a dump?"

"In front of Pastor Clive's wife," Liddy said.

"What did you do?"

"I had a shepherd clean it up, and the mother of one of the angels ran out to get carpet cleaner. I mean, what was I *supposed* to do? I never officially got approval from the school to bring in livestock."

"Wouldn't be the first time an ass went to church," Zoe said, straight-faced.

I grabbed her elbow. "Zoe, come help me in the kitchen." I dragged her through the swinging door. It smelled delicious, like gingerbread and vanilla. "No politics. You promised me."

"I'm not going to sit back while he—"

"While he does what?" I argued. "He

hasn't done anything. You're the one who made the snide comment!"

She looked away from me, petulant. Her gaze landed on the refrigerator, on a magnet printed with a fetus sucking its thumb. I'M A CHILD, said the caption. NOT A CHOICE.

I put my hands on her arms. "Reid is my only family. He may be conservative, but he's still my brother, and it's *Christmas.* All I'm asking is that, for an hour, you smile and nod your head and you don't bring up current events."

"What if he brings them up first?"

"Zoe," I begged, "please."

And for about an hour, it seemed as if we might get through dinner without a major incident. Liddy served ham and roasted potatoes and a green bean casserole. She told us about the ornaments on her Christmas tree, a collection of antique ones that had come from her grandma. She asked Zoe if she liked to bake, and Zoe talked about some lemon refrigerator pie that her mother used to make when she was a kid. Reid and I talked college football.

When "Angels We Have Heard on

High" played on the CD in the background, Liddy hummed along. "I taught this one to the kids this year for the pageant. Some of them had never heard it before."

"The Christmas concert at the elementary school is apparently the *holiday concert* now," Reid said. "A bunch of parents got together and complained, and now they won't sing anything that has even faintly religious overtones."

"That's because it's a public school," Zoe said.

Reid cut a neat little triangle of his ham. "Freedom of worship. It's right there in the Constitution."

"So's freedom of religion," Zoe replied.

Reid grinned. "You try all you want, but you can't take Christ out of Christmas, honey."

"Zoe—" I interrupted.

"He brought it up," Zoe replied.

"Maybe it's time for the next course." Liddy, always the peacemaker, jumped up and cleared the dinner plates, then disappeared into the kitchen.

"Let me apologize for my wife," I said

to Reid, but before I could finish the sentence, Zoe turned, furious.

"First of all, I'm perfectly capable of speaking for myself. Second of all, I'm not going to sit here and pretend I don't have an opinion about—"

"You came here spoiling for a fight—" I argued.

"Then I'll happily call a truce," Reid interrupted, smiling uncomfortably. "It's Christmas, Zoe. Let's just agree to disagree. Stick to topics like the weather."

"Who's ready for dessert?" The swinging door to the kitchen opened, and Liddy stepped through, carrying a homemade cake. Written across the top in white icing it read: HAPPY BIRTHDAY BABY JESUS.

"My God," Zoe murmured.

Liddy smiled. "Mine, too!"

"I give up." Zoe backed away from the table. "Liddy, Reid, thank you for a lovely dinner. I hope you have a great Christmas. Max? There's no need for you to leave if you don't want to. I'll just meet you at home." She smiled politely and headed toward the foyer to get her boots and her coat.

"What are you going to do, walk?" I called after her. Excusing myself quickly, I thanked Reid and kissed Liddy good-bye.

By the time I got outside, Zoe was already trudging down the street. The snow, unplowed, reached up to her knees. My truck barreled through it easily and stopped beside her. I leaned over and opened the passenger door. "Get in," I snapped.

She thought twice, but she climbed into the cab of the truck.

For a few miles, I didn't speak to her. I couldn't. I was afraid I might actually explode. Then, when we hit the highway—which had been plowed—I turned to Zoe. "Did you ever think how *humiliating* that was for me? Is it really too much to ask for you to make it through one meal with my brother and his wife without being a sarcastic bitch?"

"Oh, that's really nice, Max. So now I'm a bitch, because I don't feel like being brainwashed by the Christian right."

"It was a fucking family *dinner*, Zo. Not a revival meeting!"

She twisted toward me, the seat belt

cutting against her throat. "I'm sorry I'm not more like Liddy," Zoe said. "Maybe Santa could slip a lobotomy into my stocking tonight. That would help."

"Why don't you just shut the hell up? What has she ever done to you?"

"Nothing, because she doesn't have a mind of her own," Zoe said.

I'd had plenty of discussions with Liddy about whether people like Jack Nicholson and Jonathan Demme owed their success to B movies; about *Psycho*'s impact on film censorship. "You don't know anything about her," I argued. "She's a . . . a . . ."

I swung the truck into our driveway, letting my voice trail off.

Zoe jumped out of the truck. It was snowing so hard now that there was a curtain of white behind her. "A saint?" she said. "Is that the word you're looking for? Well, I can't be one, Max. I'm just a flesh and blood woman, and apparently I even suck at *that*."

She slammed the passenger door and stomped to the house. Furious, I spun the wheels in reverse and tore down the street, skidding.

Between the fact that it was Christmas Eve and the heavy storm, it seemed like I was the only one on the roads. Nothing was open, not even McDonald's. It was easy to imagine I was the last person left in this universe, because that's sure as hell how it felt.

Other men were busy building bicycles and jungle gyms so that their kids could wake up on Christmas morning and get the surprise of a lifetime, but I couldn't even manage to produce a kid.

I pulled into an empty shopping center lot and watched a plow go by. I remembered the first time Liddy had seen snow.

I reached for my cell phone and dialed my brother's house, because I knew she would answer. I was just going to hear her say hello, and then hang up.

"Max?" she said, and I grimaced—I'd forgotten about caller ID.

"Hey," I said.

"Is everything okay?"

It was ten at night, and we'd left in a

major storm. Of course she was panicked.

"There's something I need to ask
you," I said.

*Do you know how you light up a
room?*

Do you ever think about me?

Then I heard Reid's voice in the background. "Come on back to bed, honey.
Who's calling so late, anyway?"

And Liddy's response: "It's just Max."

Just Max.

"What did you want to ask?" Liddy
said.

I closed my eyes. "Did . . . I leave my
scarf there?"

She called out to Reid. "Sugar? Did
you see Max's scarf?" There was some
exchange I couldn't quite make out.
"Sorry, Max, we haven't found it. But
we'll keep a lookout."

A half hour later, I let myself into my
apartment. The light over the stove was
still on, and the little tree that Zoe had
bought and decorated herself was
glowing in the corner of the living room.
She absolutely insisted on a live tree,
even though it meant lugging it up two

flights of stairs. This year she'd tied white satin bows to the boughs. She said each one was a wish she had for next year.

The only difference between a wish and a prayer is that you're at the mercy of the universe for the first, and you've got some help with the second.

Zoe was asleep on the couch, curled beneath a blanket. She was wearing pajamas with snowflakes all over them. She looked like she'd been crying.

I kissed her, to wake her up. *I'm sorry,* she murmured against my lips. *I shouldn't have—*

"I shouldn't have, either," I told her.

Still kissing her, I slipped my hands under the edge of her pajama top. Her skin was so hot it burned my palms. She dug her fingers into my hair and wrapped her legs around me. I sank to the floor and tugged her down with me. I knew every scar on her body, every freckle, every curve. They were markers on a road I'd been traveling forever.

I remember thinking our lovemaking that night was so intense, it should have left behind some kind of permanent record, like the beginnings of a baby, except it didn't.

I remember that my dreams were full of wishes, although, when I woke up, I couldn't remember a single one.

By the time Liddy gets to wherever she's planning on going, my buzz has worn off and I'm pretty much pissed at myself and the world. Once Reid finds out that I was pulled over by a cop for drunk driving, he'll tell Pastor Clive, who'll tell Wade Preston, who'll lecture me on how easy it is to lose a trial. When all I wanted, I swear, was to quit being thirsty.

I have been riding with my eyes closed because I'm also suddenly so tired I can barely keep upright. Liddy throws the truck into park. "We're here," she says.

We are in the lot in front of the storefront that houses the administrative offices of the Eternal Glory Church.

It's after hours, and I know that Pastor Clive won't be around, but that doesn't make me feel any less guilty.

Alcohol has already messed up my own life, and here I am using it to mess up a whole bunch of other people's lives, too. "Liddy," I promise, "it won't happen again . . ."

"Max." She tosses me the keys to the church office, which she has because she is the head of the Sunday School program. "Shut up."

Pastor Clive has set up a small chapel here, just in case someone needs to come in to pray at a time other than our weekly service at the school auditorium. It's got a few rows of chairs, a lectern, and a picture of Jesus on the cross. I follow Liddy past the receptionist's desk and the copy machine into the chapel. Instead of turning on the lights, she strikes a match and touches it to a candle that's sitting on the lectern. The shadows make Jesus's face look like Freddy Krueger's.

I sit down beside her and wait for her to pray out loud. That's what we do at Eternal Glory. Pastor Clive carries on a conversation with Jesus and we all listen.

Tonight, though, Liddy folds her hands in her lap, as if she's waiting for *me* to speak.

"Aren't you going to say something?" I ask.

Liddy looks up at the cross behind the lectern. "You know what my favorite passage in the Bible is? The beginning of John 20. When Mary Magdalene was grieving after Jesus's death. He wasn't *Jesus* to her, you know, he was her friend and her teacher and someone she really cared about. She came to the tomb, because she just wanted to be close to his body, if that was all that was left of him. But she got there, and his body was gone, too. Can you imagine how lonely she felt? So she started crying, and a stranger asked her what was wrong—and then said her name, and that's when she realized it was actually Jesus talking to her." Liddy glances at me. "There are lots of times I've been sure God's left me. But then it turns out I was just looking in the wrong place."

I don't know what I'm more ashamed

of: the fact that I am a failure in the eyes of Jesus, or in the eyes of Liddy.

"God's not at the bottom of that bottle. Judge O'Neill, he'll be watching everything we do. Me and Reid, and you." Liddy closes her eyes. "I want to have your baby, Max."

I feel electricity run through me.

Dear God, I pray silently, *let me see myself as You do. Remind me that none of us are perfect until we look into Your face.*

But I am staring at Liddy's.

"If it's a boy," she says, "I'm going to name him Max."

I swallow, my mouth suddenly dry. "You don't have to do that."

"I know I don't have to, but I want to." Liddy turns toward me. "Did you ever want something so bad you think that hoping is going to jinx it?"

In all the spaces between the words, I hear ones she hasn't spoken out loud. So I grasp the back of her head, and I lean forward and kiss her.

God is love. I've heard Pastor Clive say that a thousand times, but now, I understand.

Liddy's arms come up between us, and with more force than I would have expected her to have, she shoves me backward. My chair screeches across the floor. Her cheeks are bright red, and she's covering her mouth with one hand.

"Liddy," I say, my heart sinking, "I didn't mean to—"

"You don't have to apologize, Max." Suddenly there is a wall between us. I may not be able to see it, but I can feel it. "It's just the alcohol, acting out." She blows out the candle. "We should go."

Liddy leaves the chapel, but I stay behind. For at least another minute, I wait, completely in the dark.

After my car wreck, when I let Jesus into my heart, I also let Clive Lincoln into my life. We met in his office, and we talked about why I drank.

I told him that it felt like a hole inside me, and I was trying to fill it up.

He said that hole was quicksand, and I was sinking fast.

He asked me to list all the things that made that hole bigger.

Being broke, I said.

Being drunk.

Losing clients.

Losing Zoe.

Losing a baby.

Then he began to talk about what could patch that hole in me.

God. Friends. Family.

"Yeah," I said, looking down at the floor. "Thank goodness for Reid."

But Pastor Clive, he can hear when you don't mean what you say, and he leaned back in his chair. "This isn't the first time Reid's bailed you out, is it?"

"No."

"How does that make you feel?"

"How do you think it makes me feel?" I exploded. "Like a total fuckup. Like everything comes so easy to Reid, and me, I'm always drowning."

"That's because Reid's given himself over to Jesus. He's letting someone else lead him over the rapids, Max, and you—you're still trying to swim upstream."

I smirked. "So I just let go, and God takes care of it?"

"Why not? You sure as heck haven't been doing a bang-up job lately, yourself." Pastor Clive walked behind my chair. "Tell Jesus what you want. What does Reid have that you wish you could have, too?"

"I'm not going to talk out loud to Jesus—"

"Do you think He can't read your thoughts anyway?"

"Fine." I sighed. "I'm jealous of my brother. I wish I had his house. His bank account. Even his faith, I guess."

Speaking it so baldly made me feel like shit. My brother had never done anything but help me, and here I was coveting everything he had. I felt ugly, like I had peeled off a layer of skin to find an infection underneath.

And God, all I wanted to do was heal.

I might have cried then; I don't remember. I do know it was the first time I really saw myself for the person I was: someone too proud to admit his flaws.

I left one thing off the list, though,

when I was talking to Pastor Clive. I never said I wanted Reid's wife.

I kept that secret.

On purpose.

I apologize at least fifty more times to Liddy on the way home, but she stays cool, tight-lipped. "I'm sorry," I say again, as she pulls into the driveway.

"For what?" Liddy asks. "Nothing happened."

She opens the front door and lifts my arm over her neck, so that it looks like she's supporting me. "Follow my lead," she says.

I'm still a little unsteady on my feet, so I let her drag me inside. Reid is standing in the foyer. "Thank God. Where did you find him?"

"Throwing up on the side of the road," Liddy answers. "He's got a nasty case of food poisoning, according to the ER."

"Man, little brother, what did you eat?" Reid asks, wrapping an arm around me so that he can take some of my weight. I pretend to stumble, and let him pull me downstairs to the guest room in the basement. After Reid lays me down on the bed, Liddy takes off my shoes. Her hands are warm on my ankles.

Even in the dark, the ceiling's spinning. Or maybe that's just the ceiling fan. "The doctor says he'll be able to sleep it off," Liddy says. Through slitted eyes, I notice that my brother has his arm around her.

"I'll call Pastor Clive, tell him Max got back safely," Reid says, and he leaves.

Pastor Clive was looking for me, too? A fresh wave of guilt floods over me. Meanwhile Liddy steps into the closet and reaches onto the top shelf. She shakes out a blanket and covers me. I consider apologizing again, but then on second thought, I pretend to be asleep.

The bed sinks under Liddy's weight. She is sitting close enough to touch me, and I hold my breath until I feel her hand brush my hair away from my face.

Her voice is a whisper, and I have to strain to hear it.

She's praying. I listen to the rise and

fall of her words, and pretend that, instead of asking God for help, she is asking God for me.

The morning of the first time we are scheduled to appear in the courtroom, Wade Preston shows up at Reid's front door holding a suit. "I have one," I tell him.

"Yes," he says, "but do you have the *right* one, Max? First impressions, they're critical. You don't have a chance for a do-over."

"I was just going to wear my black one," I say. It's the only suit I own; I got it from Eternal Glory's goodwill closet. It's been good enough for me to wear to church on Sundays, anyway, or when I'm out doing mission work for Pastor Clive.

The one Preston's brought is charcoal gray. There is also a crisply pressed white shirt and a blue tie. "I was going to wear a red tie," I say. "I borrowed it from Reid."

"Absolutely not. You don't want to stand out. You want to look humble, stable, solid as a rock. You want to look the way you will when you go to the kindergarten parent-teacher conference."

"But Reid will be going to that—"

Wade waves me away. "Don't be obtuse, Max. You know what I mean. A red tie says, *Notice me.*"

I pause. Wade is wearing the most perfectly tailored suit I've ever seen. His initials are embroidered on the French cuff of his shirt. He's got a pocket square made of silk. "*You're* wearing a red tie," I say.

"My point exactly," Wade replies. "Now go get dressed."

An hour later, we are crammed at one of the tables in the front of the courtroom: Liddy, Reid, Ben Benjamin, Wade, and me. I haven't spoken to Liddy all morning. She's probably the one person who could calm me down, but every time I try, Wade remembers something else he needs to tell me about my behavior in court: *Sit up straight, don't fidget, don't make faces at the judge. Don't react to anything the other side says, no matter how much it upsets you.* From what he's said, you'd think I was about to have my stage debut instead of just sitting through a legal motion.

My tie is choking me, but every time I yank at it, Wade or Reid tells me to quit.

"Showtime," Wade murmurs, and I turn around to see what he's looking at. Zoe's just walked into the courtroom, along with Vanessa and a tiny lady with bouncy black curls that ricochet in all directions from her scalp.

"We're outnumbered," Vanessa says quietly, but I can hear her all the same, and I like the idea that Wade's already thrown them off their game. Zoe doesn't look at me as she takes her seat. I bet that little lawyer gave her a bunch of rules to follow, too.

Wade quietly dials a number on his cell phone, and, a moment later, the double doors at the back of the courtroom open and a young woman who works as a paralegal for Ben Benjamin wheels a hand truck full of books down the aisle. She stacks them on the table in front of Wade, while Zoe and Vanessa and their lawyer watch. There are books of research, books of law from other states. I start reading the titles on the spines: *Traditional Marriage. The Preservation of Family Values.*

The last book she sets on top of the pile is the Bible.

"Hey, Zoe," the female lawyer says. "You know the difference between a catfish and Wade Preston? One's a slimy, scum-sucking bottom-feeder. And the other one's just a fish."

A man stands up. "All rise, the honorable Padraic O'Neill presiding."

The judge enters from another door. He is tall, with a mane of white hair that has a tiny triangle of black at the widow's peak. Two deep lines bracket his mouth, as if his frown needed any more attention drawn to it.

When he sits down, we do, too. "*Baxter versus Baxter,*" the clerk reads.

The judge slips a pair of reading glasses on. "Whose motion is this?"

Ben Benjamin stands. "Your Honor,

I'm here today on the behalf of third-party plaintiffs, Reid and Liddy Baxter. My client is joining in the effort to have them impleaded into the case, and my colleague, Mr. Preston, and I would very much like to be heard on that issue."

The judge's face crinkles in a smile. "Why, Benny Benjamin! Always a pleasure to have you in court. I get to see if you managed to learn anything I ever taught you." He glances over the paperwork in his folder. "Now, what is this motion about exactly?"

"Judge, this a custody battle over three frozen embryos that remained after the divorce of Max and Zoe Baxter. Reid and Liddy Baxter are my client's brother and sister-in-law. They wish—and Max wishes—to gain custody of the embryos for the purpose of giving them to his brother and sister-in-law to gestate and bring to term and raise as their own children."

Judge O'Neill's eyebrows knit together. "You're telling me there's a final judgment about property that the parties didn't deal with during their divorce?"

Wade stands up beside me. His cologne smells like limes. "Your Honor, with all due respect," he says, "we are talking about *children*. About pre-born *children*—"

Across the aisle, Zoe's attorney rises. "Objection, Your Honor. This is ludicrous. Can someone please tell Mr. Preston we're not in Louisiana?"

Judge O'Neill points at Wade. "You! Sit down right now."

"Your Honor," Zoe's lawyer says, "Max Baxter is using biology as a trump card to take three frozen embryos away from my client—who is one of the intended parents. She and her legal spouse intend to raise them in a healthy, loving family."

"Where's her legal spouse?" O'Neill asks. "I don't see him sitting next to her."

"My client is legally married to her spouse, Vanessa Shaw, in the state of Massachusetts."

"Well, Ms. Moretti," the judge replies,

"she's not legally married in Rhode Island. Now, let me get this straight—"

Behind me, I hear Vanessa stifle a snort. "But we're *not*," she murmurs.

"—You want the embryos." He points at Zoe. "And you want them," he says, pointing at me, and finally he points to Reid and Liddy. "And now *they* want them?"

"Actually, Your Honor," Zoe's lawyer says, "Max Baxter doesn't want the embryos. He plans to give them away."

Wade stands up. "To the contrary, Your Honor. Max wants his children to be raised in a traditional family, not a sexually deviant one."

"A man seeking embryos to give away to somebody else," the judge sums up. "Are you saying that's a traditional type of thing to do? Because it sure isn't where I come from."

"If I may, Judge, this is a complicated case," Zoe's attorney says. "As far as I know, it's a new area of the law that's never been determined in Rhode Island. Today, though, we're only convened because of the motion filed to implead

Reid and Liddy Baxter, and I strenu-
ously object to them becoming parties
in this lawsuit. I have filed a memo today stating that, and, in fact, if you
choose to allow prospective gestational
carriers to implead this case, then Vanessa Shaw should also be a party, and
I will file a motion immediately—"

"I object, Your Honor," Wade argues.
"You already said this is not a legal
marriage, and now Ms. Moretti is raising a red herring that you already tossed
out."

The judge stares at him. "Mr. Preston, if you interrupt Ms. Moretti again, I
am going to hold you in contempt of
court. This is not a TV show; you're not
Pat Robertson. This is *my* courtroom,
and I'm not about to let you turn it into
the circus you'd like it to be. I'm retiring
after this case, and so help me, I'm not
going out in a religious catfight." He
bangs his gavel. "The motion to implead is denied. This case is between
Max Baxter and Zoe Baxter, and it will
proceed in the ordinary course. You,
Mr. Benjamin, are welcome to call

whomever you like as a witness, but I'm not impleading anyone. Not Reid and Liddy Baxter," he says, and then he turns to the other lawyer. "And not Vanessa Shaw, so don't file any motions requesting it."

Finally, he turns to Wade. "And Mr. Preston. Word to the wise: think very carefully about what kind of grandstanding you plan to do. Because I'm not allowing you to run away with this court. I'm in charge here."

He stands up and leaves the bench, and we jump up, too. Being in court isn't that different from being in church. You rise, you fall, you look to the front of the room for guidance.

Zoe's lawyer walks over to our table. "Angela," Wade says. "I wish I could say it's a pleasure to see you, but it's a sin to lie."

"Sorry that didn't go as well for you as you'd hoped," she replies.

"That went just fine, thank you very much."

"Maybe that's what you all think in Louisiana, but, believe me, here you just got slammed," the lawyer says.

Wade leans on the books that were brought in by the paralegal. "The true colors of this judge will come out, darlin'," he says. "And believe me . . . they're not rainbow-striped."

	TRACK 1	SING YOU HOME
	TRACK 2	THE HOUSE ON HOPE STREET
	TRACK 3	REFUGEE
	TRACK 4	THE LAST
	TRACK 5	MARRY ME
	TRACK 6	FAITH
✓	**TRACK 7**	**THE MERMAID**
	TRACK 8	ORDINARY LIFE
	TRACK 9	WHERE YOU ARE
	TRACK 10	SAMMY'S SONG

ZOE

Lucy is drawing a mermaid: her hair long and twisted, her tail curled into the corner of the thick manila paper. As I finish singing "Angel," I put down my guitar, but Lucy keeps adding little touches—a ribbon of seaweed, the reflection of the sun. "You're a good artist," I tell her.

She shrugs. "I design my own tattoos."

"Do you have any?"

"If I did, I'd be thrown out of my house," Lucy says. "One year, six months, four days."

"That's when you're getting your tattoo?"

She looks up at me. "That's the minute I turn eighteen."

After our drumming session, I had vowed never to make Lucy meet in the special needs classroom again. Instead, Vanessa tells me which spaces are unoccupied (the French class that's on a field trip; the art class that has gone to the auditorium to watch a film). Today, for example, we are meeting in the health classroom. We're surrounded by inspirational posters: THIS IS YOUR BRAIN ON DRUGS. And CHOOSE BOOZE? YOU LOSE. And a pregnant teen in profile: NO DEPOSIT, NO RETURN.

We have been working on lyric analysis. It's something I've done before with the nursing home groups, because it gets people interacting with each other. Usually I start by telling them the name of a song—often one they don't know—and ask them to guess what it will be about. Then I sing it, and ask for the words and phrases that stood out. We talk about their personal reactions to the lyrics, and, finally, I ask what emotions the song produced in them.

Because I didn't think Lucy would

want to verbally open up, I started having her draw her reactions to the lyrics. "It's interesting that you drew a mermaid," I said. "Angels aren't usually pictured underwater."

Immediately, Lucy bristles. "You said there wasn't a right and a wrong way to do this."

"There's not."

"I guess I could have drawn some of those totally depressing animals on the ASPCA commercial . . ."

It has been running a few years now: a montage of sad-eyed puppies and kittens, with this song playing in the background.

"You know, Sarah McLachlan said the song was about the keyboard player for the Smashing Pumpkins, who OD'd on heroin," I say. I'd picked this song because I was hoping to get her talking about her previous suicide attempts.

"Duh. That's why I drew a mermaid. She's floating and drowning at the same time."

Sometimes Lucy says things that just leave me speechless. I wonder how Vanessa and all the other school counselors could have ever thought she was distancing herself from the world. She'd drawn a bead on it, better than any of us.

"Have you ever felt like that?" I ask.

Lucy looks up. "Like OD'ing on heroin?"

"Among other things."

She colors in the mermaid's hair, ignoring the question. "If you could pick, how would you want to die?"

"In my sleep."

"Everyone says that." Lucy rolls her eyes. "If that wasn't an option, then what?"

"This is a pretty morbid conversation—"

"So is talking about suicide."

I nod, giving her that much. "Fast. Like an execution by firing squad. I wouldn't want to feel anything."

"A plane crash," Lucy says. "You practically get vaporized."

"Yeah, but imagine what it's like the few minutes before, when you know you're going down." I used to actually have nightmares about plane crashes. That I wouldn't be able to turn on my phone fast enough or get a signal so that I could leave Max a message telling him I loved him. I used to picture him sitting at the answering machine after my funeral, listening to the dead air and wondering what I was trying to say.

"I've heard drowning's not so bad. You pass out from holding your breath before all the really awful stuff happens." She looks down at the paper, at her mermaid. "With my luck, I'd be able to breathe water."

I look at her. "Why would that be so bad?"

"How do mermaids commit suicide?" Lucy muses. "Death by oxygen?"

"Lucy," I say, waiting for her to meet my gaze, "do you still think about killing yourself?"

She doesn't make a joke out of the question. But she doesn't answer, either. She begins to draw patterns on the mermaid's tail, a flourish of scales. "You know how I get angry sometimes?" she says. "That's because it's the only thing I can still feel. And I need to test myself, to make sure I'm really here."

Music therapy is a hybrid profession. Sometimes I'm an entertainer, sometimes I am a healer. Sometimes I am a psychologist, and sometimes I'm just a confidante. The art of my job is knowing when to be each of these things. "Maybe there are other ways to test yourself," I suggest. "To make you feel."

"Like what?"

"You could write some music," I say. "For a lot of musicians, songs become the way to talk about really hard things they're going through."

"I can't even play the kazoo."

"I could teach you. And it doesn't have to be the kazoo, either. It could be guitar, drums, piano. Anything you want."

She shakes her head, already retreating. "Let's play Russian roulette," she says, and she grabs my iPod. "Let's draw the next song that comes up on Shuffle." She pushes the picture of the mermaid toward me and reaches for a fresh piece of paper.

"Rudolph, the Red-Nosed Reindeer" starts playing.

We both look up and start laughing.

"Seriously?" Lucy says. "This is on one of your playlists?"

"I work with little kids. This is a big favorite."

She bends over the paper and starts drawing again. "Every year, my sisters watch this on TV. And every year, it scares the hell out of me."

"*Rudolph* scares you?"

"Not Rudolph. The place he goes."

She is drawing a train with square wheels, a spotted elephant. "The Island of Misfit Toys?" I ask.

"Yeah," Lucy says, looking up. "They creep me out."

"I never really understood what was wrong with them," I admit. "Like the Charlie-in-the-Box? Big deal. Tickle Me Elmo would have still been a hit if it were called Tickle Me Gertrude. And I always thought a water pistol that shot jelly could be the next Transformer."

"What about the polka-dotted elephant?" Lucy says, a smile playing over her lips. "Total freak of nature."

"On the contrary—sticking him on the island was a blatantly racist move.

For all we know his mother had an affair with a cheetah."

"The doll is the scariest . . ."

"What's her issue?"

"She's depressed," Lucy says. "Because none of the kids want her."

"Do they ever actually tell you that?"

"No, but what else *could* her problem be?" Suddenly, she grins. "Unless she's a *he* . . ."

"Cross-dressing," we say, at the same time.

We both laugh, and then Lucy bends down over her artwork again. She draws in silence for a few moments, adding spots to that poor misunderstood elephant. "I'd probably fit right in on that stupid island," Lucy says. "Because I'm supposed to be invisible, but everyone can still see me."

"Maybe you're not supposed to be invisible. Maybe you're just supposed to be different."

As I say the words, I think of Angela Moretti, and Vanessa, and those frozen embryos. I think of Wade Preston, with his Hong Kong tailored suit and slicked-back hair, looking at me as if I am a total aberration, a crime against the species.

If I remember correctly, those toys all jump into Santa's sleigh and get redistributed beneath Christmas trees everywhere. I hope that, if this is true, I wind up under Wade Preston's.

I turn to find Lucy staring at me. "The other time I feel things," she confesses, "is when I'm here with you."

Usually after Lucy's therapy session, I go to Vanessa's office and we have lunch in the cafeteria—Tater Tots, let me tell you, are vastly underrated—but today, she's off at a college admissions fair in Boston, so I head to my car instead. On the way I check my phone messages. There's one from Vanessa, telling me about an admissions officer from Emerson with an orange beehive hairdo who looks like she fell off a B-52's album cover, and another just telling me she loves me. There's one from my mother, asking me if I can help her move furniture this afternoon.

As I get closer to my yellow Jeep in

the parking lot, I see Angela Moretti leaning against it. "Is something wrong?" I say immediately. It can't be a good thing when your attorney travels an hour to tell you something.

"I was in the neighborhood. Well, Fall River, anyway. So I figured I'd swing by to tell you the latest."

"That doesn't sound very good . . ."

"I got another motion on my desk this morning, courtesy of Wade Preston," Angela explains. "He wants to appoint a guardian ad litem to the case."

"A what?"

"They're common in custody cases. It's someone whose job it is to determine the best interests of the child, and to communicate that to the court." She shakes her head. "Preston wants one appointed for the *pre-born* children."

"How could he . . ." My voice trails off.

"This is posturing," Angela explains. "It's his way of setting forth a political agenda, that's all. It's going to be knocked out of court before you even sit down in your chair." She glances up at me. "There's more. Preston was on *Joe Hoffman* last night."

"Who's Joe Hoffman?"

"A conservative who runs the Voice of Liberty Broadcasting. A mecca for the closed-minded, if you ask me."

"What did he talk about?"

Angela looks at me squarely. "The destruction of family values. He specifically named you and Vanessa as being at the forefront of the homosexual movement to ruin America. Do you two receive mail at your house? Because I'd strongly recommend a post office box. And I assume you have an alarm system . . ."

"Are you saying we're in danger?"

"I don't know," Angela says. "Better safe than sorry. Hoffman's small potatoes, compared to where Preston's headed. O'Reilly, Glenn Beck, Limbaugh. He didn't take this case because he cares so deeply for Max. He took it because it gives him a platform to stand on while he's preaching, and because it's a current hook that gets him booked on these shows. By the time we go to trial, Preston's going to make sure you can't turn on the TV without seeing his face."

Angela had warned us that this would be an uphill battle, that we had to be prepared. I'd assumed that what was at stake was my chance to be a mother; I hadn't realized that I'd also lose my privacy, my anonymity.

"When you think about the lengths he's going to, it's laughable," Angela says.

But I don't find it funny. When I start crying, Angela hugs me. "Is it all going to be like this?" I ask.

"Worse," she promises. "But imagine the stories you'll have to tell your baby one day."

She waits until I've pulled myself together, and then tells me to be at court tomorrow to fight the motion. As I'm getting into my car again, my cell phone rings.

"Why aren't you home yet?" Vanessa says.

I should tell her about Angela's visit; I should tell her about Wade Preston. But when you love someone, you protect her. I may stand to lose my credibility, my reputation, my career, but then again, it's my battle. This is *my* ex-husband, *my* former marriage's embryos. The only reason Vanessa is even involved is because she had the misfortune of falling for me.

"I got tied up," I say. "Tell me about the beehive lady."

But Vanessa is having none of it. "What's the matter? You sound like you're crying."

I close my eyes. "I'm getting a cold."

It is the first time, I realize, I've ever lied to her.

It takes my mother and me two hours to swap all the furniture in my old bedroom and hers. She's decided that she needs a new perspective, and what better way to start each day than to see something different when she opens her eyes?

"Plus," she says, "your window opens to the west. I'm tired of waking up with the sun in my eyes."

I glance around at the same bedding,

the same bedroom set. "So basically you're your own life coach?"

"How can I expect my clients to follow my advice if I don't follow it myself?"

"And you really believe that relocating ten feet down the hall is going to revolutionize your life?"

"Beliefs are the roads we take to reach our dreams. Believe you can do something—or believe you can't—and you'll be right every time."

I roll my eyes at her. I am pretty sure there was a self-help movement not too long ago that followed that mantra. I remember seeing a high school student on a newsmagazine who subscribed to the philosophy and then didn't study for her SATs because, after all, she could visualize that perfect 2400. Needless to say, she wound up going to a community college and complaining on television about how it was really all a load of BS.

I look around the room at my mother's same old bedding, same furniture. "Doesn't it defeat the purpose of starting over when you're doing it with stuff you've had forever?"

"Honestly, Zoe, you are such a downer sometimes." My mother sighs. "I'm more than happy to give you a little life coaching, free of charge."

"I'll take a rain check, thanks."

"Suit yourself." She slides down, her back pressed to the wall, while I collapse across the mattress. When I look up, I see a freckling of glow-in-the-dark stars affixed to the ceiling.

"I'd forgotten about those," I say.

After my father died, I became obsessed with ghosts. I desperately wanted my father to be one, in the hope that I might find him sitting on the edge of my bed when I woke up in the middle of the night, or feel him whisper a shiver across the nape of my neck. To this end, I borrowed books from the library on paranormal activity; I tried to conduct séances in my bedroom; I sneaked downstairs late at night and watched horror movies when I should have been sleeping. My teacher noticed, and told my mother I might need help. The psychiatrist I'd been seeing sporadically after my father's death agreed it could be an issue to address.

My mother didn't. She figured if I wanted my father to be a spirit, I must have had a valid reason.

One night at dinner she said, "I don't think he's a ghost. I think he's a star, looking down on us."

"That's dumb. A star's just a ball of gas," I scoffed.

"And a ghost is . . . ?" my mother pointed out. "Ask any scientist—they'll tell you that new stars are born every minute."

"People who die don't become stars."

"Some Native Americans would disagree with you, there."

I considered this. "Where do stars go during the day?"

"That's the thing," my mother said, "they're still there. They're watching us, even when we're too busy to be watching them."

While I was at school the next day, my mother hot-glued little plastic stars on my ceiling. That night, we both lay down on the bed and covered ourselves with my blanket. I didn't sneak out of bed to watch a scary movie. Instead, I fell asleep with my mother's arms around me.

Now, I look at her. "Do you think I would have turned out differently if Dad had been around when I was growing up?"

"Well, sure," my mother says, coming to sit beside me on the bed. "But I think he'd be pretty proud of the outcome all the same."

After Angela left, I'd stopped off at my house. I'd gotten on the Internet and downloaded the podcast of Joe Hoffman's radio program, where I listened to him and Wade Preston rattle off statistics: children raised by homosexual parents were more likely to try a homosexual relationship themselves; children of homosexual parents were embarrassed to let their friends find out about their home lives; lesbian mothers feminized their sons and masculinized their daughters.

"My lawsuit was on Joe Hoffman's radio show," I say.

"I know," my mother says. "I heard it."

"*You* listen to him?"

"Religiously . . . pun intended. I tune in when I'm on the treadmill. I've found that, when I'm angry, I walk faster." She laughs. "I save Rush for my abdominal crunches."

"But what if he has a point? What if we have a boy? I don't know anything about raising one. I don't know about dinosaurs or construction equipment or how to play catch . . ."

"Honey, babies don't come with in-struction booklets. You'd learn the same way we all do—you'd read up on dino-saurs; you'd Google backhoes and skidders. And you don't need a penis to go buy a baseball glove." My mother shakes her head. "Don't you dare let anyone tell you what you can and can-not be, Zoe."

"You have to admit, things would have been easier if Dad was here," I say.

"Yes. I actually agree with Wade Pres-ton in one respect: every child should be raised by a married couple." She smiles broadly. "That's why same-sex marriage should be legal."

"When did you become such a gay activist?"

"I'm not. I'm a *Zoe* activist. If you'd told me you were vegan, I can't say I'd stop eating meat, but I'd fight for your right to not eat it. If you'd told me you were becoming a nun, I can't promise you I'd convert, but I'd read the Bible so I could talk to you about it. But you're gay, so instead I know that the American Psychological Association says children raised by gay parents describe themselves as straight in the same proportion as those raised in heterosexual households. I know there's no scientific basis for saying gay people are any less capable than straight parents. As a matter of fact, there are certain bonuses that come with being raised by two mommies or two daddies: compassion, for one. Plus, girls play and dress in ways that break gender stereotypes, and boys tend to be more affectionate, more nurturing, and less promiscuous. And probably because they've dealt with questions all their lives, kids raised by gay parents are better at adjusting in general."

My jaw drops. "Where did you learn all that?"

"On the Internet. Because when I'm not listening to Joe Hoffman, I'm researching what I'm going to say when I finally back Wade Preston into a corner."

No matter what Joe Hoffman and Wade Preston say, it's not gender that makes a family; it's love. You don't need a mother and a father; you don't necessarily even need two parents. You just need someone who's got your back.

I imagine my mother going after Wade Preston, and I smile. "I hope I'm around to watch that."

My mother squeezes my hand. She looks up at the stars on the ceiling. "Where else *would* you be?" she asks.

I lean over Lucy from behind and place the guitar in her arms. "Cradle it like a baby," I say, "with your left hand supporting the neck."

"Like this?" She turns in her seat, so that she is looking up at me.

"Let's hope when you babysit you don't strangle the kids quite like that . . ."

She lets up on her choke hold on the neck of the guitar. "Oh."

"Now put your left index finger on the fifth string, second fret. Put your left middle finger on the fourth string, second fret."

"My fingers are getting all tangled—"

"Playing the guitar's like Twister for your hands. Take your pick between your right thumb and forefinger. Press down on the strings with your left hand, and with your right, gently drag that pick over the sound hole."

A chord fills the small confines of the nurse's office, the space we are occupying for our session today. Lucy looks up, glowing. "I did it!"

"That's an E minor. It's the first chord I learned, too." I watch her play it a few more times. "You've got a really good sense of music," I say.

Lucy bends over my guitar. "Must be genetic. My family's really big on making a 'joyful noise.'"

I forget, most of the time, that Lucy's

family attends Max's church. Vanessa had told me months ago, when Lucy and I started working together. Most likely, they know Max and Wade Preston. They just haven't done the math yet to realize their precious daughter is spending time with the Devil Incarnate.

"Can I play a song?" Lucy asks, excited.

"Well, with one more chord you can learn 'A Horse with No Name.'" I take the guitar from her and settle it in my lap, then play the E minor, followed by a D add6 add9.

"Wait," Lucy says. She covers my hand with her own, so that her fingers match the places where mine sit on the guitar. Then she lifts my hand off the neck of the instrument, and spins my wedding band. "That's really pretty," Lucy says.

"Thanks."

"I never noticed it before. Is it your wedding ring?"

I wrap my arms around the guitar. Why is a question that should be so simple to answer *not* simple at all? "We're not here to talk about me."

"But I don't know anything about you. I don't know if you're married or if you've got kids or if you're a serial killer . . ."

When she says the word *kids,* my stomach does a flip. "I'm not a serial killer."

"Well, that's a comfort."

"Look, Lucy. I don't want to waste our time together by—"

"It's not wasting time if I'm the one who asks, is it?"

This much I know about Lucy: she is unstoppable. Once she gets an idea in her head, she won't let go. It's why she picks up so quickly on any musical challenge I toss her, from lyric analysis to learning how to play an instrument. I've often thought that this was why she was so disconnected from the world when we first met—not because she didn't care but because she cared too much; whenever she engaged, it was bound to exhaust her.

This I also know about Lucy: Although I don't think she's particularly conservative, her family is. And in this case, what she doesn't know can't hurt her. If she accidentally reveals to her mother that I'm married to Vanessa, I have no doubt our therapy sessions will come to a grinding halt. I couldn't stand knowing that my own situation in some way negatively affected hers.

"I don't understand why this is such a state secret," she says.

I shrug. "You wouldn't ask the school psychologist about her personal life, would you?"

"The school psychologist isn't my friend."

"I'm not your friend," I correct. "I'm your music therapist."

Immediately, she pulls away from me. Her eyes shutter.

"Lucy, you don't understand—"

"Oh, believe me, I understand," she says. "I'm your fucking dissertation. Your little Frankenstein experiment. You walk out of here and go home and you don't give a shit about me. I'm just business, to you. It's okay. I totally get it."

I sigh. "I know it feels hurtful to you, but my job, Lucy, is to talk about you. To focus on you. Of course I care about you, and of course I think about you when we're not meeting. But ultimately I need you to see me as your music therapist, not your buddy."

Lucy pivots her seat, staring blankly out the window. For the next forty minutes, she doesn't react when I play, sing, or ask her what she wants to listen to on my iPod. When the bell finally rings, she bolts like a mustang who's chewed through her tethers. She's halfway out the door when I tell her I will see her Friday, but I am not sure she hears me at all.

"Stop fidgeting," Vanessa whispers as I sit beside Angela Moretti, waiting for the judge to walk into the courtroom and rule on Wade Preston's motion to appoint a guardian ad litem.

"I can't help it," I mutter.

Vanessa is sitting directly behind our table. My mother, beside her, pipes up. "Anxiety's like a rocking chair. It gives you something to do, but it doesn't get you very far."

Vanessa looks at her. "Who said that?"

"I just did."

"But were you quoting anyone?"

"Myself," she says proudly.

"I'm going to tell it to one of my AP students. He actually had his car detailed to read HARVARD OR BUST."

I am distracted by the arrival of Max and his attorneys. Wade Preston walks down the aisle of the courtroom first, followed by Ben Benjamin, and then Reid. A few steps behind is Max, wearing another new suit that his brother must have purchased for him. His hair is too long, curling over his ears. I used to make fun of him when it got like that, used to say he was rocking a Carol Brady look.

If there's a physical component to falling in love—the butterflies in your stomach, the roller coaster of your soul—then there's an equal physical component to falling out of love. It feels like your lungs are sieves, so you can't get enough air. Your insides freeze solid. Your heart becomes a tiny, bitter pearl, a chemical reaction to one irritating grain of truth.

The last person in the entourage is Liddy. She's channeling Jackie Kennedy today. "Is she OCD?" Vanessa whispers. "Or are the gloves a fashion statement?"

Before I can respond, a harried paralegal rushes down the aisle with a hand truck and begins to stack reference books in front of Wade Preston, just like the other day. Even if it's all for show, it's working. I'm totally intimidated.

"Hey, Zoe," Angela says, not looking up from the notes she's writing down. "Did you know that the postal service almost put Wade Preston's face on a stamp? But they gave up when people couldn't figure out which side to spit on."

In a flurry of black robes, Judge O'Neill enters. "You know, Mr. Preston, you don't earn rewards mileage for coming to court more often." He flips through the motion before him. "Am I misreading this, Counselor, or are you asking for a guardian ad litem to be appointed for a child that does not and may never exist?"

"Your Honor," Preston says, getting to his feet, "the important thing is that we're talking about a *child.* You even just said so, yourself. And once this pre-born child comes into being, the outcome of your decision is going to determine where he or she is raised. To that end, I think you should have some input from a qualified professional who can interview the potential families and prospective parents and give you the tools to make that decision."

The judge peers over his glasses at Angela. "Ms. Moretti, something tells me you might have a different point of view."

"Your Honor, a guardian ad litem's responsibilities include interviewing the child at the center of the disagreement. How do you interview an embryo?"

Wade Preston shakes his head. "No one's suggesting that the GAL talk to a petri dish, Judge. But we feel that talking to the potential parents will give a good indication of which lifestyle might be more fitting for a child."

"Straw," I whisper.

Distracted, Angela leans closer to me. "What?"

I shake my head, silent. The embryos are kept in straws, not petri dishes. If Preston had done his homework, he would have known that. But this isn't about being thorough, or accurate, for him. It's about being the ringmaster of a circus.

"With all due respect, Your Honor, the law in Rhode Island is clear," Angela counters. "When we discuss what's in the best interests of children during a custody battle, we are talking about children that are already alive. What Mr. Preston is trying to do is elevate the status of frozen embryos to something they're not in this state—namely, humans."

The judge turns to Wade Preston. "You raise an interesting point, Mr. Preston. I'm not sure I wouldn't appreciate exploring that concept further, but Ms. Moretti is right on the law. The appointment of a guardian ad litem presumes the existence of a minor child, so I am going to have to deny your motion.

However, as concerns this court, it's in our best interests to protect innocent victims. To that end, I will hear from all the witnesses and take on the role of a guardian ad litem myself." He glances up. "Are we ready to set a date for trial?"

"Your Honor," Angela says, "my client is forty-one years old, her spouse is nearly thirty-five. The embryos have been cryo-preserved for over a year now. We'd like this resolved as soon as possible to ensure the best chances for a viable pregnancy."

"It seems that Ms. Moretti and I actually agree for once," Wade Preston adds. "Although the reason we want this brought to trial quickly is because these children deserve to be put into a loving, traditional Christian home as soon as possible."

"There's a third reason for this to be scheduled in a timely fashion," Judge O'Neill says. "I'm retiring at the end of June, and I damn well don't intend to leave this mess for someone else to clean up. We'll set the trial date for fifteen days from now. I trust both sides will be fully prepared?"

After the judge leaves for chambers, I turn to Angela. "That's good, right? We won the motion?"

But she is less enthusiastic than I would have expected. "Technically," she admits. "But I don't like what he said about 'innocent victims.' Feels slanted to me."

We stop speaking as Wade Preston approaches and hands a piece of paper to Angela. "Your witness list," she says, looking it over. "Aren't you proactive?"

He grins, like a shark. "You ain't seen nothin' yet, sugar," he says.

On Friday, Lucy is fifteen minutes late for our session. I decide to give her the benefit of the doubt, since we have been moved to the photography studio on the third floor—a room that I didn't even know existed. "Hi," I say, when she walks in. "You had trouble finding it, too?"

Lucy doesn't answer. She sits down

at a desk, takes out a book, and buries her nose in it.

"Okay, you're still mad at me. That's coming through loud and clear. So let's talk about it." I lean forward, my hands clasped between my knees. "It's perfectly normal for a client to misinterpret a relationship with her therapist—Freud even talked about it being a key to finding out something from your past that's still upsetting to you. So maybe we can look constructively at why you want me to be your friend. What does that say about who you are, and what you need right now?"

Stone-faced, she flips a page.

The book is a collection of short stories by Anton Chekhov. "You're taking Russian lit," I surmise. "Impressive."

Lucy ignores me.

"I never took Russian lit. Too much of a wimp. I have enough trouble understanding all that stuff when it's in English." I reach for my guitar and pluck out a Slavic, minor run of notes. "If I were going to play Russian literature, I think it would sound like this," I muse. "Except I really need a violin."

Lucy slams the book shut, shoots me a look of death, and puts her head down on the desk.

I pull my chair closer to her. "Maybe you don't want to tell me what's on your mind. Maybe you'd like to play it, instead."

No response.

I reach for my djembe and put it between my knees, tilted so that she can drum on it. "Are you this angry," I ask, striking it lightly, "or *this* angry?" I smack it, hard, with my palm.

Lucy continues facing in the opposite direction. I begin to play a beat, *thump-thump-thump-THUMP, thump-thump-thump-THUMP.*

Eventually, I stop. "If you don't want to talk, maybe we'll just listen today."

I set my iPod on the portable speaker system and begin to play some of the music that Lucy has reacted to before—either positively or negatively. At this point, I just want to get a rise out of her. I think I've finally cracked her shell when she sits up, twists in her chair, and digs in her backpack. A moment later, she comes up with a ratty, crushed tissue.

Lucy tears off two tiny scraps of the tissue. She balls them up and sticks them in her ears.

I shut off the music.

When I first started working with Lucy and she behaved like this, I saw it as a challenge I had to overcome, the same way I faced challenges with all my other patients. But after months of progress . . . this feels like a personal affront.

Freud would call that countertransference. Or in other words, what happens when the therapist's emotions get tangled up with a patient's. I am supposed to step back and wonder why Lucy might try to elicit this anger in me. That way, I regain control of the emotions in our therapeutic relationship again . . . and, more important, I discover another missing piece of the puzzle that is Lucy.

The thing is, Freud got it all wrong.

When Max and I first met, he took me fishing. I'd never been, and I didn't understand how people could spend entire days bobbing around on the ocean waiting for a bite that never came. It seemed silly, an utter waste of time. But that day, the striped bass were running. He baited my hook and cast the line and showed me how to hold the fishing rod. After about fifteen minutes, I felt a tug on the line. *I've got one,* I said, excited and nervous. I listened to Max carefully as he told me what to do—move rhythmically and slowly, never let up on the pull of the line—but then, suddenly, it went slack. When I reeled in, the bait was gone, and so was the striper. I was utterly deflated, and in that moment I understood why fishermen would wait all day to catch something: you have to understand what you're missing before you can really feel a loss.

That's why Lucy's boycott of this session hurts so much more than it did at the beginning. I know her now. I've connected with her. So her withdrawal isn't a challenge; it's a setback.

After a few minutes, I turn off the music, and we sit out the rest of the session in silence.

When Max and I were trying to have a baby, we had to see a social worker at the IVF clinic—but I don't remember the questions being anything like the ones that Vanessa and I are hearing now.

The social worker's name is Felicity Grimes, and she looks like she didn't get the memo that the eighties are over. Her red suit jacket is asymmetrical, with enormous shoulder pads. Her hair is piled so high it could function as a sail in the wind. "Do you really think you'll stay together?" she asks.

"We're married," I say. "I think that's a pretty good indicator of our commitment."

"Fifty percent of marriages end in divorce," Felicity says.

I am nearly certain that, when Max and I met with the social worker, she didn't question whether or not our relationship would stand the test of time.

"That's true of opposite-sex marriages," Vanessa says. "But gay marriage hasn't been around long enough to really have any statistics. Then again, considering the lengths we had to go to to *get* married, you could argue we're even more committed than the average straight couple."

I squeeze Vanessa's hand, a warning. I've tried to explain to her that, no matter how stupid the questions get, we have to just stay calm and answer them. The objective here is not to wave a rainbow banner. It's to get a social worker's check mark, so that we can move on to the next step. "What she means is that we're in this for the long haul," I say, and smile tentatively.

We had to fight the clinic director to begin the process of in vitro—in spite of the fact that a court order held the frozen embryos in limbo. She agreed to allow us to get the psychological components completed, and then—if the court ruled in our favor—to start Vanessa immediately on the drug regimen. But, she pointed out, if Max wanted Reid and Liddy to have the same privilege, she would have to give it to them.

We have already explained to the counselor how we met, how long we've been together. "Have you considered the legal ramifications of being same-sex parents?"

"Yes," I say. "I'll adopt the baby, after Vanessa gives birth."

"I assume you both have powers of attorney?"

We look at each other. Unlike straight couples, if I were in a car crash and dying, Vanessa wouldn't have the rights as my spouse to sit by me at the hospital, to make the decision to turn off life support. Because our marriage isn't federally recognized, we have to jump through all these extra legal hoops to get the same rights—1,138 of them—that come naturally to heterosexual couples who get married. Vanessa and I had been planning to sit down with a bottle of bourbon one night and ask each other questions no one ever wants to have to answer—about organ donation and hospice care and brain death—but then we were served with a lawsuit and, ironically, asking a lawyer to draft a power of attorney was moved to the back burner. "We're in the process of getting that taken care of." It's not a lie if we *meant* to do it, is it?

"Why do you want to have a child?" Felicity asks.

"I won't speak for Vanessa," I say, "but I've always wanted one. I tried for almost a decade, with my ex-husband. I don't think I'll feel complete if I don't have the chance to be a mother."

The social worker turns to Vanessa. "I see kids every day at work. Some of them are shy, or funny, or complete pains in the neck. But every single one of them is living proof that, at one point, their parents believed they'd have a future together. I want to have Zoe's baby so that she can grow up with two mothers who have moved heaven and earth to bring her into this world."

"But how do you feel about being a parent?"

"I'm obviously fine with it," Vanessa says.

"Yet you've never expressed a desire to have a child before now . . ."

"Because I wasn't with a partner I'd want to have kids with."

"Are you doing this for Zoe, then, or for yourself?"

"How can you ask me to separate those?" Vanessa says, exasperated. "Of course I'm doing it for Zoe. But I'm also doing it for me."

Felicity writes something down on her pad. It makes me nervous. "What makes you think you'd be a good parent?"

"I'm patient," I reply. "I have a lot of experience helping people with problems express themselves in a different way. I know how to listen."

"And she loves harder than anyone I've ever known," Vanessa adds. "She'd do anything for her child. And I—well, I'm a school counselor. I have to believe that will come in handy eventually with my own kid."

"She's also smart, confident, and empathetic," I say. "An amazing role model."

"So Ms. Shaw—you work with teenagers. Did you ever babysit when you were younger? Have any younger siblings you helped raise?"

"No," Vanessa says, "but I'm pretty

sure I can Google how to change a diaper if I get stumped."

"She's also funny," I interject. "Great sense of humor!"

"You know, I've come across a few teen mothers during my career," Vanessa points out. "They're close enough to childhood to remember it intimately, but I wouldn't say that makes them better equipped for parenting . . ."

Felicity looks up at her. "Are you always this sensitive?"

"Only when I'm talking to someone who's a—"

"What else?" I say brightly. "You must have some other questions for us."

"How are you going to explain to your child why she has two moms, and no dad?" Felicity asks.

I was expecting this question. "I'd start by telling her that there are lots of different kinds of families, and that one isn't any better than another."

"Children, as you know, can be cruel. What if a classmate makes fun of her for having two mothers?"

Vanessa crosses her legs. "I'd go and beat up the kid who teased her."

I stare at her. "You did *not* just say that."

"Oh, fine. We'd deal with it. We'd talk our kid through it," Vanessa says. "And *then* I'd go beat up the bully."

I grit my teeth. "What she *means* is that we would speak to the bully's parents and try to explain a way to get their child to be a little more tolerant—"

The phone rings, and the social worker answers it. "I'm sorry," she says to us. "Will you excuse me for a moment?"

As soon as Felicity Grimes steps out of her office, I turn to Vanessa. "*Really?* Did you really just say that to a social worker who is going to decide whether or not we get to use these embryos?"

"She's not deciding. Judge O'Neill is. And besides—these questions are ludicrous! There are plenty of deadbeat dads in the world who are reason enough to glorify lesbian parents."

"But the social worker has to give us the green light before the clinic will start any procedure," I point out. "You don't know how to play this game, Vanessa, but I do. You say anything and do anything you have to in order to get her to sign off on us."

"I'm not going to let someone judge me just because I'm gay. Isn't it bad enough that our relationship is being dragged through the court system? Do I really have to sit here and smile while Pam Ewing here tells me I can't be both a lesbian and a good parent?"

"She never said that," I argue. "That's just what you *heard.*"

I imagine Felicity Grimes listening in on the other side of the door, and putting a big red X through our file. *Couple can't even see eye to eye during an hour-long interview. Unfit to parent.*

Vanessa shakes her head. "I'm sorry, but I won't play this game like Max did. I can't pretend to be someone I'm not, Zoe. I spent half my life doing that."

In that moment, the anger I feel toward Max bubbles up like blisters on my tongue. It is one thing for him to take away my right to use these embryos. It's another thing to take away what makes me happy.

"Vanessa," I say, "I want a baby. But not if it means losing you."

She looks up at me as the social worker sails through the door again. "My apologies, again. Everything looks good on my end."

Vanessa and I look at each other. "You mean we're done?" I ask. "We passed?"

She smiles. "It's not a test. We don't expect you to have the right answers. We just want you to have answers, period."

Vanessa stands up and shakes the social worker's hand. "Thank you."

"Good luck."

I gather my coat and purse, and we walk out of the office. For a moment, we just stand in the hallway, and then Vanessa grabs me and hugs me so hard I am lifted off my feet. "I feel like I just won the Super Bowl."

"More like the first game of the season," I point out.

"Still. It feels good to have someone say yes instead of no."

Her arm is draped over my shoulders as we walk down the hall. "For the record," I say, "when you went to beat up that hypothetical bully? I may not have wanted to tell the social worker, but I would have been right behind you."

"That's why I love you."

We've reached the elevator, and I press the button. When the bell sounds, Vanessa and I step away from each other.

It's second nature.

It's so that the people inside have nothing to stare at.

On Tuesday mornings I go to a hospice and do music therapy with people who are dying by degrees. It is brutal, soul-draining work. And yet, I'd far rather be there than sitting next to Angela Moretti again, this time for a hearing on an emergency motion that was filed by Wade Preston just before the close of business last night. Angela is so angry, in fact, she's not even making lawyer jokes at Preston's expense.

Judge O'Neill stares daggers at Preston. "I have before me an emergency motion filed by you asking to disqualify Angela Moretti as Zoe Baxter's attorney, and a Rule Eleven motion to strike this motion, filed by Ms. Moretti. Or, as I like to call it, a whole bottle of Excedrin before noon. What's going on, Counselor?"

"Judge, I take no pleasure in bringing this information to the court. But as you can see from the attached photograph, which I'd like to enter as Exhibit A, Ms. Moretti is not only a lesbian sympathizer . . . she is engaged in this deviant lifestyle herself."

He holds up a grainy eight-by-ten that shows Angela and me, embracing. I have to squint to figure out where on earth this was taken. Then I see the chain-link fence and the lamppost and realize it is the high school parking lot.

Angela and I didn't have a scheduled meeting that day.

Which means Preston has had someone following me.

Wade Preston shrugs. "A picture's worth a thousand words."

"He's right," Angela says. "And this fallacious photo speaks for itself."

"If this is what they're willing to do in public, imagine what they do in private . . ."

"Oh, my God," Angela mutters.

"It's a little late to start praying now, darlin'. Clearly the defendant and her attorney are embroiled in an improper relationship that's in violation of the ethical rules governing attorneys in the state of Rhode Island," Preston says.

Ben Benjamin slowly comes out of his seat. "Um, actually, Wade? In Rhode Island, you can have sex with your client."

Preston whips around and looks at him. "You *can*?"

I blink at Angela. "You *can*?"

Benjamin nods. "As long as it's not in lieu of legal fees."

Undaunted, Preston faces the judge again. "Your Honor, Rhode Island notwithstanding, we all know there are ethical standards in the practice of law, and a counselor would have to be morally bereft to have a relationship with a client that crosses the boundaries of propriety as indicated by Exhibit A. Clearly, Ms. Moretti is not fit to represent her client impartially in this matter."

The judge turns to Angela. "I assume you have something to add here?"

"I absolutely, unequivocally deny that I am having an affair with my client, whose wife is sitting behind me even now. What Mr. Preston's paparazzi witnessed was an innocent embrace that followed a meeting with my client, when she became distraught after learning about Wade Preston's attempt to distort justice by filing a motion to appoint a guardian ad litem for *zygotes.* Although I completely understand why Mr. Preston would not recognize common human kindness when he sees it—since that presumes he *is* indeed human—he has completely misinterpreted the situation. In addition, Your Honor, this begs the question *why* there was someone taking a photograph of my client in the first place."

"She was in a public place, in a parking lot, in plain view," Preston argues.

"Is that a wedding ring you're wearing?" the judge asks Angela.

"Yes."

"Are you married, Ms. Moretti?"

She narrows her eyes. "Yes."

"To a man or a woman?" Wade Preston interrupts.

Angela rounds on him. "Objection! This is completely unsupportable, Your Honor. This is slander and defamation—"

"Enough," Judge O'Neill roars. "Motion denied. I'm not awarding counsel fees or sanctions to either party. Both of you, stop wasting my time."

The minute he is off the bench, Angela crosses to the plaintiff's table and shouts up at Wade Preston, who is at least eight inches taller than she is. "I swear, you malign my character like that again and I'm going to slap a civil lawsuit on you so fast you'll be knocked into next week."

"Malign your character? Why, Ms. Moretti, are you suggesting that being homosexual is an insult?" He tsks. "Shame, shame. GLAAD may have to revoke your lifetime membership card."

She jabs a finger into his skinny lapel and looks like she's going to breathe fire but, suddenly steps away and holds up her palms, a concession. "You know what? I was going to say *fuck you,* but then I decided I'd just wait for the trial to start, so you can go fuck yourself."

She spins on her heel and marches through the gate, up the aisle, and out of the courtroom. Vanessa looks at me. "I'll make sure she's not setting his car on fire," she says, and she hurries after Angela. Meanwhile, Wade Preston turns to his entourage. "Mission accomplished, my friends. When they're running defense, they can't mount an offense."

He and Ben Benjamin walk off together, speaking in muted whispers. They leave behind the stack of books that shows up every time Wade Preston does, and Max, who sits with his head bowed in his hands.

When I stand up, Max does, too. There is a clerk somewhere in the courtroom, and a pair of bailiffs, but for that moment, everyone else falls away and it is just us. I notice the first gray glints in the stubble of his beard. His eyes are the color of a bruise. "Zoe. About that. I'm sorry."

I try to remember what Max said to me the day we lost our son. Maybe I

was on sedatives, maybe I wasn't myself, but I cannot remember a single
word of comfort. In fact, I cannot remember one concrete thing he *ever*
said to me, not even *I love you.* It's as
if every conversation in our past has
grown mummified, an ancient relic that
crumbles into thin air if you get too
close.

"You know, Max," I say, "I don't think
you really are."

For two more music therapy sessions,
Lucy arrives late, ignores me, and
leaves. At the third, I decide I've had it.
We are in a math classroom, and there
are symbols on the board that are making me dizzy and slightly nauseated.
When Lucy arrives, I ask her how her
day's been, like usual, and, like usual,
she doesn't answer. But this time, I take
out my guitar and play Air Supply, "All
Out of Love."

I follow that with an encore performance of Celine Dion's "My Heart Will
Go On."

I play anything that I think will either

put Lucy into a diabetic coma or make her rip the instrument out of my hands. At this point, I'd consider that a successful interaction. But Lucy won't break.

"I'm sorry," I say finally. "But you've left me no other resort than to pull out the big guns."

I place my guitar back in its case and take out a ukulele instead. Then I begin to strum the theme song to *Barney & Friends*.

For the first three choruses, Lucy ignores me. And then finally, in one swift move, she grabs the neck of the ukulele and clamps down with her fingers so that I can't play it. "Just leave me alone," she cries. "It's what you want anyway."

"If you're going to put words in my mouth, then I'm going to put some in yours," I say. "I know what you're doing, and I know why you're doing it. I realize you're mad."

"Thank you, Captain Obvious," Lucy mutters.

"But you're not mad at me. You're mad at yourself. Because against all odds, in spite of the fact that you were so damn sure that you would hate working with me and going to music therapy sessions, they started to work. And you like coming." I put the ukulele down on a desk beside me and stare at Lucy. "You like being around *me*."

She glances up, her face so raw and open that, for a moment, I forget what I was saying.

"So what do you do? You sabotage the therapeutic relationship we've built, because that way, you get to tell yourself you were right. That this is a load of bullshit. That it would never work. It doesn't matter how you do it or what you tell yourself is the reason we're in a fight. You ruin the one good thing you've got going because if *you* ruin it, then you don't have to deal with being disappointed later on."

Lucy stands abruptly. Her fists are clenched at her sides, and her mouth is a livid red slash. "Why can't you just take a hint? Why the fuck are you still here?"

"Because there's nothing you can do or say or any way you can act that will drive me away, Lucy. I am not leaving you."

She freezes. *"Never?"* The word is like tempered glass, broken and full of beauty.

I know how hard it is for her to lay herself bare, to expose the soft center under that hard shell. So I promise. I'm not surprised when the tears come, when she collapses against me. I do what anyone else would do, in that situation: I hold Lucy until she can hold herself.

The bell rings, but Lucy makes no move to go to class. It crosses my mind that someone may need to use this space, but when a teacher comes in— her prep period finished—she sees Lucy sitting with her head down on the desk, my hand lightly rubbing her back. We make eye contact, and the teacher slips out of the room.

"Zoe?" Lucy's voice is slow and round, as if she's spinning underwater. "Promise me?"

"I already did."

"That you won't ever play Barney again."

She looks at me sideways. Her eyes are red and swollen, her nose running, but there's her smile. *I brought that back for her,* I think.

I pretend to consider her demand. "You drive *such* a hard bargain," I say.

	TRACK 1	SING YOU HOME
	TRACK 2	THE HOUSE ON HOPE STREET
	TRACK 3	REFUGEE
	TRACK 4	THE LAST
	TRACK 5	MARRY ME
	TRACK 6	FAITH
	TRACK 7	THE MERMAID
✓	**TRACK 8**	**ORDINARY LIFE**
	TRACK 9	WHERE YOU ARE
	TRACK 10	SAMMY'S SONG

MAX

———————

Nothing makes a church look better than a crisis situation. Give them a dying relative, a child having surgery, a cancer diagnosis—and suddenly everyone pitches in. You will find casseroles at your door, you will find your name on a prayer list in the bulletin. Ladies will show up at your house to clean, or watch your kids. You will know that whatever corner of Hell you are walking through, you're not alone.

For weeks now, I have been the subject of prayer for the Eternal Glory Church, so that by the time I go to court God will have gotten an earful from nearly a hundred parishioners. Today, I am sitting in the school auditorium as Pastor Clive begins his sermon.

The children of the congregation are down the hall in the art room, gluing pictures of animals into a Xeroxed copy of an ark. I know this because, last night, I helped Liddy draw the giraffes and hippos and squirrels and aardvarks for the kids to color and cut out during Sunday School. And it's a good thing they're not here, because today Pastor Clive is talking about sex.

"Brothers and sisters in Christ," he says, "I have a question for you. You know how some things just seem to go together? You can't say one without automatically thinking of its other natural half. Like salt and pepper. Peanut butter and jelly. Rock and roll. Hugs and kisses. If you only have one of the two, it feels like a wobbly stool, doesn't it? Incomplete. Unfinished. And if you hear another word—like if I said cats and parrots, instead of cats and dogs, it sounds just plain wrong, doesn't it? For example, if I say mother, you'd say . . . ?"

"Father," I murmur, along with everyone else.

"Husband?"

"Wife!"

Pastor Clive nods. "You'll notice I did
not say *mother and mother.* I did not
say *husband and husband,* or *wife and
wife.* I did not say those things because
when we hear them, we just know deep
inside they are wrong. I believe this is
especially true when it comes to understanding why God's plan does not include a homosexual lifestyle."

He looks at the congregation. "There
are those who will tell you the Bible has
nothing to say about homosexuality—
but that is not true. Romans 1:26–27,
*Because of this God gave them over to
shameless lusts. Even their women exchanged natural relations for unnatural
ones. In the same way the men also
abandoned natural relations with women
and were inflamed with lust for one another. Men committed indecent acts
with other men and received in themselves the due penalty for their perversion.* Some naysayers—the ones who
tell us God has nothing to say about

homosexuality—will tell you that Paul is talking about what went on at pagan temples in Greece. These naysayers will tell you we are missing the big picture. I say, my friends, that we *do* see the big picture." He pauses, making eye contact with all of us. "God hates homosexuality," he says.

Pastor Clive reads aloud the verse that's written in the bulletin today. It's from 1 Corinthians 6:9–10: "*Neither the sexually immoral, nor idolaters, nor adulterers, nor male prostitutes, nor homosexual offenders, nor thieves, nor the greedy, nor drunkards, nor slanderers, nor swindlers, will inherit the kingdom of God.* I ask you, friends. Could God have been any clearer? There is no eternal life for those who are deviant. Now, those naysayers, they'll tell you that the problem is the *translation* of the Bible. That the word *homosexual* doesn't really mean 'homosexual' in this passage; that it's Greek for 'effeminate call boy.' They will tell you it wasn't until 1958 that some random translator made the arbitrary decision to even type the word *homosexual* into the English-language Bible.

"Well, I tell you that decision wasn't arbitrary at all. These passages describe a society that has lost the ability to tell right from wrong. And in fact, time after time, when homosexuality is mentioned in the Scriptures, it is condemned."

Liddy slips into the pew beside me. She gets the Sunday School classes started with their teachers and then comes up for Pastor Clive's sermon. I can feel the heat of her skin, inches away from my arm.

"Tomorrow, when Max's ex-wife stands up in court before God and says her lifestyle is normal and healthy and loving, I will tell her that Hebrews 11:25 says the pleasures of sin do indeed last for a short time. But as Galatians also says, one who sows to please his sinful nature from that nature will reap destruction. Tomorrow, when Max's ex-wife stands up in court before God and says homosexuality is widespread, I will tell her that may be so, but it doesn't make it right in the eyes of God. I would rather be in the minority and be right, than in the majority and wrong."

There is a murmur of agreement from the congregation.

"Tomorrow, when Max's ex-wife stands up in court before God and says that she was born a lesbian, I will say that not a single scientific study to date has proven this, and that she simply has a tendency toward that lifestyle. After all, I like swimming . . . but that doesn't make me a fish."

Pastor Clive walks down the steps from the stage and into the aisle, stopping at my row. "Max," he says, "come and join me up here." Embarrassed, I don't move at first, but then Liddy puts her hand on my arm. *Go,* she urges, and I do.

I follow Pastor Clive up to the stage as one of his assistants sets a chair in the center. "Max is more than just our brother. He is Jesus's man on the front line, fighting so that God's truth prevails. For this reason, I pray for him."

"Amen," someone calls out.

The pastor's voice rises. "Who will come up here and pray with me?"

A dozen folks rise from their seats and walk to the stage. They lay their hands on me as Pastor Clive's voice beats like the wings of a hundred crows. "Lord, may You be sitting beside Max in that courtroom. May You help his ex-wife learn that her sin is no greater than my sin or Your sin, and that she is still welcome in the kingdom of God. May You help Max Baxter's children find their way to You."

Streams of people rise to the stage to pray over me, to touch me. Their fingers feel like butterflies that land for just a second before moving on. I can hear the whisper of their words going up to God. For anyone who doesn't believe in the healing power of prayer, I dare you: come to a church like mine, and feel the electricity of a crowd that's rooting for you to win.

The Kent County Courthouse has a long walkway that goes from the parking lot into the building, and it's packed with members of the Eternal Glory Church. Although there are a couple of police officers milling around to make sure that the peace is being kept, the protest is far from disruptive. Pastor Clive's got everyone lined up on both sides of the walkway, singing a hymn. I mean, you can't arrest someone for singing, can you?

As soon as we arrive—and by we, I mean me, flanked by Wade and Ben, and Reid and Liddy, who are just behind us—Pastor Clive breaks rank and struts right down the middle of the walkway. He is wearing a white linen suit with a pink shirt and a striped tie; he certainly stands out, but then again, he probably would if he were wearing a potato sack. "Max," he says, embracing me. "How are you holding up?"

This morning Liddy cooked a big breakfast as a send-off, and I ate it, and promptly threw up. That's how nervous I am. But before I can tell this to Pastor Clive, Wade leans toward us. "Turn to the left."

I do, and that's when I see the cameras. "Let's pray," Pastor Clive says.

We bridge the two lines of people, forming a horseshoe that blocks the entrance to the courthouse. Wade holds my right hand; Pastor Clive holds my left. As reporters shout out questions, Pastor Clive's voice is loud and steady. "Father, in the name of Jesus, it is written in Your Word to call on You and You will answer and show us great and mighty things. Today, we ask You to keep Max and his legal counsel steadfast, and to guarantee their triumph. Hide Max from those tongues that would seek to disparage him and from the false witnesses who spill lies. Because of You, Max will not be nervous. He knows, and we know, that the Holy Spirit will move him to say what must be said."

"Beep beep," I hear, and my eyes pop open. Angela Moretti, the lawyer who's representing Zoe, stands a few feet away, trapped by the barrier of our prayer circle. "I hate to interrupt your Billy Graham moment, but my client and I would really like to get into the courthouse."

"Ms. Moretti," Wade says, "surely you wouldn't be trying to take away the

First Amendment rights of all these fine people—"

"Why, no, Mr. Preston. That would go against my grain. Just like, for example, a grandstanding attorney who summons the media in advance, knowing that there's going to be some kind of forced confrontation between his party and the opposing one."

Zoe waits behind Angela Moretti, with her mother and Vanessa.

For a minute I wonder which side is going to blink first. And then, Liddy does something I am totally not expecting. She steps forward and hugs Zoe, then smiles at her. "Jesus loves you, you know," she says.

"We're praying for you, Zoe," someone else adds.

That is all it takes to break the dam, and suddenly everyone is murmuring some message of faith and hope to Zoe. It makes me think of catching flies with honey, of killing with kindness.

And it works. Caught off guard, Angela Moretti grabs Zoe's arm and barrels her toward the doors of the courthouse. Wade lets go of my hand so that she can push between us. As she does, Zoe catches my eye.

For a moment the whole world stands still. "God forgives you," I tell her.

Zoe's eyes are clear, wide, the color of a thunderstorm. "God should know there's nothing to forgive," she says.

It's different this time.

I have been to court a bunch of times now, thanks to all those motions Wade filed, and the procedure is the same: we walk down the aisle of the courtroom and take our place at the plaintiff's table; Wade's lackey stacks a dozen books in front of him that he never actually opens; the sheriff tells us to rise and Judge O'Neill blusters in.

But this time, we are not the only ones in the courtroom. There are reporters and sketch artists. There is a delegation from Fred Phelps's Westboro Baptist Church, wearing yellow T-shirts with block letters: GOD HATES FAGS, GOD HATES AMERICA, FAG = SIN, YOU'RE GOING TO HELL. I've seen pictures of them protesting at soldiers' funerals—they believe God is killing the U.S. military to punish America for all its homosexuals—and it makes me wonder just how far Wade's media effort really has gone. Is this trial, *my* trial, really on their radar?

But the Westboro folks aren't the only ones who've come to watch. Members of my church are there, too, which relaxes me a little.

And then there are the others. Men who sit with other men, holding hands. A pair of women taking turns holding a baby. Friends of Zoe's, maybe. Or of her dyke lawyer.

Judge O'Neill sits down on the bench. "Showtime," Wade murmurs.

"Before we begin," the judge says, "I want to caution everyone present—including counsel, parties, media, and observers—that in this courtroom, *I* am God. If anybody disrupts the orderly process of this court, he or she will be removed. Which is why all of you folks in the yellow T-shirts will either take them off or turn them inside out or be escorted outside immediately. And before you go off at the mouth about freedom of expression, Mr. Preston, let me reiterate that anything disruptive does not make Judge O'Neill a happy camper."

The group from Westboro Baptist puts on sweatshirts. I get the feeling they've done this before.

"Are there any preliminary matters?" the judge asks, and Angela Moretti stands.

"Your Honor, I have a motion I'd like to make before we begin—to sequester the witnesses."

"Who are your witnesses, Attorney Preston?" the judge asks. Wade offers up a list, and then so does Angela Moretti. O'Neill nods. "Any of you people listed as witnesses, leave the courtroom."

"What?" Liddy cries out behind me. "But then how will I get to—"

"I want to be here for you," Vanessa says to Zoe.

Judge O'Neill looks at both women. "Dis . . . rup . . . *tive*," he says flatly.

Reluctantly, Vanessa and Reid and Liddy prepare to exit. "You hang in there, bro," Reid says, clapping me on the shoulder before he puts his arm around Liddy's waist and leads her out of the courtroom. I wonder where they will go. What they will do.

"Do we have opening arguments today?" Judge O'Neill asks. When both lawyers nod, he looks at Wade. "Attorney Preston, you may begin."

Although this is family court and it's the judge who will be deciding this case instead of a whole jury, Wade treats the entire courtroom as his audience. He stands up, smooths his emerald tie, and turns to the gallery with a little smile. "We are gathered together today to mourn the loss of something near and dear to us all: the traditional family. Surely you remember it, before its untimely death: a husband and a wife, two kids. White picket fence. A minivan. Maybe even a dog. A family that went to church on Sundays and that loved Jesus. A mom who baked homemade Toll House cookies and was a Boy Scout den mother. A dad who played catch, who walked his daughter down the aisle at her wedding. It's been a long time since this was the norm in society, but we told ourselves that surely an institution as strong as the traditional family could survive anything. And yet, by taking it for granted, we have virtually guaranteed its demise." Wade folds his hand over his heart. "Rest in peace.

"This is not just a custody case, Your Honor. This is a wake-up call to keep alive the cornerstone of our society—the traditional Christian family. Because research and basic common sense say that kids need both male and female role models and that the absence of this can have dire consequences, from academic struggles to poverty to high-risk behaviors. Because when traditional family values fall apart, the casualties tend to be children. Max Baxter, my client, knows that, Your Honor. And that's why he is here today, to protect the three pre-born children conceived while he was married to the defendant, Zoe Baxter. All my client is asking the court to do today is to allow him to complete the original intent of these two parties—namely, to allow those children to be parented by a heterosexual, married couple. To let them thrive, Your Honor, in a traditional Christian family."

Wade points a finger, bulleting that phrase as he repeats it. "A traditional family. That's what Max and Zoe envisioned, when they took advantage of the science that is available to create these blessings, these pre-born children. Now, unfortunately, Max and Zoe's marriage is no longer intact. And Max is not at a point in his life where he has remarried. But Max recognizes that he owes his pre-born children a debt, and so he is making a decision in the best interests of the children, instead of the best interests of himself. He's identified his brother, Reid—a fine, upstanding man you will hear from—and his wife, Liddy—a paragon of Christian virtue in this community—as future parents for his pre-born children."

"Amen," someone says behind me.

"Your Honor, you've made it clear to the parties and counsel in this matter that this is the final case you will be handling after your long and distinguished career on the bench. It's fit and proper that you be put in the position of protecting the traditional family here in Rhode Island—a state that was founded by Roger Williams, who fled to the colonies for religious freedom. Rhode Island, one of the last bastions in New England—a state holding true to Christian family values. But just to play devil's advocate, let's look at the alternative. Although Max has nothing against his ex-wife, Zoe is now living in sin with her lesbian lover—"

"Objection," Angela Moretti says.

"Sit down, Counselor," the judge replies. "You'll have your chance."

"These two women had to get married in the state of Massachusetts, because this one—their *home state*—does not legally recognize their same-sex union. Neither the government nor God sees their marriage as valid. Now, let's imagine that these pre-born children wind up in that household, Your Honor. Imagine a young boy with two mommies, exposed to a homosexual lifestyle. What's going to happen to him when he goes to school and is teased for having two mothers? What's going to happen when, as studies show, he winds up gay himself because of the way he was raised? Judge, you grew up with a father. And you yourself have *been* a father. You know what these roles have meant to you. I beg you, on behalf of Max Baxter's pre-born children, don't let your decision today deny them the same opportunity." He turns to the gallery. "Once we drive that final nail into the coffin of traditional family values," Wade says, "we'll never be able to resurrect them."

He sits back down, and Angela Moretti stands up.

"If it looks like a family, talks like a family, acts like a family, and functions like a family," she says, "then it's a family. The relationship between my client, Zoe Baxter, and Vanessa Shaw is not housemates or roommates but life partners. Spouses. They love each other, they are committed to each other, and they function as a unit, not just as individuals. The last time I checked, that was a valid definition of a family.

"Mr. Preston would like to seduce you with talk of the demise of the traditional family. He raised the fact that Rhode Island is a state that was founded on religious freedom, and we could not agree more. We also know, however, that not every resident in the state of Rhode Island believes what Mr. Preston and his client do." She turns to the gallery. "Moreover, Rhode Island *does* recognize the relationship between Zoe and Vanessa. For fifteen years, the state has offered limited legal rights to same-sex domestic partnerships. This very court routinely grants second-parent adoptions for gay and lesbian families. And, in fact, Rhode Island was one of the first states in the country to have a gender-neutral birth certificate that lists not *mother* and *father* but rather *parent* and *parent.*

"Unlike Mr. Preston, however, I don't think this case is about general family values. I think it's about one particular family." She glances at Zoe. "The embryos in question today were created during the marriage of Zoe and her ex-husband, Max Baxter. These embryos are property that was not divided in the divorce settlement. There are two bio-

logical progenitors of these embryos—
the plaintiff and the defendant, and they
have equal rights to the embryos. The
difference here, though, is that Max
Baxter no longer wants to have a baby.
He's using biology as a trump card to
gain an advantage, to take the embryos
away from an intended parent and her
legal spouse. If Your Honor rules in my
client's favor, we would make every effort to include the other biological pro-
genitor of the embryos—Max—as part
of this family. We believe there can't be
too many people to love a child. However, if Your Honor rules against my client, Zoe—the mother of these embryos—will be prevented from raising
her biological children."

She gestures at Zoe. "You'll hear testimony, Your Honor, about medical
complications that have left Zoe unable
to gestate her own embryos. At this
point in her life, she doesn't have the
time left in her reproductive cycle to go
through additional in vitro procedures
to harvest more eggs. Zoe, who so desperately wants to have a baby, is being
robbed of that opportunity by her ex-

husband—who doesn't even want a child. He isn't fighting for the right to be a parent. He's fighting to make sure that Zoe *isn't* one."

Angela Moretti looks at the judge. "Mr. Baxter's attorney has raised a lot of questions about God and what God wants and what God intends a family to be. But Max Baxter is not asking for God's blessing here, to be a parent. He's not asking God what the best situation for these embryos is."

She faces me, and, in that moment, I can barely breathe. "Max Baxter is asking you to play God instead," she says.

Being on the witness stand, Pastor Clive says, is like testifying at church. You just get up there and tell your story. It doesn't matter if it's humiliating or hard to relive. What's important is that you're a hundred percent honest, because that's how people become convinced.

Pastor Clive is one of the witnesses out there waiting in whatever limbo they've been sent to, and I sorely wish that wasn't the case. I could use his strength right now, just so that I have someone to focus on while I'm on the witness stand. As it is, I have to keep wiping my palms on my pants, because I'm sweating so much.

What calms me down, actually, is the sheriff coming at me with a Bible. At first I think he's going to ask me to read a passage, and then of course I remember how every trial starts. *Do you swear to tell the truth, the whole truth, and nothing but the truth?* I rest my hand on the worn leather cover. Immediately, my heart stops its jackhammering. *You're not alone up there,* Pastor Clive had said, and sure enough, he's right.

Wade and I have rehearsed my part a dozen times. I know the questions he's going to ask, so I'm not worried about that. What's getting me all tied up in knots is what happens when he's done, when Angela Moretti has her turn to rip me apart.

"Max," Wade begins, "why have you petitioned the court for custody of these pre-born children?"

"Objection," Angela Moretti says. "It's one thing to listen to him calling embryos 'pre-born children' during his opening statement, but are we going to have to listen to this through the entire trial?"

"Overruled," the judge replies. "I don't care about semantics, Ms. Moretti. You say *tomayto,* I say *tomahto.* Mr. Baxter, answer the question."

I take a deep breath. "I want to make sure they have a wonderful life, with my brother, Reid, and his wife, Liddy."

His wife, Liddy. The words burn my tongue.

"Why didn't you negotiate custody in your divorce agreement?"

"We didn't have lawyers; we did our own divorce settlement. I knew we were supposed to divide up the property, but these . . . these were children."

"Under what circumstances were these pre-born children created?" Wade asks.

"When Zoe and I were married, we wanted to have kids. We wound up having in vitro fertilization five times."

"Which of you two is infertile?"

"We both are," I say.

"How was the in vitro done?"

As Wade walks me through our medical history, I feel a sad emptiness in my stomach. Could a marriage of nine years really come down to this: two miscarriages, one stillbirth? It is hard to imagine that all that's left behind are some legal documents, and this trail of blood.

"How did you react to the stillbirth?" Wade says.

It sounds awful to say so, but when a baby dies, I think the mother has it easier. She can grieve on the outside; her loss is something everyone can actually see in the slope of her belly. For me, though, the loss was on the inside. It ate away at me. So that, for a long time, all I wanted to do was fill myself.

God knows I tried to, with alcohol.

My eyes are tearing up; this embarrasses me. I duck my head. "I may not have shown it the way Zoe did," I say, "but it wrecked me. Completely. I knew I couldn't go through that again even though she wanted to." Looking up, I find Zoe staring right at me. "So I said I wanted a divorce."

"What was your life like after that, Max?"

Just like that, my throat seems to turn into cotton, so that I feel like if I don't have a drink I'll die. I force myself to think of Liddy, the other night, sitting on the edge of my bed, praying over me. "I went through a bad time. I missed a lot of work opportunities. And I started drinking again. My brother took me into his home, but I kept digging myself deeper and deeper into a hole. And then one day, I crashed my truck into a tree and wound up in the hospital."

"Did things change after that?"

"Yes," I say, "I found Jesus."

"Objection, Your Honor," Angela Moretti says. "We're in court, not a revival meeting."

"I'll allow it," Judge O'Neill replies.

"So you became religious," Wade prompts.

I nod. "I started going to the Eternal Glory Church, and talking to the pastor—Clive Lincoln. He saved my life. I mean, I was a complete mess. I'd

screwed up my home life; I was an alcoholic, and I didn't know anything
about religion. I thought at first that, if I
went to church, everyone would be
judging me. But I was completely blown
away. These people didn't care who I
was—they saw who I *could* be. I started
going to adult Bible study, and to pot-
luck dinners, and to the fellowship hour
after Sunday's services. They all prayed
for me—Reid and Liddy and Pastor
Clive and everyone else in the congregation. They loved me unconditionally.
And one day I sat down on the edge of
my bed and asked Jesus to be the Savior of my soul and the Lord of my life.
When He did, the seed of the Holy Spirit
was planted in my heart."

When I finish, I feel like there's light
coming out from inside me. I look over
at Zoe, who is staring at me as if she's
never seen me before.

"Your Honor," Angela Moretti says.
"Apparently Mr. Preston didn't get the
memo about the separation of church
and state . . ."

"My client has the right to testify
about what changed his life," Wade an-

swers. "Religion is what led Mr. Baxter to file this lawsuit."

"In this particular case, I have to agree," Judge O'Neill says. "Mr. Baxter's spiritual transformation is intrinsic to the matter at hand."

"I can't believe this," Angela Moretti mutters. "Literally *and* figuratively." She sits back down, arms folded.

"Just to clarify," Wade asks me, "do you still drink alcohol?"

I think about the Bible I've sworn on. I think about Liddy, who so badly wants this baby. "Not a drop," I lie.

"How long have you been divorced?"

"It's been final for about three months, now."

"After your divorce, when was the next time you thought about your preborn children?"

"Objection! If he's going to keep calling these embryos children, Your Honor, I'm going to keep objecting—"

"And I'm going to keep overruling," Judge O'Neill says.

When Wade and I practiced the answer to this question, he suggested I say, *Every day.* But I am thinking of how

I lied about drinking, and how I can feel Jesus just behind me, and how He knows when you aren't being true to yourself or to Him. So when the judge looks at me for a response, I say, "Not until Zoe came to talk to me about them, a month ago."

For a second, I think Wade Preston is going into cardiac arrest. Then his features smooth. "And what did she say?"

"She wanted to use them to have a baby with her . . . with Vanessa."

"How did you react?"

"I was shocked. Especially at the thought of my baby growing up in a house full of sin—"

"Objection, Your Honor!"

"Sustained," the judge says.

Wade doesn't even bat an eyelash. "What did you tell her?"

"That I needed time to think about it."

"And what conclusion did you reach?"

"That it wasn't right. God doesn't want two women to raise a baby. *My* baby. Every child is supposed to have a mother and a father; that's the natural order of things, according to the Bible." I think about those animal cutouts Liddy and I made for the Sunday School kids. "I mean, you don't see the animals going on the ark in girl-girl pairs."

"Objection," Angela Moretti says. "Relevance?"

"Sustained."

"Max," Wade asks, "when did you find out your ex-wife had embraced a lesbian lifestyle?"

I glance at Zoe. It is hard for me to imagine her touching Vanessa. It makes me feel like this new life of hers is a sham, or else ours was, and I just can't let myself go there. "After we split up."

"How did it make you feel?"

As if I had swallowed tar. As if I had opened my eyes and the world was suddenly only black and white, and no matter how I rubbed my eyes I could not bring the color back. "Like there was something wrong with me," I say tightly. "Like I wasn't good enough for her."

"Did your opinion of Zoe change after you learned that she is living in a homosexual lifestyle?"

"Well, I prayed for her, because it's a sin."

"Do you see yourself as anti-gay, Max?" Wade asks.

"No," I reply. "Never. I'm not doing this to hurt Zoe. I loved her, and I can't erase the nine years we were married. I wouldn't *want* to. I just need to look out for my children."

"If this court sees fit to give you back your pre-born children, what's your intention?"

"They deserve the best parents any kid could have. But I'm smart enough to realize that means someone other than me. That's why I would want my brother, Reid, to have them. He and Liddy—they've taken care of me, they've loved me, they've believed in me. I've changed so much, for the better, because of them. I know I'd be part of the babies' extended family, and that they would be raised in a Christian, two-parent household. They'd go to Sunday School and to church, and they'd grow up loving God." I glance up, just like Wade told me to, and I say what we've practiced. "Pastor Clive told me that God doesn't make mistakes, that everything happens for a reason. For a long time, I believed my life was a mistake. That *I* was a mistake. But now I know I'm not. This was God's plan all along—to bring me together with Reid and Liddy at the same time my pre-born children needed a home and a family." I nod, convincing myself. "This is what I was put on this earth to do."

"Nothing further," Wade says, and, with an encouraging nod at me, he sits down.

When Angela Moretti starts walking forward, I realize what she reminds me of: some kind of jungle cat. A panther, I guess, with all that black hair. "Mr. Baxter, through the four years of your marriage when you tried naturally to conceive, and the five years of fertility treatments—did you believe Zoe would make a good mother?"

"Of course."

"What is it today that makes her any less fit to raise a child?"

"She's living a lifestyle that I think is wrong," I say.

"It's different from yours, granted," the lawyer corrects. "Is the fact that she's a lesbian the only detriment you see to Zoe being a parent?"

"It's a pretty big deal. God explains in the Bible that—"

"This is a yes or no question, Mr. Baxter. Is that the only negative thing you have to say about Zoe's ability to be a good mother?"

"Yes," I say quietly.

"Isn't it true, Mr. Baxter, that you still have sperm with which to create more embryos?"

"I don't know. I have male pattern infertility—which means, if I do, it won't be easy."

"Yet you don't want these embryos. You want to give them away."

"I want these children to have the best life possible," I say. "And I know that means having a mother and a father."

"In fact you were raised by a mother and a father, isn't that right, Mr. Baxter?"

"Yes."

"And yet, you still ended up a drunk,

divorced loser living in your brother's guest room."

I can't help it, I come halfway out of my witness chair.

"Objection!" Wade says. "Prejudicial!"

"Withdrawn. If this court gives your brother and sister-in-law the embryos," Angela Moretti asks, "where do you fit in?"

"I . . . I'm going to be an uncle."

"Ah. How are you going to be the uncle if you're the biological father?"

"It's like an adoption," I say, flustered. "I mean, it *is* an adoption. Reid becomes the father and I'm the uncle."

"So you're going to give up your parental rights to these children at birth?"

Ben Benjamin said that, no matter what you sign, at any point, grown children might come find you. Confused, I look at him, sitting at our table. "I thought you said I couldn't ever really do that?"

"You want these embryos to go to a traditional Christian family?" the lawyer says.

"Yes."

"But instead you're suggesting that

the court give them to a biological father who is called the uncle and is living in the basement of the home of the
parents who are raising him. Does that
sound like a traditional Christian family,
Mr. Baxter?"

"No! I mean, yes . . ."

"Which is it?"

Her words are like bullets. I wish
she'd talk more slowly. I wish she'd give
me time to think. "It's . . . it's a family—"

"When you created these embryos
with Zoe, you intended at the time to
raise these children with her, correct?"

"Yes."

"Yet Zoe is still ready, willing, and
able to take these embryos and raise
them as her children. On the other hand,
you left."

"I didn't leave—"

"Did she file for divorce, or did you?"

"I did. But I left my marriage, not my
children—"

"No, *those* you're just giving away,"
Angela says. "You also testified that
between the time when you got divorced and when Zoe came to talk to

you about using the embryos, you hadn't thought about them?"

"I didn't mean it like that—"

"But that's what you said. What else have you said that you don't really mean, Mr. Baxter?" She takes a step toward me. "That you're fine with giving these embryos to your brother and taking a backseat in their upbringing? That you're a completely changed man? That you aren't instigating this entire lawsuit as a means of getting revenge on your ex-wife, whose new relationship makes you feel like less of a man?"

"Objection!" Wade roars, but by that time I am standing, shaking, my face red and a hundred angry answers caught behind my teeth.

"That's all, Mr. Baxter," Angela Moretti says, with a smile. "That's plenty."

Wade calls for a recess, to let me get control of myself again. As I leave the courtroom, the members of the Westboro church applaud. It makes me feel a little dirty. It's one thing to love Jesus with all your heart; it's another to pro-

test outside temples because you believe Jews killed our Savior. "Can you
get rid of them?" I whisper to Wade.

"Not a chance," he murmurs back.
"They're fantastic press. You've gotten
through the hardest part, Max. Seriously, you know why that lawyer had to
get you all riled up? Because she didn't
have anything else to work with. Not
the law of this land, and certainly not
the law of God."

He leads me into a tiny room that has
a table, two chairs, a coffeemaker, and
a microwave. Wade walks over to the
microwave and bends down until his
face is level with the glossy black door.
He smiles so that he can see his teeth,
uses his thumb to pick something out
from between two of them, and then
grins again. "If you think that cross-examination was ruthless, you just sit
back and enjoy what I'm planning to do
to Zoe."

I'm not sure why this makes me feel
worse.

"Can you do me a favor?" I ask. "Can
you get Pastor Clive for me?"

Wade hesitates. "As long as you're

talking to him as your spiritual counselor, and not as a sequestered witness . . ."

I nod. The last thing I want to do right
now is rehash that last hour in court.

Wade leaves, taking all the air with
him. I sink into a plastic chair and put
my head down between my knees, sure
that I'm going to pass out. A few minutes later, the door opens again and I
see Pastor Clive's white linen suit. He
drags a chair beside mine. "Let's pray,"
he says, and he bows his head.

His words run over me, catching on
all the rough patches and wearing them
down. Prayer is like water—something
you can't imagine has the strength or
power to do any good, and yet give it
time and it can change the lay of the
land. "Max, you look like you're struggling," he says.

"I just . . ." Looking away, I shake my
head. "I don't know. Maybe I should
just give them to Zoe."

"What's making you doubt yourself?"
Pastor Clive asks.

"What her lawyer said. That I'm really
the father, but I have to be like an un-

cle. If I'm confused already, how is a kid going to be able to sort it all out?"

He clasps his hands, nodding. "You know, actually, I remember a situation very similar to this one. I can't believe I haven't thought of it before."

"Really?"

"Yes. A biological dad, whose child was raised by another couple. They were handpicked by this man—just like what you're doing—because the father wanted to do what was best for his child. Yet he still managed to have a say in his child's upbringing."

"Did you know them?"

"Very well," Pastor Clive says, smiling. "And so do you. God gave Jesus to Mary to bear, and Joseph to raise. He knew it had to be done. And Jesus— well, clearly, he was able to sort it all out."

But I am not God. I'm just someone who's screwed up time and time again, who is trying hard not to make another mistake.

"It's all going to work out, Max," Pastor Clive promises.

I do what I always do when I'm around him. I believe what he tells me.

When Reid enters the courtroom, I have to admit, my doubts start to fade. He's dressed in one of his fancy Savile Row suits, with hand-sewn Italian loafers. His black hair is trimmed precisely; I know for a fact that he had a real barber do his shave early this morning. He is the sort of man who draws attention when he enters a room, not just because he's good-looking but because he is so sure of himself. As he passes by me to take the witness stand, I smell aftershave and something else. Not cologne—Reid doesn't wear any. It's the scent of money.

"Can you state your name for the record?" Wade asks.

"Reid Baxter."

"And where do you live, Mr. Baxter?"

"Newport. One-forty Ocean Drive."

"What is your relationship to the plaintiff, Max Baxter?"

Reid smiles. "I'm his big brother."

"Are you married, Mr. Baxter?"

"To my lovely bride of eleven years, Liddy."

"Got any children?" Wade asks.

"God hasn't blessed us with children," he says. "Though—I confess—it's not for want of trying."

"Tell me a little about your home," Wade asks.

"It's a forty-five-hundred-square-foot house on the ocean. There are four bedrooms, three and a half baths. We've got a basketball hoop and a huge yard. The only things missing are kids."

"What do you do for a living?"

"I'm a portfolio manager with Monroe, Flatt & Cohen," Reid says. "I've worked for them for seventeen years, and I'm a senior partner. I manage, invest, and reinvest other people's money in order to preserve and increase their wealth."

"What's your net worth, Mr. Baxter?"

Reid looks modestly into his lap. "A bit over four million dollars."

Holy shit.

I knew my brother was well off, but four million dollars?

At the very best, the most I could offer a kid was a partnership in a crappy landscaping business and all my knowledge about how to grow roses in a difficult climate. Not exactly a trust fund.

"Does your wife, Liddy, work, too?" Wade asks.

"She does volunteer work in various organizations. She's the Sunday School coordinator for our church; she serves meals at a local homeless shelter; she's involved with the Newport Hospital Women's League. She's on the board of the Preservation Society as well. But it's always been our plan for her to be a stay-at-home mom, so that she could be the one raising our children."

"Do you consider yourself a religious man?" Wade asks.

"I do," Reid says.

"What church do you attend, Mr. Baxter?"

"The Eternal Glory Church. I've been a member for fifteen years."

"Do you hold any offices or positions within the church's hierarchy?"

"I'm the treasurer," Reid replies.

"Do you and your wife attend church on a regular basis?"

He nods. "Every Sunday."

"Do you consider yourself a born-again Christian?"

"If you mean, have I accepted Jesus as my personal savior, then yes," Reid says.

"I'd like to direct your attention to the plaintiff in this case, Max Baxter." Wade gestures at me. "How would you describe your relationship with him?"

Reid thinks for a minute. "Blessed," he says. "It is so incredible to have my little brother back in my life, and on a path that's good for him."

In my first memory, I am about three years old, and jealous of Reid's secret club. It was located in his tree house, a special hideaway where he could escape with his school friends. I was too young to climb up into it, or so I was told repeatedly by my parents and by Reid, who didn't want some pesky little brother tagging along. I used to dream at night about what the inside of that tree house looked like. I pictured psychedelic walls, stockpiles of candy, *MAD* magazines. One day, even though I knew I'd get in trouble, I climbed up into the tree house while Reid was still at school. To my surprise, it was just rough wood, with some spots where he and his buddies had drawn in crayon. There was a newspaper on the floor and a few busted caps from a cap gun.

I thought it was the most magical place I'd ever seen—but then again, that's pretty much what anyone thinks about the things that are off-limits. So I hid, even though I heard my mom calling my name over and over. When Reid came home from school, like usual, he climbed up the ladder to the tree house before he even went into the house.

What are you *doing here?* he asked, just as my mother's voice rang out, and a minute later, her head popped up through the little trapdoor.

How did Max get up here? she cried. *He's not big enough to climb that tree . . .*

It's okay, Reid said. *I helped him.*

I didn't know why he was lying for me. I didn't know why he wasn't mad about me being in his tree house.

My mother bought it, although she said that she would come back to help me climb down because the last thing she needed was a trip to the emergency room. Then Reid looked at me. *If you want to be part of the club, you have to play by the rules.*

I make all the rules, he said.

I think my whole life, all I've wanted is to be part of whatever club my brother belongs to.

Wade is still questioning him when I focus my attention again. "How long have you known Zoe Baxter?"

"She sang at my wedding to Liddy. That was the first time we met, and she went on to date my brother."

"How did you two get along?" Wade asks.

Reid smiles sheepishly. "Let's just say we have different philosophies of life."

"Did you see Zoe often during her marriage to your brother?" Wade continues.

"Not more than a couple of times each year."

"Did you have knowledge of their fertility problems?"

"Yes," Reid says. "In fact, at one

point my brother even came to me for help."

I feel my pulse start to race. I had not been present at Wade's sessions with Reid, the ones where he instructed him on what to say in response to these questions. If I had, I'd have known what was about to come.

"We met for lunch," Reid explains. "I knew that he and Zoe had done in vitro a couple of times, and Max told me that not only was it taking a huge emotional toll on them as a couple . . . but it was taking an enormous financial toll on them as well." He looks up at me. "Max had told Zoe that he'd find a way to pay for a fifth cycle of IVF, but he didn't know how. He couldn't remortgage his house, because he was a renter. He'd already sold off some of his business equipment. He needed ten thousand dollars to give the clinic, and he didn't know where else to go."

I do not look at her, but I can feel Zoe's hot glare on my cheek. I never told her about this lunch. I never told her anything, except that I'd find a way for her to have that baby, no matter what.

"What did you do, Mr. Baxter?"

"What any brother would have done," Reid says. "I wrote him a check."

Angela Moretti asks for a recess. Mostly because I think she's afraid that Zoe is about to come at me with her claws bared.

It wasn't like I was trying to lie to her, or hide the fact that Reid gave us the money for that last fresh cycle we did at the clinic. But we were buried in debt; I couldn't put another ten thousand on a credit card or find any other way to leverage the cost. I also couldn't stand the thought of telling her we'd run out of money. What kind of loser would that have made me?

I just wanted to make her happy. I didn't want her thinking about what we'd owe if and when we ever had that baby.

It's not like Reid ever asked me for the money back, either. I think we both knew it wasn't a loan, more like a donation. What he said to me, as he scrawled his name across the bottom of the check, was *I know if the situation were reversed, Max, you'd do anything you could to help me.*

When Zoe comes back to the courtroom, she doesn't make eye contact with me. She stares straight ahead at a spot to the right of the judge, while her lawyer gets up to cross-examine Reid. "So you're buying a baby," Angela Moretti begins.

"No. That money was a gift."

"But you did give your brother ten thousand dollars, which was used to create those embryos whose custody you're now seeking, correct?"

"Yes."

"And you have a right to these embryos because you bought them, don't you?" Angela presses.

"I have a moral responsibility to make sure they're raised properly," he says.

"That's not what I asked. You believe you have a right to these embryos because you bought them, isn't that correct, Mr. Baxter?"

In all the time we have been talking

about Reid and Liddy having these babies, Reid has never brought up that check he wrote me. He's never said anything to make me feel like I owe him now because of what he did for me then.

Reid looks down, carefully working through his words before he speaks them. "If it weren't for me," he says finally, "these children wouldn't even exist."

When the judge decides he's had enough for one day, I jump up before Wade can stop me and I run out of the courtroom. I have to shove past a group of Westboro folks, who call out that they are on my side.

When did this become a war?

As soon as I burst out of the courthouse, a mob of reporters surges forward. When I hear Wade's voice at my back, my knees nearly buckle with relief. "My client has no comment," he says, and he puts his hand on my shoulder and steers me through the walkway toward the parking lot. "Don't you ever do that again to me," he hisses in my ear. "You go nowhere until I tell you you can go. I am not going to let you fuck this up, Max."

I stop walking and stretch to my full six feet. I jab a finger in his fancy-ass tailored shirt. *"You,"* I say, "work for *me.*"

But this isn't one hundred percent true, either. Because Reid paid for Wade, too.

This makes me want to smash my fist into something, anything. Wade's face is tempting, but instead, I flatten my hand against his chest and give him a shove, enough to make him stumble. I head to my truck and I don't look back.

I think I know where I'm going even before I get there. There is a spot in Newport near Ruggles Avenue where there are some rocks, and on days when the surf is firing, it's got the most incredible break I've ever seen.

It's also a place where you might get totally pounded.

My shortboard is in the back of my truck. I strip down to my underwear and get into the wet suit that I always keep in the backseat, just in case. Then I work my way down through the rocks and into the water, careful to keep from getting axed on the inside.

There aren't any groms bobbing in the water—it's just me, and the most beautiful curls I've ever seen.

I don't know why the problems I have on land look different in the ocean. Maybe it's the way I'm so much smaller than what's around me. Maybe it's knowing that, even if I get trashed, I can paddle out and do it all over again.

If you haven't surfed, you can't understand the pull of the sport. No matter what Pastor Clive does or says, it's the closest I've ever felt to God. It's the strangest combination of absolute serenity and mad exhilaration. There you are, in the lineup waiting until you see a wave take off. You pump your arms, paddling like crazy, until like magic the foam becomes a wing underneath you and the wave takes over. And you're flying. You're flying, and then, just when you think your heart is going to burst outside your skin, it's over.

A swell rises underneath my board, and I turn to see a tube forming behind me. I pull myself upright and sneak into the shoulder end, riding the barrel as the wave shuts down around me, and then I am falling, tumbling, underwater, not sure which way is up.

I break the surface, my lungs on fire, my hair matted down, and my ears throbbing from the cold. This, I understand. This, I am good at.

Very intentionally, I stay out after sunset. I wrap myself in a blanket and sit on the edge of the rocks and watch the moon take a few turns riding the waves. My head is pounding and my shoulder aches from a nasty fall and I've swallowed about a gallon of salt water. I cannot even begin to describe how thirsty I am, how much I'd kill for a beer. But I also know, if I get into my truck, I'll head right to a bar and have that beer, so instead I wait until it's past last call at most places, and then allow myself to drive back home.

All the lights are off at Reid's house,

which makes sense, since it's nearly three in the morning by the time I pull into the driveway. I turn the key in the lock and leave my shoes on the porch so that I won't disturb anyone while I'm creeping inside.

I sneak into the kitchen to get a glass of water, and see her sitting at the kitchen table like a ghost. Liddy's white cotton nightgown swirls around her ankles like sea foam as she stands up to face me. "Thank God," she says. "Where have you been?"

"I went surfing. I needed to clear my head."

"I tried to call you. I was worried."

I saw her messages on my cell. I deleted them, without listening. I had to, although I can't explain why.

"I haven't been drinking, if that's what you're getting at," I say.

"I wasn't. I was just . . . I wanted to call the hospital, but Reid said you were a big boy and could take care of yourself."

I see the phone book, open on the table, and feel a pang of remorse. "I didn't mean to keep you up. You have a big day tomorrow."

"Can't sleep anyway. Reid took some Ambien, and he's snoring to beat the band."

Liddy sits down on the floor, her back aligned against the wall. When she pats the spot beside her, I sit, too. For a minute we are quiet, listening to the house settle around us. "Remember *The Time Machine*?"

"Sure." It was a movie we saw a few years back, a particularly cheesy one, that was about a time traveler who gets lost in space and stuck 800,000 years in the future.

"Would you want to see the future, even if you knew you couldn't change it?" she asks.

I consider this. "I don't know. I think it might hurt too much."

When she leans her head against my shoulder, I swear I stop breathing. "I used to read these mystery books when I was a little girl, where you could choose a different path at the end of every chapter. And depending on what you picked, the outcome changed."

I can smell her soap—mango and mint—and the shampoo she uses, which sometimes I steal out of her bathroom and use myself.

"I used to skip to the back of the book and read all the endings and pick the one I liked the best . . . and then I'd try to figure it out backward." She laughs a little. "It never worked. I could never make things happen the way I wanted."

The first time Liddy saw snow, the time I was with her to witness it, she held out her hand to catch a snowflake on her palm. *Look at the pattern,* she said, and she held it out to me so I could see. By then, though, it was already gone.

"Reid told me what he said today in court."

I look down at the floor. I don't know what I'm supposed to say.

"I know that Reid can be—well, a bully sometimes. I know he acts like he owns the whole wide world. I know it better than anyone else, except maybe you. I also know that you're wondering why you're doing this, Max." Liddy comes up on her knees and leans closer, so that her hair falls forward. She puts her hand on my cheek. Then, slowly, she kisses me. "You're doing it for me," she whispers.

I am waiting to wake up from this hellish, wonderful dream; certain that at any minute I will find a doctor peering over me and telling me that last wipe-out left me with a massive concussion. I grab Liddy's wrist before she can pull it away from my face. Her skin is warm, buttery.

I kiss her back. God, yes, I kiss her back. I cradle her face in my hands and I try to pour into her everything I've never been allowed to say. I wait for her to pull away, to slap me, but in this alternate world there is enough room for both of us. I grab the hem of her nightgown and inch it up, so that her legs can wrap around mine; I yank my shirt over my head so that she can kiss the salt from my shoulder blades. I lay her down. I love her.

Afterward, when reality settles in and I can feel the hard tile under my hip and the heaviness of her draped across me, I find myself in a total fucking panic.

All my life, I've dreamed of being like my brother, and now I *am.*

Like Reid, I want something that doesn't belong to me.

When I wake up on the kitchen floor, I am alone and wearing my boxers and Reid is standing over me. "Look at what the cat dragged in," he says. "I told Liddy you had nine lives." He's dressed impeccably, and he's holding a mug of coffee. "Better hop in the shower, or you're going to be late for court."

"Where is she?"

"Sick as a dog," Reid says. "Running a fever, apparently. She wanted to stay home, but I told her she's the next witness."

I grab my clothes and hurry upstairs. I should get ready, like Reid said, but instead I knock on the closed door of Liddy and Reid's bedroom. "Liddy?" I whisper. "Liddy, you okay?"

The door opens a crack. Liddy is wearing a bathrobe. She pulls it tight at the collar, as if I haven't already seen everything underneath anyway. Her cheeks are flushed. "I can't talk to you."

I wedge my foot in the door so she can't close it on me. "It doesn't have to be like this. Last night, you were—"

"A sinner," Liddy interrupts, her eyes filling with tears. "Last night I was married. I'm *still* married, Max. And I want a baby."

"We can figure it out. We can tell the court—"

"Tell the court what? That the baby should go to the couple with the wife who's cheating on her husband? The wife that loves her husband's brother? That's not quite anyone's definition of a traditional family, Max."

But I barely hear the last sentence. "You love me?"

She ducks her head. "The guy I fell for was willing to give the most important thing ever—his *child*—to me for safekeeping. The guy I fell for loves God, like me. The guy I fell for would never think of hurting his brother. Last night didn't happen, Max. Because if it did—then you're not that guy anymore."

She closes the door, but I just stand there, unable to move. Reid's footsteps echo down the hallway as he approaches. When he sees me in front of his bedroom door, he frowns and looks at his watch. "You aren't ready yet?"

I swallow. "No," I tell him. "I guess not."

On the witness stand, Liddy can't stop shaking. She tucks her hands underneath her legs, but even then, I can see shudders going through her. "I always talked about being a mother," she says. "In high school, my girlfriends and I would make up names for the babies we'd have. I had it all planned out even before I got married."

When she says the word *married,* her voice breaks.

"I have the perfect life. Reid and I have this beautiful home, and he makes a good living as a portfolio manager. And according to the Bible, the point of marriage is to have children."

"Have you and your husband tried to conceive?" Wade asks.

"Yes. For years." She looks down at her lap. "We were just going to look into Snowflakes Adoption. But then Max . . . Max came to us with another idea."

"Do you have a strong relationship with your brother-in-law?"

Liddy's face drains of color. "Yes."

"How did you react when he told you he wanted to give his pre-born children to you and your husband?"

"I thought that God had answered my prayers."

"Did you ask him why he didn't want to raise the children himself? Maybe at a later date?"

"Reid did," she admits. "Max told us that he didn't think he'd be good at it. He had made too many mistakes. He wanted his children to grow up with a mother and a father who . . . who loved each other."

"Have you had much interaction with children?"

For the first time since she's gotten into that chair, she brightens. "I run the Sunday School program at our church.

And I organize a youth ministry camp during the summers. I love kids."

"If the court saw fit to give you these pre-born children," Wade asks, "how would you raise them?"

"To be good Christians," Liddy says. "To do the right thing." As soon as she says it, her face crumples. "I'm sorry," she sobs.

Across from me, Zoe shifts. Today she is dressed in black, like she's in mourning. She stares at Liddy as if she's the Antichrist.

Wade pulls a crimson silk handkerchief from his suit jacket pocket and hands it to Liddy to wipe her eyes. "Your witness," he says, and he turns to Zoe's lawyer.

Angela Moretti stands and tugs on the hem of her suit jacket to straighten it. "What can you give these embryos that their biological mother can't?"

"Opportunities," Liddy says. "A stable Christian home."

"So you think that money is all it takes to raise children?"

"Of course not. They would live in a loving household."

"When was the last time you spent a few hours with Zoe and Vanessa?"

"I . . . I haven't . . ."

"So you don't really know what kind of love their household is filled with, do you?"

"I know it's immoral," Liddy says.

"So it's Zoe's sexual orientation that makes her an unfit mother? Is that your testimony?"

Liddy hesitates. "I didn't say that. I just think that Reid and I—we're the better option for these children."

"What kind of contraception do you use?" Angela asks.

Liddy blushes. "I don't use any."

I have a sudden flash of last night, her head turned so that her throat was exposed, her back arched beneath me. "How often do you and your husband have sex?"

"Objection!"

"I'll allow it," the judge says. *Dirty old man.*

"Answer the question, Mrs. Baxter."

"Thursdays," Liddy says.

Thursdays? Once a week? Like clockwork? If Liddy were my wife, I'd be in the shower with her every morning. I'd grab her when she walked by me at the dinner table and pull her onto my lap—

"Do you time intercourse so that you might be able to get pregnant?"

"Yes—"

"Have you ever been pregnant?"

"Yes . . . several times . . . but I've miscarried."

"Do you even know if you *can* carry a baby to term?"

"Does anyone?" Liddy asks.

Atta girl.

"You realize that if you get these embryos and they're transferred to you, you may still not have a live birth."

"Or," Liddy points out, "I could have triplets."

"You said that, in the Bible, the point of marriage is to have children?"

"Yes."

"So if God wanted you to have children, wouldn't you have had them already?"

"I . . . I think He has a different plan for us," Liddy says.

The lawyer nods. "Of course. God wants you to become a substitute mother by depriving a biological mother of the same right."

"Objection!" Wade says.

"Let me rephrase," Angela says. "Do you agree that what you want most in the world is to have and raise a child?"

Liddy's eyes, which have been trained so carefully on Angela Moretti, slide toward me. My mouth feels like it's full of broken glass. "Yes," she says.

"Do you agree that not being able to have a biological child is devastating? Heartbreaking?"

"Yes."

"And yet, isn't that exactly the fate to which you consign Zoe Baxter, if you take her embryos?"

Liddy turns toward Zoe, her eyes full of tears. "I would raise these babies like they're my own," she whispers.

The words pull Zoe out of her seat. "They're not yours," she replies, quietly at first, and then more forcefully. "They're *mine!*"

The judge bangs his gavel. "Ms. Moretti, control your client!"

"Leave her alone!" I cry, standing up. "Can't you see she's upset!"

For a moment, the whole world stops spinning. Zoe turns with a ghost of a smile on her lips—grateful because she thinks that my words are meant for her.

And then she realizes they're not.

You cannot be married to a person for nearly a decade and not be able to read the Morse code of a relationship: Eyes that meet at a dinner party, telegraphing that it's time to make up an excuse and go home. A silent apology when you reach for her hand under the covers. An *I love you* smile, tossed at her feet.

She knows. I can tell by the way she is looking at me that she understands what I've done. That she's lost me, and potentially her embryos, to a woman she detests.

Then the freeze-frame releases and Zoe lunges toward the witness stand. A sheriff grabs her and forces her to her knees. Someone screams. "I will have order in this court, *right now,*" Judge O'Neill roars.

By now, Liddy is a blubbering mess. Wade grabs at my arm. "Shut *up* before you ruin everything."

"Zoe," Angela Moretti says, trying to push the sheriff off her client. "You need to calm down—"

"This court is in recess," the judge shouts, and he storms off the bench.

Wade waits until Angela has dragged Zoe out of the courtroom, until the bulk of the gallery has filed into the hallway to gossip about what they've seen. "What the hell was that?" he accuses.

I don't know what to say to him. I can barely understand it myself.

"It just happened," I manage.

"Well, you better make sure it doesn't happen again, if you feel like winning this trial. If your ex wants to stand up and look like a crazy nutcase, that's fantastic for us. You think a judge is going to watch that and think she'd be a good parent? If she does it again, and I pray she will, you sit with your hands folded and you make yourself the picture of calm. You *don't* stand up and defend her, for the love of God!"

I bend my head, so that he can't see the relief flooding my face.

I have no idea where Wade found Genevieve Newkirk. A licensed clinical psychologist, she's got a Ph.D. from UCLA and has published repeatedly on issues central to marriage, sexuality, and parenting. She's been on radio and TV—local and national—and has been interviewed for web and print media. She's consulted on over seventy-five legal cases and has testified in over forty of them. "Dr. Newkirk," Wade begins, once he's gotten her admitted as an expert witness, "in your work, have you had the opportunity to explore whether homosexuality is genetically inherited?"

"I have. Frankly, there have not been many studies done, so it's very easy to review all the research."

"Are you familiar with the Bailey-Pillard studies?" Wade asks.

"Yes." Dr. Newkirk turns to the gallery. "In 1991 and 1993 J. M. Bailey and R. C. Pillard set out to study homosexuality in twins. They found that fifty-two percent of identical male twins of homosexual men were also homosexual, that twenty-two percent of fraternal twins of homosexual men were also homosexual, and that eleven percent of adoptive brothers of homosexual men were likewise homosexual. Among women they found that forty-eight percent of identical female twins of lesbians were also lesbian, sixteen percent of fraternal twins of lesbians were also lesbian, and six percent of adoptive sisters of lesbians were likewise lesbian."

"What does that suggest?"

"Well, it's complicated. Some would argue that the data suggest a biological component to being gay. However, twins who are raised together have the same sort of shaping influences. In order to have a valid study, twins who were raised apart would have to be assessed—and in identical twins who *have* been raised apart, there is a zero percent correlation; in other words, just because one twin is homosexual doesn't mean the identical twin is homosexual. Moreover, if sexual orientation is genetic, how do you explain the other forty-eight percent of identical male twins and fifty-two percent of identical female twins who wind up *not* being gay?"

"Hang on," Wade says. "You're telling me that there are identical twins— twins who were born from the same exact genetic material—who grow up so that one's homosexual, and the other's not?"

"Nearly half," Newkirk agrees. "This suggests strongly that homosexuality *isn't* a genetic determination. It may very well be a genetic *predisposition*— but that's not the same thing by a long shot. Many people are born with a genetic predisposition toward depression or substance abuse and yet don't indulge in behaviors that bring them to the surface. Or in other words: the environment in which a child is raised has an enormous influence on whether or not he becomes homosexual."

"Thank you, Doctor. What about Simon LeVay's research?"

"Dr. LeVay was a neuroscientist at the Salk Institute, and he set out to find a physiological basis to homosexuality by studying the brains of forty-one people: nineteen homosexual men, sixteen heterosexual men, and six heterosexual women. He found that a little batch of neurons in the hypothalamus—a batch thought to control sexual behavior—is smaller in homosexual men than it is in heterosexual men. Moreover, he determined that it was approximately the size of a heterosexual woman's hypothalamus—which had previously been shown to be half the size of a heterosexual man's."

"Does this show a biological basis for homosexuality?" Wade asks.

"No. First, the hypothalamic region demonstrates considerable range—in some homosexual men the region was the same size as a heterosexual man's; in some heterosexuals the region was as small as a homosexual's. Moreover, the control group was quite small, and the study hasn't been repeated. Finally, we have to wonder whether the brain structure causes sexual orientation—or changes because of it. For example, a National Institutes of Health study showed that, for people who read Braille after becoming blind, the part of the brain that controls the reading finger actually expands."

"What about Dean Hamer's 1993 study?" Wade says. "Didn't he find a 'gay gene'?"

"Not exactly," Dr. Newkirk replies. "He found that gay brothers shared a piece of the X chromosome—Xq28— more often than straight brothers did. But again, this study hasn't been replicated."

"So none of these esteemed scientists have been able to conclusively prove that a person is born gay?"

"No," the psychologist says. "It's certainly not like skin color, for example. You can't do anything to change your skin color—Michael Jackson notwithstanding. But sexual orientation isn't all nature. There's a hefty dose of nurture tossed in as well."

"That brings me to your most recent article, 'Beyond Love: Why Same-Sex Marriage Harms Children.' Can you tell us what led you to write it?"

"There's copious evidence that it is in a child's best interest to be raised by two heterosexual parents," Dr. Newkirk says. "Lesbian partners may indeed be wonderful mothers, but they simply cannot be fathers."

"Can you elaborate?"

Dr. Newkirk nods. "There are four primary reasons why it's critical for a child to be loved by both a mother and a father. First, the attachment a parent of each sex has to its child—though equally important—is significantly unique. A mother's unconditional love and a father's conditional love complement each other and influence the way a child grows up. A relationship with both sexes in a child's formative years allows the child to interact with the world more easily in later years. Second, it's a well-established fact of child development that there are different stages of growth psychologically. For example, although babies of both sexes at first respond better to the care of a mother, at a certain point, to hone his masculine identity, a boy must detach from his mother and identify with his father instead, to learn how to channel his aggression and control his emotions. The father relationship is important to the growing young lady, as well—it becomes a safe place to have her femininity validated. Without that father figure in her life, she is more likely to satiate a hunger for male attention in a way that makes her sexually adventurous in inappropriate ways."

"And the third reason?" Wade prompts.

"Same-sex relationships have been documented to cause sexual confusion in children, and promiscuity. The message sent is that all choices are equally desirable, that it doesn't matter who you marry. For this reason young people raised in same-sex-relationship households tend to be both sexually active and sexually indiscriminate."

"You mean they're more likely to form homosexual relationships themselves?"

"Exactly. Think of ancient Greece, for example. Homosexuality ran rampant—not because of a gay gene but because society condoned it. Condoning this kind of behavior only leads to a proliferation of the behavior."

"And the final reason same-sex marriage is detrimental to children?"

"Because it paves the way for even more socially unacceptable relationships. Polyamorous couplings, for example. Can you imagine the emotional ramifications suffered by a child who has a single father but multiple mommies? With whom would that child bond? And if we extrapolate from this—imagine what happens when those marriages disintegrate and then there are remarriages—well, conceivably there could be children with two fathers and six mothers . . ." She shakes her head. "That's not a family, Mr. Preston. That's a commune."

"Let me ask you, Dr. Newkirk, do your objections stem from an inability of a homosexual couple to provide love to a child?"

"Absolutely not. Certainly homosexual couples can create just as loving an environment as heterosexual couples. However, kids need more than love. They need the complementary experiences of having a male and a female parent for guidance, instruction, and psychological development."

"Naysayers will ask what your evidence is," Wade says.

Dr. Newkirk smiles. "Five thousand years or so of parenting, Mr. Preston. Putting children into a newfangled social experiment could be absolutely devastating to the next generation." She looks over at Zoe. "I have nothing but compassion for homosexuals who want to raise a family. But I can't allow my compassion for them to trounce the needs of innocent children."

"As a result of all your research, Dr. Newkirk, do you have an expert opinion as to which home would be a more fit and proper placement for these preborn children?"

"Yes, I do. I firmly believe that these children would be much better off in the home of Reid and Liddy Baxter."

"Thank you, Doctor," Wade says, and he turns to Angela Moretti. "Your witness."

"You say homosexuality isn't genetic, right, Doctor?" Angela begins.

"There's no evidence to support that."

"You said the Bailey and Pillard study isn't valid because not every identical twin who identified as gay had a gay twin, correct?"

"That's right."

"Are you aware that, even though identical twins share many identical traits, there are certain biological factors that differ between them? Fingerprints, for example?"

"Well—"

"And, Doctor, you discounted the LeVay study because it hasn't been confirmed yet with a similar study."

"That's right," the psychologist says.

"Are you familiar with the research done on the eight percent of domestic rams who are solely interested in having sex with other rams?"

"No."

"Well," Angela Moretti says, "in fact researchers discovered in those rams a bunch of neurons in the hypothalamus that were smaller than they tended to be in heterosexual rams. In fact, the findings were very reminiscent of Simon LeVay's study. Doctor, you also criticized Dean Hamer's research because it hasn't been replicated, correct?"

"Yes."

"Does that mean that at some point the study *might* be replicated?"

"Naturally I can't predict the future."

"Are you aware of the Swedish study that identified the differences in the way the brains of straight men and gay men responded to male and female phero-mones, which suggested a strong phys-iological component to homosexual-ity?"

"Yes, but—"

"Do you know that scientists in Vi-enna have identified a genetic switch for sexual orientation in fruit flies? And that, when they tampered with the switch, female fruit flies ignored males and instead tried to mate with other fe-males by mimicking the mating rituals of male fruit flies?"

"I was not aware of that, no," the psychologist admits.

"And did you know, Dr. Newkirk, that there's currently a two-point-five-mil-lion-dollar study underwritten by the National Institutes of Health to do ge-netic screenings of a thousand pairs of gay brothers, in order to better understand the genetic component of homo-sexuality? You and I both know that government rarely muddies its hands in research regarding sexuality, Doctor. Wouldn't this suggest that even an es-teemed institution like the NIH is vali-dating the biological basis for homo-sexuality?"

"Anyone can have a hypothesis, Ms. Moretti. Research, though, doesn't al-ways back it up."

"Then how about Dr. William Reiner, at the University of Oklahoma," Angela asks. "Are you aware that he's studied hundreds of cases of children born with sexual differentiation disorders—such as a baby boy with an undeveloped penis or no penis at all? Typical proto-col has involved surgery to castrate the infant, who is then raised as a girl. Did you know, Doctor, that not a single one grew up to be sexually attracted to males? That the majority of those gen-der-reassigned babies transitioned back to being males, because they were sexually attracted to women? I'd say that's a very clear example of nurture *not* trumping nature, wouldn't you?"

"Counselor," the psychologist says, "I assume *you* are familiar with Darwin's principle of natural selection?"

"Of course."

"Then you know that it's an established scientific belief that the primary goal for all species is to pass along the strongest genes to future generations. Since homosexuals produce only twenty percent of the offspring that heterosexuals do, wouldn't this gay gene you're suggesting have long been wiped out by natural selection?" She smiles. "You can't play the biology card if you can't justify that."

The lawyer brushes off her comment. "I'm just a humble attorney, Dr. Newkirk. I wouldn't presume to dabble in either science *or* pseudoscience. Now, one of your justifications for raising children in heterosexual unions is that not having both a mother and father is problematic, correct?"

"Yes."

"So if one parent in a heterosexual couple dies, is it your position to advocate removing the child and putting him in the home of a different heterosexual couple?"

"That would be ludicrous. The *optimal* living situation for any child involves having both a mother and a father, but obviously that can't always be the case. Tragedies happen."

"Such as keeping an embryo from going to its biological mother?"

"Objection—"

The judge frowns. "Sustained."

"I'll withdraw," Angela Moretti says.

"Actually, I'd like to answer," Dr. Newkirk says. "I can point Ms. Moretti to numerous studies that prove a boy who grows up without a father is more likely to become a delinquent, and to end up incarcerated."

"What about your claim that same-sex marriage opens the door for polygamy? In the years since gay marriage has been legal in Massachusetts, has anyone petitioned the legislature for a polygamist union?"

"I don't follow the legislation in that state . . ."

"I'll help you out. The answer's no,"

Angela says. "And no one's asked to get married to a rock or a goat, either." She begins to tick off points on her fingers. "Let me just sum up what I'm hearing from you, Dr. Newkirk. Homosexual parenting leads to all sorts of devastating developmental downfalls for the children involved. Homosexuality isn't innate, it's learned. If you have homosexual parents, you're likely to experiment with homosexual relationships. If you grow up with heterosexual parents, you will grow up to be heterosexual."

The psychologist nods. "That's about right."

"Then maybe you can explain something else to me," Angela Moretti says. "How come most gay people have straight parents?" She turns around and walks back to her seat while the psychologist is still trying to find a response. "Nothing further."

Angela Moretti *really* doesn't want Pastor Clive to take the stand. "Your Honor," she says, "if Mr. Lincoln is a character witness for Max Baxter, there's no need to qualify him as an expert in his field. The study of Max Baxter is not an academic discipline."

"Pastor Clive is a religious leader and scholar," Wade argues. "He's traveled all over this country preaching the word of God."

"And you know the one place he can't preach it? In a court of law," Angela replies.

"I think I want to hear what he has to say," Judge O'Neill says.

"Of course you do," Angela mutters.

The judge scowls. "I beg your pardon, Counselor?"

She looks up. "I said I'm a Jew."

"Well, I never would have made that assumption, given the fact that your last name comes straight from Federal Hill. But thanks for sharing," he adds. "It puts some of your earlier objections in a much different light. Attorney Preston, you may call your witness."

When Pastor Clive walks in from wherever he's been sequestered, accompanied by a sheriff, the gallery reacts. The members of the Eternal Glory

Church call out hallelujahs and amens; the Westboro Baptist group starts clapping. For his part, Pastor Clive ducks his head humbly and walks down the aisle.

He asks to be sworn in on his own Bible.

"Please state your name for the record," Wade says.

"Clive Lincoln."

"What do you do for a living?"

"I'm the pastor of the Eternal Glory Evangelical Church of God."

"Do you have a family, Pastor?"

"Yes," Pastor Clive says. "I have a wonderful wife, and God's seen fit to bless us with four beautiful daughters."

Three of them I know—they're fresh-scrubbed preteens who wear matching dresses and sing with Pastor Clive on Sundays. The other one sits in the back during services and doesn't say a word. Rumor has it she hasn't accepted Jesus as her Lord and Savior. I can't imagine what a personal embarrassment that must be for someone like Pastor Clive.

I guess we all have our crosses to bear.

"Do you know the plaintiff in this matter?"

"I do. Max joined our congregation about six months ago."

"Are you familiar with Reid and Liddy Baxter as well?" Wade asks.

"I've known Reid for fifteen years. He's a business whiz, frankly—he's managed the church's finances for over a decade. We may have been the only nonprofit that made money during the recession." Pastor Clive rolls his eyes upward. "Then again, we just might have had Someone looking out for us in the stock market."

"How long have you been the pastor of this church?"

"Twenty-one glorious years."

"Pastor, what does your church teach about homosexuality?"

"Objection," Angela Moretti says. "I don't see how this testimony furthers his understanding of the plaintiff's character."

"Overruled."

"We believe in the word of God,"

Pastor Clive says. "We interpret the Bible literally, and there are multiple passages that state marriage is meant to be between a man and a woman, for the purpose of procreation—and many others that directly condemn homosexuality."

"Can you elaborate?"

"Objection!" Angela Moretti stands. "The Bible isn't relevant in a court of law."

"Oh, really?" Wade says. He gestures to the King James Bible the clerk keeps on his desk for swearing in.

Angela Moretti ignores him. "Your Honor, Mr. Lincoln's interpretation of Bible verses is a direct melding of religion and justice—which violates the very principles of our legal system."

"On the contrary, Your Honor, this is entirely relevant to the best interests of the pre-born children, and the sort of home in which they wind up."

"I'll allow the testimony," Judge O'Neill says.

A man in the back of the gallery who's wearing a shirt that says CLOSETS ARE FOR

CLOTHES stands up. "Go fuck yourself, Judge!"

O'Neill glances up. "Motion denied," he says drily. "Sheriff, please remove this man from my courtroom." He turns toward Pastor Clive. "As I was saying, you may proceed. But I'll limit you to choosing a single verse as an example. Ms. Moretti is right about one thing: this is a trial, not a Sunday School session."

Pastor Clive calmly opens his Bible and reads aloud. *"Do not lie with a man as one lies with a woman; that is detestable. And if a man lies with a man as one lies with a woman, both of them have done what is detestable. They must be put to death; their blood will be on their own heads.* I know those are two verses, but they're practically on the same page."

"How would you and your congregation interpret those passages?" Wade asks.

"I don't think it's just me and my congregation," Pastor Clive says. "It's spelled out to anyone who reads it—

homosexuality is an abomination. A sin."

"For Pete's sake," Angela Moretti says, "I object. For the hundredth time."

"I will give his testimony the weight it deserves, Counselor," Judge O'Neill says.

Wade turns to Pastor Clive. "I'd like to direct your attention to the pre-born children at the root of this case," he says. "When did you learn about them?"

"Max came to me for counseling, very upset after having a conversation with his ex-wife. Apparently, she is now living a life of sin—"

"Objection!"

"Please strike that from the record," the judge says.

"Max's ex-wife wanted to get custody of these pre-born children so that she could transfer them to her lesbian lover."

"How did you advise Max?" Wade asks.

"I told him that this might be God's way of trying to tell him something. We discussed what sort of family he wanted his children to grow up in—and he said a traditional, good Christian one. When I asked him if he knew anyone like that, he immediately mentioned his brother and sister-in-law."

Liddy, I think and feel a pang in my chest.

What if I suggested we raise the babies together? We could tell Wade, and he could tell the judge, and then all of a sudden the biological father—me— would be added to the equation. Then I wouldn't be giving the babies away; I'd be keeping them for myself.

Except that Wade's made a whole case about me not being ready to be a father.

And Liddy.

Even if she was willing, I couldn't take her away from everything she's got. The money, the home, the security. How could I even come close to measuring up to Reid?

Reid, who's never done anything but help me and who gets, in return, a brother who sleeps with his wife.

Yeah, I'm the perfect father. A real, upstanding role model.

"Reid and Liddy have been praying

for children for years," Pastor Clive says. "They'd recently considered adopting through the Snowflakes agency. When Max came to me, I thought that maybe God was offering us a different solution, one that would benefit everyone involved. That perhaps Liddy and Reid were the best parents for these particular pre-born children."

"How did Max react?"

"He was cautiously optimistic." Pastor Clive looks up. "We all were."

"Thank you, Pastor," Wade says, and he sits back down.

Angela Moretti starts talking before she even rises from her chair. "A solution that would benefit everyone involved," she repeats. "Is that what you thought?"

"Yes."

"Doesn't seem like much of a benefit for Zoe, the biological mother of these embryos."

"As much as I understand the need to cater to Ms. Baxter's concerns, what a child needs is far more important," Pastor Clive says.

"So you think that picking nonbiological parents for these embryos is a better choice than picking a parent who has a direct gametic relationship to them."

"What I think matters far less than what God thinks."

"Oh yeah?" Angela asks. "When's the last time you talked to him?"

"Objection," Wade says. "I won't let her mock my witness."

"Sustained . . . watch yourself, Counselor."

"You said you've known Max for half a year, Pastor?"

"Yes."

"And you've never met Zoe Baxter—you've only just seen her in this courtroom, correct?"

"That's right."

"You have no information about them when they were a married couple?"

"No. They were not members of my church at the time."

"I see," Angela says. "But you *do* know Reid and Liddy Baxter quite well?"

"Yes."

"You had no trouble coming into this

court and saying that, in your opinion, they are the preferred custodial couple for these embryos."

"Yes," Pastor Clive says.

"You have a professional relationship with Reid Baxter, too, right?"

"He manages the church's funds."

"He's also one of the biggest contributors to your church, isn't he?"

"Yes. Reid's always been very generous."

"In fact, your church recommends tithing income for its members, doesn't it?"

"Many churches do that . . ."

"Isn't it true that you receive a grand total of about four hundred thousand dollars a year from your friend Reid Baxter annually?"

"That sounds about right."

"And coincidentally, here you are today recommending that he be awarded custody of these embryos, correct?"

"Reid's generosity to the church has nothing to do with my recommendation—"

"Oh, I'll bet," Angela Moretti says. "When you spoke with Max about his ex-wife's request to have custody of the embryos, you were the one who in fact suggested that he consider Reid and Liddy as potential parents, weren't you?"

"I opened his mind to the possibility."

"And you even went a step further, didn't you—by finding him an attorney?"

Pastor Clive nods. "I would have done the same for any member of my congregation . . ."

"In fact, Pastor, you didn't just find Max a lawyer. You found him the biggest hotshot attorney in the United States with a reputation for protecting the rights of the pre-born, right?"

"I can't help it if Max's predicament attracted the attention of someone so prestigious."

"Mr. Lincoln, you stated that the purpose of marriage is to procreate?"

"Yes."

"Does the Bible have anything to say about heterosexual couples who are unable to have children?"

"No."

"What about heterosexual couples too old to have children?"

"No—"

"How about people who remain single? Does the Bible condemn them as unnatural?"

"No."

"Even though, by your own logic, they are not procreating?"

"Plenty of other passages in the Bible condemn homosexuality," Pastor Clive says.

"Ah, yes. That lovely bit you read from Leviticus. Are you aware, Mr. Lincoln, that Leviticus is a holiness code that was written over three thousand years ago?"

"Of course I am."

"Do you know that holiness codes had a very specific purpose? That they weren't commandments but prohibitions of behaviors that people of faith would find offensive at a certain time and place? Are you aware, Pastor, that in the case of Leviticus, the code was written for priests in Israel only, and meant to hold them more accountable than priests from other countries, like Greece?"

"It's quite clear what's right and wrong when you read that passage. And you may try to explain it away historically, but it's still morally relevant today."

"Really. Did you know that, in Leviticus, there were many other prohibitions listed? For example, there's one against wild haircuts, did you know that?"

"Well—"

"And one against tattoos." She smiles. "I've got one myself, but I'm not gonna tell you where." The lawyer walks toward Pastor Clive. "Is that a silk tie against a cotton shirt? Did you know that there's another prohibition against wearing garments made of mixed fabric?"

"I fail to see how—"

"And hey, there's another one saying you shouldn't eat pork or shellfish. You like shrimp scampi, Pastor?"

"This isn't—"

"There's another prohibition against getting your fortune told. And how about football? You like football, right? I mean, who doesn't? Well, there's a prohibition against playing with the skin of a pig. Wouldn't you agree, Pastor, that many of those prohibitions are indeed historically outdated?"

"Objection," Wade says. "Counsel is testifying!"

The judge tilts his head. "What's good for the goose is good for the gander, Mr. Preston. Overruled."

"The Bible is many things to many people, but it is not a sex manual, correct?"

"Of course not!"

"Then why on earth would you turn to it for recommendations about appropriate sexual activity?"

Pastor Clive faces the lawyer. "I look to the Bible for *everything,* Ms. Moretti. Even examples of sexual deviance."

"What does it have to say about butt plugs?"

Wade rises. *"Objection!"*

"Really, Ms. Moretti?" the judge says, scowling.

"Should we assume then that there might be things not mentioned in the Bible that are still sexually deviant?"

"It's entirely possible," Pastor Clive

says. "The Bible is just a general out-line."

"But the ones that *are* mentioned in the Bible as being sexually deviant—that, in your opinion, is God's word? Completely and utterly inviolable?"

"That's right."

Angela Moretti picks a Bible off the defense table that has been littered with Post-it notes. "Are you familiar with Deuteronomy 22:20–21?" she asks. "Could you read this out loud to the court?"

Pastor Clive's voice rings through the room. *"If, however, the charge is true and no proof of the girl's virginity can be found, she shall be brought to the door of her father's house and there the men of her town shall stone her to death."*

"Thank you, Pastor. Can you explain the passage?"

He purses his lips. "It advocates stoning a woman who isn't a virgin at the time of marriage."

"Is that something you'd advise your flock to do?" Before he can answer, she asks him another question. "How about Mark 10:1–12? Those passages forbid divorce. Do you have any members of your congregation who are divorced? Oh, wait—of course you do. Max Baxter."

"God forgives sinners," Pastor Clive says. "He welcomes them back into His fold."

Angela flips through her Bible again. "How about Mark 12:18–23? If a man dies childless, his widow is ordered by biblical law to have sex with each of his brothers in turn until she bears her deceased husband a male heir. Is that what you tell grieving widows?"

I hate myself for it, but I think of Liddy again.

"Objection!"

"Or Deuteronomy 25:11–12? If two men are fighting and the wife of one of them tries to rescue her husband by grabbing his enemy's genitals, her hand should be cut off and no pity should be shown to her—"

Seriously? I had joined an adult Bible study at Reid's suggestion, but we never read anything as juicy as that.

"Objection!" Wade smacks the table with his open hand.

The judge raises his voice. "Ms. Moretti, I will hold you in contempt if you—"

"Fine. I'll withdraw that last one. But you must admit, Pastor, that not every decree in the Bible makes sense in this day and age."

"Only because you're taking the verses out of historical context—"

"Mr. Lincoln," Angela Moretti says flatly. "You did first."

	TRACK 1	SING YOU HOME
	TRACK 2	THE HOUSE ON HOPE STREET
	TRACK 3	REFUGEE
	TRACK 4	THE LAST
	TRACK 5	MARRY ME
	TRACK 6	FAITH
	TRACK 7	THE MERMAID
	TRACK 8	ORDINARY LIFE
✓	**TRACK 9**	**WHERE YOU ARE**
	TRACK 10	SAMMY'S SONG

ZOE

_____

For the first five seconds after I wake up, the day is as crisp as a new dollar bill—spotless, full of possibility.

And then I remember.

That there is a lawsuit.

That there are three embryos.

That today, I am testifying.

That for the rest of my life, Vanessa and I will have to jump twice as high and run twice as fast to cover the same ground as a heterosexual couple. Love is never easy, but it seems that, for gay couples, it's an obstacle course.

I feel her arm steal around me from behind. "Stop thinking," she says.

"How do you know I'm thinking?"

Vanessa smiles against my shoulder blade. "Because your eyes are open."

I roll over to face her. "How did you do it? How does *anyone* ever come out when they're younger? I mean, I can barely handle what's being said about me in that courtroom, and I'm forty-one years old. If I were fourteen, I wouldn't just be in the closet—I'd be gluing myself to its inside wall."

Vanessa rolls onto her back and stares up at the ceiling. "I would have rather died than come out in high school. Even though I knew, deep down, who I was. There are a million reasons to not come out when you're a teen-ager—because adolescence is about matching everyone else, not standing out; because you don't know what your parents are going to say; because you're terrified your best friend will think you're making the moves on her—seri-ously, I've been there." She glances at me. "At my school now, there are five teens who are openly gay and lesbian, and about fifteen more who don't want to realize they're gay and lesbian yet. I can tell them a hundred million times that what they're feeling is perfectly normal, and then they go home and turn on the news and they see that the military won't let gay people serve. They watch another gay marriage referendum bite the dust. One thing kids *aren't* is stupid."

"How many people have to say there's something wrong with you before you start believing it?" I muse out loud.

"You tell me," Vanessa says. "You're a late bloomer, Zo, but you're just as brave as the rest of us. Gays and lesbians are like cockroaches, I guess. Resilient as all hell."

I laugh. "Clearly that would be Pastor Clive's worst nightmare. Cockroaches have been around since the dinosaurs were walking the earth."

"But then Pastor Clive would have to believe in evolution," Vanessa says.

Thinking of Pastor Clive makes me think about the gauntlet we had to run yesterday to get into court. Last night, Wade Preston had been on the Hannity show. Today there will be twice as much media. Twice as much attention focused on me.

I'm used to it; I'm a performer after all. But there's an enormous difference between an audience that's watching you because they can't wait to see what comes next and an audience that's watching you because they're waiting for you to fail.

Suddenly nothing about Pastor Clive seems funny at all.

I roll onto my side, staring at the buttery light on the wood floor, wondering what would happen if I phoned Angela and told her I had the flu. Hives. The Black Plague.

Vanessa curves her body around mine, tangles our ankles together. "Stop thinking," she says again. "You're going to be fine."

One of the hidden costs of a courtroom trial is the amount of time that your real life is entirely interrupted by something you'd much rather keep secret. Maybe you're a little ashamed; maybe you just don't think it's anyone's business. You have to take personal time off work; you have to assume that everything else is on hold and this takes precedence.

In this, a lawsuit is not much different from in vitro.

Because of this—and because Vanessa's taking off just as much time as I am—we decide that we will spend an hour at the high school before we have to go to court for the day. Vanessa can clear her desk and put out whatever fires have sprung up since yesterday; I will meet with Lucy.

Or so we think, until we turn the corner from the school parking lot and find a mob of picketers, holding signs and chanting.

FEAR GOD, NOT GAYS
JUDGMENT IS COMING
NO QUEERS HERE
3 GAY RIGHTS: 1. STDS 2. AIDS 3. HELL

Two cops are standing by, warily watching the protest. Clive Lincoln is standing smack in the middle of this fiasco, wearing yet another white suit—

this one double-breasted. "We are here to protect our children," he bellows. "The future of this great country—and those at greatest risk to becoming the prey of homosexuals—homosexuals who work in this very school!"

"Vanessa." I gasp. "What if he outs you?"

"After all this media coverage, I hardly think that's possible," Vanessa says. "Besides, the people I care about already know. The people I don't care about—well, they'll have to just deal with it. They can't fire me because I'm gay." She stands a little taller. "Angela would *drool* to take that case."

A school bus pulls up, and as the baffled kids stream out of it, the church members yell at them, or shove signs in their faces. One small, delicate boy, wearing a hooded sweatshirt that has been yanked tight around his face, turns bright red when he sees the signs.

Vanessa leans closer to me. "Remember what we were talking about this morning? He's one of the other fifteen."

The boy ducks his head, trying to become invisible.

"I'm going to run interference," Vanessa says. "You okay on your own here?" She doesn't wait to hear my answer but barrels through the crowd—shoving with a linebacker's force until she reaches the boy and carefully steers him through this forcefield of hate. "Why don't you get a life?" Vanessa yells at Pastor Clive.

"Why don't you get a *man*?" he replies.

Suddenly Vanessa's face is just as red as the boy's. I watch her disappear into the school doors, still trying to refocus the student's attention.

"Homosexuals are teaching our children—trying to convert them to their lifestyle," Pastor Clive says. "What irony is it that *guidance* is being provided to these impressionable youth by those who live in sin?"

I grab the sleeve of a policeman. "This is a school. Surely they shouldn't be protesting here. Can't you get rid of them?"

"Not unless they actually do something violent. You can blame the liberals for the flip side of democracy, lady. Guys like this get to blow their horn; terrorists move in the neighborhood. God bless the U.S.A.," he says sarcastically. He looks at me, cracks his gum.

"I have nothing against homosexuals," Pastor Clive says. "But I do not like what they do. Gays already have equal rights. What they want are special rights. Rights that will slowly but surely take away from your own freedoms. In places where they have prevailed, speaking my mind, like I am right now, could land me in jail for hate speech. In Canada and England and Sweden, pastors and ministers and cardinals and bishops have been sued or sentenced to prison for preaching against homosexuality. In Pennsylvania, an evangelical group carrying signs like you were arrested for ethnic intimidation."

Another busload of students walks by. One of them throws a spitball at Pastor Clive. "Dickhead," the kid says.

The pastor wipes it calmly off his face. "They have already been brainwashed," he says. "The school systems now teach even babies in kindergarten that having two mommies is normal. If your child says differently, he'll be humiliated in front of his peers. But it doesn't stop in schools. You could wind up like Chris Kempling—a Canadian teacher who was suspended for writing a letter to the editor stating that gay sex poses health risks and that many religions find homosexuality immoral. He was just stating the facts, friends, and yet he was suspended without pay for a month. Or Annie Coffey-Montes, a Bell Atlantic employee who was fired for asking to be removed from the e-mail list of gays and lesbians in her company that advertised parties and dances. Or Richard Peterson, who posted Bible verses about homosexuality on his office cubicle at Hewlett-Packard and found himself out of a job."

He is a cheerleader for the cheerless, I realize. Someone who doesn't gather people to his cause as much as drive them there with paranoia.

There is a rumble of disturbance at

the edges of the crowd, an undulation like a puppy under a quilt. I am elbowed by a woman who has a large gold cross hanging between her breasts.

"Your right as a Christian to embrace your own beliefs is being curtailed by the homosexual agenda," Pastor Clive continues. "We must fight back now, before our religious and civil freedoms are a casualty, trampled by these—"

All of a sudden, he is knocked over by a blur of black. Immediately, three of his suited thugs pull him to his feet, at the same time that the two cops grab the attacker. I think he's just as shocked as I am to see who it is. "Lucy!" he cries. "What on earth are you doing!"

I can't figure out how he knows her name at first. Then I remember that she goes to his church.

Apparently under duress.

Shoving through the crowd, I step between Clive and the policemen, who are totally going for overkill with Lucy. Each of them has one of her arms twisted behind her back, and she weighs all of a hundred pounds. "I'll take this from here," I say, my voice brimming with so much authority that they actually let her go.

"You and I aren't finished," Clive says, but I shoot him a look over my shoulder as I lead Lucy into the school.

"Take it up with me in court," I tell him.

I bet Lucy's never been so glad to have the doors of the school close behind her. Her face is flushed and mottled. "Take a deep breath," I tell her. "It's going to be all right."

Vanessa comes out of the main office and looks at us both. "What happened?"

"Lucy and I need a place to calm down," I say, keeping my voice as even as possible, when what I really want to do is call the ACLU or Angela or a proctologist, anyone who has experience in dealing with assholes like Clive Lincoln.

Vanessa doesn't even hesitate. "My office. Take as long as you need."

I march Lucy into the main office—a place where she's spent far too much time, being disciplined by the assistant principal—and into Vanessa's cozy space. I close the door behind us. "Are you all right?"

She wipes her mouth on her sleeve. "I just wanted him to shut up," Lucy murmurs.

She must know, by now, that I am the center of this storm. There have been articles in the papers about the trial. Last night when I was brushing my teeth, there was my face, on the local late-night news. And now, there's picketing on the steps of the school. I may initially have tried to keep my private life from her because of our therapy relationship, but now, doing so would be like trying to sandbag the ocean.

It makes sense that Lucy's heard about all this. That people at her church are bad-mouthing me, and that she feels torn.

Torn enough to tackle Clive Lincoln.

I pull out a chair so she can sit down. "Do you believe him?" she asks.

"Frankly, no," I admit. "He's like something out of a circus sideshow."

"No." Lucy shakes her head. "I mean . . . do you *believe* him?"

At first I am shocked. It's hard for me

to imagine anyone who can listen to Pastor Clive and not take his words as utter lies. But then again, Lucy is only a teenager. Lucy goes to an evangelical church. She's been spoon-fed this rhetoric all her life.

"No, I don't believe him," I say softly. "Do you?"

Lucy picks at the unraveling black threads of her leggings. "There was this kid who went to school here last year. Jeremy. He was in my homeroom. We all knew he was gay even though he never said it. He didn't have to. I mean, everyone *else* called him a faggot often enough." She looks up at me. "He hanged himself in his basement just before Christmas. His stupid fucking parents blamed it on a D he got in Civics." Lucy's eyes glint, hard as diamonds. "I was so jealous of him. Because he got to check out of this place for good. He left, and no matter how many times I try, I can't."

I taste copper on my tongue; it takes a moment for me to realize this is fear. "Lucy, are you thinking of hurting yourself?" When she doesn't answer, I stare at her forearms, to see if she's cutting again, but even in this mild weather she's wearing a long-sleeved thermal shirt.

"What I want to know is where the fuck is Jesus," Lucy says. "Where is He when there's so much hate it feels like concrete drying up around you? Well, fuck you, God. Fuck you for going when the going gets tough."

"Lucy. Talk to me. Do you have a plan?" It is basic suicide counseling— get someone to talk about her intentions, and it's possible to diffuse them. I need to know if she's got pills in her purse, a rope in her closet, a gun under her mattress.

"Can someone stop loving you because you're not who they want you to be?"

Her question stops me cold. I find myself thinking of Max. "I guess so," I admit. Has Lucy had her heart broken? It could certainly account for her latest downslide; if I know anything about this girl, it's that she expects people to leave her, and blames herself when they do. "Did something happen with a boy?"

She turns to me, her face as open as a wound. "Sing," Lucy begs. "Make this all go away."

I don't have my guitar. I've left everything for music therapy in the car—the crowd that had gathered outside commanded my attention. The only instrument I have is my voice.

So I sing, slowly, a cappella. "Hallelujah," the old Leonard Cohen song from before Lucy was born.

With my eyes closed, with every word a brushstroke, I do the kind of praying people do when they don't know if there is a God. I hope, for Lucy. For me and Vanessa. For all the misfits in the world who don't necessarily want to fit in. We just don't want to always be blamed, either.

When I finish, I have tears in my eyes. But Lucy doesn't. Her features might as well be stone.

"Again," she commands.

I sing the song twice. Three times.

It is on the chorus, on the sixth round, that Lucy starts to sob. She buries her face in her hands. "It's not a boy," she confesses.

When I was small I got the strangest Christmas gift from a distant aunt: a twenty-dollar bill inside an acrylic puzzle. You had to pull knobs and twist levers in different machinations until you found the sequence that would release the catch and let you take the bounty. I was tempted to smash it open with a hammer, but my mother convinced me that the pieces would fall into place, and, once they started, it seemed I couldn't make a wrong move. Boom boom boom, one door or latch opened after another as if they'd never been locked in the first place.

The same thing happens now—a curtain pulled back, a sentence turned on its edge to reveal a different meaning: the suicide attempts. Pastor Clive's speech. Lucy's angry tackle. Jeremy. *Can someone stop loving you?*

It's not a boy, Lucy had said.

Maybe that's because it's a *girl*.

If there is one cardinal rule of music therapy, it's that you come into a patient's life at the place she needs you, and you leave her at a different place. You, as the therapist, are just a catalyst. A constant. You do not change as part of the equation. And you most certainly do not talk about yourself. You're there solely for the patient.

It's why, when Lucy asked me whether I was married, I didn't answer.

It's why she knew nothing about me and I know everything about her.

This isn't a friendship—I've told Lucy that before. This is a professional relationship.

But that was before my future became a snack for public consumption. That was before I sat in a courtroom with the stares of strangers needling between my shoulder blades. Before I listened to a pastor I did not know or like tell me I was a reprobate. Before I went to the ladies' room and had someone slip me a novena card underneath the stall wall with a message scribbled on the back: *I am praying for you, dear.*

If I have to run this gauntlet because I happen to love a woman, let it at least do someone else some good. Let me pay it forward.

"Lucy," I say quietly. "You know I'm gay, right?"

Her head snaps up. "Why—why are you telling me this?"

"I don't know what you're thinking or feeling, but you need to understand that it's completely normal."

She stares at me, silent.

"You know how, when you go back into a preschool classroom, you sit down in the tiny chairs at the tiny tables and feel like Alice in Wonderland? You can't imagine ever being small enough to fit the space? That's what it feels like to come out. You look back and can't imagine squeezing inside again. Even if Pastor Clive and his entire church are shoving as hard as they can."

Lucy's eyes are so wide I can see rims of white around the irises. She leans forward, her breath caught, as there is a knock on the door.

Vanessa pokes her head inside. "It's eight-forty-five," she tells me, and I jump out of my seat. We are going to have to fly if we want to get to the courthouse on time.

"Lucy, I have to go," I say, but she is not looking at me. She's looking at Vanessa, and thinking about what Pastor

Clive said about her, and putting my life together as seamlessly as I just did hers.

Lucy grabs her backpack and, without a word, runs out of Vanessa's office.

I didn't realize how much of being a witness involves being an actor. Just as if I'm in a stage play, I've been well rehearsed for this moment—from learning the lines through the intonation of my voice to the costume which Angela herself picked out for me (a navy blue sheath dress with a white cardigan; so incredibly conservative that when Vanessa saw me she started laughing and called me Mother Baxter).

Yes, I have been prepared. Yes, I am technically ready. And yes, I'm certainly used to performing.

But then again, there's a reason I play and sing music. Somehow, I get lost in the notes, adrift in the melodies, and forget where I am while I'm doing it. When I play for an audience, I can totally believe that the benefit sits squarely with me, instead of the people listening. On the other hand, the last time I was in a play, I was ten years old and cast as a cornstalk in *The Wizard of Oz,* and thirty seconds before I had to walk onto the stage, I threw up on the director's shoes.

"My name is Zoe Baxter," I say. "I live at six-eighty Garvin Street in Wilmington."

Angela smiles brightly at me, as if I've solved a differential calculus problem, instead of just reciting my name and address. "How old are you, Zoe?"

"Forty-one."

"Can you tell the court what you do for a living?"

"I'm a music therapist," I say. "I use music in a clinical setting to help patients alleviate pain or change their moods or engage with the world. Sometimes I work in senior centers with patients with dementia; sometimes I work in a burn unit with children who are having dressings changed; sometimes I work in schools with autistic kids— there are dozens of different ways music therapy can be implemented."

Immediately, I think of Lucy.

"How long have you been a music therapist?"

"For a decade."

"And what's your salary, Zoe?"

I smile a little. "About twenty-eight thousand dollars a year. You don't go into music therapy because you have dreams of living the high life. You do it because you want to help people."

"Is that your only income?"

"I also sing professionally. At restaurants, bars, coffeehouses. I write my own material. It's not enough to make a living, but it's a nice supplement."

"Have you ever been married?" Angela asks.

I've known this question is coming. "Yes. I was married to the plaintiff, Max Baxter, for nine years, and I am currently married to Vanessa Shaw."

There is a faint hum, like the buzz that sits over a bee colony, as the gallery digests this answer.

"Did you and Mr. Baxter have any children?"

"We had a lot of fertility problems, as

a couple. We had two miscarriages and one stillborn son."

Even now I can see him, blue and still as marble, his nails and eyebrows and eyelashes still missing. A work of art in progress.

"Can you describe for the court the nature of your infertility, and what steps you took as a couple to conceive?"

"I had polycystic ovary syndrome," I begin. "I never had regular periods, and wouldn't ovulate every month. I also had submucosal fibroids. Max had male pattern infertility—which is genetic. We started trying to get pregnant when I was thirty-one, and nothing happened for four years. So we started IVF when I was thirty-five."

"How did that work?"

"I followed a medical protocol with various hormones and injections, and they were able to harvest fifteen eggs from me, which were injected with Max's sperm. Three weren't viable. Eight got fertilized, and of those eight, two were transferred to me, and three more were frozen."

"Did you become pregnant?"

"Not that time. But when I was thirty-six, those three frozen embryos were thawed. Two were transferred and one was discarded."

"Discarded? What does that mean?" Angela asks.

"The way the doctor explained it to me, they're not pretty enough to be considered viable for pregnancy, so the clinic chooses not to save them."

"I see. Did you become pregnant this time?"

"Yes," I say. "And I miscarried a few weeks later."

"Then what happened?"

"When I was thirty-seven we did another fresh cycle. This time I had twelve eggs harvested. Six were fertilized successfully. Two were transferred and two were frozen."

"Did you get pregnant?"

"Yes, but I miscarried at eighteen weeks."

"Did you continue to pursue IVF?"

I nod. "We used the two frozen embryos for another cycle. One was transferred, and one didn't survive the thaw. I didn't get pregnant."

"How old were you at the time?"

"I was thirty-nine. I knew I didn't have a lot of time left, so we scrambled to squeeze in one last fresh cycle. When I was forty, I had ten eggs harvested. Seven were fertilized. Of those seven, three were transferred, three were frozen, and one was discarded." I look up. "I got pregnant."

"And?"

"I was the happiest woman in the world," I say softly.

"Did you know the gender of the baby?"

"No. We wanted it to be a surprise."

"Did you feel the baby moving inside you?"

Even now, her words evoke that slow roll, that lazy aquatic somersault. "Yes."

"Can you describe how you felt, being pregnant?"

"I loved every minute of it," I say. "I'd waited my whole life for it."

"How did Max react to the pregnancy?"

She has told me not to look at him, but magnetically, my gaze is pulled toward Max, who is sitting with his hands folded. Beside him, Wade Preston sporadically writes notes with a Montblanc fountain pen.

How did we get here? I wonder, looking at Max.

How could I not have seen this coming, when I looked into your eyes and vowed to be with you forever?

How could I have not known that one day I would love someone else?

How could you have not known that, one day, you would hate me for who I've become?

"He was excited, too," I say. "He used to stick the earphones of my iPod into my belly button so that the baby could hear the music he liked the most."

"Zoe, did you carry that baby to term?" Angela asks.

"No. At twenty-eight weeks, something went wrong." I look up at her. "I was at my baby shower when I started having really bad cramps, and bleeding. A lot. I was rushed to the hospital and put on a monitor. The doctors couldn't find a fetal heartbeat. They brought in an ultrasound machine and tried for five minutes—but it felt like five hours. Finally they told me that the placenta had sheared away from the uterus. The baby . . ." I swallow. "The baby was dead."

"And then what?"

"I had to deliver it. They gave me drugs to start labor."

"Was Max there?"

"Yes."

"What was going through your mind at the time?"

"That this was a mistake," I say, looking right at Max. "That I would have the baby and they'd see how wrong they were, when it came out kicking and crying."

"What happened when the baby was delivered?"

"He wasn't kicking. He wasn't crying." Max looks down at the table. "He was so tiny. He didn't have any fat on him yet, not like you see on other newborns. And he didn't have fingernails yet, or eyelashes, but he was perfect. He was so incredibly perfect, and so . . . so still." I find that I am leaning forward on the witness chair, perched with my hands held in front of me, as if I'm waiting for something. I force myself to sit back. "We named him Daniel. We scattered his ashes into the ocean."

Angela takes a step toward me. "What happened after your son died?"

"I had more medical complications. When I stood up to go to the bathroom, I got dizzy and short of breath. I started having chest pains. It turned out that I had a blood clot that had developed postpartum, which had settled in my lungs. I was put on heparin, and during blood tests, the doctors learned I had a genetic condition called an AT III deficiency—basically, it means I'm susceptible to blood clots, and the pregnancy probably made it worse. But the first question I asked was whether I'd still be able to have a baby."

"What was the answer?"

"That this could happen again. There could be even more severe complications. But that ultimately if I wanted to try to conceive again—I could."

"Did Max want to try to have another baby?" Angela asks.

"I thought so," I admit. "He always had been on the same page as me before. But after the visit at the doctor's office, he told me that he couldn't be with me because I wanted a baby more than anything in the world—and that wasn't what he wanted."

"What *did* he want?"

I look up. "A divorce," I say.

"So you were still reeling from the death of your child, and dealing with all these medical complications, and then your husband told you he wanted a divorce. What was your reaction?"

"I really can't remember. I think I went to bed for about a month. Everything was a blur. I couldn't focus. I couldn't do anything, really."

"What did Max do?"

"He moved out, and went to live with his brother."

"Who represented you in your divorce?"

I shrug. "We represented ourselves. We didn't have any money or property, so it didn't seem as if it was going to be complicated. I was still so numb back then, I barely even remember going to court. I signed whatever papers came in the mail."

"Did the three frozen embryos at the clinic ever cross your mind during the divorce proceedings?" Angela says.

"No."

"Even though you still wanted a child?"

"At the time," I explain, "I wanted a child with a spouse who loved me. I thought that was Max; I was wrong."

"Are you married now?"

"Yes," I say. "To Vanessa Shaw." Just saying her name makes me feel like I can breathe easier. "She's a school counselor at Wilmington High. I'd met her years earlier, when she asked me to do some music therapy with an autistic child. I ran into her again, and she asked me to work with another child—a suicidal teenage girl. Gradually, we began to hang out as friends."

"Did something happen that brought you closer together?"

"She saved my life," I say flatly. "I was hemorrhaging, and she was the one who found me and called an ambulance. I needed a D & C, and as a result of the procedure I learned that I had endometrial cancer and needed a hysterectomy. It was a very, very difficult time for me."

I am not looking at Max, now. I'm not sure how much of this he even knows.

"I knew, once I had that hysterectomy, I'd *never* have a baby," I say.

"Did your relationship with Vanessa change?"

"Yes. She took care of me, after the surgery. We spent a lot of time together—hanging out, running errands, cooking, whatever—and I started to realize that when I *wasn't* with her, I really *wanted* to be. That I liked her as more than an ordinary friend."

"Zoe, had you ever had a same-sex relationship before?"

"No," I say, carefully picking my words. "I know it seems strange, but when you are attracted to people, it's because of the details. Their kindness. Their eyes. Their smile. The fact that they can get you to laugh when you need it the most. I felt all those things for Vanessa. The fact that she was a woman—well, it was unexpected, but it was really the least important part of the equation."

"That seems hard to understand, given the fact that you were married to a man . . ."

I nod. "I think that's why it took me a while to realize I was in love with Vanessa. I just didn't get it. I'd had female friends before and never felt like I wanted a physical relationship with them. But once our relationship *did* take that turn, it felt like the most natural thing in the world. As if not having her in my life would be like asking me to stop breathing air and start breathing water instead."

"Do you call yourself a lesbian now?"

"I call myself Vanessa's spouse. But if I have to wear someone else's label in order to be with her forever, then I will."

"What happened after you fell in love?" Angela asks.

"I moved into her house. This April, we got married in Fall River."

"At some point did you two talk about having a family?"

"On our honeymoon," I say. "I had assumed, after my hysterectomy, that I'd never have children. But I had three frozen embryos with my own genetic material in them . . . and, now, a partner with a uterus who could carry those babies to term."

"Did Vanessa want to gestate the embryos?"

"She was the one who suggested it," I say.

"What happened next?"

"I called the clinic and asked to use the embryos. I was told that my spouse had to sign off on it. But they didn't mean Vanessa—they meant Max. So I went to him and asked for his permission to use the embryos. I knew that he didn't want a baby—that was why he'd asked for a divorce. I honestly believed he would understand."

"Did he?"

"He said that he'd think about it."

Angela folds her arms. "Did Max seem different to you at that meeting from the man you used to know?"

I look at him. "Max used to be a surfer dude. A laid-back guy who didn't wear a watch and didn't have an agenda and was always a half hour late. He'd get his hair cut only because I reminded him to do it; he never remembered to wear a belt. But when I went to talk to Max about the embryos, he was at work. And even though he was doing manual labor—landscaping—he was wearing a tie. On a Saturday."

"Did Max get back to you regarding the embryos?"

"Yes," I say bitterly. "He had papers served, suing me for the right to use them."

"How did that make you feel?" Angela asks.

"I was angry. And confused. He didn't want to be a father; he'd told me so himself. He didn't even have a relationship with anyone, as far as I knew. He didn't want the embryos. He just didn't want *me* to have them."

"When you were married to Max, did he have a problem with homosexuality?"

"We didn't really talk about it. But I never knew him to be judgmental before."

"During your marriage," Angela asks, "did you often see his brother?"

"Not very often at all."

"How would you describe your relationship with Reid?"

"Contentious."

"And with Liddy?" Angela asks.

I shake my head. "I just don't get that woman."

"Did you know that Reid had paid for your fifth cycle of IVF?"

"I had no idea, until I heard him testify. It was a huge stress for us, because we didn't know how we could afford it—and then one day Max came home and said he had it all figured out, that he had found a credit card with zero interest, and I believed him." I hesitate, correct myself. "I was *stupid* enough to believe him."

"Did Max at any point tell you that he wanted the embryos to go to his brother and sister-in-law?"

"No. I learned about that when a motion was filed."

"And what was your reaction?"

"I couldn't believe he'd do that to me," I say. "I'm forty-one. Even if my eggs were still worth anything, insurance won't cover fertility treatments for me to harvest them again. This is literally my only chance to have my own biological child with someone I love."

"Zoe," Angela says, "have you and Vanessa talked about what Max's relationship to these embryos might be if you receive the court's permission to gain custody, and you have children?"

"Whatever Max wants. Whatever he's ready for. If he wants to be a part of the babies' lives, we'd understand; and if he doesn't want to, we will respect that."

"So . . . you're willing to let the children know that Max is the biological father?"

"Of course."

"And be involved in their lives, as much as Max is comfortable doing so?"

"Yes. Absolutely."

"Do you think you'd be given the same courtesy, if the court awards the embryos to Max?"

I look at Max; I look at Wade Preston. "I've spent two days hearing how deviant my lifestyle is, how vile *I* am for choosing it," I reply. "They won't let those kids within five miles of me."

Angela looks up at the judge. "Nothing further," she says.

Angela and I go to get a cup of coffee during the recess. She won't let me travel through the courthouse alone, for fear I'll be ambushed by one of Wade's special interest groups. "Zoe," she says, pushing the buttons on the vending machine, "you did great."

"You were the easy part," I tell her.

"That's true," she says. "Wade is going to come after you like Bill Clinton on an intern. But you sounded calm, and smart, and very sympathetic." She hands me the first cup and is about to put coins in for the second cup when Wade Preston walks up and puts in fifty cents.

"I hear you're not getting paid for this one, Counselor," he says. "Consider this my contribution."

Angela ignores him. "Hey, Zoe? You know the difference between Wade Preston and God?" She waits a beat. "God doesn't think he's Wade Preston."

I laugh, like I always do at her jokes.

But the laughter jams in my throat this time. Because two feet away from Reid, staring at me, is Liddy Baxter. She's come down here with Max's lawyer, presumably for the same reason I have.

"Zoe," she says, taking a step forward.

Angela speaks on my behalf. "My client has nothing to say to you." She steps between us.

In a completely uncharacteristic move, Liddy says, "But I have something to say to her."

I don't really know Liddy well. I never wanted to. Max always told me I was missing out—that she was funny and smart and knew all the dialogue to *Attack of the Killer Tomatoes!* for whatever that was worth—but I couldn't see past a woman who, in this day and age, actually waited for her husband to come home from work so that she could ask him about his day and feed him a meal. Max used to say we should go out shopping, or to lunch, get to know each other—but I figured we'd run out of things to talk about before we'd backed out of her driveway.

She seems, though, to have developed a little bit of a spine. It's amazing what taking away someone else's embryos can do for one's self-esteem, I guess.

"Thanks, but I've reached my prayer quota for the day," I tell her.

"No prayers. Just . . . well . . ." She looks up at me. "Max isn't trying to hurt you."

"Yeah, I'm only collateral damage. I get it."

"I know how you must be feeling."

I am amazed at her nerve. "You have *no* idea how I'm feeling. You and I," I spit out, "have absolutely nothing in common."

I shove past Liddy, Angela hurrying beside me.

"You giving your clients lessons in charm, Counselor?" Wade calls out.

Liddy's voice rings down the hallway after me. "We do have something in common, Zoe," she says. "We both already love these babies."

That stops me in my tracks. I turn around again.

"For what it's worth," Liddy says quietly, "I always thought you'd make a great mother."

Angela loops her arm through mine and drags me down the hallway.

"Ignore them both," she says. "You know the difference between a porcupine and Wade Preston driving in his car? The prick's on the outside."

But this time, I can't even crack a smile.

I do not remember my mother going on many dates when I was growing up, but one sticks out in my mind. A man had come to the door bathed in more perfume than my own mother had on and took her out to dinner. I fell asleep on the couch watching *The Love Boat* and *Fantasy Island* and woke up sometime during *Saturday Night Live* to find her in her stocking feet, with mascara smudged under her eyes and her hair tumbling out of its updo. "Was he nice?" I remember asking, and my mother just snorted.

"Never trust a man who wears a pinkie ring," she said.

I didn't understand, back then. But now I agree: the only jewelry a guy should wear is a wedding band or a Super Bowl ring. Anything else is a clue that it isn't going to work out: a high school ring says he never grew up; a cocktail ring says he's gay and doesn't know it yet. A pinkie ring says he's too polished for his own good; a Truman Capote wannabe concerned more with how he looks than with how you do.

Wade Preston wears a pinkie ring.

"You certainly have had your fair share of health complications, Ms. Baxter," he says. "One might say it's almost Job-like."

"Objection," Angela says. "One might *not* say that."

"Sustained. Counsel will refrain from personal commentary," Judge O'Neill says.

"Many have been life-threatening, isn't that true?"

"Yes," I say.

"So there's a chance that, if this court awards you the pre-born children, you might not even be around to see them grow up, right?"

"Right now, I am completely cancer-free. My chance of recurrence is less than two percent." I smile at him. "I'm healthy as a horse, Mr. Preston."

"You do understand that, if the court somehow awards you and your lesbian lover these pre-born children, there's no guarantee a pregnancy will occur?"

"I understand that better than anyone," I say. "But I also understand that this is my last chance to have a biological child."

"You now live with Vanessa Shaw in her home, is that correct?"

"Yes. We're married."

"Not in the state of Rhode Island," Wade Preston says.

I fix my gaze on him. "All I know is that the state of Massachusetts gave me a marriage certificate."

"How long have you been together?"

"About five months."

He raises his brows. "That's not very long."

"I guess I knew something good as soon as I saw it." I shrug. "And I wanted to be with her forever."

"You felt the same way when you married Max Baxter, didn't you?"

First blood. "I wasn't the one who wanted a divorce. Max left me."

"Just like Vanessa could leave you?"

"I don't think that will happen," I say.

"But you don't know, do you?"

"Anything's possible. Reid and Liddy could get a divorce." As I say the words, I glance at Liddy in the gallery. Her face drains of color.

I don't know what the story is between her and Max, but there is one. I could feel threads between them, invisible as they were, during her testimony, as if I'd walked through a spiderweb stretched across an open doorway. And then her words downstairs in the snack room: *Max isn't trying to hurt you.* As if she'd discussed this with him.

Max couldn't be in love with her.

She's as different from me as a person could possibly be.

At that thought, I have to smile a little. Max could clearly say the same thing about Vanessa.

Even if Max has a crush on his sister-in-law, I can't imagine it going anyplace.

Liddy is far too caught up in being the perfect wife, the ideal church lady. And as far as I can tell, there's no wiggle room for a fall from grace.

"Ms. Baxter?" Wade Preston says impatiently, and I realize I have completely missed his question.

"I'm sorry. Could you repeat that?"

"I said that you resent Reid and Liddy for the life they lead, don't you?"

"I don't resent them. We just place importance on very different things."

"So you're not jealous of their wealth?"

"No. Money isn't everything."

"Then you resent the fact that they're such good role models?"

I smother a laugh. "Actually, I don't think they are. I think they buy what they want—including these embryos. I think they use their Bible to judge people like me. Neither of which are qualities I'd want to pass down to a child."

"You don't go to church on a regular basis, do you, Ms. Baxter?"

"Objection," Angela says. "Perhaps we need a visual." She takes two legal books and smacks one down in front of her. "Church." She moves the second book to the opposite edge of the defense table. "State." Then she looks up at the judge. "See all the nice room in between."

"Cute, Counselor. Please answer the question, Ms. Baxter," the judge says.

"No."

"You don't think much of people who go to church, do you?"

"I think everyone should be entitled to believe what they want. Which includes not believing at all," I add.

Vanessa doesn't believe in God. I think her mother's attempts to pray away the gay in her closed the door on organized religion. We've talked about it, in the folds of the night. How she doesn't really care much about an afterlife, as long as she gets what she needs in her present one; how there's an evolutionary component to helping people that has nothing to do with a Golden Rule; how even though I can't subscribe to an organized religion, I also can't say with certainty that I don't believe in some higher power. I'm not sure if this is because I actually still

cling to the vestiges of religion, or because I'm too afraid to admit out loud
that I might not believe in God.

Atheism, I realize, is the new gay. The
thing you hope no one finds out about
you—because of all the negative assumptions that are sure to follow.

"So you wouldn't plan to raise these
pre-born children with any religion?"

"I don't know," I say honestly. "I'm
going to raise a child to be loved and
to show love; to be self-respecting and
open-minded and tolerant of everyone.
If I can find the right religious group to
support that, then maybe we will join
it."

"Ms. Baxter, are you familiar with the
case of *Burrows v. Brady*?"

"Objection!" Angela says. "Counsel
is referencing a custody case, and this
is a property issue."

"Overruled," Judge O'Neill says.
"Where are you going with this, Mr.
Preston?"

"In *Burrows v. Brady,* the Rhode Island Supreme Court ruled that, when
parents are divorced, each parent who
has custody has the right to raise the

child in the faith they think is in the child's best interests. Moreover, *Pettinato v. Pettinato* said that the moral character of each potential custodial parent must be considered—"

"Is counsel trying to tell the court how to do its job," Angela asks, "or does he actually have a question for my client?"

"Yes," Wade replies. "I do have a question. You testified, Ms. Baxter, that you went through several in vitro procedures, all of which resulted in disaster?"

"Objection—"

"I'll rephrase. You did not actually carry a baby to term, did you?"

"No," I say.

"In fact you had two miscarriages?"

"Yes."

"And then a stillbirth?"

I look into my lap. "Yes."

"It's your testimony today that you've always wanted a child, correct?"

"That's right."

"Your Honor." Angela sighs. "All this has been asked and answered."

"Why then, Ms. Baxter, did you murder your own child in 1989?"

"What?" I say, stunned. "I have no idea what you're talking about—"

But I do. And his next words confirm it: "Did you or did you not have a voluntary abortion when you were nineteen years old?"

"Objection!" Angela is out of her seat immediately. "This is irrelevant and occurred prior to my client's marriage, and I move that it be stricken immediately from the record—"

"It's completely relevant. It informs her desire to have a baby now. She's trying to make up for past sins."

"Objection!"

My hands have gone numb.

A woman stands up in the gallery. "Baby killer!" she yells, and that is the hairline crack it takes to break the dam. There is shouting—by the Westboro contingent and by the Eternal Glory congregants. The judge calls for order, and about twenty observers are hauled through the double doors of the courtroom. I imagine Vanessa watching on the other side. I wonder what she's thinking.

"Mr. Preston, you may continue your line of questioning, but without the editorial comments," Judge O'Neill says. "And as for the gallery, if there is one more disruption, I will turn this into a closed session."

Yes, I tell him. I had an abortion. I was nineteen, in college. It wasn't the right time to have a baby. I thought— stupidly—that I'd have many more chances.

When I finish, I am gutted. I have only spoken once of the procedure since it happened, and that was at the fertility clinic, when I had to be completely honest about my reproductive history or compromise my chances of conceiving. It has been twenty-two years, but suddenly I feel the same way I felt back then: Shaky. Embarrassed.

And angry.

The clinic could not legally have released that information to Wade Preston. Which means that it must have come from the only other person who was at the clinic the day I gave my medical history.

Max.

"Is there a reason you were hiding this information from the court?"

"I wasn't hiding—"

"Could it be because you thought, correctly, it might make you seem a little disingenuous when you start sobbing about how much you want a baby?"

"Objection!"

"Have you ever considered," Wade Preston presses, "that the fact that you haven't been able to have another child was God's judgment on you for killing your first?"

Angela is furious. She goes after Wade with a verbal streak of fire. But even once he has withdrawn his question, it hangs in the air like the letters of a neon sign after you close your eyes.

And even if I don't have to reply out loud, I may just have already answered silently.

I don't want to believe in a God who'd punish me for having an abortion.

But that doesn't mean I haven't wondered if it's true.

"You want to tell me what the hell that was all about?" Angela asks the minute the judge says that we are adjourning for the day. "How did he get your medical files?"

"He didn't have to," I say flatly. "Max must have told him."

"Then why didn't you tell *me*? It would have been much less damaging if we'd been able to bring it up on direct instead of cross!"

Like Max's alcoholism. Everyone likes a reformed sinner. If we'd been the ones to bring up his drinking, it would have looked like he had something to hide.

Which is exactly how Wade Preston has painted me today.

Preston has finished packing up his briefcase; he smiles politely as he walks by. "Sorry you didn't know about the skeleton in your client's closet. The literal one, that is."

Angela ignores him. "Is there anything else I need to know about? Because I *really* do not like surprises."

I shake my head, still numb, and follow her out of the courtroom. Vanessa is waiting with my mother—both of them still sequestered. "What *happened* in there?" Vanessa asks. "How come the judge threw out half the gallery?"

"Can we talk about it in the car? I really just want to go home."

But the moment we open the front door of the courthouse and step outside, there is a hail and volley of questions.

I'm expecting this. Just not the ones they ask.

How far along were you when you had the abortion?
Who was the baby daddy?
Do you still keep in touch with him?

A woman walks up to me. From her yellow T-shirt I realize she is from Westboro Baptist Church. She's holding a recyclable plastic bottle filled with some kind of fruit punch, but it looks like blood from here.

I know she's going to throw it at me the moment before she actually does. "Some choices are wrong," she cries.

I step back, shielding myself, so that the liquid only lands on my right foot. I completely forget about Vanessa until I hear her voice beside me. "You never told me."

"I never told anyone."

Vanessa's eyes are cold. She glances at Max, walking between his attorneys. "Somehow," she says, "I don't believe you."

My mother wants to go after Wade Preston for dragging up my history; it takes Angela's interference and the magic word (*grandchild*) before she agrees to go home without putting up a fight. She tells me she will call me later to make sure I'm all right, but it's pretty clear to her that I don't want to talk right now. To anyone except Vanessa, that is. The whole ride home, I try to explain what happened during my testimony. She doesn't say a word. When I mention my abortion, she flinches.

Finally, by the time we park the car, I can't stand it. "Are you going to give me the silent treatment forever?" I yell, slamming the car door and following Vanessa into the house. I strip off my panty hose, which are still sticky. "Is this some Catholic thing?"

"You know I'm not Catholic," Vanessa answers.

"But you used to be—"

"This isn't about the damn abortion, Zoe. It's about *you*." She is facing me now, her hands still clutching the keys to the car. "That's a pretty big bit of history to leave out of a relationship. It's like forgetting to tell someone you have AIDS."

"For God's sake, Vanessa, you can't catch an abortion like an STD—"

"Do you think that's the only reason to disclose something incredibly personal to the people you love?"

"It was a horrible decision to have to make, even if I was lucky enough to be able to make it. I don't particularly enjoy reliving it."

"Then tell me this," she argues. "How is it that Max knew, and I didn't?"

"You're jealous? You're actually jealous that I told Max about something horrible in my past!"

"Yeah, I am," Vanessa admits. "Okay? I'm a selfish bitch who wishes that my wife opened herself up to me as much as she opened herself up to the guy she used to be married to."

"And maybe I'd like *my* wife to show a little compassion," I say. "Considering I was just raked over the coals by Wade Preston and that I'm now Public Enemy Number One for the entire religious right."

"There's more than just a *u* in *us*," Vanessa says. "Not that you seem to realize it."

"Great!" I yell, tears springing to my eyes. "You want to know about my abortion? It was the worst day of my life. I cried the whole way there and the whole way home. I had to eat ramen noodles for two months because I didn't want to ask my mother for money; and I didn't tell her I'd done it until I was back home for the summer. I didn't take the medicine they gave me for the cramps afterward because I felt like I deserved the pain. And the guy I was dating—the guy who decided with me that this was the right thing to do—broke up with me a month later. And in spite of the fact that every doctor I've ever seen tells me that my infertility has nothing to do with that procedure, I've never really been able to believe it. So how's that? Are you happy now? Is that what you wanted to know?"

By the time I finish, I am crying so hard I can barely understand my own words. My nose is running and my hair is in my face and I want her to touch me, to take me in her arms and tell me it's all right, but instead she steps back. "What else don't I know about you?" she asks, and she leaves me standing alone in the entryway of a house that no longer feels like home.

The actual procedure took only six minutes.

I know, I counted.

They had talked to me about all my options. They had given me lab tests and a physical. They had given me a sedative. They had opened my cervix with dilators. They had given me forms to sign.

This took a few hours.

I remember the nurse fitting my feet into the stirrups, telling me to scoot down. I remember the shine of the speculum as the doctor lifted it from its sterile napkin. I remember the wet-vac sound of the suction device.

The doctor never called it a baby. She never even called it a fetus. She referred to it as *tissue.* I remember closing my eyes and thinking of a Kleenex, balled up and tossed in the trash.

On the way back to campus, I put my hand on the stick shift of my boyfriend's old Dodge Dart. I just wanted his palm to cover mine. Instead, he untangled my fingers. "Zoe," he said. "Just let me drive."

Although it was only two in the afternoon when I got back to my dorm room, I put on my pajamas. I watched *General Hospital,* honing my focus on the characters of Frisco and Felicia, as if I would have to pass a test on them later on. I ate an entire jar of Jif peanut butter.

I still felt empty.

I had nightmares for weeks, that I could hear the fetus crying. That I followed the sound to the courtyard outside my dorm window and crouched down in my pajama bottoms and torn tank to dig with my bare hands in the ragged ground. I pulled up hunks of sod, chipped my fingernails on stones, and finally uncovered it:

Sweet Cindy, the baby doll I'd buried the day my father died.

I can't unwind that night. I hear Vanessa moving around above me, in the bedroom, and then when it gets quiet I assume she's fallen asleep. So instead, I sit down at my digital keyboard and I start playing. I let the music bind me like a bandage. I sew myself together note by note.

I play for so long that my wrists begin to cramp. I sing until my voice frays, until I feel like I'm breathing through a straw. When I stop, I lean my forehead so that it rests on the keys. The silence in the room becomes a thick cotton batting.

Then I hear clapping.

I turn around to find Vanessa standing in the doorway. "How long have you been there?"

"Long enough." She sits down beside me on the piano bench. "This is what he wants, you know."

"Who?"

"Wade Preston. To break us apart."

"I don't want that," I admit.

"Me neither." She hesitates. "I've been upstairs doing math."

"No wonder you've been gone so long," I murmur. "You suck at math."

"The way I figure it, you were with Max for nine years. I plan to be with you for the next forty-nine years."

"Just forty-nine?"

"Stick with me, here. It's a nice round number." Vanessa looks at me. "So by the time you're ninety, you'll have spent over half your life with me, as opposed to ten percent of your life with Max. Don't get me wrong—I'm still wicked jealous of those nine years, because I can't ever have them with you, no matter what I do. But if you hadn't lived them back then with Max, maybe you wouldn't be here with me now."

"I wasn't trying to keep a secret from you," I tell her.

"But you should be able to. I love you so much that there's nothing you could possibly tell me that would change that."

"I used to be a guy," I say, straight-faced.

"Deal breaker." Vanessa laughs, and she leans forward and kisses me. She puts her hands on either side of my face. "I know you're strong enough to do this alone, but you don't have to. I promise not to be an idiot anymore."

I settle closer to her, rest my head on her shoulder. "I'm sorry, too," I say, an apology as wide as the night sky, with no limits.

VANESSA

My mother used to say that a woman without lipstick was like a cake without icing. I never knew her to go without her signature color, Forever After. Every time we went to a drugstore to get aspirin or tampons or asthma medication, she picked up a couple more tubes and stashed them in one of her dresser drawers—one that was completely filled with the small silver tubes. "I don't think the company's gonna run out," I used to tell her, but she, of course, knew better. In 1982, they stopped making Forever After. Luckily my mother had stockpiled enough to carry her forward a decade. When she was in the hospital, so drugged for the pain that she couldn't remember her own mantra, I made sure she was always made up. When she took her last breath, she was wearing Forever After.

She would have found it incredibly ironic that I had turned out to be her cosmetic guardian angel, since I had been running away from her mascara wand since I could walk. Whereas other little girls liked to sit on their mothers' bathroom counters and watch them transform themselves into works of art, I couldn't stand the feel of anything other than soap on my face. The one time I let my mother come near me with eyeliner, it was to pencil in a Gomez Addams mustache on my upper lip for a school play.

I mention all this to duly underscore the fact that at 7:00 A.M. I am poking my eye out with Zoe's eyeliner applicator. I am grimacing in the mirror so that I can roll Hot Tamale lipstick over my mouth. If Wade Preston and Judge O'Neill want to see the traditional woman who stays at home and does her nails and cooks roasts for dinner, I'll become one for the next eight hours.

(Unless I have to wear a skirt. That is *just not happening.*)

I lean back with spots dancing before my eyes (it is really hard to not go cross-eyed while you're putting on liquid liner) and scrutinize my handiwork in the mirror. Just then, Zoe stumbles into the bathroom, still half asleep. She sits down on the closed toilet seat and blinks up at me.

Then she gasps, horrified. "Why do you look like a scary clown?"

"Really?" I say, rubbing my hands over my cheeks. "Too much blush?" I frown into the mirror again. "I was going for that nineteen fifties pinup look. Like Katy Perry."

"Well, you got Frank-N-Furter from *Rocky Horror,*" Zoe says. She stands and pushes me down on the seat instead. Then she takes makeup remover, squirts it on a cotton ball, and wipes my face clean. "You want to tell me why you've suddenly decided to use makeup?"

"Just trying to look more . . . feminine," I answer.

"You mean less like a dyke," Zoe corrects. She puts her hands on her hips. "You know you look fine without a drop of anything on your face, Ness."

"See, this is why I'm married to you instead of Wade Preston."

She leans forward, sweeping blush along my cheekbone. "And here I thought it was because I had—"

"An eyelash curler," I interrupt, grinning. "I married you for your Shu Uemura."

"Stop," Zoe says. "You're making me feel so cheap." She tilts up my chin. "Close your eyes."

She brushes and dabs at me. I even let her use the eyelash curler, although I nearly wind up blind in the process. She finishes by telling me to let my mouth hang open, and she swipes it over with lipstick.

"Ta da," Zoe says.

I am expecting a drag queen. Instead, I see something entirely different. "Oh, my God. I've turned into my mother."

Zoe peers over my shoulder, so that we are both looking at our reflections.

"From what I hear," she says, "it happens to the best of us."

Angela pays a janitor twenty bucks to let us into the courthouse through the delivery door in the back. We walk in spy-novel silence past the boiler room and a supply closet stocked with paper towels and toilet tissue before he leads us into a rickety, grimy service elevator that will take us up to the main floor. He turns the key and pushes a button and then looks at me. "I got a cousin who's gay," he says, this man who hasn't spoken more than four words to us the whole time he's been with us.

Because I don't know what he thinks of that cousin, I don't say anything.

"How did you know who we are?" Zoe asks.

He shrugs. "I'm the custodian. I know everything."

The elevator belches us out into a corridor near the clerk's office. Angela winds her way through the maze of hallways until we are at the door of our courtroom. There is literally a wall of human media facing away from us, toward the door, waiting for our entrance up the front steps of the courthouse.

While we're actually standing right behind the morons.

I think I have more respect for Angela at that moment than I ever had before.

"Go get a granola bar or something in the snack room," she advises. "That way you'll be outta sight, outta mind while Preston's coming into court, and the reporters won't come after you." Because I'm still sequestered—at least for the first few minutes of today's court session—this makes sense. I watch her safely tuck Zoe inside the courtroom and then slip down the hallway unnoticed while the rest of the counsel arrives.

I eat a pack of Nutter Butters, but they make me queasy. The truth is, I'm not good when it comes to public speaking. It's why I'm a school counselor and not up in front of a classroom. The fact that Zoe can sit on a stool and sing her heart to shreds in front of an audience leaves me in awe.

Then again, watching Zoe load the dishwasher pretty much takes my breath away, too.

"You can do this," I say under my breath, and by the time I come back to the double doors of the courtroom, a bailiff is waiting to bring me inside.

I do the whole rigmarole—the swearing on the Bible, the name and age and address. Angela walks toward me, looking much more poised and intense than she does when she's not in front of a judge. To my surprise, she drops her pad of notes about a foot in front of me. "You know how Wade Preston sleeps?" she whispers quickly. "He lies on one side and then he lies on the other." When she sees me smother a laugh, she winks, and I realize she didn't fumble that pad at all.

"Where do you live, Ms. Shaw?"

"In Wilmington."

"Are you presently employed?" Angela asks.

"I work as a school counselor at Wilmington High School."

"What does that entail?"

"Counseling students in grades nine

through twelve. I make sure they're academically on track, I see if there are problems at home, keep an eye out for depression or substance abuse, and I help guide kids through the college application process."

"Are you married?"

"Yes," I say, smiling. "To Zoe Baxter."

"Do you have any children?"

"Not yet, but I hope that will be the outcome of this litigation. Our intent is to have me gestate to term the embryos that are biologically Zoe's."

"Have you had any experience with small children?"

"To a limited degree," I say. "I've taken care of our neighbor's kids for a weekend here and there. But from what I hear from friends, parenthood is trial by fire no matter how many books you've read by Dr. Brazelton."

"How would you and Zoe be able to support this child financially?"

"We both work, and we'd both continue to work. Luckily our schedules allow for flexibility. We plan to raise the children equally, and Zoe's mother lives ten minutes away and is delighted at the thought of helping us out."

"What, if any, is your relationship to Max Baxter?"

I think of the argument Zoe and I had last night. My relationship to this man is that, forever, we will be linked together through her. That there will be parts of her heart she's already given to someone else.

"He's my spouse's ex-husband," I say evenly. "He's biologically related to the embryos. I don't really know him; I only know what Zoe's told me about him."

"Are you willing to allow him to have contact with any child that might result?"

"If he wants to."

Angela faces me directly. "Vanessa," she says, "is there anything that prevents you from being considered a fit and proper person to have custody of a child?"

"Absolutely not," I reply.

"Your witness," Angela says, turning toward Wade Preston.

Today he is wearing an outfit that

shouldn't work—and believe me, if *I'm* making a fashion commentary, it must be truly hideous. His shirt is checkered, purple and white. His tie is striped, lilac and black. His black suit jacket is flecked with bits of gray and silver and purple. And yet what should look like a nasty eighties anachronism somehow looks, with his spray-on tan and his bling, like a *GQ* spread. "Ms. Shaw," he begins. I actually look down to see if he's left a trail of oil as he comes closer. "Does your employer know you're a lesbian?"

I square my shoulders. If he wants to play hard, I'm ready.

After all—I'm wearing my lipstick.

"It's nothing I've volunteered. Teachers don't normally sit around the break room talking about their sex lives. But it's nothing I hide, either."

"Don't you think parents have a right to know what sort of guidance their children are getting?" He absolutely sneers the word *guidance.*

"They don't seem to be complaining."

"Do you ever talk about sex with these teens?"

"If they bring it up. Some kids come to me because of relationship problems. Some of them have even disclosed to me that they might be gay."

"So you're recruiting these innocent teenagers to your lifestyle?" Preston says.

"Not at all. But I am offering them a safe place where they can talk when other people"—I pause for effect—"are not being particularly tolerant."

"Ms. Shaw, you testified on direct examination that you believe you're a fit and proper parent for a child, is that right?"

"Yes," I say.

"You're saying there's nothing about you that suggests, for example, an inability to cope?"

"I don't believe so . . ."

"I'd like to remind you that you're under oath," the lawyer says.

What the hell is he getting at?

"Isn't it a fact that you were hospitalized for a week in 2003 in the Blackstone Hospital psychiatric ward?"

I go very still. "A relationship had ended. I voluntarily checked myself in for a week to deal with the stress. I was put on medication and have not had another episode like that."

"So you had a nervous breakdown."

I lick my lips and taste the wax of the cosmetics. "That's an exaggeration. I was diagnosed with exhaustion."

"Really? That's all?"

I lift my chin. "Yes."

"So it's your testimony that you did not try to kill yourself?"

Zoe's hand is pressed to her mouth. *Hypocrite,* she must be thinking, after last night.

Turning to Wade Preston, I meet his gaze. "Absolutely not."

He holds out his hand, and Ben Benjamin leaps up from the plaintiff's table to give him a file. "I'd like to have these marked for identification only," Preston says, handing them to the clerk for a stamp and then giving a copy to Angela and another to me.

They are my medical records from Blackstone.

"Objection," Angela says. "I've never

seen this evidence before. I don't even know how Mr. Preston could have legally obtained them, since they're protected by HIPAA—"

"Ms. Moretti is welcome to follow along with her own copy," Preston says.

"Your Honor, under our confidentiality statute, I should have received three weeks notice of this prior to the records being subpoenaed. Ms. Shaw is not even a party to this action. There's no way these records should be admissible in this courtroom."

"I'm not entering these records as evidence," Preston says. "I'm just using them to impeach the witness who has testified falsely under oath. Since we are talking about a potential custodial parent, I think it's critical to know this woman is not just a lesbian—she's also a liar."

"Objection!" Angela roars.

"If Ms. Moretti needs a brief recess to review the records, we're perfectly willing to give her a few minutes—"

"I don't need a recess, you windbag. I have no question in my mind that not only are these records irrelevant but that Mr. Preston obtained them through an illegal missive. He comes into this courtroom with unclean hands. I don't know what they do in Louisiana, but here in Rhode Island we have laws to protect our citizens, and Ms. Shaw's rights are being violated at this very moment."

"Your Honor, if the witness would like to recant her testimony and admit that she did attempt suicide, I am happy to dismiss the records entirely," Preston says.

"Enough." The judge sighs. "I will allow the records in for identification purposes only. However, I'd like counsel to explain how he obtained them before we go any further."

"They were pushed under the door of my hotel room," he says. "God works in mysterious ways."

I highly doubt that God was the one running the Xerox machine at Blackstone.

"Ms. Shaw, I'm going to ask you again. Did your suicide attempt lead to your stay at Blackstone Hospital in 2003?"

My face is flushed; I can feel my pulse hammering. "No."

"So you accidentally swallowed a bottle of Tylenol?"

"I was depressed. I didn't have a plan to kill myself. It was a long time ago, and I'm in a very different place now than I was back then. Frankly, I don't understand why you're even on this witch hunt."

"Is it fair to say that you were upset eight years ago? In crisis?"

"Yes."

"Something unexpected happened that rattled you to the point where you ended up hospitalized?"

I look down. "I guess."

"Zoe Baxter has testified that she had cancer. Are you aware of that?"

"Yes, I am. But she's healthy now."

"Cancer has a nasty way of recurring, doesn't it? Ms. Baxter could get cancer again, couldn't she?"

"So could you," I say.

Preferably in the next three minutes.

"This is a terrible thought," Preston says, "but we do need to press through all possibilities here. Let's say Ms. Baxter got cancer again. You'd be upset, wouldn't you?"

"I'd be devastated."

"To the point of another breakdown, Ms. Shaw? Another bottle of Tylenol?"

Angela stands again, objecting.

Wade Preston shakes his head and tsks. "In that case, Ms. Shaw," he says, "who's gonna take care of those poor children?"

As soon as I step down from the witness stand, the judge calls a recess. Zoe turns to the seat I've taken behind her in the gallery. We both stand; she wraps her arms around me. "I'm so sorry," she whispers.

I know she is thinking of Lucy, how I went above and beyond the call of a school counselor's duty to find that girl something that would keep her tethered to this world instead of checking out of it. I know she's wondering if I saw myself in her.

From the corner of my eye, I see a flash of purple. Wade Preston heads up the aisle. Gently I disengage myself from Zoe's embrace. "I'll be back."

I follow Preston down the hallway, drawing into shadows as he glad-hands congregants and gives sound bites to reporters. He whistles, too full of himself to even notice that he's got a shadow. He turns a corner and pushes open the door to the men's room.

I go in right after him.

"Mr. Preston," I say.

He raises his brows. "Why, Ms. Shaw. I would think a person with your sort of lifestyle would be the last one to make the mistake of walking into the facility with the picture of a man on it."

"You know, I'm an educator. And you, Mr. Preston, are sorely in need of an education."

"Oh, you think so?"

"I do." I quickly glance under the stall doors, but, fortunately, we are the only ones in the room. "First, homosexuality? It's not a lifestyle. It's who I happen to be. Second, I didn't choose to be attracted to women. I just am. Did *you* make a choice to be attracted to women? Was it during puberty? When you graduated from high school? Was it a question on the SATs? No. Homosexuality isn't a choice any more than heterosexuality is. And I know this because why on earth would anyone choose to be gay? Why would I want to put myself through all the bullying and name-calling and physical abuse I've faced? Why would I want to constantly be looked down at and stereotyped by people like you? Why would I willingly pick a *lifestyle,* as you call it, that's such an uphill battle? I honestly cannot believe someone who has traveled the world as much as you have, Mr. Preston, could have his eyes so tightly shut."

"Ms. Shaw." He sighs. "I'll keep you in my prayers."

"That's touching. But since I'm an atheist, it's also irrelevant. In fact, I'd hope that you might consider reading up on homosexuality with a text that's a little more current than the one you've been using—the Bible. There's been a lot more literature written on the subject since five hundred A.D."

"Are you finished yet? Because I came in here for a reason . . ."

"Not yet. There are a lot of things I'm not, Mr. Preston. I'm not a pedophile. I'm not a softball coach or a biker chick, any more than gay men are always hairstylists or florists or interior decorators. I'm not immoral. But you know what I *am*? Intelligent. Tolerant. Capable of parenting. Different from you, but not lesser," I say. "People like me, we don't need to be fixed. We need people like *you* to broaden your horizons."

When I finish, I am sweating. Wade Preston is blissfullly, utterly silent.

"What's the matter, Wade?" I ask. "Not used to getting beat up by a girl?"

He shrugs. "Say what you want, Ms. Shaw. You can even pee standing up if you like. But your balls, mark my words, are never gonna be bigger than mine."

I hear him unzip his fly.

I cross my arms.

A standoff.

"Are you going to leave, Ms. Shaw?"

I shrug. "You won't be the first dick I've run across in my life, Mr. Preston."

With a quick indrawn breath, Wade

Preston zips his pants again and storms out of the bathroom. I smile so wide it hurts, and then I turn on the faucet.

When a bailiff I've never seen before comes into the men's room, he sees a strange, tall woman washing off her makeup in the sink, patting her face dry with cheap paper towels. "What?" I accuse when he stares at me, and I saunter out the door. After all, who's he to say what's normal?

Before Zoe's mom testifies, she wants to talk to her glass of water.

"Ms. Weeks," the judge says, "this isn't a performance space. Can we please just get along with the trial?"

Dara faces him, still holding the glass in one hand. The pitcher that sits beside the witness stand is half full. "Don't you know, Your Honor, that water can feel positive and negative energy?"

"I wasn't aware that water could feel anything except wet," he mutters.

"Dr. Masaru Emoto has done scientific experiments," she says, huffy. "If human thoughts are directed at water before it's frozen, the crystals will be either beautiful or ugly depending on whether the thoughts were positive or negative. So if you expose water to positive stimuli—like beautiful music, or pictures of people in love, or words of gratitude—and then freeze it and look under a microscope, you get ice crystals that are symmetrical. On the other hand, if you play a Hitler speech to your water or show pictures of murder victims or say *I hate you* and then freeze it, the crystals are jagged and distorted." She looks up at him. "Our bodies are made up of more than sixty percent water. If positive thoughts can impact an eight-ounce glass of water, imagine the effect they might have on all of us."

The judge rubs his hand down his face. "Ms. Moretti, I assume since this is your witness you don't mind if she praises her water?"

"No, Your Honor."

"Mr. Preston?"

He shakes his head, dumbfounded. "Frankly, I don't even *know* what to say."

Dara sniffs. "All in all, that's probably

a real blessing from the water's point of view."

"You may proceed, Ms. Weeks," the judge says.

Dara raises the glass. "Strength," she says, her voice rich and full. "Wisdom. Tolerance. Justice."

It should seem precious, wacky, New Age. Instead, it's riveting. Who among us, no matter what we believe personally, would stand against those principles?

She tilts the glass and drinks every last drop. Then Dara glances at Judge O'Neill. "There. Was that really so bad?"

Angela walks toward the witness stand. She refills Dara's glass—not out of habit but because she knows it will keep everyone thinking what words are being said in front of that water that might alter it, much the way having a toddler in the room acts as a deterrent for lewd conversation. "Can you state your name and address for the record?"

"Dara Weeks. I live at 5901 Renfrew Heights, Wilmington."

"How old are you?"

Blanching, she looks at Angela. "I really have to tell you that?"

"I'm afraid so."

"Sixty-five. But I *feel* fifty."

"How far away do you live from your daughter and Vanessa Shaw?"

"Ten minutes," Dara says.

"Do you have any grandchildren?"

"Not yet. But . . ." She knocks the wood of the witness stand.

"I take it you're looking forward to the prospect, then?"

"Are you kidding me? I'm going to be the best grandmother who ever lived."

Angela crosses in front of the stand. "Ms. Weeks, do you know Vanessa Shaw?"

"I do. She's married to my daughter."

"What do you think of their relationship?"

"I think," Dara says, "she makes my daughter very happy, and that's what has always mattered most to me."

"Has your daughter always been happy in her relationships?"

"No. She was miserable after the stillbirth, and during her divorce. Like a zombie. I'd go over to her place, and she'd still be wearing the same clothes I left her in the day before. She didn't eat. She didn't clean. She didn't work. She didn't play guitar. She just slept. Even when she was awake, she seemed to be sleeping."

"When did that start to change for her?"

"She began to work with a student at Vanessa's school. Gradually, she and Vanessa went to lunch, to movies, to art festivals and flea markets. I was just so glad Zoe had someone to talk to."

"At some point did you learn that Zoe and Vanessa were more than just friends?"

Dara nods. "One day they came over and Zoe said she had something important to tell me. She was in love with Vanessa."

"What was your reaction?"

"I was confused. I mean, I knew Vanessa had become her best friend—but now Zoe was telling me she wanted to move in with her and that she was a lesbian."

"How did that make you feel?"

"Like I'd been hit with a pickax." Dara hesitates. "I don't have anything against gay people, but I never thought of my daughter as gay. I thought about the grandchildren I wouldn't have, about what my friends would say behind my back. But I realized that I wasn't upset because of who Zoe fell in love with. I was upset because, as a mother, I would never have picked this path for her. No parent wants her child to have to struggle her whole life against people with small minds."

"How do you feel now about your daughter's relationship?"

"All I can see, whenever I'm with her, is how happy Vanessa makes her. It's like Romeo and Juliet. But without Romeo," Dara adds. "And with a much happier ending."

"Do you have any qualms about them raising children?"

"I couldn't imagine a better home for a child."

Angela turns. "Ms. Weeks, if it were up to you, would you rather see Zoe's children parented by Max or Vanessa?"

"Objection," Wade Preston says. "Speculative."

"Now, now, Mr. Preston," the judge replies. "Not in front of the water. I'm going to allow it."

Dara looks over at Max, sitting at the plaintiff's table. "That's not my question to answer. But I can tell you this: Max walked away from my daughter." She turns to me. "Vanessa," she says, "won't let go."

After her testimony, Dara sits down in the seat I've saved beside me. She grips my hand. "How did I do?" she whispers.

"You were a pro," I tell her, and it's true. Wade Preston had nothing of merit to use during his cross-examination. It felt like he was spinning his wheels, grasping at straws.

"I practiced. I was up all night aligning my chakras."

"And it shows," I reply, although I have no idea what she's talking about. I look at Dara—her magnetic bracelet, her medicine-bag pouch necklace, her healing crystals. Sometimes I wonder how Zoe grew up the way she did.

Then again, you could say the same thing about me.

"I wish my mom could have met you," I whisper back to her, when what I really mean is, *I wish my mother had had a heart even half as big as yours.*

Dr. Anne Fourchette, the director of the fertility clinic, arrives with a milk crate full of files—Zoe's and Max's medical records, which have been copied for the lawyers and are handed out by the clerk of the court. Her silver hair brushes the collar of her black suit, and a pair of zebra-striped reading glasses hangs from a chain around her neck. "I've known the Baxters since 2005," she says. "They began trying to have a baby back then."

"Did your clinic assist them with that?" Angela asks.

"Yes," Dr. Fourchette says, "we provided IVF services."

"Can you describe the process for a

couple that comes in for IVF treatments?"

"We begin by doing a medical workup—lots of testing to determine the causes for the infertility. Based on those causes, we chart a course of treatment. In the Baxters' case, both Max and Zoe had fertility issues. For this reason we had to inject Max's sperm individually into Zoe's eggs. For her part, Zoe was on hormone therapy for weeks that allowed her to produce multiple eggs, which were harvested at a very precise time and fertilized with Max's sperm. For example, during their first cycle, Zoe produced fifteen eggs, eight were successfully fertilized, and of those eight that were fertilized, two looked good enough to be transferred and another three looked good enough to be frozen for a future cycle."

"What do you mean, 'looked good enough'?"

"Some embryos just look a little more uniform, more regular than others."

"Maybe someone's playing them beautiful music or whispering words of gratitude," Preston mutters. I glance over, but he's poking through the medical file.

"Our policy is to only transfer two embryos per patient, three if she's older, because we don't want her winding up with multiples like the Octomom. If there are additional embryos that look good enough for future use, we freeze them."

"What do you do with the ones that aren't 'good'?"

"They are discarded," the doctor says.

"How?" Angela asks.

"Since they are medical waste, they're incinerated."

"What happened during Zoe's last fresh cycle?"

Dr. Fourchette slides her glasses onto her nose. "She became pregnant at forty and carried the fetus to twenty-eight weeks, at which point it was delivered stillborn."

"Were there embryos remaining after that procedure?"

"Yes, three. They were frozen."

"Where are those embryos now?"

"They're at my clinic," the doctor says.

"Are they viable?"

"We won't know until we thaw them," she replies. "They could be."

"Following that last procedure," Angela asks, "when was the last time you saw Zoe?"

"She came to the clinic asking to use the embryos. I explained that, according to our policy, we could not release the embryos to her without her ex-husband's signed consent."

"Thank you, nothing further," Angela says.

Wade Preston taps his finger on the plaintiff's table, considering the doctor before he goes in for the kill. "Dr. Fourchette," he says, "you say the embryos that aren't 'good' are discarded. Incinerated?"

"That's correct."

"Incinerated means 'burned,' does it not?"

"Yes."

"Which is in fact," he says, standing, "what we sometimes do with people who die. Cremate them. Right?"

"True, but these embryos are not people."

"And yet they're treated in the same manner as a deceased person. You don't flush them down the toilet—you reduce them to ash."

"It's important to note that sixty-five percent of embryos actually are abnormal and die on their own," the doctor says. "And that both parties in this lawsuit actually signed a contract with the clinic agreeing to the incineration of embryos that were not appropriate to be transferred or frozen, among other things."

At the word *contract,* Wade Preston turns. Angela, in front of me, snaps erect. And Judge O'Neill leans toward Dr. Fourchette. "Excuse me? There's a *contract*?"

He asks to see it, and Dr. Fourchette hands over the document. The judge scans it for a few moments in silence. "According to this contract, in the event of divorce of these parties, any embryos that remain shall be destroyed by the clinic. Dr. Fourchette, why was this contract not carried out?"

"The clinic was unaware of the Baxters' divorce," the doctor says. "By the time we learned of it, it was clear that a lawsuit was about to be filed."

The judge glances up. "Well. This makes my job a lot easier."

"No," Zoe breathes, at the same time that both Angela and Wade Preston leap up, shouting their objections.

"Your Honor, we need a recess—" Angela says.

"A chambers conference," Preston interrupts.

Judge O'Neill shakes his head. "I do believe enough of my time has been wasted. Counsel, approach the bench."

Zoe turns around, frantic. "He wouldn't do that, would he? I can't lose this baby to a technicality."

"Ssh," I say, but I'm not just trying to comfort her. The lawyers are in a heated discussion, and I'm close enough to hear. "Why did counsel not know about this contract?" the judge demands.

"My client never said anything about it, Your Honor," Angela replies.

"Nor did mine. We didn't even know this contract existed," Preston adds.

"And yet both of your clients initialed this," the judge points out. "I can't just ignore the fact that a contract exists."

"Circumstances have changed since the time it was signed," Preston says.

"And there's case law—"

The judge holds up his hand. "You have one day. Tomorrow at nine A.M. we'll reconvene in a hearing about the enforceability of the contract."

Angela reels back. "What?"

"We need more time," Preston insists.

"You know what I need?" the judge storms. "I need attorneys who actually do their homework before walking into my courtroom. I need counselors who know basic contract law, something a 1L student would have easily flagged in this case. What I do *not* need are two whining, contentious attorneys who could be using their time to better advantage!" The clerk scrambles forward to make his announcement as Judge O'Neill strides off the bench, so that we all rise, too, like some magnetic aftereffect of his anger.

Angela finds a small conference room on the upper level of the courthouse and Zoe, Dara, and I follow her into it. "Talk," she demands, sitting across from Zoe, who is a mess.

"He can't really order the clinic to destroy the embryos if we both want them, right?" Zoe sobs.

"A contract's a contract," Angela says flatly.

"But this was a consent form. Like when you have anesthesia and they make you sign something just before you go under. All we wanted to do was have a baby. I figured we had to check off all the boxes if we were even going to be considered."

Angela raises her brows. "So you didn't read through the whole thing?"

"It was twenty pages long!"

Angela closes her eyes and shakes her head. "Great. Fabulous."

"How long could this postpone the judge's decision?" I ask. "That could affect the embryos, too."

"He might be incredibly speedy," Angela says. "He might just follow the damn contract and be done with it by nine-fifteen tomorrow morning. This certainly gives him an easy out, a legal precedent to follow. And it wouldn't hurt his reputation any to have his judgment compared to the judgment of Solomon." She stands and grabs her briefcase. "I'm outta here. I have a shit-load to do before tomorrow morning."

As the door closes behind her, Zoe buries her face in her hands. "We were so close," she whispers.

Dara leans down to kiss the crown of Zoe's head. "You need something to eat," she says. "There is very little in this world that Oreos cannot solve."

She goes to forage in a vending machine downstairs. Meanwhile I rub Zoe's back, feeling utterly helpless. "Who the fuck is Solomon?" I ask.

A small laugh bubbles up from Zoe's throat. "Really?"

"What? Is he some famous lawyer or politician I should know?"

She sits up, wiping her eyes. "He was a biblical king. Super smart. When two women came to him with a baby, each claiming to be the mom, Solomon suggested cutting the baby in two with a sword so they could each have a piece. One woman got hysterical and said she'd rather give up the baby than kill it, and that's how Solomon figured out who was the real mother." Zoe hesitates. "I'd do that, you know. I'd give Max these embryos before I'd let them be destroyed." She wipes her eyes. "You would have been such a fantastic mom, Vanessa."

"It ain't over till it's over," I reply.

I say this, because it's what Zoe needs to hear.

But I'm already missing something I never even had.

MAX

When I come upstairs to the kitchen the next morning, Wade Preston is pouring maple syrup on a waffle. He looks well rested and sharp, which is more than I can say for me. I don't think I got five minutes of sleep last night. Then again, I'm sure Wade has minions to do his legal research for him. He probably watched Leno and called it a night.

"Morning, Max," Wade says. "I was explaining contract law to Reid, here."

I smell mango and mint, like summertime, as Liddy leans over me to set a plate down. She is wearing a bathrobe. All the hair on the back of my neck stands up.

I wonder briefly why Wade is explaining his legal strategy to my brother instead of me. "If the old goat decides to follow the letter of the contract," Wade says, "I can mobilize every pro-life group in this country. He'll retire in the middle of the biggest shitstorm imaginable. He knows I've got that kind of pull, which leads me to believe that he'll think twice before giving his ruling."

"Then again," Reid says, "if the church is the victim in this, it puts us in a very sympathetic light."

I look at him. "Not the church."

"I beg your pardon?" Wade asks.

"Not the church. Me. These are *my* embryos. *My* pre-born children."

"Now, Max." Wade takes a long sip of coffee, staring at me over the rim of his mug. "Don't let the judge hear talk like that. *You* have no attachments here. These babies are destined to belong to your brother and his wife."

There is a clatter in the sink. Liddy has dropped a spoon. She places it on the dish rack and turns to find us all staring at her. "I need to get dressed," she says, and she leaves the kitchen without meeting my gaze. While Wade continues talking, I stare at the sunlight that fills the space where she stood.

Pastor Clive is missing. Today, of all days, when I could have used his support in the courtroom, the seat he's always taken directly behind me is conspicuously empty.

I imagine Zoe is feeling the same way. Because it's 9:05 and court's in session and her *lawyer* is MIA.

"I'm here, I'm here," Angela Moretti shouts, bursting through the double doors. Her blouse is untucked, and she's wearing sneakers with her suit instead of heels. There is a smudge on her cheek that could be jam or blood. "Kid fed bacon to the minivan CD player," she explains. "Sorry for the holdup."

"You may begin anytime, Counselor," Judge O'Neill says.

Angela sifts through her briefcase. She pulls out a SpongeBob coloring book, a *Cooking Light* magazine, and a novel before locating her brief. "Your

Honor, there's only one case in this country where a consent form like the one the Baxters signed was actually enforced. In *Kass v. Kass,* both parties signed forms that stated in the event of divorce, if they were unable to agree on the placement of their embryos, the clinic would dispose of the embryos, and a court upheld that agreement. If the parties were willing to be bound to the agreement back then, the court reasoned, they could enforce it now. However, the rest of the cases in this country regarding embryo donation—and they're a slim group—rule primarily in favor of the party wishing to avoid procreation. In *Davis v. Davis,* the mother originally wanted the embryos but then decided to donate them—and that tipped the court in favor of the father, who did not wish to become a parent. The court said that, if there had been a contract, it would be upheld—but if not, you have to balance the rights of the party wishing to be a parent with those of the party that does not. In *A.Z. v. B.Z.* in Massachusetts, forms filled out gave the wife use of embryos in the case of divorce or separation. However, the ex-husband sought an injunction against allowing her to use them. The court said that the contract that had been filled out was trumped by a person's choice, post-divorce, to not procreate. Namely, although a contract *did* exist, the circumstances had changed so drastically from the time of signing it that enforcement wouldn't be legitimate. Plus, the court said that, as a matter of public policy, it was wrong to enforce an agreement that would compel one of the donors to become a parent against his or her will."

Angela buttons her suit jacket. "In the case of *J.B. v. M.B.* in New Jersey, there was a contract stating that, in the event of divorce, embryos would be destroyed. By the time the divorce occurred, the ex-wife wanted them destroyed, but the ex-husband now said that was a violation of his religious beliefs and his right to become a parent. The court did not uphold the contract—not because they felt it was contrary to public policy, as in Massachusetts, but because a person had a right to change his mind up till the point of use or destruction of the embryos. The contract had to be a formal, unambiguous record of the intent of both parties, and since that wasn't the case, the court said the party wishing not to have children would prevail, since the father could go on to have children in the future."

She turns to look at Zoe. "The difference between those cases and *this* case, Your Honor, is that *neither* party wishes to destroy these embryos. For different reasons, both Zoe and Max want them. Yet, as in those other cases, there is a prevalent theme throughout which is applicable here, Your Honor: when there's a change of circumstances from the time that the consent form is signed—due to divorce or remarriage or religious beliefs—then a contract is no longer legally binding. Today—when both parties want to give these embryos a chance at life—for you to enforce a contract that is no longer relevant would simply be bad case law."

There is a racket at the back of the courtroom. I turn and see Pastor Clive barreling down the aisle. His face is nearly as white as his suit. He leans over the gallery railing, between Ben Benjamin and me, as Wade stands up.

"I can sink her," Pastor Clive whispers.

"I am surely glad you're sitting, Your Honor, because for once we agree with everything Attorney Moretti said," Wade begins.

Ben turns in his seat. "Seriously?"

Pastor Clive nods. Ben gets up and walks toward Wade, who's still speaking. "We are of the opinion, in fact, that it would be preferable to have the embryos go to a lesbian couple than it would be to send them to the incinerator—" He breaks off as Ben leans over and murmurs into his ear. "Your Honor?" Wade asks. "Might we have a recess?"

"What the hell?" Angela Moretti says.

"My co-counsel informs me that some new evidence has come to light, evidence that might affect Your Honor's decision in this matter."

The judge looks at him, and then at Angela. "Fifteen minutes," he pronounces.

The courtroom empties. Wade pulls Angela Moretti aside and speaks quietly with her; a moment later she gathers Zoe and ushers her out of the courtroom. "We couldn't have asked for a better Hail Mary moment if we'd designed it ourselves," Wade says, coming back toward me.

"What's going on?"

"Your ex-wife is about to be charged with sexually harassing a student," he says. "Or in other words, you can go out and buy a stroller or a bassinet. No judge is going to give a baby to someone who sexually abused a kid. As far as I'm concerned, you just won this case."

But I keep hearing the first part of his statement. "Zoe would never do that. It can't be true."

"Doesn't matter if it's true," Ben says. "It just matters that the judge hears it."

"But this doesn't feel right. Zoe could lose her job—"

Wade waves away my concern, batting at my words like they're mosquitoes. "Max, boy," he says. "Eyes on the prize."

ZOE

"Please tell me you've never heard of a girl named Lucy DuBois," Angela says.

Immediately, I picture Lucy, with her long red hair, her chewed fingernails, the ladder-back scars of her arms. "Is she all right?"

"I don't know." Angela's voice sounds too tight, like a spring. "Is there something you want to tell me?"

Vanessa pulls up a chair and sits down next to me. We are back in the conference room from the other day, but it is raining. The world outside the window looks ripe and lush, the grass so green it hurts to look at it. "She's a student who suffers from severe depression," Vanessa explains to Angela, and then she touches my arm. "Didn't you say she was upset two days ago?"

"She was talking about killing herself. Oh, my God, she didn't do it, did she?"

Angela shakes her head. "Her parents have accused you of sexual assault, Zoe."

I blink, certain I haven't heard correctly. "What?"

"They say you came on to her on two separate occasions."

"That's absolutely ridiculous! Our relationship is completely professional!" I turn to Vanessa. "Tell her."

"She's a seriously disturbed girl," Vanessa says. "Surely whatever Lucy's said would have to be taken with a grain of salt the size of a salt lick."

"Which is why it's particularly damaging that someone named Grace Belliveau has apparently signed a statement indicating she saw Zoe and the girl in a compromising position."

My bones feel like they are floating loose inside me. "Who the hell is Grace Belliveau?"

"She teaches math," Vanessa says. "I doubt you've ever even met her."

I have a brief and vivid flash of a teacher with short black hair, poking her head into the room at the end of a particularly emotional session with Lucy. My hand on Lucy's back, rubbing slow circles.

But she had been sobbing, I want to say.

It's not what you think.

I had played Barney's theme song on the ukulele. I'd told Lucy that I knew the truth, that she was shutting me out so that I couldn't shut *her* out. I'd told her I wouldn't leave her. Ever.

"The girl alleges," Angela says, "that you told her you're gay."

"Give me a break." Vanessa shakes her head. "After all this media coverage, who *doesn't* know? Whatever this is, whatever he's got on Zoe—it's all fabricated."

"I did tell her I was gay," I confess. "The last time I saw her. It's the last thing you're ever supposed to do as a music therapist—bring yourself into the therapy—but she was so upset over what Pastor Clive was saying about homosexuality. She was talking about suicide again, and . . . I don't know. I just had the sense that maybe she was questioning her own sexuality, and that it wasn't something her family would really be supportive about. That maybe it would help her to realize that someone she respected—someone like me—could be a good person and still be a lesbian. I wanted to give her something to hang her hat on, you know, instead of the sermons she probably hears at church."

"She goes to Clive Lincoln's church?" Angela asks.

"Yes," Vanessa says.

"Well. That solves the mystery of how Pastor Clive got this scoop."

"So the accusation isn't public yet?" Vanessa asks.

"No," Angela says. "And surprise, surprise. Wade says that he might be able to *persuade* the family to keep it private. Someone in Lucy's family must have gone to the pastor for counseling. Maybe even brought Lucy there herself."

It's not a boy, Lucy had said.

It was a girl.

Could it have been me? Had her attachment to me gone further than friendship? Could she have said something, sung something, written something that was misinterpreted by her parents?

Or had Lucy done nothing at all, except finally gotten the courage to come out . . . only to have her parents twist it into a lie that was easier for them to accept?

"What's the mother like?" Angela asks.

Vanessa glances up. "Meek. Does what her husband says. I've never met him."

"Has Lucy got siblings?"

"Three younger ones coming up through the middle school," Vanessa says. "It's a second marriage, from what I understand. Lucy's biological father died when she was a baby."

I turn to her. "You believe me, don't you? You know I'd never do what she's saying I did?"

"*I* believe you," Angela says. "Maybe even the judge will believe you. But by that time, Zoe, you'll have been dragged through the coals in a courtroom. The allegation will be all over the newspapers. And even if the case comes out in our favor, the fact that you were accused might be what sticks in everyone's minds."

I get up from my seat. "I need to talk to Lucy. If I could just—"

"I don't want you anywhere near her," Angela yells. "Do you know what a field day Wade will have with that?"

Stunned into silence, I fall back into my chair.

"You have a lot to think about, Zoe," she says. "Because you might get these embryos—but it could cost you your career."

Angela requests a day to digest the new information before the trial resumes. My mother and Vanessa and I sneak down to the parking lot via the custodian's elevator again, but this time, instead of feeling like we've outsmarted the other side, it only feels like we're hiding.

"Take a walk with me," my mother says, as soon as we are outside.

We are in the rear of the courthouse near the loading dock. I tell Vanessa I'll meet her at the car, and then I follow my mother to a big green Dumpster. Two women wearing summer dresses that make them look like sausages stuffed into casings are smoking cigarettes. "Dwayne's an ass," one of them says. "When he comes back, I hope you'll tell him to go jump in a lake."

"Excuse me," my mother says. "We need a little privacy."

The women look at her as if she's crazy, but they leave us alone. "Do you remember when I found out I was making four thousand dollars less than Hudd Sloane when we were both working at the travel agency?"

"Vaguely," I say. I was about twelve at the time. I remember my mother saying a strike was a strike, even if your union was a party of one.

"And do you remember what I did when your kindergarten class read *If I Ran the Circus* and I fought against the message it sent about animal cruelty?"

"Yes."

"And you know I'm the first one out there with a sign when it comes to campaigning politically for any female candidate," she adds.

"You are."

"I'm telling you this because I want you to remember that I'm a fighter."

I look at her. "You think I should take Wade Preston on."

My mother shakes her head. "Actually, Zoe, I think you need to let this go."

I just stare at her. "So you're advocating letting the family of a teenage girl spread lies about me. Doing nothing."

"No, I'm thinking of you and what's best for you. People in a small town— and Rhode Island functions as one, honey—they remember things. Not accurately, either. I remember the mother of a kid in your graduating class who somehow had convinced herself your father died of a heart attack while in bed with his mistress."

"Daddy had a mistress?" I say, shocked.

"No. That's the point. But this woman was so sure of it because that's how she recalled it. And even if you were absolutely right to hug that sad little girl when she was crying; even if you are the only person in her life who showed her any kindness for who she truly is— that's not what people in the community will remember. Years from now, you'll still be the one who was accused of getting too close to one of your students." My mother hugs me. "Give Max the embryos. And move on. You'll still have a beautiful partner who can have kids. You'll have your music."

I feel a lone tear streak down my face as I turn away from her. "I don't know what to do."

She smiles sadly. "You can't lose if you're the one who walks away from the game before it's over."

It is, I realize, exactly what Lucy would say.

Instead of driving home, Vanessa drives to the Point Judith Lighthouse. We take off our shoes and walk across the

grassy carpet that borders the structure. We take a picture for a vacation-
ing elderly couple. We shield our eyes
from the sun and try to see if the ferry
is coming from or going to Block Island.
In the adjacent park, we sit on a bench
and hold hands, even though one
woman who sees us frowns and abruptly
turns the other way.

"I have to tell you something," Vanessa finally says.

"That we can adopt?" I guess.

She tilts her head, as if that's not at
all what she was thinking about. "I lied
on the witness stand."

"I know. I was there, remember?"

"Not about the suicide attempt. I
mean, I lied about that, too. But I lied
about the reason I was in the psychiatric hospital." She looks at me. "I said
that a relationship had ended. It's a
half-truth, really, I guess. It was a relationship, but it was a professional one."

"I don't understand . . ."

"I was a counselor at a private school
in Maine," Vanessa says. "And I happened to be the field hockey coach,
too. The team won a huge game against

a rival academy, so I had the kids over for dinner, to celebrate. I was renting a house from a teacher who was with his family in Italy, on sabbatical. It was still so new I didn't know where to find things, like dishwasher detergent and extra paper towels. Anyway, a few girls wandered downstairs to the basement, and they found a wine cellar. Apparently, one of them cracked open a bottle and drank, and a teammate who was suffering an attack of conscience told the headmaster. Even though I told him I had no idea the girls were doing that downstairs—even though I didn't know there was a wine cellar in the house, for God's sake—he gave me a choice. I could be fired quite publicly, or I could very quietly resign." She looks up at me. "So that's what I did. And I hated every minute of it. Of being punished for something that wasn't my fault, at best, and was an accident, at worst. That's why I got so depressed. It took nearly killing myself to realize that I couldn't live in that moment anymore. I couldn't change it; I couldn't change what had been said by those girls, and I certainly couldn't spend the rest of my life wondering when it was going to come back to haunt me." She tucks my hair behind my ear. "Don't let them take your career away from you. If that means you want to fight back, then fight back. But if it means you trade those embryos for Wade Preston's silence—then know I understand." She smiles. "You and me, we're already a family. With or without children."

I look up at the lighthouse. There is a plaque here that says it was built for the first time in 1810. That, after a hurricane in 1815, it was built again, bigger and stronger, this time of stone. In spite of the lighthouse, wrecks continued with great regularity.

Safety is relative. You can be so close to shore that you can practically feel it under your feet, when you suddenly find yourself breaking apart on the rocks.

After I lost my baby at twenty-eight weeks, after I went home from the hospital into a house with no music, I received a phone call.

Is this Mrs. Baxter? a woman asked.

I barely knew who I was anymore, but I said yes.

Daniel's here. Your son is waiting for you.

The first time, I thought it was a cruel joke. I threw the receiver across the room, and when the phone immediately rang again, I disconnected it. Max found it that way when he came home from work, and I shrugged. I told him I didn't know how that had happened.

The next day there was another phone call.

Mrs. Baxter, please, Daniel's waiting.

Was it really that easy? Could I move into an alternate universe just by completing the one act I hadn't: finding my son, picking up where we had left off? I asked for an address, and that afternoon, I got dressed for the first time since I'd been home. I found my car keys and my purse. I drove.

I marveled at the white pillars, the grand staircase leading up to the building. I parked in the circular drive, black as a tongue, and slowly made my way inside.

"You must be Mrs. Baxter," the woman at the reception desk said.

"Daniel," I said. My son's name, in my mouth, was as smooth and round as a sweet. A Life Saver. "I'm here for Daniel."

She disappeared into the back room and returned a moment later with a small cardboard box. "Here he is," she says. "I'm so sorry for your loss."

It was no bigger than a watch box, and I could not reach for it. I thought if I touched it, I might faint.

But then she was offering it to me and I saw my hands folding around it. I heard my voice saying *Thank you*. As if this was what I'd wanted all along.

I have not been to Reid and Liddy's house in a few years. There is a profusion of color in the front yard—mostly roses, Max's handiwork. There is a new gazebo on the lawn, painted white, with heliotrope crawling up its side as stealthily as a jewel thief. Max's battered truck is parked behind a gold Lexus.

When I ring the doorbell, Liddy answers. She stares at me, speechless.

She has tiny lines around her eyes and her mouth, now. She looks tired.

I want to ask her, *Are you happy?*

Do you know what you're getting into?

But instead, I just say, "Can I speak to Max?"

She nods, and a moment later, there he is. He's wearing the same shirt he had on in court, but there is no tie. And he's wearing jeans.

It makes this easier. It makes me able to pretend I am talking to the old Max.

"Do you want to come inside?"

In the back of the foyer, I can see Reid and Liddy hovering. The last thing I want to do is go into that house. "Maybe we could go over there?"

I nod to the gazebo, and he steps onto the front porch. He is barefoot but follows me to the wooden structure. I sit down on the steps. "I didn't do it," I say.

Max's shoulder is touching mine. I

can feel the heat of his skin through his dress shirt. "I know."

I wipe at my eyes. "First I lost my son. Then I lost you. Now I stand to lose the embryos, and most likely my career." I shake my head. "There won't be anything left."

"Zoe—"

"Take them," I say. "Take the embryos. Just . . . promise me that it ends, here. That you'll keep your lawyers from bringing Lucy into court."

He bows his head. I don't know if he's praying, or crying, or both. "You have my word," Max says.

"Okay." I rub my hands over my knees and stand up. "Okay," I repeat, and I walk briskly back to my car, even though I hear Max calling my name.

I ignore him. I get into the car and back out of the driveway and park near the mailbox. Even though I can't see them from here, I imagine Max going into the foyer and telling Reid and Liddy. I picture them embracing.

All the stars fall out of the sky and rain on the roof of my car. It feels like a sword between my ribs, the loss of these children I will never know.

Vanessa is waiting for me, but I don't drive home right away. Instead I take aimless left and right turns until I find myself in a field somewhere on the back side of T. F. Green Airport, beyond where the courier planes sleep at night. I lie on the hood of the car in the dark with my back against the sloped windshield and stare up as the jets scream down to the runway, so close it seems I can touch their bellies. The noise is absolutely deafening; I can't hear myself think or cry, which is perfect.

So it makes no sense that I go into the trunk for my guitar. It's the same one I used at the school to teach Lucy. I was going to let her borrow it, for a while.

I wonder what she said. If this allegation was the distance between who she was and who her parents needed her to be. If I had been completely off the mark and had interpreted her comments the wrong way. Maybe she wasn't questioning her sexuality; maybe that was simply on my mind, because of the trial, and I painted my own thoughts over the blank canvas that Lucy actually was.

I take the guitar out of its case and crawl back onto the hood of the car. My fingers settle over the neck, stroking frets as lazily as they'd move across an old lover, and my right hand goes to strum. But there is something bright, fluttering, caught between the strings; I fish it out carefully so that it won't fall into the sound hole.

It is the chord progression for "A Horse with No Name." In my handwriting. I'd given it to Lucy the day we were learning the song.

But on the back, in green marker, five parallel lines have been drawn. A musical staff. On the top bar, two slanted lines break through, like train tracks.

I do not know when Lucy left me this message, but that's what it is. Of all the musical symbols she might have drawn, Lucy's chosen a caesura.

It's a break in the music.

A brief, silent pause when time isn't counted.

And at some point, when the conductor decides, the tune resumes.

MAX

In court the next morning, Angela Moretti's face is pinched shut as tight as a lobster claw. "My client is withdrawing her objection, Your Honor," she says. "We ask that the embryos not be destroyed per the contract and that they be released to Max Baxter's custody."

There is clapping in the courtroom. Ben grins at me. I feel like throwing up.

I've felt this way since last night. It started when Zoe bolted out of the driveway. And then when I walked back into the house, blinking because the lights were so suddenly bright, and told

Liddy and Reid that Zoe was going to give in.

Reid lifted Liddy in his arms and danced her around the foyer. "Do you know what this means?" he asked, grinning. "Do you?"

And suddenly I did. It meant that I would have to sit by quietly and watch Liddy getting bigger and bigger with my baby inside her. I'd have to hang out in the waiting room while Reid took part in the delivery. I'd have to watch Reid and Liddy fall in love with their baby, while I was the third wheel.

But she looked so goddamned happy. She wasn't pregnant, and there was already a glow to her cheeks and a shine to her hair. "This calls for something special," Reid said, and he left me standing alone with her.

I took a step forward, and then another. "Is this really what you want?" I whispered. When Reid came back, we moved apart. "Congratulations, Sis," I said, and I kissed her cheek.

He was holding an open bottle of champagne, still foaming, and two glasses. In his pocket he'd tucked a bottle of root beer. Clearly, that was for me. "Drink up," he said to Liddy. "From here on in, it's going to be soy shakes and folic acid." He handed me my root beer and said, "I say we toast. To the beautiful mother to be!"

I drank to her. How couldn't I?

"To Wade!" Reid said, hoisting his glass again. "To Lucy!"

Confused, I glanced at him. "Who's Lucy?"

"Clive Lincoln's stepdaughter," Reid said. "Zoe sure picked the wrong girl to mess with." He drained his champagne, but I didn't drink. Instead I set my bottle down on the bottom step of the staircase and walked out the front door.

"I need some air," I said.

"Let me go with you—" Liddy took a step toward me, but I held up my hand. I walked blindly to the gazebo, where I'd been sitting with Zoe just a few minutes before.

I had met Pastor Clive's wife a hundred times. And his three girls, who stood up there with her on the stage and sang. None of them was anywhere near old enough to be in high school.

And none of them, I knew, was named Lucy.

But there was another child. A black sheep, who suffered through services and never stayed for fellowship. If she was his stepdaughter, she could have had a different last name from Clive. It was entirely possible Zoe would never have made the connection.

Had this girl really come to Zoe for help because she was worried about being gay? Had she tried to tell her mother and stepfather? Had Clive heard all this, and immediately assumed Zoe had tried to recruit his stepdaughter to her lifestyle—because any other interpretation would only reflect poorly on *him*?

Or had Pastor Clive—knowing that we needed ammunition in court, knowing how much a victory would mean to the beliefs he preached daily—pressed this accusation out of his stepdaughter? Had he made her the fall guy so that I'd win? So that *he'd* win?

I sat with my head in my hands, puzzling this out, until I realized that *how* the accusation came about didn't matter.

All that mattered was that it had happened at all.

Judge O'Neill looks over at Zoe, who is staring down at the square of wood between her hands on the defense table. "Ms. Baxter," he says, "are you doing this freely and voluntarily?"

She doesn't answer.

Behind her, Vanessa raises her hand and rubs Zoe's shoulder. It's the tiniest gesture, but it reminds me of the day I first saw them together in the grocery store parking lot. It is the kind of comfort you offer, out of habit, for someone you love.

"Ms. Baxter?" the judge repeats. "Is this what you want?"

Zoe slowly lifts her head. "It is not what I want," she says. "But it's what I'm going to do."

After about an hour in the gazebo, I saw a ghost.

It moved like a memory across the grass, slipping between the trees. I thought it was saying my name.

Max, Liddy said again, and I woke up.

"You can't sleep out here," she said. "You'll freeze to death."

She sat down next to me, a cloud of billowing cotton nightgown.

"What are you two doing in there? Poring over the baby name books?" I asked.

"No," Liddy said. She looked up at the sky. "I've been thinking."

"What's there to think about?" I asked. "It's all good news."

Liddy smiled a little. "That's what the word *gospel* means, you know. Spreading the good news of Jesus."

"If you'll excuse me," I said, starting to get up, "I'm not really in the mood for a Bible lesson."

She continued as if I hadn't even spoken. "You know what the greatest commandment in the Bible is, don't you? *Love your neighbor as yourself.*"

"Great," I said sourly. "Good to know."

"Jesus didn't make exceptions, Max,"

Liddy added. "He didn't say we're supposed to love ninety-eight percent of
our neighbors . . . but hate the ones
who play their music too loud or who
always drive over our lawn or who vote
for Ralph Nader or who get tattooed
from head to toe. There may be days I
don't really want to love the guy whose
dog ate the heads off my daylilies, but
Jesus says I don't have a choice."

She held out her hand, and I pulled
her to her feet. "It's not love if there are
conditions," she said. "That's what I've
been thinking."

I looked down at our clasped hands.
"I don't know what to do, Liddy," I admitted.

"Of course you do," she said. "The
right thing."

Ironically, we have to sign a contract.
That the information Clive received will
not be released by the plaintiff or the
church, or be discussed with any party
in the future. Pastor Clive signs a stipu-
lation that Wade Preston writes on a
piece of lined paper. The judge scans it

and pronounces me the sole custodian of the three frozen embryos.

By now, there is nobody left in the gallery. They're all outside, waiting for me to appear on the steps and give them a big smile and thank God for the outcome of this trial.

"Well," Wade says, grinning. "I do believe my work here is done."

"So they're mine now? One hundred percent legally mine?" I ask.

"That's right," Wade agrees. "You can do anything you want with them."

Zoe is still sitting at the defense table. She is the center of a flower, surrounded by her mother, her lawyer, and Vanessa. Angela hands her another tissue. "You know how many of Max's lawyers it takes to plaster a wall?" she says, trying to cheer Zoe up. "Depends on how hard you throw them."

I wish I could have done it some other way, but I didn't know how. Wade would have had something up his sleeve. The truth is, this was never what I had intended. Somewhere along the way, this became about politics, and religion, and law. Somewhere along the way, it stopped being about people. About Zoe, and me, and these children we once wanted to have.

I walk toward my ex-wife. Her entourage parts, so that I find myself standing in front of her. "Zoe," I begin. "I'm sorry—"

She looks at me. "Thanks for saying that."

"You didn't let me finish. I'm sorry that you had to go through all this."

Vanessa moves closer to Zoe.

"They'll have a good life," Zoe says, but it sounds like a question. "You'll make sure of that?" She is crying, now. Shaking with the effort of holding herself together.

I'd take her into my arms, but that's someone else's privilege now. "The best," I promise, and I hand her the legal document Wade Preston just gave me. "Which is why I'm giving them to you."

	TRACK 1	SING YOU HOME
	TRACK 2	THE HOUSE ON HOPE STREET
	TRACK 3	REFUGEE
	TRACK 4	THE LAST
	TRACK 5	MARRY ME
	TRACK 6	FAITH
	TRACK 7	THE MERMAID
	TRACK 8	ORDINARY LIFE
	TRACK 9	WHERE YOU ARE
✓	**TRACK 10**	**SAMMY'S SONG**

SAMANTHA

Even at age six, there are many things Sammy knows for sure:

That peanut butter makes her dog, Ollie, look like he's talking real words to her.

That at night her stuffed animals come to life, or how else would they move around her bed while she's sleeping?

That inside Mommy Zoe's arms is the place in the world where she feels the most safe.

That when she was riding on Mama Ness's shoulders once she *actually* touched the sun, and she knows for sure because she got a blister on her thumb.

That she hates hates hates getting shots at the doctor's office and the smell of gasoline and the taste of sausages.

That whoever invented glitter was just *asking* for a mess.

That she can write her whole name. Even the long version.

That Annie Yu is her best friend in the whole world.

That storks don't *really* bring babies. But to be honest, she doesn't really believe Annie Yu's description of what actually happens, either.

That bologna sandwiches are better with the crusts off.

That the best day of the year is the first time it snows every winter.

That her daddy wrapped branches from two different rosebushes together, and this summer, when the flowers come, they will look different from any other rose ever seen in the world, and he's going to name it after her.

That when he marries Liddy, she will get to be the flower girl. (Liddy promised her this when they made a fort last weekend under the kitchen table with blankets. Even though, she said, Sammy's father hadn't asked her yet and what on earth was he waiting for.)

That it is not a good idea to put marshmallow Peeps in the microwave.

That when Jack LeMar made fun of her when her moms came to the winter concert, and Sammy told him he was so dumb he thought M&M's were really W's, it made her moms laugh *really* hard.

That Mama Ness is the tooth fairy. Sammy peeked.

That one day she wants to be an astronaut. Or maybe a figure skater. Or both.

That she can hold her breath underwater in the bathtub for a ridiculous amount of time and today at recess she is going to ask Annie Yu if it's possible to be part mermaid.

That when she fell out of a tree and broke her arm and woke up in the hospital, her moms and her dad were all standing around her bed and they were so happy she was okay they forgot to yell at her for climbing the tree in the first place.

That most kids have just one mom and just one dad, but that she is not "most people."

That, really, she is the luckiest girl in the world.